REBELLION, BATTLE AND TRUCE

REBELLION, BATTLE AND TRUCE

IN HER PARANORMAL MAJESTY'S SECRET SERVICE™
BOOK TWO

MICHAEL ANDERLE

REBELLION, BATTLE & TRUCE TEAM

Thanks to the Beta Readers
James Caplan, Larry Omans, John Ashmore, Kelly O'Donnell, Mary
Morris

Thanks to the JIT Readers

Micky Cocker
Dave Hicks
Debi Sateren
Jackey Hankard-Brodie
Jeff Goode
Larry Omans
Diane L. Smith
Deb Mader
Dorothy Lloyd
Paul Westman
Jeff Eaton

If I've missed anyone, please let me know!

Editor
The Skyhunter Editing Team

LMBPN Publishing
PMB 196, 2540 South Maryland Pkwy
Las Vegas, NV 89109

First US Edition, February 2020
Version 1.01, May 2020
ebook ISBN: 978-1-64202-728-0
Print ISBN: 978-1-64202-729-7

DEDICATION

*To Family, Friends and
Those Who Love
to Read.
May We All Enjoy Grace
to Live the Life We Are
Called.*

— Michael

GENEVIEVE KING'S UK TO US TRAVEL GUIDE

An insight into how the Americans butcher the queen's English

UK (Correct) — *US (Wrong)*

- **Aluminium (*ah-luh-min-ee-um*)** — Aluminum (*ah-loo-min-uhm*...WHAT?)
- **American Football** — *Football*
- **Bathroom / Toilet / Loo** — *Restroom*
- **Biscuit** — *Cookie*
- **Bonnet (Car)** — *Hood*
- **Broadsheet** — *Newspaper*
- **Car Park** — *Parking Lot*
- **Chips** — *French Fries*
- **Crisps** — *Potato Chips*
- **Dual carriageway** — *Highway, freeway*
- **Dummy** — *Pacifier*
- **Duvet** — *Blanket (yes there are duvets, but not in this story)*
- **Extension lead** — *Extension cord*
- **Flat** — *Apartment*
- **Football** — *Soccer*
- **Garden** — *Yard*
- **Holiday** — *Vacation*
- **Ice lolly** — *Popsicle*
- **Jumper** — *Sweater*
- **Knickers** — *Panties*
- **Lift** — *Elevator*
- **Lorry** — *Truck*
- **Mad** — *Insane / Crazy*
- **Motorway** — *Highway*
- **Mummy** — *Mommy*
- **Nappy** — *Diaper*
- **Number Plate** — *License Plate*

- **Oregano (*or-i-gah-no*)** — *Oregano (or-eh-ga-no...I mean, come on!)*
- **Pants** — *Underwear*
- **Pavement** — *Sidewalk*
- **Peckish** — *Hungry*
- **Police / Bobbies / Pigs / Boys in Blue** — *Cops / Police*
- **Potato (*poh-tah-to*)** — *Potato (pah-tay-to)*
- **Rubbish** — *Trash*
- **Shop** — *Store*
- **Sofa** — *Couch*
- **Sweets** — *Candy*
- **Torch** — *Flashlight*
- **Tomato (*toh-mah-to*)** — *Tomato (tah-may-to)*
- **Trainers** — *Sneakers*
- **Trollied** — *Drunk/plastered*
- **Trousers** — *Pants*
- **Tube** — *Subway*
- **Waistcoat** — *Vest*
- **Wardrobe** — *Closet*
- **Windscreen** — *Windshield*

CHAPTER ONE

<u>**Route 295, New Jersey, USA**</u>

The 2011 Ford Crown Victoria cruised on down Route 295.

Rookie Special Agent Jack Hansen stared out of the rolled-down window of the passenger side of the car as flashes of green and orange blurred past. Although Fall was in the air, the sun gave off a steady heat, and there was calm all around.

He turned to the driver's seat where his partner, Special Agent Clive Bannon, sat with his steely gaze fixed on the road.

Clive was exactly what Jack imagined when he had pictured an agent. An older man with wrinkles set deep into the grooves of his face. Tanned, leathery skin and a scratchy layer of stubble. His hair was on the final steps of turning gray, drawing attention to the fact that he had been through the wars and knew what he was doing when it came to getting the job done. These days, he was considerably closer to retirement than he was to any other part of his career.

Jack knew that that was all in appearance only.

Neither of them really knew what purpose the SIA was supposed to serve beyond investigating incidents that would have been laughed off a year or so earlier. Things had changed considerably in the last year. Even more so since the Times Square incident, which was why they were driving far away from home in order to investigate the report. Jack had wondered if the supernatural existed, but never truly believed in it until his transfer to the agency.

Clive silently signaled his turning and made his way through Haddon Heights and onto Route 30. The radio clipped to the dashboard called out instructions for one of their operatives in a tinny voice, which they ignored. They were too far away from Washington at this point to consider assisting.

Besides, they were on a top-secret mission. One of the first of its kind to leave DC. Even if a thousand jobs arose, they'd stay focused on the assignment at hand.

Jack let his head fall back against the headrest and let out a long breath. They had been silent for the better part of an hour, and he had learned pretty quickly that Clive hated music in the car. Said it dulled his senses.

Maybe age will do that to you, too.

"Something the matter?" Clive asked, breaking the silence at Jack's exhalation.

Jack considered the question. He supposed that *everything* was the matter after the things he'd been shown during his recruitment briefing. Ever since the lab geeks had taken them into the clean white rooms and showed them a whole new world, everything had changed. His entire understanding of what was real and what wasn't had been flipped upside down, and there was no way of going back.

Jack thought about telling Clive this. Thought about bringing up the impossible sights they'd seen. Thought of telling him that, at age thirty-four, he'd expected himself to find a steady girl by now. That he'd expected to graduate from the Academy and be rolling around the streets and pulling in the bad guys as a local cop until retirement came around. That being headhunted by the government and getting recruited into a top-secret division of the US Government hadn't been high on his agenda.

The SIA had needed fresh meat after the Times Square Incident exposed the spectral world. People who had excelled in the mortal realm and were able to adapt their training in order to understand

and operate in this new world with success. To be biased by training was something Jack had learned may or may not lead to him getting killed somewhere along the way.

Sure...If they can even kill us.

Instead of answering with the truth, Jack merely shook his head as he turned back to the window and muttered a soft, "No. Nothing's the matter."

"Good," Clive replied, his lips barely moving. "Good."

The Crown Victoria was near enough silent. Soon the little town of Haddon Heights was lost to trees, and the first signs of the forest unfolded before them.

The conifers and pines grew thickly around them, blocking out the setting sun. The oranges were thrown into dazzling embers of light above the canopy. Small wisps of white clouds floated lazily among a pink canvas above.

They skirted the edge of the forest, following the long road ahead. The roads were virtually empty on their side, with the only traffic they saw leading away from the forest. A gentle trickle of tourists who had come, seen, and conquered the sights of the park.

Soon enough, the small town came into sight. Night fell in a sheet of black, and the sodium arcs illuminated the sleepy place.

Clive navigated the streets as if he'd been here before, expertly taking the correct turnings until they parked outside a restaurant. Jack had once asked how he was so good with directions, and Clive had replied with a simple shrug, followed by a grunted, "I study."

They ate a modest meal of spaghetti and meatballs, served at the locally famous Joe Italiano's. They drank their fill of black coffee and water and eventually threw a forty percent tip onto the table for the young waitress, who had been ogling Jack all night.

"You could have her, you know," Clive told him as the chill night air blew on their faces. "Fish in a barrel."

"I prefer the chase," Jack replied. "More fun that way. Gives me the open ocean."

"See how that's served you so far?" Clive chuckled, the effects of forty years of smoking decorating the sound. "When this is all over,

I'll make myself scarce if you want to get your stick wet. God knows I'd do the same in your shoes if I were ten years younger."

"I'm twenty years younger than you."

Clive just looked at him.

While Jack climbed back into the Crown Victoria, Clive popped the trunk and checked that the contents were still inside. Satisfied, he climbed in beside Jack, started the engine, and slowly exited the village. The next road would take them straight into the forest. For twenty-five minutes or so, it would be nothing but them and nature.

And whatever else lies out there.

Jack tapped his fingers against his thighs. The silver moon shone down on them, a large crescent in the sky.

Clive smirked. "Nervous?"

"Yeah," Jack replied firmly. "You aren't?"

Clive shook his head. "A job's a job."

Jack gave a derisive snort. "Maybe you should be."

"Listen, kid. I've been in this business for a long time. Longer than you've been alive. I've seen it all, and then some. There's no fucker in Washington who's going to startle me into being scared or nervous on a mission. A job's a job. We do what we came to do, we leave. Simple as that."

"This isn't just a job," Jack replied. "Don't play this off like this is just another day at the office. You saw what they showed us. You read the files. This is *nothing* like we've encountered before." Jack gave another snort. "Spectral Intelligence Agency… Like that is going to catch on."

"You really bought all that?" Clive asked incredulously.

Jack raised an eyebrow. After several hours in the car with Clive, now was the time he was telling Jack he doubted the authenticity of their mission. "You don't?"

"Holograms." Clive laughed. "Technology has come pretty far these days." He turned to Jack, whose face did not reflect his sentiment. "Oh, come on. Think how ridiculous that all was. 'Put on these goggles; now you can see ghosts.' It's all just VR. Training for the next chapter."

Jack hadn't considered that before. "I suppose…"

"I *know*," Clive stated. He drew out a pack of cigarettes, shook the box until one white stick slid out, and clamped it between his teeth. He reached into his pocket and pulled out his lighter, doing his best to maintain his view of the road while he fought with the zippo to light it. He rolled down the window and exhaled smoke into the forest.

"Look," he told Jack, the cigarette bouncing as he spoke. "Back in '89, they did the same thing. Brought a bunch of us rookies out into the field under pretense in order to assess our mettle. Two dozen were 'specially selected' for training, and only three made it through. You know what happened to those three?"

Jack shook his head. "No."

"They hit the big leagues. Got accepted straight into an acceleration program, and now they're the ones giving us orders on where to go and what we're supposed to do."

"You mean..."

"Yep," Clive confirmed. He pushed his head back against the headrest. "If only I had tried a little harder back then, I could've been in a swanky office instead of wasting away my final years cruising out here with a damn rookie."

"I'm not a rookie," Jack protested.

"Are you a pro?"

Jack thought of responding but decided against it. Clive wasn't one to back down from an argument, and now wasn't the time to enter one.

"Trust me, kid. All that spectral world shit, it's exactly that. AR, or VR bullshit. You watch. The minute we arrive at this village, it's going to be all laser guns and...and..."

Clive's words trailed away as a glimmer of something pale and white shot out of the forest beside them. It was quick, galloping between the trees and carving its way deeper into the forest.

The sight only lasted a few moments, but it was enough to make both of their jaws drop.

"Was that..." Jack asked.

Clive answered by pushing his foot harder on the gas and

propelling them forward. His knuckles had gone white, gripping the steering wheel, but he didn't seem to notice.

"Clive?" Jack asked softly.

Clive slowly shook his head. "Let's get this shit over with."

Small, crooked signs indicated the way to the Batsto Village, a quaint hamlet set deep into the heart of the forest. Clive switched off the headlights and parked the Crown Victoria around half a kilometer away from the village in a small recess off the road.

Jack took a deep breath as he climbed out of the car and met Clive at the trunk. He opened it up and saw the array of new technology the lab rats had provided them both. Gleaming silver equipment was tucked into the dark black cases Clive selected.

Clive grabbed the goggles and hooked them around his neck. He then grabbed a retro-looking revolver that reminded Jack of the types the cowboys held in Western flicks.

Clive examined the revolver. "Six in the chamber. Not the best, but given the resources being poured into this thing, I guess it's the best they've got."

"Will six be enough?" Jack frowned, then corrected his expression when Clive's eyes met his.

"Course it will. This is all bogus, remember? A practice exercise. We'll need one of these paint pellets, at most."

Jack picked up his own revolver and examined it closely. It sure looked real to him. He set up the holster around his waist.

Exactly like in the Westerns.

Now they took to the road, keeping tight to the shadow of the trees. Jack could hear his heart beating. The town was deathly still. If there really were a band of lawbreakers hiding out here, they were great at keeping themselves quiet.

When the trees broke, they moved like wraiths across the open landscape. Several houses were in sight, and they tucked behind these, clinging to the walls with their hands near their guns. Clive led the operation, using hand signals that Jack had memorized. Soon, they had made their way over a small bridge across a chuckling stream. They stopped when they reached the church.

The church was the pinnacle of the town. A great spire pointed into the sky—the only sign that a town even existed here when viewed from a distance.

Clive cocked an ear. Jack followed suit. They could hear the sounds of nature: trees whispering, birds taking flight, crickets, and other singing insects.

"Told you, new blood. Nothing to fear," Clive muttered.

Then why are you still whispering? Jack wondered.

Clive lifted a hand to his neck and pulled the goggles over his eyes. He pressed the button on the side and a small ring of green LEDs lit around each eyepiece.

Clive gasped. "Holy shit. Get your goggles on, kid."

Jack placed his own goggles on and followed suit. The minute the goggles activated, he could see them with crystal clarity.

Small white orbs hovered inches from their faces, like floating lanterns. Jack looked beyond the orb directly in front of them, and saw several more in a line, leading away from the church and into the forest to where several bright, glowing creatures stood alert.

"VR?" Clive asked, sounding more uncertain than before.

"I don't—"

Gunfire broke the silence, eliminating any chance of Jack's reply being heard.

CHAPTER TWO

New York City, USA

Jennie King had only been back in New York for a few days and she was already preparing to leave. She looked around Radio City Music Hall and smiled, not quite believing how much had changed in so short a time.

For years, Jennie had operated on her own. She had gone out solo and brought the bad guys to justice with her bare hands. For years she had shunned making friends, ignored the call to be social, and earned her reputation as the one the specters called "Rogue."

Now, though…

Now Jennie was in the heart of it all, surrounded by more specters than she had ever seen packed into a single venue. Celebrating their triumph. Basking in the glory of Jennie and her company's latest victory over the queen.

Signs hung up on the wall, painted in scrappy lettering. Some which sported the phrase, All hail the King's Court! Others read, Death to Winter, bring on Summer.

Jennie's cheeks hurt from smiling. She flushed red from the warmth of the celebration—and the volume of alcohol inside her. Baxter and Tanya really had known what they were doing when they had gathered all available specters from the Spectral Plane—and, indeed, any specter who fancied joining their celebrations—to Baxter's old haunt and set the whole shebang up.

Specters had come from all over New York. Some of them were filled with curiosity as to what the celebration was for, others had the determined intention of personally congratulating Jennie and those closest to her on emancipating themselves from the Crown. A small number of those in attendance were Obake who had followed Jennie from England under the impression that a better life lay ahead, and there were even some who had traveled from nearby towns and cities to pledge oaths to the mysterious Rogue.

Which she downright refused. No longer would specters in the United States feel as if they had to tie themselves to unrealistic promises in the name of servitude.

Jennie joined in with the festivities, dancing, singing, and laughing until she was out of breath, and by the time the morning rolled around, she was exhausted.

The specters dissipated, and the hall emptied. Jennie roamed back down the long streets with Carolyn, Baxter, Feng Mian, George, Tanya, Lupe, and Sandra, and soon they were back in her apartment at the Plaza.

The sun was crowning as they walked into the apartment, filling the world with a golden glow. Central Park dazzled under the first rays, its oranges and browns aglow like earthen fire.

"You can't say that Jennie doesn't know how to throw a party," Carolyn remarked, finding a chair and kicking her feet over the side. "Is it possible that my feet are killing me? I really feel like they're killing me."

"They can't kill you." Lupe smirked when Carolyn looked at him. "You're already dead."

Carolyn snorted and gave a half-assed glare.

"Besides," Lupe continued, "you've got Tanya and Baxter to thank for the party. Not Jennie. Jennie had zero input on that one."

"Hey!" Jennie sounded hurt.

Lupe raised his eyebrows.

"I brought the punch…"

"Which only you, Tanya, and I can drink," Lupe reminded her. "The specters could float through it and smell it, but they couldn't get drunk."

"Man, being dead *sucks*!" Carolyn whined.

"Not as bad as hearing you complain about it." Jennie grinned. "Seriously, guys. Thanks for all of that. That's certainly one way to spread the word that there's a new power in town. Even those loyal to the crown will have something to consider when they hear about what went down tonight."

"That was one hell of a speech, too," Baxter enthused, finding a seat beside Carolyn on the plush couch. "Really got them all riled up."

Jennie made her way to the fridge. "It's a new age. They've got to be excited. Let's be honest; with Tanya at the helm, they're more supportive than ever. I don't know what you've done to them all while we've been away."

"What *we've* done," Sandra corrected, snuggling into Tanya's arms. "We're a team, right, Mom?"

Jennie, who had the neck of a bottle in her mouth as she chugged the last of its contents, choked and nearly spat out her mouthful. "Mom?"

Tanya beamed. "Sandra says that, because her mom's not around anymore, she'd need a new one. I guess you were right about imprinting, huh?"

Jennie laughed. "I guess so, *mom*." She shook her head and busied herself making another cocktail.

"Another?" Baxter asked. "Shouldn't you be getting some sleep?"

"Hair of the dog," Jennie replied. "Ahead of the morning. This won't shift the hangover completely, but I've found that mixing a *lot* of fruit juices and ice cubes, with a dash of something stiff will take the edge off come the morning. We've got a long drive ahead of us, and I want to be alert."

"By drinking more alcohol?" Baxter asked.

"Have you met Rogue?" George chuckled.

Feng Mian sat silently, watching the others speak with his usual passive demeanor.

"I'll be fine," Jennie assured them. "This isn't my first rodeo. It certainly won't be my last."

She finished shaking her cocktail and poured the thick, maroon-colored liquid into a pint glass. She downed the whole thing in one, then placed a hand to her temple and gasped. "*Argh*, brain freeze."

"Do you really have to go tomorrow?" Sandra asked. Since Jennie had come back, she'd noticed that the girl had really come out of her shell. Where before she had been nervous and shy and hadn't wanted to stick around in the modern world, Tanya had turned all of that around. Now she joked, laughed, and played like a regular young girl.

Jennie wondered how long it would all last. She'd known a few specters who were children when they died, but she had never stuck around long enough to know if they ever really grew up at all. Maybe they spent their days as Peter Pans, flying around and never truly growing older.

"We've stayed here long enough," Jennie told Sandra softly, her smile fading. "Just because we've come back from the UK and we've taken what we want, it doesn't mean that the hard part is over."

"It was fucking hard, though," Carolyn blurted.

Jennie blew air through her lips. "Are you kidding? That wasn't even the hardest thing I've done this week."

They all looked at her.

"Oh, come on. Another seven-hour plane ride with a crying baby? Now, *that* was painful."

She smiled at the others and winked. They shook their heads and chuckled.

"So, do you think you're ready for the next chapter?" George asked. "How much do you know about the US Government?"

"Not that much," Jennie admitted. "But if they're smart, then they've spoken to the paranormal court, so they'll certainly have heard of me by now. Several specters at the hall told me that there were agents poking around a day or two after the Times Square incident. They're nowhere near as developed with their spectral departments as the UK is, but that's where I come in. I plan to offer my services. Forge connections. See what the king's court can add to the equation."

"You want to work *with* them?" Carolyn asked.

"Sure. Why not?" Jennie replied. "An agency helping an agency. Makes sense."

Carolyn seemed a little disappointed.

"What's the problem?" Jennie inquired.

Carolyn's nose wrinkled in disappointment. "I thought we were going to dominate the world. Take on the big bad guys. Be the number one organization people come to for help."

Jennie grinned. "All in time, young Padawan. All in good time."

"Really? Star Wars, again?" Baxter exclaimed.

Jennie stuck out her tongue.

Route 295, New Jersey, USA

Jennie didn't waste any time in grabbing her things and getting on the road when morning rolled around. Accompanied by Baxter, she left the others behind so that they could watch over the city and start their work.

The goodbyes were hard, but they were only temporary. If all went to plan, Jennie and Baxter would be at Washington DC in a few hours' time, and there they could begin their work. Jennie had spent time over the last few days getting as up to speed with the United States' governmental structure in order to try to determine the best "in" she could find for her plan.

Lupe and Tanya would watch over the Spectral Planes and ensure that the city remained in a state of neutrality. While specters could have factions, no one division could dominate the state. There still was some work there to do with the crown, but with George on their side. they had an expert diplomat to diffuse situations before they began to arise.

Now, Jennie and Baxter cruised down the 295 in the black EcoBoost Jennie had stored in one of the many underground carparks of NYC. She was pleased to see her Mustang was still in mint condition. The engine growled like a lion when she pressed on the gas. Heads turned as they sped past cars on the freeway, and soon New York City was far behind them both.

"Do you really think it's going to be as simple as walking straight in and showing them what you can do?" Baxter asked, staring at the bridges and off-ramps as they snaked over and around the freeway.

Jennie laughed. "You've never truly been outside of NYC, have you?"

Baxter blushed. "Except for London, you mean? Is it that obvious?" He sat straight in the car and rested his head back. "I never really saw any need for it. New York was and is my home. I was happy as a specter, examining the ever-changing structure of the city, seeing technological advancements. All my life, I'd been told New York was the pinnacle of modern civilization, so why would I journey anywhere else?"

"You weren't even tempted to hop on a bus and travel to your brother cities? Philly? Boston? Rochester?"

"You certainly know a lot about New York State," Baxter remarked.

"Philly isn't in—"

"I know where Philly is!" Baxter interrupted. "Don't try to out-American me, British girl."

Jennie smirked. "I read up on everything I can before I go anywhere. It's one of the things that's gotten me this far in life. I learn fast, and I go deep. While you played around in the cockpit and the engine room on the flight, I spent several hours checking my geography and planning ahead. Given that you've hardly ever left your own city, I'd be surprised if I don't already know more than you."

Baxter fixed Jennie with a stare as if assessing that what she was saying was true. Eventually, he looked away and said, "I was never tempted to travel because I never understood what else was out there. I didn't get inducted into the spectral world the same as most others. I was left alone to fend for myself. All I heard about the neighboring cities were horror stories of dark creatures and wandering souls, and I decided it was better for me to stay where I know it's safe and where

I know things. That plan worked out well for me for a century…until you came along."

Jennie frowned. "You say that like it's a bad thing."

"No, it's not." Baxter sighed. "If anything, it makes me regret my choice. My fear stood in the way of my exploration. That's not something to be proud of."

Jennie nodded and turned onto the outer lane, speeding past a trio of yellow buses filled with high school kids. They waved at her as she passed, and she responded by blaring the Mustang's horn.

When they were in front of the coaches, Jennie pulled away and returned her attention to Baxter. "To answer your question, no, I don't think it'll be as easy as walking into their office and showing them what we can do. This operation has to be sophisticated. We've got to approach this properly. We're getting involved in a government operation about a world they hardly know about."

"They know about us?" Baxter asked.

"Enough that they've begun forming departments. Over the last few months, the queen—or, at least, the Obake bitch who was posing as the queen—had put in a lot of legwork to bring the US into her clutches." She pointed at herself. "Exhibit A. One of the other approaches was to negotiate a collaborative relationship with the government, in much the same way that the mortal intelligence agencies have."

Baxter smirked. "So, a for-real spook agency?"

Jennie nodded to confirm. "From what I understand, she's had some success, but it's still early days. Here's where we grab our opportunity to slide in with Uncle Sam's spooks before they get too involved with Queeny."

Baxter smirked. "Induct them into the king's court?"

"Something like that," Jennie replied. "Something like that…"

CHAPTER THREE

Route 206, New Jersey, USA

Baxter tried to keep as straight a face as possible, but the smile wouldn't stop creeping along the edge of his lips. "Just admit it. We're lost."

Jennie scowled at Baxter. "No. We're not lost. We've just…taken a detour."

"Check your phone, Miss 'I-know-America-Better-Than-You.'"

Jennie pulled the car onto the hard shoulder and tapped her phone on the dashboard. She turned the music down and pulled up the "Maps" app. Immediately a small icon appeared, showing that they were now located several miles further south than where they were meant to be.

"You're kidding," Jennie exclaimed, her face a picture.

Baxter couldn't hold it in anymore. His laughter filled the car. He laughed so hard that small spectral tears glittered in the corner of his eyes.

Jennie played with the screen, moving the map around to try to figure out where they were and the best way to get back on track. According to the map, they had turned off the freeway too early and were heading into the center of New Jersey.

She looked around the car and saw nothing bordering the stretch of road except for quaint houses and trees. "I thought New Jersey was meant to be a shit-hole. This place is beautiful."

"Don't discount an entire state because of TV," Baxter managed at last. "Everywhere has its sweet spots."

"Still…" Jennie looked at the estimated time of arrival on her phone. The ETA had gone up by hours. "I can't understand how this happened."

"That's what happens when someone gets too confident and decides to try to make their way along a four-hour journey by heart," Baxter replied smugly. "I told you to have the map open the entire time."

"It's fine," Jennie told him. "Means we can see more of this delightful country of yours." Her stomach growled. "How about we find some food first and then set about a U-turn."

"You want to drive all the way back to where we were?" Baxter asked. "Why not carry on this scenic route of yours and join back up with the freeway later?" He pointed to the map, where a thin road some miles ahead would save them another couple of hours of retracing their steps.

"Fine," Jennie agreed begrudgingly. "We'll keep on pushing until we find a suitable place to eat."

"You mean, for you to eat?"

"Of course." Jennie smiled. "You can sit there and smell it."

Twenty minutes later, Jennie was tucking into a Big Mac and fries. The tray was piled with empty wrappers, from the chicken nuggets, McChicken Sandwich, extra fries, and Quarter Pounder she had ordered alongside it. Two large drinks cups had been drained of their Coke, and Baxter and the surrounding customers stared at Jennie in disbelief.

"Get over it," Jennie told Baxter between mouthfuls. "I'm hungry, okay?"

A group of children stared at her, wondering who she was talking to.

Baxter waved his hands over the destruction Jennie had wrought to the mountain of fast food. "Yeah, but there's hungry, and then there's *this*."

Jennie shrugged. "It's who I am. When I eat, I eat big, okay? Worthington complained about my appetite and look at how he ended up. Do you want to tread that same path?"

Baxter fell silent, then laughed and waited patiently. The children nearby sidled back to their parents and occasionally threw her looks.

Satisfactorily full, Jennie looked up at the ceiling and exhaled loudly. Her hand found the small round bump of her stomach, which she stroked like a pregnant woman feeling for her baby's kick.

"You know, I had my first McDonald's in 1974," Jennie told him. "I never looked back. It's been pretty much the same ever since. That's how you win a woman's heart—consistency. Be there. Be dependable. Be delicious."

Baxter laughed. "That should be their new slogan."

"You ever eaten a Maccy D's?" Jennie asked.

Baxter thought about it, then shook his head. "They didn't exist in my day. I'm sure I don't remember seeing them really until the Rat Pack made the scene. That must've been around the sixties. By then, I had no taste buds and no stomach. Guess I missed that train, huh?"

"You really did," Jennie sympathized. "Cheap, fast, and dirty."

"Just how you like it," Baxter teased.

Jennie winked. "Don't you just know it."

Jennie was about to lift her tray up to tidy the contents in the already over-spilling trash cans when she picked up snippets of someone else's conversation.

"No, I'm saying go *around* it. Haven't you been reading the papers? It's a no-go zone."

Jennie glanced out of her periphery at the elderly couple sitting at a nearby table. The woman was short and looked to be in her seventies, with a thick perm of hair and milk-bottle glasses. She dug into her purse and drew out a small tabloid paper.

The man was as tall as she was short. His combover did nothing to hide the gaping bald circle on his crown, but his suit was pristine and sharp. Jennie always admired the elderly who made an effort in society. Those who cherished their appearance as much in later life as they did in their youth.

"You really going to let the tabloids add time onto our journey? Marianne, I'm seventy-eight next week. I've only got so much life left in me. You want to take the long way around, then take the long way. But I'm going to save precious seconds of my life by going the fastest route possible."

"It's dangerous," Marianne hissed. "Harold, you'll get us in trouble."

She spread out the pages of the newspaper and rotated it so Harold could see.

He spent a few seconds examining the page before rolling his eyes and pushing the newspaper back in her direction. "Black magic? You've got to be kidding me."

"That's what it says!" Marianne urged. "Black magic. You know how I feel about the arcane."

"Yes, dear. After forty-one years of marriage, you've made it quite clear about your thoughts on the occult and the paranormal."

Marianne's ears turned red. "Don't take that tone with me."

"I'm sorry, honey," Harold apologized, and to his credit, he looked like he truly meant it. "But pushing a glass around on a Ouija board, seeing a psychic twice a week, and thinking that you can see your mother floating above the ottoman every time there's a full moon doesn't change the truth that this magic spiel is bullshit."

Marianne grabbed the paper and shoved it indelicately into her bag. "Then explain why the paper says the area's cordoned off."

Jennie glanced at Baxter, then walked over to the elderly couple. She stopped at their table and said in her most sickly-sweet voice, "Excuse me, I'm sorry to eavesdrop, but I heard you two from over there."

Marianne slapped Harold's hand. "See what you've done? You've caused a scene."

Harold gasped. "Me?"

Jennie interrupted before they could continue. "Honestly, it's fine. It's just, I couldn't help but hear you say something about a town being cordoned off? Is that true?"

Blushing, Marianne retrieved the paper from her purse, the pages all now creased and disheveled. "It's right here, dear. Page sixteen. *Black Magic Ritual hits Batsto.*"

"Can I take a closer look?" Jennie waited for Marianne to nod before picking up the paper and moving it closer to read. Baxter towered behind her, squinting to see better.

One-quarter of the page was filled with a dark, blurry image of what appeared to be the front section of a church. The floor was covered in a burning pentagram. Several dark hooded figures could be seen in the fire's glow, their hands linked as they underwent some kind of ritual.

Harold rolled his eyes. "It's all bull. There've been whack jobs like that roaming around for years."

"They might be the Shadows," Marianne exclaimed with a gasp.

"Not this again," Harold groaned. "They're nothing more than grown-ass men toying around with candles and scripts."

"You think these are the Shadows?" Jennie asked, handing her the paper.

Marianne took the paper and had a closer look. "I suppose they could be."

"It's all bull," Harold protested again, although neither woman paid him any attention.

"Where is this place?" Jennie asked casually. "Is it going to be blocking our way?"

Marianne shook her head. "Not unless you're planning on heading down the 206 and off to the south to find the beaches. They're on the other side of the forest, hon. If that's the way you're heading, you're screwed. No one can get in or around that area unless you're law or otherwise."

Harold folded his arms. "We're going."

"We are not," Marianne declared.

Jennie took one more look at the paper then handed it back. "I think we should be fine." She flashed a winning smile. "I just didn't want to add unnecessary time to a journey if it didn't need it. Thank you for your kindness."

She turned and exited the restaurant, walking quickly to her car.

Baxter laughed. "*You* don't want to add unnecessary time to your journey?"

Jennie latched onto him and froze him in place in the middle of the road. A car curved out from the drive-thru and drove straight through him. "Don't play with me, specter. Remember who's got the power here."

She released Baxter, whose smile slipped slightly. "Remember that you need me in order to use your powers."

Jennie climbed into the car, and Baxter slipped through the door. "Still, I can survive without you."

Baxter gave her a pointed look. "Can you, though?"

Jennie gave him a hard stare, then her face softened into a grin. "Why would I want to?" She tapped the unlock code on her phone and scrolled through the list of local towns to find what she was looking for.

The words "Batsto Village" filled the screen.

Baxter chuckled. "I knew you wouldn't be able to resist."

"Hey, it's hardwired in my nature. See a problem linked with the spectral world, and fix it. Judging by the article in that paper, it's nothing more than a bunch of lowlifes playing around in an arena that they don't fully understand. I can straighten that out."

"What if it's not?" Baxter suggested. "These 'Shadows' sound like they've been around the block. Maybe they do know what they're doing."

Jennie chewed her lip as she started the car. "Well, then. All the more reason for us to jump in and see what's going on, don't you think?"

Baxter grinned. "I can't think of a reason not to."

Jennie reversed out of the spot and pulled onto the road again. "Besides, it won't take us too long. We take a short drive to the village, threaten the idiots with the Big Bitch. If we're lucky, we'll be back on the road to DC by nightfall."

"My favorite time of the day," Baxter told her.

"The *night*," Jennie corrected.

Baxter's grin widened. "Pedant."

CHAPTER FOUR

Wharton State Forest, New Jersey, USA

The forest was beautiful, and the roads were dead. Jennie and Baxter trailed cautiously down the 206 and skirted the forest until they saw the signs for Batsto Village.

The sky was clear, and the air was fresh. In the UK, Jennie had been to the Lake District, had visited the Peaks, and been to Sherwood Forest, and none of them had the sheer scale or scenic-postcard beauty Wharton State Forest had.

Jennie looked both ways at the crossroads and hooked left when they reached a junction that told them to turn. She only made it a few more meters when she saw something white glowing through the gaps in the trees.

Her hand found Baxter's shoulder. "Bax, what's that?"

Baxter followed her eyes, and he froze. Jennie pulled the car over to the side of the road and leaned forward to get a better look. "Is that a deer?"

The stag was tall, its antlers stretching either side of its head with pride. It stared at them like some knowing sentinel, frozen in time on the verge.

"It looks like one," Baxter replied. "Actually, more like a stag. But it's…"

"Spectral," Jennie finished, opening her door and climbing out of the car. She shut the door behind her, and the stag's ear twitched. She took a few tentative steps forward, now confirming what she was seeing.

"I've never seen spectral animals before," Baxter marveled. "In all my years of living in the city, you'd think perhaps I'd have seen a fox, or mouse, or squirrel. Hell, a rat would have been enough to open my eyes."

Jennie placed a finger over her lips and edged closer to the stag. The creature was about fifty feet away. Her feet padded softly on the grass as she inched toward it, wondering how close she could get before it took off and dashed into the shadowed canopy of the forest.

Because that's what deer did, right? They feared humans, and they ran for cover when one got too close. It was how they survived, and how they acted in life.

But what about in death?

The stag pawed the ground impatiently with a hoof as Jennie got closer. When she was no more than ten feet away, she stopped and rubbed two fingers together.

"Hey, big guy," she whispered, letting the silence of the forest carry her words. Many more faint spectral shapes took form behind the stag—rabbits, possums, raccoons, and a plethora of birds. They lit up the shadows like fireflies in the deep of a cave.

Jennie smiled. "Lots of guys, I see. Well, hello there."

Baxter stopped close behind Jennie.

The stag stared him in the eye and dragged its hoof across the floor.

"Careful there, Bax," Jennie warned. "He thinks you're competition."

"Me?" Baxter asked in surprise. "Why?"

Jennie shrugged. "You're a big guy. He's a big guy. Relax, you don't want to get yourself into a stand-off, do you?"

Baxter's shoulders softened. "I suppose not. What exactly are they?"

Jennie half-turned her head but kept her eye on the stag. "Yokai."

Baxter didn't have a chance to ask Jennie to expand before the stag suddenly reared up on its hinds, lowered its head, and charged straight at them.

The stag was fast, closing the distance in seconds.

Jennie was prepared. She bent her legs, ready for the collision. Baxter leapt sideways, clearing himself from the impact, and got to his feet just in time to see Jennie twist and jump.

She grabbed the stag by the neck and swung her legs around, using the stag's momentum to give her leverage. Her face was steeled as her legs hooked over its back.

Jennie laughed as the stag put on a burst of speed, then turned back on itself and charged straight for Baxter.

Baxter's eyes grew wide as he rose back to his feet and prepared to dodge again.

Jennie calmed herself and felt around for a connection with the stag, but before she had a chance to make one, the stag bucked.

The movement was so sudden that it shocked Jennie and broke her grip. She was bounced off its back and flew through the air, landing with an uncomfortable thump moments later. The deer continued its trajectory toward Baxter, skidding as it tried to turn, then paused once more near the tree line.

Baxter backed away with his hands up, taking big steps backward until he reached Jennie.

"Angry 'lil thing, isn't it?" Baxter remarked.

Jennie eyed the stag warily. "You can say that again."

Baxter winked. "Angry—"

Jennie shoved her index finger in Baxter's face. "*Don't.*"

The stag stared at them for a few moments longer from the trees, then turned its head and began to gallop back into the forest. When it was on the edge of their vision, it paused and waited expectantly.

"I think it wants us to follow it," Jennie told Baxter. She took a few steps forward.

"You're not serious?" Baxter asked. "After what just happened, you're going to trust it to lead you into the forest? You'll get lost."

Jennie shrugged, her face a mask of silent confidence. "*We'll* get lost."

Baxter rolled his eyes. "Fine. But if we can't find our way back here, I'm haunting you for the rest of your life."

"That's exactly what the ghost of Elvis told me." Jennie chuckled. "He grew bored with it long before I did. Now, c'mon."

The forest grew thicker around them as they progressed. Whilst the edge of the great mass of trees had been well-maintained and touched by the hands of man, the farther into the forest they followed the spectral creatures, the wilder the forest became.

Dense foliage covered the forest floor, creating small traps that hooked and tugged at Jennie's feet. Logs and bracken barred her way, and Jennie was forced to use the Saber of the Holy Divinity to hack their way through on several occasions.

The animals continued to walk with them, keeping a healthy distance from the pair who clearly didn't belong in their domain. They glowed like lanterns around them—a sight which humans would never truly be able to appreciate. At one point, a swarm of fireflies illuminated the way before them.

Jennie felt as though she were in a strange dream. She knew that many mortals believed in spirit animals, but didn't truly understand the true nature of the Yokai. A sentiment that was reflected when Baxter asked, with mouth agape, "What is this place?"

"The true realm of the natural dead," Jennie told him quietly. "There are few spots in the world in which the Yokai may go to find peace. I don't know much about the selection process of spectral animals, but I do know that you wouldn't find this kind of thing in the man-made structures of places like Central Park."

"It's beautiful," Baxter marveled.

Jennie followed his gaze toward where several deer were trotting alongside them. An owl flew from branch to branch above them, its great wings spread out in a hypnotizing spectral array. "The Yokai are famed among those who have seen them for guiding the lost to their destination," she continued. "They can take most forms in the woodlands and are said to only appear when there is danger nearby."

Baxter turned to Jennie. "You failed to include that part before we followed it into the woods."

"Would it have changed your mind?" she asked.

Baxter thought about it for a moment. "I suppose not."

Jennie lifted her hands. "Exactly. You know you're safe with me. Now, hush up and follow."

They headed ever deeper into the forest. The stag didn't once turn back to check they were following. They crossed over a small stream in which the faint shimmer of a school of minnows could be seen battling against the current.

Jennie thought back to the first time she had encountered Yokai, way back near the start of the twentieth century. She had been on a mission in England and found herself in the heart of the Peak District —a large expanse of natural land filled with hills, mountains, woods, and brooks. Even back then, the Yokai had been mystical, leading her into the heart of the trees to where a hiker had fallen into a small sinkhole and struggled to escape.

Jennie had helped free his swollen ankle and taken him to the roadside, where she called an ambulance and waited the hour until he was collected. In that time, the hiker spoke of the wisps that had led him astray, and how he had been captivated enough to blindly follow them into the darkness.

Now, Jennie was doing exactly the same thing, only following the good over the bad. Will-o-the-wisps were bad news; she knew that. Beacons of flame-like white light that lured lone travelers into the darkness.

The Yokai, on the other hand, were the natural force that opposed the wisps. Creatures with golden hearts and a moral compass which followed them even into death.

Except for maybe some of the darker predators which lurked in the forest. Wolves and bears never really changed their tune.

The sky grew dark around them. Jennie snatched glimpses between breaks in the trees as the canvas turned black, dotted with stars. She wondered how much farther it would be before the Yokai stopped, then, at the moment she was reaching into her pocket to check the GPS on her cell, she heard a soft groan in the forest ahead.

Jennie and Baxter exchanged glances, then sped up. Jennie dropped the hand that had been reaching for her cell to her pistol, preparing for possible danger. The groans were pained whimpers that hardly carried at all.

A moss-covered boulder appeared at the end of their path, and Jennie climbed to the top. The Yokai stopped and watched silently as Jennie scanned the forest, hardly able to see anything in the dark.

Following a moment of inspiration, Jennie drew her cell phone out of her pocket and thumbed her pin code. She tapped the flashlight app, and a cone of light lit the area around them.

Jennie gasped, realizing how lucky it had been that she had climbed the boulder, and why the Yokai had stopped where they had.

A shallow crevasse opened up on either side of the ground beyond the boulder—a dark, thin slit.

Jennie shone the flashlight into what appeared to be an underground cave system. A nearby stream dropped its contents down the hole like a mini waterfall. The crevasse stretched into the darkness.

"Help…"

The voice was weak.

Carefully lowering herself from the boulder, Jennie followed the source of the voice.

"Help… Please…"

The voice came from directly below her. She found the edge of the crevasse and peered down, stunned to see a man a couple of feet below the edge, clinging to a thick knot of tree roots with his bare hands.

"Shit, hold on," Jennie told him, looking around for something to grab so she could reach for him and not fall in alongside him. When nothing came to her, she caught Baxter's eyes and decided to improvise.

"Baxter, hold onto that tree."

Baxter obeyed without question, although there was doubt in his eyes. Jennie latched onto Baxter and felt the tendril of energy close between them. She used the energy to anchor herself while she reached down and took the man's hand.

His palms were clammy, and his grip wasn't strong, but she grabbed the material of his cuffs and used that. He kicked weakly against the wall, helping as much as possible. Jennie's muscles strained, and she gritted her teeth to lever him up. Baxter held fast against the tree.

After a short struggle, the man's stomach made it onto the surface. She retained her grip on him until his whole body was out of the crevasse.

He got to his hands and knees, gasping for breath.

Jennie wiped her hands on her top and drew her cell out again. She shone the light on the man's face and felt a chill run down her spine.

He was wearing all black and had a retro-looking revolver strapped to his hip. There was a set of goggles around his neck, and thick white letters spelled the acronym SIA across the back of his jacket.

The man slowly pushed himself to his feet. "Thank you, ma'am. I wasn't sure how much longer I was going to be able to hold on there." He offered Jennie a hand. "Jack Hansen."

"Jennie King," she replied. "How long were you down there?"

"Hours," Jack told her. "I lost count." He shook his hand. "My fingers were reaching the end of their tether. If you hadn't come along, I don't know what condition I'd be in." He looked around the forest as if trying to track something down, then looked at Jennie with confusion. "Aren't there more of you? I thought I heard you talking to someone."

Jennie glanced at Baxter, then turned back to Jack. "No. It's just me."

"Oh." Jack shrugged. "Okay. Well, how did you find me?"

Jennie took a breath. "That's a tough one to explain."

CHAPTER FIVE

They sat on the boulder for a while and let Jack recover his strength. Jennie found a small, hollowed-out rock and used it as a makeshift bowl to carry water from the stream to quench Jack's thirst.

"I never imagined I'd fall into a massive crack in the ground," Jack told her as he sipped. "Did you know there's a cave system below the forest? Me neither. Still, the evidence is right there, as dark as night."

Jennie asked what Jack was doing in the forest in the first place. The man was clearly from the authorities. Only those in positions of power sported the kind of attire he was wearing.

Not to mention the gun strapped to his waist.

"I'm afraid I can't go into those details, ma'am." Jack tensed up, his face straightening. "It's on a need-to-know basis, and you don't need to know."

Jennie nodded. "Okay, then. How about those goggles around your neck? That revolver that clearly isn't standard issue for a man of authority such as yourself? What's all that about?"

"Can't say," Jack repeated, this time seeming apologetic as he responded.

Jennie pinched the bridge of her nose. "Look, I understand if you're on some sort of top-secret agency business, but if you want to stand a hope in hell of finding your way out of this forest and back to…wherever you came from, you're going to have to trust me." She held up her cell. "I have a cell phone here with GPS on that should be able to track our position and guide us back to safety. So, if you need to find a way out of this forest fast, then trust me. I'm not here to hurt you."

Jack raised an eyebrow and spun around to face her better. "Then why are you here? I mean, I know why I'm here, but how does a young lady like you find her way into the middle of the forest and stumble across a man in trouble?" He paused, eyes widening slightly. "Did they find you, too?"

Jennie looked back into the forest toward the place the animals had guided her to. She wasn't surprised to see that there were no more Yokai in sight. The forest was nothing more than a dense shade of black beyond the break in the canopy that spilled silver starlight onto them.

"Did what find us?" Jennie asked.

"The will-o'-the-wisps," Jack asked eagerly before realizing he was letting on too much and falling into his authoritative demeanor again. "I mean…"

"You saw will-o'-the-wisps?" Jennie asked. "Where?"

Jack pointed toward a part of the forest Jennie hadn't yet explored. "They appeared like small lanterns in the air and guided us away from danger." His eyes grew glassy. "They were mesmerizing. I couldn't believe it. I'd never seen anything like it in my life. We thought those sentient balls of spectral flame could guide us away from the danger zone."

Jennie nodded. "Yeah, will-o'-the-wisps can be good like that."

"Well, not all good," Jack continued. "Before I knew it, I was alone and deep in the woods, yet I couldn't tear my eyes away. I reached the place where the final wisp stopped, and that's when I stepped into thin air and fell down the crevasse."

"Yeah." Jennie nodded again. "Will-o'-the-wisps can be dicks like that, too."

Jack raised his head. "You know about them?"

"I know something about them." Jennie smiled. "Let's just say that I'm a researcher of all things paranormal. I've studied will-o'-the-wisps at great length. Even tried to track them a few times."

"A researcher?" Jack said, impressed. "Wow, talk about a stroke of luck."

Jennie looked at him questioningly.

Jack opened his mouth, then considered what he was about to say. He closed his mouth and shook his head. "It doesn't matter."

Jennie's ass began to grow numb on the rock. She stood up and stretched, then looked back down at the agent. "You said 'us' earlier. I'm guessing that means that you've got a partner around here somewhere who might be in as much danger as you were in?"

"Maybe," Jack replied. "That depends on whether or not his theory about our mission was true."

Jennie stared at him expectantly.

"I'm sorry, I can't." Jack rose to his feet and brushed himself down. He turned back to the forest and steeled himself with a deep breath. He stood up straight and extended a hand to Jennie. "Miss King, I thank you for rescuing me, but I have to go on alone. I can't compromise the mission I was sent here for, so I wish you well, and thank you again for your assistance."

Jennie slapped his hand away and rolled her eyes. "You men are all the same," she told him. "Think you can brave it alone without any help from anyone, but what are you going to do in the dark, eh? How are you going to know where you're going?"

"I can guide myself by the stars," Jack informed her hotly. "Basic training."

"How are you going to avoid the potholes?"

"Tread carefully."

Jennie sighed. "You're going to make it all of two hundred yards before something gets you, be that a pothole, a stump, a root, or a predator. You may have your pretty little gun there, but that's not going to make your way any easier." She moved the flashlight on her phone and lit the way ahead. "Let's at least stick together until we find the road again, then you can head on your way, and that'll be that."

Jack considered that for a moment, hand moving involuntarily to shield his revolver. For Jennie, that made his rookie status painfully clear. The logical option was obvious. If he'd put his stubbornness aside, they'd be halfway back to the road already.

"Fine," he conceded. "Until we get to the road."

"There we go," Jennie told him more cheerfully than she felt. "Maybe putting on your night vision goggles will give you a better chance of seeing in the dark."

Jack looked at her in surprise. Jennie grinned.

"I wish they were night-vision goggles," he told her.

Jennie's curiosity was piqued. "What are they?"

"Nothing to concern yourself with," he replied. "My business, okay?"

Jennie shrugged. "Okay." She turned to Baxter and subtly waved him over.

Jennie raised her cell phone to her face and opened the Maps app. The screen showed the loading icon for several seconds before a message appeared on the screen.

Location services currently unavailable.

"Oh, great," Jennie muttered.

"What?" Jack asked.

"We're too far out in the sticks to receive any signal," Jennie replied. "Guess it's down to you and your star-gazing, Captain. Lead the way."

There was something incredibly beautiful about seeing the inside of the altar alive with the glow of flames.

Controlled flame, that was. Seeing the round circle with the five-sided star overlapping itself in the middle was a work of beauty that had taken years to refine. A steady hand, lighter fluid, and the careful dexterity to ensure that no liquid splashed on you were the key components here.

Meister Donavon stood up straight, the long black folds of his cloak shrouding all but the twinkle in his eye. The small flames did nothing to alleviate the chill in the night air, yet he was warm from excitement.

"At last, after thirteen long years, it's going to happen. I can *feel* it."

A woman shuffled beside him, her eyes deep emerald as she turned to him and nodded. He could feel her smile. Knew what lay beneath that cloak and could already imagine them in the throes of passion. His hands sliding over her body, her mouth desperately finding his. When had he become so lucky to find someone who shared his passions in mind, body, and spirit?

Meister Donavon shook his head. He couldn't allow himself the distraction. Not now. Not when all was so close to fruition.

Smoke gently rose into the air. The rest of the order were gathered in a circle around the pentagram, with small silver blades in their hands. The tips were as sharp as a filed dragon's tooth, although less than half the size.

The Meister closed his eyes and took a deep breath through his nose. The air was pregnant with excitement, his member pushed dangerously against his robe as it stiffened with the thought of what was to come. Once the sacrifice had been delivered, they would be here. He would draw them to him, and he would command them. Lead the order with his new pets and show the world why they should never laugh in the face of a progressive occultist.

A door opened and closed. Someone screamed through a gag. The Meister turned with wicked avarice and spread his arms wide. "At last. The final piece of our puzzle is here." He practically glided down the aisle toward the two muscular figures dragging the older man across the floor.

The man's face was blackened and bruised. One eye was almost closed, thanks to the swelling on his face. Duct tape covered his lips, and there was a thin gash which trailed small rivulets of blood down his cheek.

"To think, you arrived at exactly the right time," Meister Donavon crooned. He loomed over him and beamed down. "The texts have been against us all these years, but we've finally cracked it, don't you know? We've finally figured out what was missing all along, and it was the very thing that bound us to the law that has been the blockade of our order."

The gagged man screamed a muffled response. He kicked against his muscular captors, but it was a wasted effort.

Meister Donavon crouched until he was in the man's line of sight. "Do you understand what's going to happen tonight? Do you?"

The man's eyes were wide, and small red veins decorated the whites. He shook his head wildly.

"You're going to die," Meister Donavon told him simply. He stood and walked back up the aisle, raising his voice as his thugs pulled the man along behind them. "It's all for a grand cause, my friend. We've initiated the residents of this village and silenced all those who opposed our goals, and now we have nothing but time to ensure that we do this right. Death…that is the key that will unlock the other side. Bloody murder in the form of sacrifice." He tapped his head. "I don't know why we didn't realize it before."

He arrived back at the pentagram and took a step to the side. The thugs dragged the man across the burning flames and into the center of the image and tied his hands and feet to large stakes that had been jammed into the floor. The flames were inches from the man's body.

The man struggled, but it was all for nothing. The cloaked individuals stared at him passively. When the thugs were done, they returned to their places in the circle and held hands with their comrades.

"Well, well," Meister Donavon murmured with glee in his eyes. "The formalities are over. I suppose we should begin."

They had been trekking through the forest for the better part of an hour, and there was still no sign of the road.

There had been no more sign of the Yokai either, nor had Jennie seen any wisps, as she might have expected. The forest was a silent cloak around them, one they were both eager to leave.

"Are you sure he's taking us in the right direction?" Baxter hissed.

Jennie glared at him but ignored him.

Despite the situation they found themselves in, Jennie found that she was enjoying Jack's company. Although he couldn't speak about what had brought him to the forest in the first place, he had opened up to Jennie about certain elements of his life, and in return, she had spoken about particular parts of her life—within reason.

Jack was a young man with a good heart and a great personality. He was honorable and valued the truth, which was something that couldn't be said for a lot of people. After he asked Jennie what brought her to the forest and she had avoided the question, he had chosen not to pursue the subject.

We've all got our secrets, Jennie thought, glancing back to see Baxter watching the forest over his shoulder as if something might jump out and attack him.

"So, what brought you to this side of the Atlantic?" Jack asked. When Jennie curved her eyebrow, he added, "Your accent. It's British, right?"

"I was a major in history at London Metropolitan University," Jennie told him, resurrecting one of the many cover stories she had concocted over the years to convince those who didn't live in her world that she was ordinary. "Passed my exams, got caught up in American culture and history, and found a section in the campus library dedicated to the paranormal. Followed those books down a dark path and found that there were sites in the US where black magic was practiced."

"Really?" Jack asked. "What kinda places?"

"Salem is the main one," Jennie told him. "Everyone and their auntie has heard about the Salem witch trials, and there may have been some truth to the accusations against those women. But what people don't know is that there were towns all over where the locals heard about the trials and began to seed their own cults. Small communities who welcomed black magic."

"Woah," Jack told her. "So, you're really knowledgeable about this kind of stuff?"

"Let's just say, I've been around," Jennie agreed.

Jack laughed. They stepped over a fallen log and wove around some trees.

"Now you've got to give me something," Jennie urged. "Those goggles around your neck. What are they, swimming goggles?"

Jack shook his head.

Jennie continued to press. "If they're not for swimming, and they're not for seeing in the dark, then what are they for?"

"VR," Jack replied but decided to say no more.

Jennie was about to probe with another question when she heard a loud howl nearby. She paused. The sound raised her skin in goose-flesh, and her hand went instinctively to the weapons at her hip.

Jack stopped and looked around. "What is it?"

"Didn't you just hear that?" Jennie asked.

"Hear what? You think there's something out there?"

"Er, Jennie?" Baxter cut in. "I don't think that was a regular howl."

Baxter backed toward the pair as several spectral shapes came into sight. At first, they were nothing more than flares of light, but soon they coalesced into a pack of large, disgruntled wolves.

Their fur was matted, and their eyes blazed a deep red. Many had gashes and wounds across their spectral forms, and some had patches were there was no flesh or fur, nothing more than hollowed bone.

"*Fuck*," Jennie cursed, drawing her sword. She broke the connection to Baxter that prevented the sword from manifesting and held it before her.

"What the..." Jack took a step back, seeing a woman who had made a sword appear staring into the shadows. "What are you doing?"

"It's a little bit hard to explain," Jennie told him. "Just lay low. I got this."

CHAPTER SIX

The wolves snarled and snapped their teeth. Glowing spectral saliva dripped onto the forest floor. There were at least a dozen wolves surrounding them. Where they had come from, Jennie had no idea. Perhaps they had been stalking them for miles, waiting for a moment they were alone and vulnerable.

"Seriously, where did you get that?" Jack asked. He drew his pistol and aimed it hesitantly at Jennie.

"I'd lower that gun if I were you," she told him.

Jack paid no attention. "Jennie King, lower your weapon. I'm not gonna ask again."

But Jennie's attention wasn't on Jack, it was with the wolves slowly closing in on them. Baxter had taken out his pistol and wrench and readied them.

Jennie side-mouthed to Baxter. "Whatever you do, don't shoot. The sound might attract others."

Baxter nodded.

"I don't want to, but you're going to make me," Jack warned, eyes darting into the gloom. "Jennie, don't ignore a federal agent."

Jennie took slow steps toward the wolves. They snarled and growled at her, their hackles raised. The alpha that led the group in front of her was at least double the size of the others. Jennie reached down and drew her pistol, and she aimed it at those to her side.

Jack grew serious at the sudden appearance of the gun. He tightened his grip on the revolver and thumbed back the catch. "This is your last warning, Jennie. I don't know what kind of fucked-up magic trick you're playing, but if you don't lower that weapon by the count of three, I'm going to have to use force."

"If you really want to protect yourself, you'll do as I say," Jennie yelled without turning back. "Stay back, and let me take care of this."

Jack started counting. "One…"

One of the wolves to her left jumped forward, then leapt back, jaws sounding like a movie clapperboard.

"Two…"

The alpha stopped and allowed its brethren to continue.

"Thre—"

One of the wolves broke from the back and streamed toward Jennie and Baxter. Jennie planted her feet as she raised the sword and swung it in a sweeping arc toward the wolf.

The instant the blade connected with the wolf's flesh, blinding white light sparked in the forest. Jennie, Baxter, and Jack shielded their eyes as the glow bloomed, then faded into darkness, leaving no trace of the wolf behind.

Jack crouched, shocked by the sudden flash. His gun was still aimed at Jennie, but now his eyes darted in all directions. "Jennie? What the hell was that?"

"No time to explain," Jennie told him, dodging out of the way of another wolf as it sprang at her. All of the wolves were angered by the painful light and the loss of their pack member.

Behind her, Baxter swung his wrench and smashed the skull of a wolf. Another came at him from behind and bit into his leg, causing him to cry out in pain. He aimed and fired his pistol, eliciting a yelp from the wolf, who released its hold on his muscle and fell to the ground, twitching.

Baxter stood shakily on one good leg and let off several more shots. Some found their targets, while many went through the trees and off into the distance.

Jennie, meanwhile, dived to the ground and turned her momentum into a well-executed roll. She rose to her feet and slashed at two more wolves, producing two more blinding bursts of light.

Using the light as a distraction, she moved away from the wolves so she could get an accurate headcount. There was more than a handful left, and they were growing angrier with each light surge.

Baxter was busy defending against the next wolf that attacked him, while Jennie prepared to face the multiple wolves that were advancing quickly toward her.

Her eyes were drawn to the alpha, which was watching silently from a short distance away. It remained motionless, even when members of its pack were lost.

Jennie narrowed her eyes and sprinted for the big boy. If she could take him, perhaps the rest would flee.

<hr>

Jack couldn't understand what the hell was going on. At first, he'd thought Jennie had gone crazy. Maybe she had been stranded in the woods for too long. Perhaps her story about black magic and paranormal activity had been a cover-up for a girl with a deranged mind who had stumbled into the woods.

But the moment the flash of light had appeared, he no longer questioned her. While he wasn't entirely sure what was going on, there was definitely something afoot here, and she clearly knew what she was doing.

Jack watched while Jennie fought with the air, her sword swings sporadically met with an explosion of light that burned his retinas and faded, only to leave painful red after-burns in his vision.

He brought his hands up to shield his eyes, and the goggles around his neck moved with him. He felt their presence on his neck and stretched the flexible band to view the lenses. They were tinted, which might shade some of the blinding light. However, he looked at them cautiously, wondering whether the VR technology would bring back the wisps, who would try to lead him elsewhere.

Another blinding flash made him decide to take the chance. He strapped the goggles to his face and adjusted them until they were comfortable, then turned around.

His jaw dropped. Where before there had been nothing more to see than Jennie slicing at imaginary objects in the air, there were now a number of wolves around Jennie that emanated a strange blue radiance.

Wolves? Jack's mind scrambled to keep up. *How is this even possible? Is she...part of the game, too?*

Then another figure caught his attention—a large man, made of the same ghostly substance as the wolves. He stood at least six and a half, maybe seven feet in height. His shoulders were broad and his arms were thick, and in his hands were a large wrench and a pistol.

Jack observed the pair of them for a few moments, stunned into silence. It was only when he found the strength to move and took a step forward that he realized his mistake.

In moving, he had drawn the attention of a nearby wolf. The creature turned to him with a hungry look, rearing back on its haunches.

Shit, Jack. What the hell have you gotten yourself wrapped up in?

Jennie sprinted forward as fast as she could, her attention trained on the big guy.

The wolf didn't flinch. It merely watched her as though she were a plaything.

Jennie darted out of the way of the attacking wolves, moving as fast as her legs would allow. When she was within closing distance of the alpha, she leapt with her sword held like a skewer in front of her. She shouted, preparing to feel the fleshy squish of the wolf as it was impaled on the blade...

But nothing happened.

In fact, the wolf was gone.

Jennie looked around wildly and spotted the wolf ten feet or so away from her. She jumped again, and once more the wolf vanished at the last moment, only to reappear in another location.

"Spectral translocation?" Jennie muttered, focusing her effort on her connection with Baxter. "How…and how do I kill it?"

A wolf smacked into her side. She fell to the ground, crushed beneath its weight as the wolf trained its maw on her throat. Jennie held its jaws open with her bare hands and twisted to throw it away from her.

She was on her feet before the wolf came for the final bite. She became material and slid to the side as the creature overcommitted. When she was behind the wolf, she turned immaterial again and drove her saber into its back.

The wolf managed half a howl before it too was exorcized.

"Stay back!" Jack's voice carried across the forest.

Jennie turned her head and saw that the man was in danger as a spectral wolf came straight at him.

Without hesitation, she aimed her pistol and fired at the wolf. The report caused all the other wolves to flinch. The bullet found its mark in the center of the wolf's skull in midair and the impact forced the creature away from its mark.

Jack gave her a thankful nod.

Jennie returned the gesture, suddenly aware of the wolves closing on her again.

More gunshots, and this time they weren't Jennie's. Jack moved rapidly closer, the rims of his goggle's lenses blinking with strange green lights. The bullets bit the dirt around her, sending up sprays of dirt and debris.

Not one of his shots hit the wolves.

"What the hell?" Jack exclaimed. He looked at his gun, then opened fire once more. The gun clicked empty. He muttered another, "Shit," then threw the gun on the ground.

The wolves were in a frenzy.

Baxter moved closer to Jenny to guard her back. They whirled around each other, Baxter knocking wolves aside with swings of the wrench, both of them sending bullets into their bodies, and Jennie's sword causing others to erupt into bursts of light.

They were breathless when they finished.

"All right," Jack murmured softly. "Okay. They're gone."

Jennie shook her head. "You've forgotten the big boy."

Jack glanced around, nonplussed. "The big boy?"

Baxter nodded, then pointed over Jack's shoulder to where the alpha waited before them, somehow even larger than he was before.

Jennie cocked her head to the side. "At least its troops have gone. One on one seems like better odds to me."

"There are three of us," Jack stated, looking uncertainly at Baxter as though he wasn't sure if he was real. He pawed the air, and his hand passed through Baxter's head.

Baxter glared at him. "Do you mind?"

Jennie broke free of the pair and held the saber out to her side. The wolf's mouth creased into something that could be mistaken for a grin. At his full height, his back was as tall as the top of her head.

Jack moved to follow her.

Baxter held a spectral arm out, which, while it didn't make an impact, paused Jack in his tracks. "She said, one-on-one."

Jennie's eyes narrowed. The wolf had a determined expression on his face. There was a glint of intelligence in his large black eyes. Whatever was going on, killing him wasn't going to be easy. Creatures who would fall easily tended to leap straight into battle. This creature bided his time.

"C'mon, pup," Jennie soothed. "Don't tell me you're frozen stiff? I'm just a puny little chew-toy. Surely even you can see that?"

The wolf snarled in response.

"Fine," Jennie conceded. "Have it your way."

A thin tendril of ethereal energy shot from Jennie and latched onto the wolf. She broke the stillness and ran, using the Yokai's energy to propel her forward. Her back arched and her teeth gritted, she held the sword in front of her and went for the wolf's neck.

Before she could make contact, the forest around her vanished. It reappeared a moment later, only the wolf was now behind her. Jennie landed awkwardly in the underbrush and used her free hand to steady her fall.

Deciding now was the time to strike, the wolf lunged at her. Inspired by her recent trip, Jennie made a snap decision. She latched onto the wolf and imagined herself next to Baxter and Jack.

The wolf's mouth closed around her, but his teeth snapped on thin air.

Jennie wobbled on her feet, using the two men for support. "Thanks, guys. I knew you'd come in handy."

Baxter grinned. "Whatever you need, Jennie."

Jack merely stared, mouth agape.

The wolf howled, then turned his head and planted his feet firmly. He looked set to charge at Jennie once more. In a blink, she latched onto the creature and translocated to the other side of the wooded area, drawing his attention away from her companions.

The wolf shot her that almost human grin again. This time, something strange happened.

Small orbs materialized on the ground in the places where the remaining wolves had been injured. The lights grew in intensity as the beasts turned amorphous and lost their form. They liquified into a shimmering substance which now shot toward the alpha wolf, joining with its form the instant they touched its flesh.

The wolf grew impossibly large, his head now scraping the canopy overhead, and howled once more.

Jennie sighed. "Rule Thirty-One, Genevieve. Slay your enemies, don't play with them."

The wolf jumped at her, the ground shaking as its massive paws hit it. Jennie sidestepped, then ran beneath the wolf, the sword directly in front of her as she went for a long slice across his stomach.

The wolf turned on his front paws and aimed his bite at Jennie. She materialized at the exact moment the teeth should have shredded her, then ran through the wolf's spectral form and found the place she wanted to strike.

"Don't you know what happens when you wolf down your

dinner?" Jennie snarked, drawing her strength together. "You get a severe stomach ache!"

This time the wolf was too slow to move. Jennie became immaterial and stabbed the blade into his belly. There was no resistance whatsoever as the blinding light erupted in front of her. This time she could feel its heat, the light looking as though it was going to swallow them both.

The wolf whined and yelped, scrambling his giant paws against the earth as his body was taken by the blade's power. Jennie dropped to the ground and covered her eyes, only now hearing the wolf's pain.

A final blast of heat pulsed from the sword's entry point, then silence fell thick over the forest.

Jennie raised her head from her arms and saw the sword lying a few feet away from her. She reached for it, stood, brushed herself off, and then looked for the others.

Jack removed his goggles and placed them atop his head, his mouth hanging open.

Baxter tucked his wrench and pistol away and gave Jennie a round of applause.

CHAPTER SEVEN

<u>**Wharton State Forest, New Jersey, USA**</u>

Meister Donavon's hand trembled as he clutched the knife, which was inches away from the man's heart. His forehead bore a sheen of sweat, and his eyes were wide and wild. One motion and the man would be dead. The ritual would begin. His blood would spill and activate the magic.

Or would it?

He gritted his teeth, mind whirling with doubts.

Suppose the magic doesn't activate? Suppose I'm just killing a man for the sake of it? What then? What would that make of me if I snuffed out a life and got nothing in return? I'd be nothing more than a criminal. A lowlife murderer.

What he didn't dare voice even in his mind was that his entire belief system would be shattered. He pushed the doubt away.

But what if it does *work? What if you're able to trigger the darkness and bring her back to life? What then?*

His followers waited, staring patiently at their leader. The chanting had stopped the minute he had crouched over the man, bathing them in a heavy silence. The only disturbances were the weak whimpers of the man on the floor, his sounds masked by the duct tape over his mouth.

Meister Donavon took a deep breath and closed his eyes. When he opened them again, he raised the knife high above his head, drove it down…

And stopped again.

This time he let the hand holding the knife drop to his side. The other he used to punch the man in the stomach, venting his frustration at the inconvenient intrusion of his conscience.

You're doing this for her. *Think of her sweet little fingers, fingers that never got to grasp yours. Think of her…*

"I can't," he admitted through gritted teeth.

"You can," Julia urged.

Meister Donavon looked up and into Julia's eyes. Even in the darkness, her eyes gleamed like jewels. She broke free of the circle, stepped carefully over the flames, and placed a hand on his back.

"No one will ever understand the pain we've gone through to get here," she whispered, her lips a hair's breadth from his ear. Each syllable sent a tingle through his body. "No one will understand why we have to do what we're doing. But you do, don't you, my love? Do you understand it all? Life is only a fleeting thing. A butterfly in a snowstorm, beating its wings before the sweet chill of death embraces it. That's all this is. You're the snowstorm, he's the butterfly. Embrace the cold."

The Meister stared down at the man, whose wrinkles carved deep grooves in his forehead. His eyes were filled with fear.

"He's already close to death," Julia soothed. "You're not snatching a child or a mother in her prime. You're preventing the slow decline of this man's health by rewarding him with death. He has lived, and now, so must she."

Donavon's stare hardened. He gave a curt nod, then kissed Julia deeply.

She smiled and returned to her place in the circle.

Donavon stared once more at the point the knife would puncture. One swift jab; that was all it would take. Like ripping off a band-aid, the task needed to be performed swiftly to minimize the pain to himself.

A growl escaped his throat. The sound escalated into a triumphant roar. His arm coiled above his head, then he screamed at the top of his lungs and drove the knife down, his hands gripping so hard that the knuckles were white.

———

Clive stared up in horror as the cloaked figures finished their chant. His hands were bound and his mouth was taped; there was nothing he could do.

He looked around for some means of escape. The figures blocked the view of anything that might be useful. He had trained for years to escape hostage situations, yet, outnumbered and incapacitated, what was there to do?

He scanned all of the cloaked figures' faces in turn, eyes desperately trying to connect with theirs. Each one he looked at was more passive than the next.

Until he came to the girl.

A sudden flare of fire illuminated the softness of her features. The doubt in her eyes. She bit her lip and glanced at the others, uncertainty all but hijacking her features. Where the others stood as still as gargoyles, her fingers twitched and rubbed her palms.

An out? Clive wondered. *Please?*

Clive stared at her with desperation, doing what he could to ignore the figure who crouched over him with a steel blade glinting in the firelight. He moaned and shouted, trying to catch her attention.

Please, just look at me. Please!

And then she did. Her eyes locked onto his, and at that moment, he saw a single tear roll down her cheek.

The man struggled and fought with his own inner demons, teasing Clive with the blade just inches away from his stomach. Seconds later, a woman broke free and muttered something into his ear.

You're running out of time, Clive thought, trying to pass the message telepathically to the girl. *Any second now.*

The man nodded and steeled himself. He held the knife high above Clive's stomach and drove it down fast…

The girl broke from the pack and delivered a swift kick to the man's temple.

A sudden flash of pain bloomed in Donavon's head. He saw stars where he should've seen blood and death. The Meister fell sideways, his head cracking on the hard floor.

The knife fell from his limp hands. Fire chewed at his sleeve. As he struggled to push himself off the floor, he became aware of footsteps and a sudden rush of movement.

A dark shape leapt over him and sprinted down the aisle of the church, cloak flying behind him while his followers gave chase.

The door opened. Even the dribble of moonlight was enough to reinitiate the pain. His head pounded, and he almost screamed. The shouts were too much. Donavon closed his eyes, only aware a few moments later that Julia had dragged him into the nest of her lap and was cradling his head.

"What was that?" Donavon managed, rage building inside him. He looked at the pentagram and was distressed to see that the shape had been disturbed by the trampling feet.

"A traitor," Julia informed him in a soft voice. "One more despicable piece of shit to expel from our order. Don't worry, she'll come to justice soon enough."

She ran as fast as her legs could carry her.

The village was dark, every house and building cloaked in shadow. Dotted around the spaces between were cloaked figures patrolling the streets, wandering with torches aflame in their hands. The air was chilly, the night peaceful.

Until the shouts came from behind.

She ducked around the side of the church, praying to God that her way wouldn't be barred. She had done the unspeakable; she had betrayed her coven. The group she had bound herself to for the last two years were now enemies she had backstabbed on the cusp of all they had wanted to achieve.

Yet there wasn't an ounce of remorse in her heart as she stuck to the shadows and hid at the back of an old brick building. There wasn't a part of her that felt guilty for saving the man's life. Playing with magic had been awesome to begin with, and she had loved the possibility that more existed beyond death. However, things had taken a turn in recent weeks, and murder was something she wouldn't be an accessory to.

The coven poured out of the church. Alarms were raised. The citizens of the village would no doubt open their eyes and remember the situation they were in, with their town hostage to the coven. She had to flee. Had to run and fast.

Maybe the man wouldn't survive the night. Maybe her actions wouldn't be enough to give the man the gift of living another twenty or thirty years. Maybe, when she was either captured or the coven had given up their search, they would simply return to the ritual and start again.

But she wouldn't die with it on her conscience. She'd done what she could to grant the man a new lease of life, and by God, she hoped he lived long enough to take advantage of that gift.

She slipped away in the shadows, her cloak swallowed in the darkness. With carefully timed dashes between buildings, and her knowledge of the town's layout, she slipped away from the pitchforks and flaming torches and made her way toward the forest.

CHAPTER EIGHT

Buckingham Palace, London, UK

Footsteps echoed loudly around the throne room. A number of mortal men in pressed dark suits strode confidently down the red carpet, each carrying a thick briefcase in one hand. On their faces were pairs of thick, round goggles that glowed with green light around their edges.

Queen Victoria leaned forward on her throne, her fingers laced together in her lap. Her sour expression had been replaced with a look of keen interest, and she studied the mortals as they approached.

On either side of her throne was a specter—her new number twos, burly men with dark eyes and muscles beneath the thin cotton of the clothing they had died in.

Leading the congregation of suited men was SIS Agent Oliver Clark. He stopped several feet in front of Victoria and took a knee. He stared at the floor, the silence pressing on them all, and waited until he was given the command to rise. There were no goggles on his face.

The other four men followed suit.

"You may rise," Victoria finally allowed, enjoying the power she had abandoned and left for so long to the control of those greedy no-good little shits who couldn't even run the goddamn country properly.

They did so.

"Present your cases," Victoria ordered, putting thoughts of Porter and Yasmine aside.

Agent Clark nodded, then gave the command to his men. They laid their suitcases neatly on top of the tables set up along either side of the aisle, then took a step back and crossed their hands behind their backs.

Agent Clark waited until each was ready, then set about thumbing the combination into the lock of each suitcase. When a small click came, he pulled a set of keys from his inner breast pocket, placed it in the lock, and turned it. When the next click came, a quick placement of his thumb against a dark pad sprang the catch, and the case opened to reveal the contents inside.

When all four cases were open, he nodded to Victoria, who held out her hands on either side to allow her henchmen to aid her to her feet. An unnecessary maneuver, but one which added to her show of power.

She walked over to peer into the cases, which were lined with a soft, velvety material. Each one displayed a strange array of sleek metallic objects.

Victoria picked up a small pistol and weighed it in her palm. The metal was cool to the touch, far below the temperature of the room. "These are the latest tech?"

"They are," Agent Clark replied. "Fresh off the press and tested against your..." he searched for the right word, "er, donations."

Agent Clark moved closer to Victoria and held out his hand. She gave him the pistol. "The very latest in spectral technology. Weapons, distractions, and gear for mortals to aid in the hunt for specters who wrong the crown." He rotated the pistol in his hand and thumbed a catch, and the magazine slipped into his hand. He flipped it over to reveal gleaming silver bullets inside.

"Imbued with spectral energy and able to penetrate a specter from a hundred yards," Agent Clark enthused. "Rapid-fire, lightweight, 9mm caliber."

"You've come a long way over the last few…" Victoria paused, the momentary slip almost enough to give away her position. No one else besides Jennie and her crew and Porter and Yasmine knew the truth behind the true queen's absence, and there Victoria was, about to say something as simple as "You've come a long way over the last few years."

She had almost slipped on several occasions already. Getting up to speed properly on the duties she had neglected over the last few decades was starting to take its toll. One minor slip would be enough to shake the court's confidence in her leadership, and now, when the spectral world was already on thin ice—particularly given Jennie's efforts to ignite a new faction in the US—she really needed to keep it together.

"Months," Victoria finished with a curt nod. She crossed to another briefcase and stared intently at the agent standing beside it, who had dark-lensed goggles on his face. "And these are?"

"We call them SI Goggles," Agent Clark replied. "Spectral Intelligence goggles, which allow the user to tap into spectral frequencies."

Victoria indicated the goggle-wearers with a wave. "So, these men are not conduits like you?"

Agent Clark shook his head. "They're nothing more than mortals in possession of great technology."

"So, they can see me?"

Agent Clark gave a small hiss of breath. "In a sense. At the moment, the technology allows them to make out the outline of nearby specters, but nothing more. We're still working on drilling down to the finer details. Imagine looking at yourself through a steamed-up window and seeing a glowing white reflection with basic facial features."

"Impressive." Her eye was drawn to another pistol, smaller than the last. "Am I to assume this one is all the better for concealment? A weapon which can be hidden from concealment easily and drawn when needed?"

Agent Clark gave Victoria a strange look. Didn't she know this was the same weapon he had drawn on Rogue during the final showdown between the agent and the wraiths?

But he knew it wasn't wise to question the queen's memory. "That's correct, Your Majesty."

He led Victoria over to the other cases, showcasing an array of gas grenades which he explained could not be seen by mortals, as well as various tasers, rifles, and even a pair of leather gloves that had been implanted with nodes and wires that gave off a small hum when switched on.

"These allow mortals to make contact with specters," Agent Clark informed her. "Put on the glove, and the wearer can touch, hold, restrain, or choke any specter who crosses his path. No longer will specters have the advantage against mortals of being able to control their material state. We can fully control the process."

"Amazing," Victoria marveled, unable to believe how far technology had truly come in the last few decades. If there was one thing Porter, Yasmine, and Alexandria had done right, it was funding spectral technological development. "Have you thought about a wider range of clothing?"

"Researchers are working on a suit of armor as we speak. Their timeline isn't clear at the moment, but soon SI armor will be standard issue for the SIS and any other agency dealing with specters.

"Excellent," Victoria praised. The truth was, even though she had allowed Jennie her chance to go back to the US and away from bothering the finer parts of her spectral kingdom, she didn't feel safe anymore. With her secret in the hands of Jennie and her group, how long would it be before they started trying to leverage her past against her? Could she really trust the group to stay where they were and be quiet with that power in their hands?

Power does crazy things to people, particularly those who have wielded it for the longest.

She didn't see the irony in her thoughts.

"How long until these items become standard issue among the troops?" Victoria asked.

"I've been told a few weeks are needed to issue out the items to those who will need them," Agent Clark replied. "A manufacturing process has still yet to be established given the nature of the spectral imbuement. I've been asked to request an additional number of spectral donations in order to achieve the desired effect."

Victoria waved a hand. "Take as many as you need. We've got them by the thousands, ready to donate their lives for a greater cause. It's not like they're doing much with their second chances anyway."

Agent Clark nodded, then gave the order for his men to close the cases. When they were all standing and awaiting their next orders, Victoria spoke again.

"One more thing before you go."

"Yes, Your Majesty?"

"My earlier instructions were followed, correct? The US has been informed?"

Agent Clark told her they had. "Down to the letter. They are aware, and schematics for our technology have been shared with them. If I may be allowed to speak frankly, Your Majesty?"

Victoria indicated that he could.

"With the technology in American hands, there is a chance that they'll accelerate everything we've created so far. Their resources are greater than ours, and they have more staff."

"Your point?" Victoria stated.

"Just that the Americans have a history of going big with anything new. If they run away with this, there might soon be an even bigger army across the Pond with technology we can only dream of."

Victoria pondered that. "True. But when that moment comes, the Americans will have to remember who opened their reality and gave them insight into the spectral world. By that time, we'll have the ultimate negotiating assets."

Agent Clark looked doubtful.

"Besides," Victoria told him. "We've already laid the groundwork with the SIA. Who do you think they're going to follow—her Royal Paranormal Majesty, or some renegade from the slums?"

· · ·

Wharton State Forest, New Jersey, USA

Jennie looked down at the dark ribbon of road. It was a welcome sight after the sheer number of trees they had navigated through. "I suppose this is where we part ways?"

Jack stood beside her, still as pale as the moment the wolves had appeared. He had kept the goggles on the entire way back, asking Jennie question after question about what had happened back there.

Jennie had grinned and given Jack the lowdown on the spectral world, imparting only as much information as she was sure that his brain could handle. Initiating newbies into the world had a tendency to fry their circuits if they learned too much too soon, so she gave him the abridged version.

"Though, I'm judging by your technology that you're hardly ignorant of the entire spectral world?" Jennie had asked after several minutes of discussing her ability to see and communicate with Baxter, and the process of turning spectral.

"Well, no, not entirely ignorant," Jack replied, his ears turning red. "It's just, my partner thought that this was some kind of training exercise. Virtual reality to aid in the induction of new blood into a new government division. I didn't know what to believe until you showed me different."

"Virtual reality?" Jennie asked.

"It's a type of technology in which false images are displayed in a hyper-realistic—"

Jennie grinned. "I know what VR is, you idiot."

"Oh." Jack deflated, unable to work out how best to respond to Jennie's insult, even if it was playful. "Well, you can understand my confusion, then? Transferred to a new department and given strange, never-before-seen technology. Put on these goggles, and strange glowing shapes appear in front of me. With the way the world is going, why wouldn't this be an ultra-advanced training system?"

Jennie nodded. It was true that things had certainly come a long way in the last hundred years or so. Virtual and augmented reality technologies had been incorporated by the army, the navy, and the Air

Force, with simulated scenarios becoming the most effective way to train new cadets without risk.

Jennie had eyed Jack's technology the rest of the way out of the forest, at one point handling it herself and looking through the dark lenses. With the goggles on, she was surprised he could see anything of the forest. It was a wonder he hadn't tripped over anything. When she looked through them, she could still see Baxter as clear as day, but she had no idea if that was because of the tech or her abilities.

Jack looked along the road's dark length in either direction and waited for Jennie's phone to get a signal. When her map finally loaded, they knew which way they needed to go.

Jennie waited for a long moment, watching Jack consider his options.

"You waiting for something?" Jennie asked.

"I'm just thinking," Jack told her. "Before, when I was heading back to save my partner, I thought I needed to be alone. That the white ghosts I'd seen—"

"Wisps."

Jack smiled. "Yeah, wisps. I thought they were all a part of the simulation. Now I'm aware that there has to be something spectral going down in the village."

Jennie winked. "Oh? Is the super-cautious Agent Jack finally going to tell me his mission?"

The SIA agent's brow wrinkled. "Understand that this is top secret information, and what I'm telling you now could result in my dismissal."

Jennie was enjoying playing with him. "Then why are you telling me?"

Jack frowned. "Because I need your help."

He told Jennie the situation, from sneaking into the village to investigate the reports of a coven practicing dark and dangerous magic to Clive being taken by the coven.

"If we don't find them soon, I'm worried what they're going to do to him."

Jennie's face straightened. "You were lucky that the wisps led you away from danger. That's not always characteristic of their nature."

"They led *me* away from danger," Jack reminded her. "Clive wasn't so lucky. He's older and was overrun far quicker. There was nothing I could do in their trance."

Jennie sighed. "Why do I have a feeling that there's something bigger going on here?" She turned to Jack. "You better fill me in on everything. Much like you government types, I need to know every possible nugget of information before we dive in. The last thing we need is to run in there all guns blazing and find out it's a trap."

Then came the sound of footsteps and heavy breathing. Jennie drew her pistol in a flash and trained it down the road at where a dark figure was running toward them.

"Friend of yours?" Jennie asked without looking away.

Jack had his own gun drawn. "Not one of mine."

The shadow loomed closer. The figure ran straight toward them with no concern about the two guns pointed in their direction.

Jennie's finger tensed on the trigger.

One wrong move and it's bye-bye to you.

The figure waved its arms and struggled for breath. It wore a dark cloak, which made it difficult to identify.

Jennie took a step forward. "If you value your life, I recommend you stop and put your hands behind your head."

The figure continued walking.

Jack moved forward with Jennie. "Federal agent," he barked. "You get one chance. *Stop and put your hands on your head.*"

The figure reluctantly obeyed. Its hands moved to the top of its head, where they gripped the hood and pulled it down to reveal a beautiful young woman.

Jennie and Jack cautiously approached.

"Who are you, and what's your business?" Jennie asked.

The woman craned her head to the sky and gasped for breath, chest rising and falling rapidly. Her lips moved, but no words came out. She tried to speak again, managing only guttural choking before her knees collapsed and she folded to the ground.

CHAPTER NINE

They managed to bring the woman around with some water scooped from a nearby stream. Jack indelicately splashed her face, causing her to gasp and jackknife to a sitting position.

"Where am I?" she asked.

Jennie knelt beside her, still gripping her pistol firmly. If there was one thing she'd learned over the last century, it was never to let your guard down for a pretty face.

"You're in the woods," Jennie told her. "Well, technically, you're on a road parallel to the woods. You've been running for a while, it seems."

The woman moved her hands to the ground to straighten out her legs, but the maneuver forced Jack and Jenny to raise their guns again.

"Hands where we can see them," Jack told her.

"Who are you?" Jennie asked.

"My name's Ruby," she told them, moving one hand as she rubbed her eye with her palm. "I was running away from…" Her eyes grew wide when she saw the letters on Jack's uniform. "You're with him. I mean, he's with you. You're one of *them*?"

Jack and Jennie exchanged glances.

"In English, please?" Jennie asked.

Ruby pointed at Jack's breast. "SIA. It's the same initials as the older guy." She looked him in the eyes. "Are you from the government?" She spat the words out like they were dirty.

Jack moved closer, taking a knee beside Jennie. "You've seen Clive?"

Ruby nodded.

"Where is he?" Jack urged. "Is he okay? Where did you see him? What are they doing to him?"

"He's okay for now," Ruby told him. "I saved him. I…" Tears welled in her eyes. "I saved him, but it was at a great cost."

Ruby went on to explain that the coven was on the verge of completing their ritual. That their leader, Meister Donavon, had shown signs of madness over the last several months when other attempts had failed. How desperate he was to prove that there was something greater out there and that black magic was more than just grown-ups playing pretend.

"He'll stop at nothing to prove he's right," Ruby told them. "What he wanted to do to your partner only goes to show that. I was on board with everything he did until he turned to murder as the final step of his plan."

"Murder?" Jack repeated, his face turning pale. "They're going to kill him?"

"Almost did," Ruby whispered. "Until I charged the Meister's altar and caught him off-guard with a kick to the face."

Jennie gave a curt nod. "Human sacrifice. It's a staple of many dark rituals. Only in the spilling of human blood and the meeting of certain requirements can humans who aren't blessed with the gift see the dead. Even then, it's only temporary. Unless…"

"Unless what?" Ruby asked.

Jennie thought back to past situations she'd dealt with. In her mind's eye, she could see the black veil of smoke covering the victim of a ritual long in the past. Could see the rising excitement of the cult members before the creature emerged and created chaos.

"Should the ritual occur over a flaming pentagram, and the correct Latin be muttered, then things can take a hairy turn."

"What are we talking about here?" Baxter asked. "Poltergeists?"

Jennie shook her head. "No. Something darker."

Ruby gave her a strange look, not understanding why Jennie had continued to talk to herself. She looked at Jack for an answer, but he too was staring through his goggles into the empty space behind them.

Jennie turned her attention back to Jack and Ruby. "Black magic is real, and it can have a profound impact on a new spectral life. With the right manipulation, reality can shatter, and darkness can be born where light should flourish." She looked down the road. "We need to get to them and fast."

Ruby's eyes widened. "Are you kidding? I can't go back! They're already out there looking for me. You think I'll be able to just sneak back in there unnoticed without severe consequences?"

The sound of rumbling engines came from down the road.

"The way I see it," Jennie told her, "you've got two choices. Either head on down the road the way you were going and walk miles to the nearest accommodation where you might be safe for a short while until they find you, or come with me and finish what you started."

Headlights broke the horizon of the road. Jennie ran to the verge and waited by the tree line. "Your call."

Jack immediately followed, but Ruby hesitated a moment longer. When the full beams were about to come into view, she steeled her face and dashed into the woods.

Several cars sped by as they walked parallel to the forest. When asked how Ruby had out-raced the cars, she told Jennie that the Shadows wouldn't have believed she could run far and would have aimed their search at the nearby woods where no cars could drive.

When the possibility of finding her grew slimmer, maybe they had taken to the roads in the hope of reaching nearby houses and towns before she could make it to them and tell her tale.

Jack grew antsy as they walked, armed now with the knowledge that his partner was in mortal danger. What had started as a strange VR experience had turned into an encounter with specters, and then into a genuine threat from which he needed to save Clive.

As they walked, they kept the road in sight. Jennie pressed Ruby for everything she knew about the coven. She asked questions about her involvement, and why Ruby had had a sudden change of heart in the middle of the direst situation.

Ruby sighed and told Jennie that all of her life, she had been aware of faint lights around her and presences she couldn't understand. At night she would hear people whispering, faint sounds of talking, yet they would fall silent when she replied. At sleepovers and on late-night walks, she would see floating orbs or quick flashes of things that she knew couldn't be real.

It was at a party when she had just turned sixteen that she had decided to invite a few friends over to her house to play with a Ouija board. For the first few hours of the party, they had listened to music and laughed and danced as teens should do. But when the clock struck midnight, and her parents went upstairs for the night, things had taken a turn.

Ruby told them how the girls hadn't really wanted to take part in the Ouija board. They'd heard stories about them, and would rather have gone to sleep. Powered by her curiosity, Ruby had encouraged them to get involved, and within a few moments of play, things had begun to take effect.

"Our hands moved against our will, I swear it. The pieces of the board moved and told us what they wanted to tell us."

"What did they say?" Jack asked.

"They spelled out the names of people who had once lived in the house, followed by 'Help us.' Suzie Dutton was the first to freak out, and she left the living room and locked herself in the bathroom. Amber and Tyrene continued playing, too curious to do anything but."

After half an hour of communicating with the dead, things became more physical. The girls began to ask for specific things—signs to show the dead were really there. The first was the striking of the clock several minutes before it was due to chime the hour. However, Amber put that down to faulty mechanics.

Next was a sudden gust of wind that rattled the glass windows in their frames and sent a chill into the house none of them could explain.

"The final sign came when Suzie started screaming. She was locked in the bathroom, and we couldn't get to her. She kept shouting for help, and it was only after Dad woke and shouldered through the door that we found her curled up on the floor as if she was asleep."

"She wasn't asleep, was she?" Jennie asked.

"No, she was," Ruby told her. "She came around when Dad offered her a glass of water and scooped her onto the sofa. She remembered none of it. Couldn't recall screaming, let alone the reason why."

"That must have been terrifying," Jack commented. "To be helpless like that."

"That's not the end of it," Ruby told him. "After everyone had calmed down and we had hidden the board, we laid down and tucked ourselves into our sleeping bags in the living room. What we didn't realize was that we had broken the one rule of the Ouija—the most fundamental thing to contain the power within."

Jennie nodded, the bright beams of a headlight streaming past as she murmured, "Never break contact."

"Never break contact," Ruby repeated. "They say you should never release your finger from the board until you've had time to commit to a goodbye."

"So, what happened?" Jack asked.

"They came back," Ruby replied. "We were all on the verge of sleep when the chill returned, and before we had a chance to ask each other if the cold was in the house or just in us, the living room window exploded in a rain of glass. The whole thing was blown out of its frame in a heartbeat. Nothing came through it, no rock, no brick, no nothing. It just...smashed."

Jack gave Ruby a strange look. "And after all of that, you decided to join a bunch of black magic enthusiasts in a cult and chase ghosts?"

Ruby shrugged. "What can I say? It was evidence, wasn't it? Proof that things live beyond the veil. All those signs and strange occur-rences weren't me going crazy. Now I had others who believed in the other side, too."

"Man, she sounds just like Tanya," Baxter commented, unknown to Ruby.

Jennie smiled. "So, where do the Shadows come into it?"

"The Shadows had put out a call on an online forum, searching for new members. They told stories of people like me who had witnessed the paranormal. Promised to find ways to seek to provide solid evidence of life after death. For two years, I lied to my parents and told them I had after-school classes and meetings when really, I was out with a bunch of adults who all believed in the same things I did. They promised evidence, and I went along for the ride."

"Until now," Jack finished.

"Until now," Ruby agreed.

Jennie took a long step over a tangle of thorns. In her peripheral vision, she could see the faint shape of the Yokai once more. She wondered what it meant that they were gathered near her observing.

"This Meister Donavon," Jennie asked. "What's he like?"

Ruby thought about that for a few minutes. "He was kind. Gentle, loyal, a real leader. To begin with, he was just one of us. The person who brought us together. But then, he changed."

"Why?" Jack asked. "People don't just change for no reason. There's usually something that flips the switch."

Ruby looked down her nose at him. "What do you think?"

Jack touched his chin. "Well, in my experience, it's women. Women change men."

"Bingo."

"That was her name?" Jennie grinned.

"Her name is Julia," Ruby continued. "She joined the cult...I mean, coven, around six months ago. Since then, she's been spewing poison into his ears, digging out old texts and promising she'll deliver the one thing that he wants. The one thing he's never quite been able to attain. She's the reason he's doing the things he's doing."

"That's why you're going to kill a US federal agent?" Jack asked. "Just to prove that ghosties exist?"

"I wouldn't expect a non-believer to understand," Ruby contested, fixing Jack with a glare. "All my life, I've dealt with you clean-shirt types, with your bulging pecs and your chiseled jaws. I know what I know, and everything I've said is true. Believe whatever the fuck you want because this here is the real deal. This is happening, whether we like it or not. Meister Donavon is going to raise the dead and have them speak to us."

Jack held up his hands. "Hey, calm down. I'm on your side, remember? And despite what I may have truly thought a few hours ago, I'm a believer, too. These goggles here on my face? They're not just decoration. They're…" he paused and turned to Jennie as if for confirmation of what he was about to do. "They're Spectral Intelligence Goggles. With these on, I can see the dead. So don't peg me for a non-believer when you don't know me."

Ruby blew a raspberry from her lips. "Yeah, sure. Like I'm ever going to believe something as ludicrous as that."

Jack laughed. "Oh, you can believe ghosts shattered your window and mentally scarred your friend, but you can't believe that this piece of equipment gives me the ability to see the things you've wanted to see your whole life?"

Now Ruby paused, curiosity taking over. "You're telling me that if I look through those, I'll be able to see ghosts?"

Jennie grinned. "They prefer to be called specters."

Ruby's mouth dropped. "You've seen them too?"

"I see one right now," Jennie told her. "Baxter, hold up a number of fingers on your hand and I'll tell her how many there are."

Baxter rolled his eyes, then held up seven fingers.

"Seven."

Ruby turned from Jack to Jennie then back again. He held out the goggles, which she eagerly took and placed on her face. The lenses activated with their green rims and Ruby took several stunned steps backward, tripping over a root and falling on her ass.

Baxter held up seven fingers, then lowered them and waved at her with a big smile on his face.

"That's… There's…something's there," Ruby stuttered.

"That's a specter," Jennie told her. "Ruby, meet Baxter. Baxter, say hi to Ruby."

Baxter waved again.

Ruby rose unsteadily to her feet and took a few tentative steps forward. She stopped in front of Baxter and looked him up and down like an elderly lady scanning a cake counter through glasses that were way outside of her prescription. "Is he…"

"Real? Yes," Jennie answered. "As real as you and me."

Ruby reached out as if to touch his stomach, then let out a strange chuckle as her hand passed through him. "He's cold."

"Yeah, that's the chill you've likely felt before. I don't know the science behind it, but suffice it to say, a specter's body temperature is considerably lower than yours and mine."

Ruby now waved her hand more enthusiastically through Baxter's body, and his smile slipped from his face. She twirled her hand around as if mixing ingredients until she felt Jennie's hand on her shoulder.

"It may be fun for you," Jennie told Ruby, pulling her a few steps backward, "but specters don't take kindly to being played with. This isn't a TV sitcom."

As if to emphasize her point, a car sped past with several cloaked figures hanging out the window and shouting into the forest. "Come out, come out, wherever you are!" someone yelled as the others laughed darkly.

Ruby's smile faded. "How is this all possible?" She removed the goggles and gave them back to Jack. "You can see specters without help, and technology exists that lets us see them too?"

"My story is a long one," Jennie told her.

"Mine is pretty short, but I'm not telling you," Jack added. "Classified."

Ruby nodded appreciably. "This is all insane." She looked at the floor, then a sudden realization popped into her head. "You were both on your way to the village, weren't you? You already knew something was going on down there."

Jennie nodded. "I read about the interference in the paper."

"But if it's in local news, how come we haven't seen any authorities coming our way? I would have thought the police would have come to investigate, considering we...I mean, *they* have taken over the entire village.

"The *whole* village?" Jennie hadn't considered the whole community would be involved. "Well, this gets more interesting. Jack, any ideas?"

Jack stared at them both for a while, his gaze dark and serious. "My only guess, based on the information that I have, is that the SIA has forewarned local authorities that this is a government issue to address. I was here with my partner to scout the situation and diffuse anything that we came across. Clearly, the full information hasn't leaked to the wider population, or the whole place would be surrounded by cops. I'm assuming things escalated rather quickly?"

Ruby nodded. "We arrived the day before yesterday and began acquiring pieces for the ritual. We only captured the surrounding villages earlier this afternoon when Meister Donavon appeared to get a fresh injection of crazy juice and decided to turn this place and his organization upside-down."

"There you go," Jack said, eyes darting toward something familiar beyond the trees.

Jennie saw it, too—a 2019 Crown Victoria perched at the side of the road. It was at the center of an impressive bonfire.

"No," Jack groaned. "Not the Vic! The paperwork..."

There were several shouts from near the car before a large group of cloaked figures came into sight. They scoured the tree line, looking for movement.

"Come on," Jennie urged. "Deeper into the forest. We must be getting close."

Jack nodded, ducked, and waved for Ruby to follow them.

CHAPTER TEN

Wharton State Forest, New Jersey, USA

Clive couldn't believe this shit.

Things had been heated for a while. After the girl had saved his life, the remaining members of the cult inside the church had gone ballistic.

Their leader had screamed orders at his followers, and they had blindly obeyed.

As embers that had been kicked across the wooden floor glowed dangerously close to the pews, the leader had let out an almighty roar of frustration.

His face had turned crimson, and all sense had left his eyes. He stared at Clive and looked as if he was about to deliver a painful blow to his ribs when the woman who had whispered in his ear during the ritual grabbed him and hauled him away in an impressive display of strength.

Now Clive had no idea where they were. All was dark inside the old shack he had been thrown into, a small outbuilding that might once have been a storage facility for the town. His only access to the outside world were the calls and chatter outside and the thin cracks in the wood through which he could make out the bright beams of headlights.

Clive rested his head against the wood and stared at the dark ceiling. Had he been in worse scrapes than this? Sure, he had. Dealing with local nutcases who had formed psycho cults was his bread and butter. Usually, these were nothing more than twisted individuals whose reality had been altered by lies and fake news, nothing a slap on the wrist and some truth shoved in their faces couldn't fix.

But their leader, the figure in the dark cloak who had hovered over him with the knife?

There had been a look in his eye that Clive had seen in only a few others, and the slow descent into madness nobody came back from added a dangerous possibility to all this. He would have to be clever, and he would have to deploy ultimate diplomacy if he were to have any chance of escaping his situation.

Clive now knew that not everyone followed the leader's rule. If one girl could break ranks and turn on them the way she had, others would, too. The only problem was that as leaders of cults tightened their grip on their crew and lost their grip on reality, the power of fear strengthened within their ranks.

It was a tactic that the Neo-Nazis used—a tactic deployed in politics and battle strategies throughout human history. If Clive wasn't able to convince the other members of the cult there was another way that didn't end in homicide, as well as numerous kidnapping and false imprisonment charges based on how he had heard the gang outside discussing the residents of the village who were currently holed up in their homes, this could easily turn into a bloodbath.

He closed his eyes and thought back to the moment of his capture. The gunshots had rung out as clear as the church bell, and Jack had found a way to escape.

Clive hadn't been so lucky. In the confusion and chaos, arms had appeared as if from nowhere and taken him captive. They had chased Jack, and he had sprinted into the forest, navigating the trees as if he knew them by heart.

He had no idea if Jack had made it. There hadn't been gunshots, but it didn't take a silver bullet to kill a man.

Clive hoped he was okay. Maybe he was somewhere out there in the woods, putting in the call to HQ. Calling for reinforcements to help rescue him from this sticky situation.

"If only I'd believed them," Clive muttered to himself. "Rhone is going to have a field day with this one."

Time was running out. It wouldn't be long before the leader returned and the ritual began again. Given the look in that man's eyes, nothing was going to stop his ritual from taking place.

"Sorry, Meister. There's no sign of them." The man's head was lowered, his hands shaking.

Meister Donavon's lip curled as he glared at his inferior. "Well, look harder! Send a troop into the forest. Find her! We can't afford to have *any* loose ends out there, and we currently have *two?*"

Meister Donavon sat on the bed and rubbed his head. His hood was lowered, revealing a shiny bald dome that reflected the moonlight streaming through the window.

"The other agent will be long gone by now," the man countered. "Even if we sent a search party into the woods, there's no guarantee he'll be found. We've stationed cars at each intersection surrounding the main forest roads, so we have the escape routes covered. If any of them show up outside the woods, we'll know."

The Meister closed his eyes and took a breath. It was bad enough that they'd had to exert so much effort to capture the village, but to have to divide their resources because of some backstabbing bitch who had stolen his glory at the moment his dreams should have been realized…

That was a truth with a sting.

The Meister turned to address the woman sitting on the bed beside him, one arm placed delicately on his back. "Who was it?"

"Ruby Armstrong," Julia told him. "A girl fresh out of her teens who has been a member of our group for two years now—"

"Yes, yes, I know Ruby," the Meister interrupted. "I'm pissed off, not senile. Of course, I noticed her. Young, pretty face, and…"

His voice trailed away under the scolding glare from Julia.

"Go find the bitch," he ordered, turning to his lackey once more. "I don't want any excuses. If any of this shit leaks, we're done for. We only have a limited amount of time to make this happen, so either you find them, or I cut you open and bleed you out into the altar."

The man gulped and nodded, then turned and left, leaving the Meister and Julia in relative darkness.

The Meister rested his head in his hands. Car engines revved outside among the general chatter of his crew.

Julia shifted along the bed and wrapped her legs around him, kneading his back with her delicate fingers. "Don't worry, my love. Soon all will be as we want it to. I promise you, tonight will be your night. The night we break the world with the truth of the beyond. Tonight it happens." She placed a kiss on his neck. "Be strong."

The Meister leaned his head back against her, his entire body softening. "It will?"

Julia gave a dark smirk he couldn't see. She playfully nibbled his ear. "Of course, my love. Your people are resetting the altar as we speak. Give them a short while to get things back in order, and this time don't hesitate with that knife. You know what you need to do to make this happen." She reached around and grabbed his crotch with one hand, finding him alert and ready. "Just stick it in, and earn that sweet release."

Meister Donavon let out a moan. He melted onto the bed as Julia shifted from behind him and straddled him, her lips locking with his. Before he knew it, they were both free of their clothes and wrapped in each other's arms.

"Are you sure we have time for this?" the Meister whispered. "The door's not even locked."

Julia gave a coy smile and kissed down his body. "The night is still young, my love. Still very, very young."

Julia worked her magic on the Meister, leaving him in a state of ecstasy. Neither of them paid much attention to the bundle in the corner of the room that contained the dark SIA jacket and the pair of dark-lensed goggles, their lights deactivated.

There were dozens of them in the tiny village, a whole congregation of cloaked figures strolling around the place and keeping guard. A few of them held firearms loosely in their grip as they scoured the perimeter and stared into the dark of the forest.

"Security has really tightened since my last visit," Jack murmured. "Before, me and Clive just ran from shadow to shadow until we found everyone."

"The congregation has broken," Ruby told them. "Most of the Shadows had gathered in the church. The Meister was cocky. He believed this would be an easy job. In and out in one night, and the world would know."

"I guess that plan went down the shitter." Jennie smirked. "They didn't expect federal agents to break up their party, let alone one of their own to fuck it all up."

They stopped talking and ducked as a beam of torchlight sliced the area nearby. Jack was only inches away from Ruby and couldn't help but admire the scent of her perfume. "One question. Why are they using Clive for the ritual? Surely if they have the village under lock-down, they could use any of the hostages?"

Ruby shrugged. "I don't know what's going on in that guy's mind. Random hostages would have been easier, but I suppose he might figure that taking out an agent who would otherwise be his ticket to prison is the right thing to do."

"Even after I'd escaped?" Jack asked.

Ruby shrugged. "Again, I don't know his mind."

"Whatever's going on, we need to get inside." Jennie's eyes narrowed. "We need to have a look around and see what's going on in there. They look like they're getting things sorted in the church." She pointed ahead to where members of the cult filed back into the church in a neat line. "If we don't hurry, they'll just start it all up again."

"Affirmative," Jack agreed. "We'll need to scan the surrounding area, find any blind spots they have. Maybe if we can take one of them out, we can steal their cloak and go undercover. They'd never know it was us."

"That would be a great idea," Jennie started. "Only…"

"Only what?"

"Your plan would take too much time, and I have another suggestion for how we can run a quick surveil without detection."

Jack chuckled quietly. "Oh, yeah? What are you going to do, turn invisible and walk into the village?"

Jennie gave a small tilt of her head, latched onto Baxter, and vanished from sight.

Ruby and Jack both stared at where Jennie had been, open-mouthed.

"You've got to be kidding me," Ruby gasped.

Jack, who was beginning to realize that the woman was full of surprises, just shook his head.

Jennie reappeared with a large smile on her face. "It's one of my gifts. Don't ask me about it; there's no time. Lay low until I'm back. I'll be as quick as possible."

Jack fidgeted with his pistol, clearly not comfortable with sitting tight and not taking action. "If you're not back in fifteen minutes, I'm going in."

"Fifteen?" Jennie laughed quietly. "I can do it in less than ten."

"You're on." Jack clicked the timer on his watch. Before he had looked up again, Jennie had faded from sight.

CHAPTER ELEVEN

The call to Hansen's cell was met with no response. For two minutes, they had repeatedly redialed Bannon and been met by a voicemail that played on the loudspeaker to the three agents in the SIA boardroom.

Special Agent Alan Rhone's brow was furrowed. His finger hovered over the keypad to redial. Never in his eight years of service had he had trainee operatives out on the field and out of contact. The mission had been a simple one. They should have checked in by now.

Senior Special Agent Tom Hopkins frowned, the glare from his steel-blue eyes piercing. From the moment they had put out the call, he had been silent, but it was clear a thousand thoughts were being processed behind those eyes.

A woman who looked as though she would have dominated every match on a high school wrestling team was sitting beside the senior special agent. She was more muscular than Rhone, with a shaved head, and an expression that could only be likened to a pit bull. Special Agent Holly Daggro had been one of the first agents to enlist in the Spectral Intelligence Agency, and it was her seal of approval that had gotten Rhone his rank.

Now she looked at him with a doubtful glare.

"Any idea on what might have transpired?" SSA Hopkins asked, offering Rhone the opportunity to respond before assumptions were made. That was the kind of nicety that wasn't often offered by a ranking official.

"Complications," was all Rhone could offer.

"Complications on a trainee mission?" SSA Hopkins responded with a slight flick of his eyebrow. "Agent Daggro, should there really be complications on a mission of this nature? Was I not briefed that the assignment was fit for rookies? A chance for our trainees to experience the other side and gain incremental exposure into the world beyond our own we know to exist?"

Daggro sat up straighter in her chair, her face sour. She referred to a neat piece of paper in front of her. "Initial reports detailed a rogue cult playing with black magic, a slap-on-the-wrist procedure raised by the local authorities in New Jersey. Since our introduction into the spectral world, all local authorities in our neighboring states have been told to report all dealings with the paranormal to our dedicated line but haven't been informed as to why.

"This mission as described in this correspondence between Agent Rhone and me was an investigation in which minor exposure to the spectral realm might be a factor. The agents are both trained in their fields, with Trainee Agent Clive Bannon running point as a long-serving agent within the mortal departments of the FBI. Under Agent Bannon's leadership and guidance, both agents will remain vigilant and disband any activity currently occurring in the village of Batsto with minimal interruption to daily proceedings in the neighboring villages."

"And the target?" Hopkins nudged.

"The Shadows, sir," Rhone added. "A cult interested in the resurrection of the dead and experimentation with black magic. A group who has no history of major criminal activity, but has been issued warnings about public disturbances and charged with a few instances of trespassing and petty theft."

Hopkins gave a curt nod, his expression difficult to read. "So, an in-and-out job?"

"That's correct, sir," Rhone and Daggro replied simultaneously.

"Then what happened?" he asked.

"We're looking into it, sir," Rhone confirmed under the stare of Daggro. "In the absence of contact and the concern of disappearance, I have already assembled our team to head on-site and investigate. They should be prepped and ready for orders by the time this meeting is adjourned."

Hopkins sat back in his chair and exhaled loudly. "I shouldn't need to remind you both that the success of every single operation we run is critical to the continuation of this agency's operation. The oversight committee will not react well to agents going missing. The spectral world is an entirely new beast, something that our agents are still adjusting to dealing with. Hell, I struggled when the evidence of specters was presented to me. Yet, here we are."

"We fully understand, sir," Daggro interjected.

"Do you?" Hopkins retorted. "Because it seems to me that we've currently got two trainee agents MIA and out of communication. Do you know what kind of message that would send to the oversight committee? Do you understand the impact that would have on the SIA? We're a fledgling team looking to find our place, taking the lead from a group of people we would normally dismiss as crackpots who have proven to us that specters exist. Who could have known that many issues and problems in the world are actually caused by ghosts who have influence over the mortal realm? Ghosts who can communicate with some mortals, some ghosts who can touch and manipulate and, in some extreme cases, possess our agents and the citizens we're here to protect."

Daggro and Rhone sat patiently, respecting their senior agent's need to vent.

Hopkins placed his fingertips together and leaned closer to them. "For forty-three years, I have dedicated my life to serving this country. I fought in Iraq, I served in 'Nam. I've sat at the President's table and offered my two cents on tactical and strategic maneuvers in warfare. Never in a million years did I truly believe there was a greater enemy out there than man, but here we are. Specters are real. Our research teams are building technologies based on blueprints sent over by an organization within British Intelligence known as the paranormal court. The spectral world has been blown wide open, and only a select number of mortals in a governmental capacity are aware of it."

Hopkins paused for a moment, deep in thought.

"We have the opportunity here to build something historic, something that goes beyond the realm of typical secrecy. Something beyond the enigma of Area 51. Here we are training our agents and equipping them with the knowledge to handle the other side—the first wave of special agents to deal with and conquer the paranormal world." He stood up and slammed a fist on the table so suddenly that Rhone and Daggro jumped. "Find your men, and don't fuck it up. That is an order."

Agent Alan Rhone nodded and rose from his own seat. "Affirmative, sir. It's under control."

"It had better be," Hopkins growled. "Or else you'll *both* have to deal with the consequences."

Wharton State Forest, New Jersey, USA

Jennie wasn't entirely sure what to expect from scouring the village, but it was certainly worse than she had feared.

The sleepy village of Batsto appeared to exist in its own little bubble. A quaint, New England village consisting of cottages, churches, local-run stores, and streams, the place was almost entirely self-sufficient. It was no wonder this was such an easy place to take when the residents of the town were miles away from the big city, and there were only a few paths and roads that led into its heart.

Jennie melted through walls and examined houses in which civilians were crammed into rooms and kept under constant watch by members of the cult. Children slept fitfully in the arms of tired parents. The elderly sat quietly and gently rocked themselves. All the while, they remained under the threat of a single Shadow with a pistol or, on the rare occasion, an assault rifle.

The farther Jennie went around the village and observed the patterns and locations of the Shadows and their hostages, the more she had begun to think that there was a lot more to it than even Ruby had initially thought. No run-of-the-mill cult would have armed themselves so heavily if they were only down to initiate a small ritual and see what would happen.

Whether she'd believed it or not, Ruby and likely several of the Shadows had been hoodwinked to blindly follow their leader into the abyss.

Jennie overheard snippets of conversation, too. She and Baxter wandered undetected past Shadows who whispered in clusters, catching pieces of conversation that cast doubt on the whole operation. It was clear that not everyone was on board, but there wasn't yet enough steam for an overthrow or rebellion.

We'll see what we can do about that.

"You mortals are strange," Baxter muttered as they ran through another house and saw yet another gaggle of hostages. "Why would you bother to play with the other side when there are a thousand issues mortals have yet to face?"

"What?" It occurred to Jennie that the deep roots of folklore she was used to coming across in Europe might not be so widespread in America. "You're telling me that you never came across anything like this in the US? No black magic cults, or those dealing with paranormal instances?"

Baxter scoffed. "Are you kidding? My mind was on technology. On the invention of new things. I spent my days dissecting the work of others and looking at ways to improve the services and creations that might benefit the world."

"Until you blew yourself up?"

Baxter nodded. "Exactly."

When they melted out of the final house, Jennie checked her watch. She still had one minute and fifty-three seconds left.

"Best make a dash back to the others," Jennie suggested. "I don't want that agent to feel like he's got one up on me."

They ran across the village, on a few occasions passing through

Shadows. As they ran, Jennie began, "I keep meaning to ask. With all this talk of inventions and the inventor's lifestyle, did you ever create anything of note?"

Baxter laughed. "I thought you'd never ask. To be honest, nothing huge. Greater minds than me had already made all the big stuff. I did, however, have some influence over the invention of the modern bra."

Jennie stopped in her tracks. "Excuse me?"

"I thought that might get your attention." Baxter laughed. "True story, too. I won't go into the specifics since I don't want to tarnish my ex's legacy, but I once dated a lady who suffered from… Let's just say that her chesty gifts were something of a burden to her day-to-day life and she was in need of…*support*."

"Go on." Jennie looked at her watch again. Forty-three seconds.

"I suggested a solution that might alleviate her discomfort and provide more shape. She slapped me, called me a pig, and left me several weeks later."

Jennie didn't blame the woman. "Let me guess. Your ex-girlfriend was the inventor of the modern bra?"

"Not quite," Baxter replied. "Although she and Caresse Crossby crossed each other's paths a few years later. I have it under strong authority that there was collaboration on the project, but Caresse took the credit."

"Wow!" Jennie laughed, delighted. "I suppose I'll never have to ask if you're a boob or an ass man, then?"

Baxter laughed along. "I guess not. How long left?"

Jennie glanced at her watch. "Minus twelve seconds."

"We're late?"

"Doesn't matter. What's a few seconds over?"

"I'm guessing you've never met federal agents before?" Baxter scoffed. "I mean, I haven't personally, but I've watched a lot of TV."

Jennie rolled her eyes. "Shut up and hurry."

They ran in a straight line toward where they'd left the others, passing through a number of houses which blocked their way. When the church appeared nearby, they found themselves sprinting through a small outhouse that appeared no larger than a utility closet. Jennie's eyes were fixed on the church so she could have a quick look inside before returning to the others.

They passed through it so quickly that they almost missed him. It was only when the man hidden inside shuddered that Jennie stopped and retraced her steps.

She dragged Baxter back into the outbuilding and stopped in the darkness. It didn't take Jennie's eyes long to adjust enough to see the man shivering in the corner, his face black and blue.

Jennie adjusted her feet so that she wasn't standing in his legs, then dropped her connection to Baxter and became material.

The man was so dazed he almost didn't notice. It was only when Jennie crouched before him and placed a hand over his mouth to stifle his surprise that he noticed her arrival.

Jennie held his mouth in a firm grip. The man was older, and his stubble scraped the skin of her palm. She placed a finger over her mouth and whispered, "I'd strongly advise you be silent. We might be your only hope for getting out of here."

The man stopped making noises and nodded.

"Am I right in believing you're Agent Clive?" Jennie moved her hand away from his mouth.

The agent looked up at her in disbelief. "It's actually Agent Bannon. We don't use our Christian names for—"

"Yeah, yeah, enough of that," Jennie interrupted. "I'm not here for a lesson in federal etiquette. I'm already over my time limit to return to your buddy and give him an update on the situation."

"Agent Hansen is okay?" Bannon replied. "Where is he?"

"Again, no time for that," Jennie urged. "I'm going to get you out, but not just yet. First I need to investigate what's happening with this ritual, then we've got to find a route out of here."

The agent looked at the floor as if processing all that had just happened. "You appeared from nowhere. How did you do that?"

"Mr. Bannon?"

"*Agent* Bannon."

"Again, no time," Jennie told him. "It's good to see you alive. Now, I'm going to do everything I can to ensure that that remains your state of existence. Trust me, and everything will be okay."

With that, Jennie vanished from view before the agent could say anything. She had one more place to examine before she committed to a plan for rescue.

Jack tsked and lowered his watch. "They're fifteen minutes late."

Ruby looked at Jack, her attention drawn away from the group of men gathered around a black SUV just beyond the trees. She had been watching with curiosity as they huddled close and spoke in hushed tones, one of them occasionally breaking ranks and sweeping the surrounding area with his flashlight.

Although she had been with them for a couple of years, she still struggled to recognize individuals in their cloaks.

She supposed that was half the point.

"Shouldn't we give her more time?" Ruby's eyelashes fluttered rapidly, a tic she knew occurred when she was nervous or unsure. "Just a couple more minutes. She'll be back by then, I'm sure."

"Are you psychic?" Jack asked, his face straight.

"What? No."

"Then how do you know she'll return?"

"I..." Ruby searched for the answer but found none. "I don't know."

"One of the first rules of training is that you cannot sit around and wait for things to happen. Action is the only way to move forward, you got that?"

Ruby looked as if she was about to argue, then thought better of it.

Jack continued. "Every second we spend hanging around and waiting is a second wasted in saving my partner. Do you think I'll be happy that I sat on my ass when I find out he died in the hands of those monsters?"

"Hey!" Ruby exclaimed a little louder than she'd planned. The nearby Shadows stopped talking and cocked their ears to the forest. She lowered her voice. "I'm not one of them anymore."

"Sure," Jack hissed. "Another rule of mine. Never trust someone who switches sides. Allegiance means nothing to them. As far as I'm concerned, you're still a liability."

"I rescued your friend," Ruby protested. "I ran away from them—"

"You ran when the going got tough," Jack clarified. "What's going to happen if I'm in a position where I need to kill to survive and end this charade? Are you going to leave all your emotions at the door and let me do my thing? No."

He turned, and his face softened at the hurt in her eyes. "Look, you're a good kid. Even I can see that. But morals don't mean squat in situations like this. Either you attack and win, or you hesitate and die. We need to strike and rescue my partner before anything bad happens to him, hear me?"

Ruby nodded and folded her arms. "I'm not a monster."

"Nobody intends to become a monster," Jack told her resignedly, his tough composure losing a little of its edge. "We all have monsters inside of us, hidden somewhere in the dark. It's the decisions we make and choices we are given which determine whether the monster breaks free." He placed a hand on her shoulder. "For the record, your decision today kept the monster at bay for a little longer."

She gave a weak smile.

"But that doesn't mean you're out of the woods." He cast a glance around. "So to speak."

Ruby let out a weak chuckle and wiped a tear from the corner of her eye. "Today hasn't gone the way I thought that it would."

"That's the problem with psychotic cultists," Jack preached. "Sooner or later they all break, and they bring every brick in the wall down with them." He took her hand and ducked when the flashlight beam scoured above their heads again. "C'mon. Let's take action."

Ruby followed without question.

"Oh, one final thing," Jack added. "If the choice comes down to my death or the deaths of others, I'm protecting myself to my final breath, you got that?"

Ruby nodded.

"Good. Let's go."

CHAPTER TWELVE

Wharton State Forest, New Jersey, USA

Black-cloaked cultists lined the pews, dozens upon dozens of Shadows ready to watch the ceremony. At the front of the congregation, a huddle of cloaked figures set about lighting the candles around the large circle with a five-pointed star in its center they'd made with aromatic oil.

A pentagram. Jennie had seen a fair few in her time. The arcane symbol was said to grant the user access to the dark dimension. When lit and the correct words were spoken, the middle would soak up the sacrifice and unlock the door to the darker realm.

"Funny," Jennie muttered to Baxter.

"What?" he asked.

"No one ever seems bothered enough to create a door to lead to God. A pentagram has stood as the doorway to the dark side, but surely that would mean there's an equivalent to lead to the Lord Almighty."

"Are you suggesting that no one has ever seen God because we haven't figured out the symbol that opens the door to Heaven?" Baxter scratched his chin. "Isn't the church the doorway to Heaven?"

Jennie ignored the end of Baxter's comment. "Maybe it's a

diamond shape with an octopus in the center, or perhaps a unicorn in the middle of a dodecahedron. I bet God would be elaborate like that. He admires the finer parts of the craft, not quite reflecting on the simplicity of Satan's preferences." She scoffed. "A star in a circle? *Puh-lease*. Any idiot can draw that. But a unicorn in a dodecahedron? Now there's something elaborate enough to earn the approval of God."

Baxter gave Jennie an incredulous look. "Are you okay?"

"Sorry." Jennie grinned. "Churches make me a bit loopy."

"Join the club," Baxter muttered as the Shadows lit the final candles and touched the flames to the poured oil. The back of the church grew alive with the sentient flame of the pentagram. "I guess it's almost time."

Jennie gave a small murmur of agreement. "How many of them would you say are in here, total?"

Baxter performed a quick count. "Maybe fifty. Possibly sixty."

"How many guns do you see?"

Again, Baxter scanned the crowd. It was almost impossible to make an accurate count, given that those sitting in the pews were shadowy figures. Whatever they had on their persons was hidden under their cloaks.

"No idea."

"Good. It's best when you're honest. None of that bullshit Worthington used to pull, pretending to know more than you do."

Baxter raised an eyebrow, unsure if he was being complimented or insulted. "Thanks?"

"You're welcome."

Jennie studied the crowd in silence for a little longer, weaving through the Shadows and sending chills down their spines. A few of the cult members became cold enough to search for the source of the draft.

By the time Jennie had scanned the entire congregation, two members of the Shadows left under whispered orders to "Fetch the Meister. It is time."

She returned to Baxter. "It's impossible to count guns, but that doesn't matter now anyway. We're running out of time."

"What do we do?" Baxter asked. "Don't we need to go back to the others?"

"Yeah," Jennie mused as two figures broke free of the pack and walked down the aisle toward the doorway. Before they reached the front of the church, Jennie ran over to the pentagram and swept a hand across a section of the candles, extinguishing the flames in a gust of wind.

The cloaked figures around the pentagram knelt and took hold of some of the candles that were still lit. They began re-igniting the ones that had gone out, but before they could, Jennie swept another hand around the area, bathing them all in darkness once more.

"Hold on," a particularly large cultist called to the pair at the door.

"What is it?"

"Must be a draft," the man replied.

One of the cultists brought out a lighter and began working on one of the candles. The minute the flame came alive, Jennie waved a hand through it and put the fire out.

"What the..." The figure shook the lighter and studied it closely.

"Is there a problem?" one of the pair grunted, now immediately behind the figure with the lighter.

"No," he replied uncertainly. "No. The lighter is full."

"Well, give it here, then." The larger of the pair snatched the lighter, shook it, and thumbed the striker. With a smug grunt, he lit a candle, then threw the lighter back to its owner.

"There. Light the rest from that candle," he growled.

The figure holding the lighter examined it closely, the glow from the candle enough to showcase the expression on his face.

Jennie waited until he touched the candle to another and lit the flame before fanning her hand one final time and extinguishing both lights.

A ripple of murmurs reverberated around the crowding figures. The larger cultist came storming back, shouting expletives so loud that no one heard as Jennie laughed and ran from the church to find the others.

"That'll buy us a bit of time."

Baxter grinned and sped out behind her.

When they got back to the spot they had left Jack and Ruby, there was no one there.

"Oh, for crying out loud!" Jennie exclaimed. "You give mortals *one* instruction, and they run off before you get back."

Baxter raised a finger. "You did say you'd be ten minutes."

"I wasn't much longer than ten."

"How long has it been?"

Jennie glanced at her watch. "Shut up."

"He did say he'd leave after fifteen," Baxter affirmed. "He's a government agent, true to his word."

"He's an idiot." Jennie squinted into the dark village. "He's going to get himself killed. We did him a favor buying time before they bring his partner back in, and now we have to waste time finding him too?"

Baxter patted Jennie's shoulder.

"What is it?"

He pointed ahead. "I don't think we'll have to hunt for long."

Jack and Ruby crept swiftly through a clearing ahead, finding a hiding spot behind the dark shadow of a large townhouse. Jennie rolled her eyes and sighed. "Guess we didn't miss them by much."

"They're too close to the cloaks," Baxter muttered. "Over there, look. There are at least fifteen of them between the church and their location. How do they think they're going to get past?"

"If there's one thing I've learned about government-types, it's that their egos far exceed their logic, particularly with newbies to any department. The moment they took Clive from him, it became personal. He's got something to prove."

Baxter grunted. "Seems like a smart way to do business."

Jennie latched onto Baxter and turned immaterial. "Time to go undercover again and pull them out of the situation." She stared at the stars. "Just once, I wish people would listen to me and trust me when I give orders. This is why I work alone."

"*Used* to work alone," Baxter reminded her. "Maybe people don't listen to you because you never stick to a leadership position long enough for people to trust your commands?"

Jennie contemplated that, wondering if it was true. Besides the fact that these two mortals knew nothing about her history or what she was capable of, they also had only met her that night. Could she blame Jack for following his own protocol and ignoring orders from a stranger?

Probably not.

"Fine," Jennie conceded. "Let's get them out of there."

***

Jack's eyes narrowed as he assessed the situation.

Sneaking past the perimeter guards was a doddle. Clearly, they were dealing with a group of amateurs who had never arranged anything like this before in their lives and took their entire inspiration from a selection of TV shows, films, and games where hostages had been taken.

There was no pattern to their guard. No rigidity. For long periods no one would so much as glance at the forest, meaning that there was plenty of time to penetrate the cult.

Until they got closer, that is.

The majority of the cultists surrounded the church. From where Jack stood, he could see a group of over a dozen standing and talking. Occasionally, cloaked figures would enter or exit the church. Over by one particularly grandiose-looking house, a huddle of figures stood guard. Jack looked up and saw a shirtless man looking out at the church from the top window. A woman with dark hair was holding him from behind.

He knew from training that amateur cults could be incredibly simple to disband, or chaotically problematic. Organized crime gangs had their patterns. There were tactics law enforcement could employ that were sometimes as easy to operate and navigate as a game of Monopoly.

Whereas with amateur groups, one quick shock could scare the inexperienced into a series of dangerous actions. Uncontrollable fear could drive civilians to make stupid decisions, and before you knew it, you had three bullet holes in your body and a civilian turning the gun on themselves.

Which is it going to be today? Jack wondered. He ducked back around the corner and closed his eyes. He always thought best in the dark. Ruby breathed heavily beside him, her eyes wide with the realization that she was right back where she didn't want to be.

"Will you control your breathing?" Jack whispered. "They're going to hear you wheezing soon enough. It's like a beacon for anyone looking for us."

"I'm sorry," Ruby snapped. "Am I not calm enough for you? Did you think I wanted to be right back in the center of the place where I fucked up our leader's ambitions? Oh, yeah. This is the *perfect* place to be calm."

Jack peered around the corner again. The door to the church opened, then slammed shut a second later. The man at the window of the house was gone.

"You're doing a good deed," Jack tried to soothe her. "Heroes aren't born, they're formed by the choices they make. If you want to be a hero and join me, then calm down. If you want the chance to exit this situation, then run on back through the town and escape...again. You've done it once, why not try it once more?"

Ruby clung to Jack's arm. "No, thanks. I'd rather take my chances with you. At least you're trained."

"Not in one-armed combat." Jack regretted his retort when Ruby's face crumpled."I'm sorry, you were only trying to help. But I need you to stay calm. Control your breathing and let me figure this out."

He studied the situation for a few more minutes before finding his resolve. "Okay, there's an opening over toward the back of the church. If we can navigate around the back, there may be a place to climb in and use the element of surprise—"

Jack turned mid-sentence and his heart jumped when he saw

Jennie standing where Ruby had been. Ruby was now tucked behind Jennie's back.

"Really?" Jack hissed. "Do you know how close I was to shouting in surprise?"

"Not a tough man like you, surely?" Jennie grinned. "Aren't you trained for things like this?"

Jack glared at her. "Of course, I am. That's why I *didn't* shout."

"You're so brave."

"What the fuck are you doing here?"

Jennie cocked her head. "Well, when we realized that you'd run off to play hero, we decided to come and find you. You know I have a bunch of intel, right? I can help us here. Why don't we try working as a team?"

Jack continued to smolder. "You were late."

"You were honest."

Jack's glare broke into a soft smile. "I'm always true to my word."

"And you're still determined to rescue your friend?"

"Of course."

Jennie gave a resolute nod. "Then let's make sure your word remains true." She poked her head around the side of the building. "You're thinking of the back entrance?"

"He's government-issue. I bet he's always thinking about the back entrance," Baxter quipped.

Jennie had to cover her mouth to hold in her laugh.

Jack raised an eyebrow. "What's so funny?"

"Nothing, it's… Don't worry."

"*He* said something, didn't he?" Jack brought his goggles to his face and searched for Baxter.

"Forget it," Jennie told him. "Let's focus on the task at hand. You were talking about the back passage?"

"The back entrance," Jack corrected, his face straight. Behind Jennie, Ruby laughed into her hand. "If we can get across there, we might stand a chance of breaking this up and finding Clive."

Jennie touched her chin. "That could work, or we could go to the place where your buddy is being held." At Jack's questioning look, she pointed at the outbuilding just beyond the church.

"He's in there?" Jack asked.

Jennie nodded. "Yep. You might want to go free him before the others finish setting up, though. Believe me, you don't have long."

She explained what she'd seen in the church and the trick she'd played on the Shadows.

When Jennie finished, Jack clenched his teeth and checked the clearing again. "Fine. Let's move."

Staying as close to the buildings as possible, they managed to sneak over to the other side of the large townhouse without being seen. They had to suddenly duck behind large crates or in the dark recesses of the buildings on a few occasions, but they made it eventually.

Time was pressing. The outbuilding was about forty feet away. Four Shadows stood guard around the small building, fingers laced behind their backs.

"Shit, they're coming out," Jennie hissed, reappearing from around the corner. "The head cult guy—I just saw him leave the house and head toward the church. We're running out of time."

"We need a distraction," Jack urged. "Something to get rid of the guards. Then it's in, get him, and get out."

"I've got you covered." Jennie became immaterial and ran out of hiding.

She picked up a large stone and threw it down the street, the rock making a loud clapping noise as it landed. The guards' ears pricked up, and one of them broke free to investigate.

When he made it to the rock, Jennie flickered into view. She remained material for half a second before disappearing again. All the cultist saw was a woman on her knees with a sad expression on her face before she vanished.

"Huh?"

Jennie flickered into view again, this time on the cultist's other side. He turned his head, but she was gone.

He stood up, suddenly more frightened than he'd ever been. Jennie appeared before him, and he took a few steps back.

"Guys?" he called uncertainly.

Jennie cocked her head and threw a pebble at his face. It hit him on the cheek and set off a pulse of pain.

Now the other guards could see her and had taken an interest. They walked over, and the minute they realized someone else was there, they chased her.

Jennie turned on her heel and fled toward the forest.

"Get her!" one of the guards shouted at the top of his lungs.

Jack watched from the darkness as they tore after Jennie, impressed that the smile hadn't left her face. Drawn by the shouts, more cultists appeared on the street and sprinted after Jennie.

Rogue ran until she was at the tree line, then, the minute the shadows cloaked her, she disappeared. Baxter caught up with her, panting. She moved out of the way of the sprinting cultists and returned to Jack, surprised by how quickly the situation had spiraled into panic.

Cultists ran past by the dozen, determined to at least catch one of their enemies tonight. The head Shadow ducked quickly into the church, surrounded by his henchmen, and soon the clearing was almost vacant.

Jennie took the opportunity to hurry over to the outbuilding. Taking a small vial from her back pocket, she poured the liquid on the lock and waited as the acidic concoction ate through the metal. When the lock dropped free, she opened the door and…

Found that the outbuilding was empty.

Son of a bitch, Jennie thought. *They've already dragged him inside.*

CHAPTER THIRTEEN

<u>Wharton State Forest, New Jersey, USA</u>

Meister Donavon could hear the ruckus outside and knew his time was short. In his mind, he imagined the worst. He saw red and blue lights, a whole fleet of cops, and helicopters filled with agents in black. Soon they would have him.

Time was short.

Even the serotonin rush of sex had faded as his blood turned to ice, and now his mind was doing strange things to him.

His excitement was mixed with fear, and his heart raced. His men huddled around him, and this time he knew it would happen. No matter what was going on outside, this was his time to make reality shift. As long as he completed the ritual, he would be able to command the darkness, and he would be safe.

The other side would protect him from harm.

"Go, my love," Julia whispered, providing him with a sharp nudge toward where the agent was once more strapped to the floor, surrounded by candles in a pentagram.

The Meister's eyes lit with excitement as the chanting began. He reached into his pocket and found the cold steel blade of the knife.

This time, he would not hesitate.

With one party of cultists off in the woods and the rest surrounding the front door, Jennie led Jack and Ruby toward the back entrance of the church.

Darkness was their friend, and soon they were in a position to see the rear of the church.

"Damn. More of them," Ruby whispered as the four hooded figures shuffled nervously in the darkness.

"Leave it to me," Jennie told them, not pausing for an answer as she slipped onto the spectral plane and navigated between them.

When she was in the center, she appeared before them, startling them enough that she could work her magic. A hundred and twenty years of combat training had made her senses sharp and her reactions quick. With precision and speed, she jabbed fingers into each of their throats hard enough to disable their vocal cords temporarily.

When they clutched their necks, she grabbed the hoods of two of the cultists and banged their heads together, causing them to fall to the ground unconscious.

The cultist behind her was less lucky. This one she elbowed on the bridge of her nose, causing an eruption of blood from her nostrils. The cultist folded to her knees.

Jennie pulled out a vial filled with silver powder, cupped the powder in her palm, and blew it into the final cultist's face.

The cultist blinked stupidly for a few seconds, then fell to the ground, snoozing.

To finish her attack, Jennie knelt before the bleeding cultist and jabbed two fingers into the soft crook between her neck and shoulders, causing her to pass out beside her comrades.

Jennie rose to her feet and brushed the powder off her hands.

The others stepped out of the darkness and toward the back door, their faces filled with wonder.

"That was…" Ruby started. "Where did you…"

"Nice work." Jack tried his best to hide how impressed he was. "That was…" he struggled to find the words, "good work."

Jennie gave a swift thanks, then opened the door and ushered them into the back of the church.

The room would have been pitch-black if it hadn't had been for the faint glow of candles gently piercing the gaps in the wooden wall before them. Jennie snuck over and peeked through a hole where a knot of wood had once been.

"They're starting."

"You couldn't get that from the chanting?" Baxter commented.

Jennie stared at him.

"What?"

"What are they chanting?" Jack asked, oblivious to Baxter's comment.

"It's Latin," Ruby answered softly. "An ancient petition to the Lord of Darkness. A prayer requesting the resurrection of the being of death through a vessel of mortality sacrificed in His name."

Jack's nose curled. "And not once did you think that was a bad thing to be doing?"

Ruby shook her head. "You go with the flow. It never used to entail murder."

At that word, Jack steeled himself and approached the door. He placed a hand on the handle, stopping only when Jennie placed a hand on his shoulder.

"What's your plan, Jack?" she asked. "Go in there, all guns blazing, and end it?"

"Something like that?" he agreed. "They're off-guard. One look down the barrel of my gun and the situation will be under control."

"How about we consider a two-pronged approach?" Jennie replied, easing Jack's rookie nerves by assuming command. "You take that door, I'll take this one, and we'll come from either side. Two guns are always going to be better than one."

Jack considered that was true. Soon the cultists would stop chanting, and the sacrifice would begin. "Fine. Just get there quick. We're running out of time."

Jennie crossed the room to where a second door led to the main area of the church. She placed her hand on the handle, then held up three fingers. She counted these down to one, then lowered her final finger.

They shouldered the doors and jumped into the room, guns trained on the figures in the center of the altar.

Meister Donavon could see nothing but the man on the floor. Beads of sweat dripped down his body. The knife was slick in his hand.

Almost showtime, he thought, heart racing faster than he could ever remember it beating.

The chanting reached its crescendo. The moment his people stopped, he raised the knife high above his head, all of his mind focused on driving that sucker down and ending the ritual. Calling the demons forth and starting his new life.

But the crash of two doors smacking against the wall halted that effort. Meister Donavon gasped when the man in the SIA uniform pointed a gun at his head.

"Federal agent! Drop the knife, scumbag!" Jack shouted in the most authoritative tone he could muster. "Now!"

The leader of the Shadows froze, the look on his face almost inhuman—an empty look devoid of emotion or intent. The knife in his hand shook.

Jennie stepped forward, drawing his attention behind him. "You heard him. Drop the knife."

The gathered cultists stood almost perfectly still. They formed a half-perimeter around the leader, blocking any easy escape through the front door. The leader refused to obey the command.

Jennie glanced at Jack and saw him grow more desperate. With two hands on his pistol, he stepped closer. "I said, drop it!"

The leader stared intently at Jack. "You don't know what you're doing. It's too late to go back. We're so close."

Jack jerked the barrel of his gun at the leader. "I don't give a shit what you're close to. You move that knife away from that agent before I splatter your brains over your posse."

"I'd listen to him," Jennie warned. "Bullets travel faster than blades. If you like, we can make a whole Jackson Pollock and shoot at the same time?" She nodded at the cultists. "Watch out, folks. Front two rows are a splash zone."

The leader hesitated for a moment before slowly lowering his hand. He deflated, still staring longingly at Clive with that hungry look on his face. "Very well."

Jennie and Jack exchanged looks, then advanced. Jack knocked over some of the candles as he moved close enough to unbind Clive. Jennie took a position behind the leader with her pistol kissing the back of his head.

"Not a single move, arsehole," she muttered.

The leader took a sharp breath.

Jack assisted Clive to his feet, where he wobbled precariously for a few seconds. He supported his weakened partner with an arm around his shoulder and returned his aim to the leader.

"We're taking this man to safety," Jack announced. "If you're thinking of doing anything stupid or trying any heroics, I should tell you that the church is surrounded."

Jennie was impressed by this guy's bravado. A bold lie, and one that could easily pay off.

"A dozen police and SIA cars are outside waiting to take you all into custody and iron out whatever the fuck kind of weirdness was going to happen here tonight," Jack continued. "Those who cooperate will receive considerably lesser charges. Remain where you are."

He indicated for Jennie to follow and shuffled back toward the door, his pistol still trained on the leader.

Jennie had only taken two steps when a voice called from the front of the crowd, "This is bullshit! There's no one outside. We'd have heard them from miles away."

The caller lowered their hood to reveal a stunning woman with a shadow across her face. In a flash, she revealed a Glock 17 from the sleeve of her robe and fired two shots at Jennie.

Jennie dived out of the way, rolling and thumping into the wall. Jack leapt backward, dragging Clive with him. He managed to make it to the doorway before all hell broke loose.

The cultists broke their tableau and ran for the intruders. A few of them drew guns and aimed, but it was almost impossible to get a straight shot without the possibility of accidentally shooting one of their own.

Jennie ducked out of sight and turned immaterial at the last second, avoiding the clutches of a large man who lunged at her and tried to capture her.

Jack slammed the door shut behind him and held it fast, allowing Ruby to support and take Clive toward the back door.

"Go! Now!" Jack called, straining against the door as several dozen cultists pushed against it from the other side.

Jennie hunted through the crowd for the bitch who had shouted at her and broken their illusion. It was often said that behind every great man was a great woman, and it seemed like that might just be the case in this situation, too.

The flurry of movement was chaotic. Cult members darted in all directions, many afraid to look outside for fear of the police but prepared to attack their attackers. Twice tonight, they had been robbed of their glorious moment, and that frustration drove them.

When Jennie found her, the woman was shouting at the man kneeling on the floor over a cultist. The candles Jack had kicked over had caught the oil, and the floor was alight. In the midst of it, the shape of the pentagram could still be seen burning brighter than the rest.

Jennie made a move toward the pair, the hair on her neck standing on end when she heard the screamed instructions from the woman and saw the resolute expression on the leader's face.

The knife was raised in the air, its tip hungry and looking for blood.

Her words tickled Meister Donavon's ears. She was absolutely right. Why were they concerning themselves with the target when any blood would do?

The pentagram was smudged, but its shape remained. If they were going to get caught and taken away by the authorities, this would be the last chance to perform the ritual.

Maybe the last chance ever, depending on what happened after this. Donavon didn't know a great deal about the law, but he expected the repercussions for plotting to murder a federal agent would be severe.

He narrowed his eyes. The chaos around him sucked away reality like a whirlwind. The world was a blur of cloaks, screams, and Julia's shouts.

He raised his hand high and drove the blade down, slashing several times before the blade found its target.

It jarred the Meister's wrist, and rivulets of blood decorated his arm as the victim jolted and collapsed to the floor face-down.

The Meister liked it that way. At least face-down, he wouldn't have to see the haunted expression on the woman's face as she faded from life and crossed into the beyond. She hadn't even managed to let out a scream before it was all over.

Then the haunting began.

CHAPTER FOURTEEN

The chaos stopped the minute someone let out an ear-piercing scream. Julia stared coldly at the woman on the floor with the knife buried deep in her back.

The Meister grinned hungrily, rising to his feet as he waited for the impossible to happen.

Jennie had seen it all. She'd been too slow to save the woman's life, and now she was gone. Her soul was passing into the spectral beyond.

The woman's specter sat up inside her body, her glowing white face a mask of confusion.

She patted her back as if the knife would still be there. Then, seeing Jennie and Baxter, she asked the question Jennie had heard a thousand times before.

"Am I dead?"

Jennie gave a solemn nod. "I'm sorry."

To her surprise, the woman smiled. "Don't be. This is all we've ever wanted—evidence of a beyond." She laughed and held her hands in front of her face while the cultists stared at her body. She passed her arms through her old peers and continued laughing. "It's real. It's all real, just as we envisioned."

Jennie remained quiet, wondering how long it would take.

The woman turned to her. "Are you two dead, too?"

"She isn't, I am," Baxter replied. "Long story. I'm sure you'll have time for all the gory details soon enough."

I doubt that, Jennie thought.

The woman pushed to her feet and stared around in wonder. She moved closer to the Meister and punched his head, her hand sinking through his skull. "Son-of-a-bitch."

"I thought you were okay with death?" Baxter questioned.

The woman shrugged and laughed again. "Doesn't mean I appreciated getting stabbed in the back. I always thought I'd go in my sleep, or maybe in a car accident."

Her voice trailed away as her image flickered. She screwed her eyes shut and took a step back, hit by a sudden wave of something strange.

Here it comes.

Jennie readied the Big Bitch in her hand.

"Sorry, I don't know what came over me." The woman grunted in pain. "I… Eurgh… What's…"

Words were lost as she clutched her stomach. She doubled over in pain as her spectral body flickered again. The white glow shrouding her began to darken, turning dark gray bordering on black.

"What's happening?" Baxter gasped.

Jennie's steely expression remained fixed on the specter. "The ritual is taking effect. This is what happens when a specter's soul has been tarnished by the black magic of mortals who don't have a clue what they're doing."

"She's changing?"

Jennie nodded. "She's changing, and the end result won't be pretty. You've seen poltergeists and wraiths, right?"

Baxter grunted his confirmation.

"They're not the only variations on spectral life," Jennie continued. "Did you know that the word 'poltergeist' comes from the German words *'poltern'* and *'geist,'* which means 'disturbance ghost?'"

"Is now really the time for a language lesson?" Baxter asked, staring at the cloud of darkness swirling around the woman, unbeknown to the mortals present.

Jennie ignored Baxter, her voice rising as a small storm began to kick up. "Over the years, there have been many instances of different forms of poltergeist appearing across Europe. There's the *wirbelgeist*, a specter that can harness the power of the wind."

The woman shrieked, her body losing its shape in the dark clouds now pulsing with electricity.

"Also the *monsungeist*, and the *flüstergeist*." Jennie continued. "The first is a specter that can manipulate water and cause storms indoors, flooding and often drowning its victims, and the other whispers to its victims, driving them to the brink of insanity."

Now the mortals in the cloaks began to notice a disturbance. The darkness began to cross the veil and break into the mortal frequency, manifesting as a small cloud. They muttered and pointed excitedly as it appeared above the body of the girl.

"So, what does that make this one?" Baxter asked with concern. "It doesn't seem to fit your profile of the other geists."

"A *sturmgeist*." Her voice softened. For the first time since Baxter had known her, Jennie looked tired. "I've only encountered one before, and that fight took all my strength to win." She patted her side in the place where her sword was hidden by the spectral camouflage cast by Baxter. "Although I didn't have this baby last time."

The hilt of the sword fit comfortably in her hand. Jennie could swear she could feel something akin to a heartbeat in the metal, as though the energy the blade was imbued with gave the sword its own life force.

"I don't understand. Why don't you stop it before it finishes forming?" Baxter urged with a hint of desperation in his voice. "Get it before it gets us."

"It doesn't work like that." Jennie planted her feet as the cloud began to take its final form. "Spectral weapons only work on a fully formed specter. There needs to be substance, and the metamorphosis of the spectral state has its own protection. It's not something I can fully explain, but there it is."

"And there *it* is," Baxter breathed.

Hovering before them was the dark shape of the woman. The skin of her exposed torso had transformed, now made of shadow. Her eyes were pure white, and she floated on a dense black cloud that jolted with electric charges.

The *sturmgeist* met Jennie's stare.

"Fuck," Jennie muttered. "Here we go again.

Meister Donavon couldn't believe it.

It had worked. By God, it had worked. After years of trial and error, years of his hope diminishing day by day, it had worked. There was something there. A small something, admittedly, but something everyone could see.

The dark cloud was no bigger than a soccer ball. It roiled and hovered several feet above where the dead body lay. He had never seen anything like it, but he knew it was somehow connected to the other side.

"We've done it," he whispered. Then, more explosively, *"We've done it!"*

He laughed and punched the air with his bloodstained hand. The gathered cultists weren't focused on the dead body on the floor; their eyes were fixed on the cloud. The strange, inexplicable, impossible cloud of darkness that hung before them as if awaiting instructions.

Julia clawed Donavon's shoulders from behind as if preparing to perch on them. She leaned over and whispered, *"You've* done it, my love. Now, control it."

"What do you mean?" Donavon asked without turning. With the thing floating before them, it was impossible to process anything else.

"Instruct it," Julia cooed. "It will obey your every command. That's what the spell is for, remember?"

The Meister gave a goofy laugh and deliberated his first instruction. He waved a hand, then said, "Float higher."

The cloud wobbled for a second, then rose several feet higher in the air.

The Meister laughed again. Several Shadows joined in.

"Come down," he ordered.

The cloud obeyed.

Tears pricked the Meister's eyes. Julia nibbled his ear and whispered, "Test its strength."

Meister Donavon's eyes sought the door where the others had escaped. The door was slightly ajar, and through it, he could see the glint of the second agent watching the ordeal.

The Meister leered with satisfaction. Between barely parted lips, he whispered, "Destroy the agent."

The *sturmgeist* didn't hesitate. One minute, it was staring intently at Jennie, the next second it was obeying the command.

The cloud sped toward the door, its increase in size apparent to the mortals. Jennie could see the whole of the fearsome specter.

The *sturmgeist* moved with the rapidity of lightning, and the door exploded in a rain of splinters. Jack jumped back just in time to avoid the worst of it. Somewhere in the darkness, Ruby screamed.

The *sturmgeist* crashed through the wall, then gunned for Jack. He yelled in surprise as it covered him, swallowing him whole in its darkness.

Jennie reached out and latched onto the *sturmgeist* and sped toward its presence. Within a second, she had joined Jack inside the storm, able to see everything he saw.

It was as if they had been transported to another world. The church was gone, and in its place was a wall of wind. They floated in the eye of a tornado as the chilly wind whipped their faces and ate at their exposed skin. Lightning crashed around them, illuminating their pale faces and threatening to jolt their bodies.

"What's happening?" Jack shouted, even though the storm did its best to rip the words away.

"It's going to be okay!" Jennie called. "We just have to get out of its heart, and then we can attack its mind."

"It's always heart versus mind with chicks!" Jack managed to make light despite his fear.

Jennie tried to laugh, but her breath was sucked away. She closed her eyes and focused on exiting the vortex, and when she opened them again, she was standing on the wooden boards of the back room.

Ruby ran to her, but Jennie stopped her with a look.

Jennie stared up at the *sturmgeist*. The woman had lost all humanity and was now nothing more than a monster. Wind whipped around her in a cyclone, picking up bits of debris.

Jennie decided to go for broke and aimed the Big Bitch at the *sturmgeist*'s chest. She pulled the trigger, and the report added another thunderclap to the din.

She expected the bullet to do some damage, but the *sturmgeist* was unfazed. Her body opened around the bullet's trajectory and closed again once it had passed, letting the roof take the brunt of the damage as more splinters rained and joined the ghost's maelstrom.

"With every bit of collateral, she's growing," Jennie yelled. "We need to go straight to the source."

"What do you mean, source?" Ruby called out, shrinking against the wall beside Clive.

Jennie ignored her and sprinted toward the *sturmgeist*, her brow furrowed against the growing winds. With every second that passed, more debris was picked up and caught in the storm. Soon there were boxes and chairs and candles flying around the back room. The heads of the Shadows who had opened the doors and fought for a view of the battle disappeared, closing the door firmly behind them as the damage radius grew.

Jennie hoped the door would break and the leader of this frigging cult would get sucked into the tornado.

When Jennie reached the ghost, she leapt as high as she could and held the sword high. The blade shone a brilliant white as it cut through the air. Jennie prepared for the blinding flash of exorcism as the blade met with the specter...

But nothing came.

Instead, the wind dropped as suddenly as it had come, leaving behind dead silence in the room as detritus and bric-a-brac fell to the floor.

Jennie landed with a *thud* on the floor and looked around for the *sturmgeist*, but there was no trace of it. Jack was gone, too.

"Where did it go?" Ruby shook as she stepped forward. "Where's Jack?"

Her question was answered when shrieks and cries came from next door.

Jennie and Baxter dashed through the wall in spectral form and emerged into insanity.

With more room to grow, the *sturmgeist* now accommodated a large section of the empty space above the pews. The woman's laughs were thunder and lightning, and she threw her head back as she folded her arms and wreaked havoc.

Jennie stared up with mouth agape, unable to believe how quickly the thing had grown. From what she remembered, *sturmgeists* grew in proportion to the chaos they created. The more bodies they swallowed, the larger they would become.

Figures in dark cloaks orbited the *sturmgeist* like planets around the sun. They kicked their legs and flailed their arms, and occasionally some disappeared inside the clouds and out of sight.

Meanwhile, the leader of the Shadows stood at the altar and barked his commands.

"Yes! Yes, my pet! None of them believed me, but now they shall learn! Take them. Take them all!" His laughter was maniacal, the sound made by a man who had lost all sensibility.

The woman stood beside him, her eyes wide with wonder. Jennie wasn't sure who looked crazier, but each had their own style.

"Call it off!" Jennie shouted before realizing she was immaterial. She disconnected from Baxter and stormed over to the leader, surprised to see that the mortals were seeing only a large black nondescript mass vacuuming their cult. "Call the damn thing off before it swallows the whole building."

The leader of the Shadows slowly turned to her, his eyes blank. He shook his head. "I was right! All along they said I was crazy, but I was right. There's life beyond death. I knew it all along!"

Jennie took his shoulders in her hands and shook him violently. "Yes, and soon you'll know more about life beyond death than you've ever imagined. You know why? Because I'm going to kill you. Call it off before it's too late."

A flicker of doubt crossed over the leader's mind, but it was quickly erased when Julia shoved Jennie, her face a picture of rage.

"You *dare* touch the mighty Meister Donavon? Who do you think you are?"

Jennie clicked her fingers in the woman's face. "Your worst nightmare, bitch. Do you really want to start this?"

The woman slapped Jennie, leaving a bright red handprint on her cheek.

Jennie's hand moved to her face. When she turned back to the woman, her scorn was so powerful that Julia's confident demeanor faded instantly.

The woman retreated behind Meister Donavon and whispered in his ear. The Meister turned to Jennie and grinned, then pointed and shouted, "My pet! Absorb her. Absorb her now and remove this nuisance from my perfect moment."

Jennie took that moment to scowl before disappearing from sight and startling the pair. As she dipped into the spectral world, she felt the *sturmgeist*'s eyes on her before she saw them.

Immediately the pressure grew, and she had to fight to stay grounded. She latched onto Baxter, using him as a kind of reverse belay while the *sturmgeist* tripled its efforts to absorb Jennie into its mass.

Jennie concentrated every ounce of willpower she had to hold on, but even she had her limits. As she floated suspended in the air, she tried to think back to her last encounter with a creature of this magnitude. The memory was hazy—it *was* almost eighty years ago, after all—but something was there. A small nugget of information.

A helpful nugget.

Taking a deep breath, Jennie released her hold on Baxter and was sucked into the specter.

CHAPTER FIFTEEN

The storm had grown and was now violent.

It had happened so fast, too. Whatever ritual those idiots had enacted, it had been powerful. It grew in power faster than she'd thought imaginable, and the inside of the *sturmgeist* was now a scene from an apocalyptic movie.

The wind whipped in enormous circles, catching everyone inside in the vortex. It seemed impossible that such a large specter could fit inside the main chamber of the church, but Jennie supposed that was the magic of the spectral illusion.

Debris spun with Jennie. Her hair whipped her face and stung her eyes. Where before the *sturmgeist* had held only Jack and had been nothing more than a premature tornado, this was a damn hurricane.

There was no bottom. No ground to speak of. Jennie floated, growing more nauseated as she was spun. She tried her best to regain her balance and some sort of control, and after a few moments of swimming and flailing her arms, she managed to work into a rhythm and was able to focus on the center of the specter.

The woman was small compared to her storm. She hung suspended in her full glory in the center of the hurricane, holding her arms out as she looked at the sky. Jennie couldn't help but compare this vision to the religious symbols she'd seen in churches.

The *sturmgeist* was as naked as the day she was born. Her skin was a liquid black. Dark smoke filtered from her fingertips and fueled the storm, and each flutter of her eyelids shot lightning.

There's a power I'd love to be able to absorb, Jennie thought, ducking as a half-destroyed chair whirled above her head.

Knowing she only had a limited amount of time to rescue Jack and everyone else absorbed by the storm, Jennie gritted her teeth and began her work.

Maintaining control over her body while sending out her spectral feelers was a chore, to say the least. Jennie focused her attention on the small woman in the center of it all, knowing she could end this if she could get close enough. The spectral frequencies thrummed around her, and soon she felt the first connection as a dark tendril crept from the woman and wormed its way toward her.

The moment it made contact with Jennie, the *sturmgeist's* eyes twisted toward her. Her face showed no emotion, but there was a sudden change in her demeanor. The ghost tensed, blank white eyes fixed on Jennie.

Jennie channeled spectral power through the tendril and used it to move closer to the middle. Like a child on a merry-go-round, the closer she got to the center of the storm, the more powerful the force became.

And the easier it was to strengthen her connection.

Jennie's heart raced. Her head pounded from the exertion. She made infinitesimal progress as more Shadows were swept into the storm.

The *sturmgeist* sent a streak of lightning down the ever-thickening tendril to shock Jennie and force her back.

Not today.

Jennie was a solitary mountaineer climbing Everest. Unbeknownst to the dozens of figures whirling in the black spectral mass around her, their savior was making progress.

When she was ten feet away, Jennie forced another spectral

connection, then another, binding the ghost. Now she could feel the ghost's panic.

The vortex began to slow as the *sturmgeist* focused her efforts on the invader.

Blue and white bolts of electricity tore down the connections, causing Jennie's body to go rigid. She clamped her teeth shut and held on, knowing the pain wouldn't last forever.

Meister Donavon and Julia watched in the mortal world with apprehension as the swirling cloud shot bolts of lightning in all directions around the church, striking the wooden pews and starting small fires as well as shattering antique ornaments and statues of Jesus and his disciples.

Eventually, the lightning stopped. The *sturmgeist* stared at Jennie with white-hot hatred. Through the connections that bound them together, Jennie could feel it doing whatever it could to manipulate her, trying to use the spectral tethers to control Rogue and remove the nuisance.

Jennie fought the power and reached for her blade. The movement of lowering her hand to her side felt like she was fighting through mud to get there.

When Jennie grasped the blade at last, she let out a roar of primal rage as she drew the sword and thrust it toward the sturmgeist.

In the moment before the blade connected, Jennie felt pulses of energy leave the specter. Small white balls of lightning flew in all directions, shocking the Shadows caught in her vortex.

Then the blade connected, and the church was filled with blinding light. Jennie screwed her eyes shut and gasped as the vortex collapsed in an instant. One moment she was suspended in the air, fighting the storm, the next she felt the firmness of wooden flooring as she landed on her back in the real world.

From all around her came thuds and moans as the Shadows were released from the *sturmgeist*'s grasp. Some landed awkwardly on the pews, others fell face-first to the floor. A few landed in the fires that had sparked around the church and were frantically patting the parts of their bodies that had caught fire.

Jennie pushed herself off the floor. A short way in front of her, Jack lay unconscious. Clive and Ruby ran out of the back room and knelt by his side. They rolled him onto his back and felt for a pulse.

Before Jennie could go over to check on him, a body crashed into her side.

"You spiteful bitch!" Meister Donavon spat as he straddled her and held the knife above her body. "You evil, cruel, stupid little wench! You ruined everything!"

He raised the knife high and was about to drive it into her chest when Jennie reacted so suddenly that he froze in place. Her draw of the Big Bitch was so quick, he had barely seen her move. The barrel now stared him in the eyes, her finger poised on the trigger.

"Think about sticking me with that prick and it's all over for you."

Meister Donavon hesitated, although his mind continued to work. His hands shook. His mouth curled into a sneer. She could see the debate in his eyes as he contemplated the effects of just going for the stab, but armed with the knowledge of how fast she was, he knew he could never do it in time.

His face softened, but he still held the knife above her. His words were soft. "The spectral world is real. It's true. We made it happen…"

"And you almost killed everyone in the process," Jennie accused. "Was it really worth it just to find out?"

Meister Donavon nodded, eyes wide. "Without a doubt. What's been done once can be done again. Armed with this knowledge, there's no stopping us. We can bring specters to the public's notice and—"

The Meister stopped talking as every door in the church slammed open at once. Bodies clothed in black with riot helmets burst into the church, assault rifles leading the way and trained on the civilians in the room. The bold white letters SIA decorated their jackets.

The shouts of the newcomers bought everyone to their knees. Commands of "Federal agents! Freeze!" and "Get on the floor!" echoed around the small church.

The Shadows obeyed without question, lacing their hands behind their heads and folding to their knees, their hoods lowered to reveal frightened faces. Many of them sobbed, still in shock from what had transpired.

Rough hands ripped Meister Donavon from on top of Jennie. She stood up slowly, hands held out in surrender.

"We said get on the floor, lady," a rough voice shouted at her.

From the ranks of SIA operatives, a man and woman approached. They were the only ones not wearing helmets.

It was the woman who had spoken. Her surly face spoke of years of service and dealing with assholes.

"You above the law?" she hollered. "On the ground before we force you."

"I'd like to see you try," Jennie returned, meeting her hardened stare.

"It's okay, Holly," Clive called, appearing at her side. "She's good. We've got her to thank that we're alive."

The woman's lip curled. "It's Agent Daggro to you. Show some damn respect to your superior."

Clive gritted his teeth but nodded anyway. "Apologies."

"What the hell happened here?" the second agent, a man in his mid-forties with a bald spot at the back of his head, asked. "Where's Agent Hansen?"

Clive led the pair over to Jack, who was now sitting against the wall with his eyes closed. Jennie was glad to see his chest rising and falling once more.

"Agent Hansen, the boss wants to see you."

Jack opened his eyes and gave a half-hearted smile. "Agent Daggro. Agent Rhone."

"Are you okay, Agent?" Rhone asked, crouching next to Jack. Agent Daggro stood with her arms folded, clearly not as empathetic as her associate.

Jack gave a small nod. "I've been better. So much for a training mission, huh?"

Agent Rhone laughed softly and stood once more. "Let's clear the area and get the wounded some medical attention," he told Daggro. "We'll keep all associates of the cult in custody until we get a full picture of the events that transpired here tonight. Agent Hansen, Agent Bannon, you come with us."

"Hold on, sir," Jack asked. "With respect, you're going to want Jennie to come with us. If you want answers, she's in the best position to give them. She saved all our asses tonight."

The pair eyed Jennie. Daggro looked a lot more mistrustful than Rhone.

"Very well," Rhone agreed. "Ma'am, come with us."

As Jennie left, she saw Meister Donavon in handcuffs, the knife now in possession of one of the agents, although she didn't see any sign of the woman who had clearly been infatuated with the Meister.

The church was cleared, and the Shadows were taken into the various cars waiting outside. All the vehicles were black and had snuck into the village like shadows. The villagers were set free, although a small squadron of SIA agents remained behind to ask questions and get a clearer picture of events. Fires were extinguished, and ambulances called from the nearest hospital.

"I've got to say, I was not expecting this to be my night," Jennie muttered to Baxter as she waited patiently by Agent Rhone's car for the pair to return. The lead agents had excused themselves to organize the scene containment efforts and said they would be back soon for questioning.

"A *sturmgeist*." Baxter shook his head solemnly. "I've been a specter for over a hundred years, and there's still so much I don't know."

"Me, too," Jennie told him. "I don't think we'll ever know all there is to know about what lies in the great beyond and the forces that govern it all."

Baxter sighed. "That's sad."

"No," Jennie replied, "that's exciting. A world in which we're always learning. What's sad about that?"

She stopped talking to Baxter when Jack and Clive approached the car. Jack had sat in the back of an ambulance for a short time while they attended to his wounds and checked that he was okay. He now wore a sling and had several band-aids covering the cuts on his face and arms.

"That looks fun," Jennie commented, nodding to his arm.

"Oh, it's just a precaution. Likely a shoulder sprain from the fall." He looked at the stars, the dark sky beginning to lighten as dawn set in. "I've got to say, if tonight hasn't been a total dream, I'm not sure what's real and what isn't anymore."

"You mean, you've never ridden a whirlwind inside a *sturmgeist* before?" Jennie grinned. "Man, you haven't lived."

Jack scoffed.

"What are you?" Clive asked abruptly, scanning Jennie's face. "What was all that in there? How is everything you did possible?"

Jennie shrugged. "If I'm honest, I'd rather wait for your bosses to get back to answer those questions. I've answered them a lot in my life, and I hate to repeat myself. You think you can wait until then?"

Clive looked over his shoulder to where Agent Rhone and Agent Daggro were deep in talks with a handcuffed Meister Donavon and the other agents holding him.

"I guess so." Clive rubbed his tired eyes. "Maybe we should grab some shut-eye first."

"We can sleep in the car," Jack told him. "It's a three-hour trip from here to DC. Perfect for a catnap."

"Sounds good to me," Jennie agreed, trying to stifle a yawn. She didn't realize how tired she was. "Wait, did you say DC?"

"I did," Clive confirmed.

Jennie turned to Baxter and smiled. "How fortuitous. That was where we were heading." Her smile faded. "Oh, my car. Can we hitch a ride? "

Jack laughed. "Jennie, given everything that's happened tonight, I don't think you have a choice."

CHAPTER SIXTEEN

Washington DC, USA

SSA Tom Hopkins strode down clinical white halls with an extra jolt of fuel in his step.

Colleagues lowered their eyes as he passed. Doors yielded to a quick retinal scan, and soon the boardroom came into sight—the place he seemed to spend most of his time these days.

The night had reportedly been eventful, but it wasn't all good news. While his men and women had arrived in the nick of time and resolved the situation, it shouldn't have become a situation in the first place.

For the last year, SSA Hopkins had been weighed down by the knowledge of things he almost couldn't believe. From the moment the special agent in charge had inducted him into the Spectral Intelligence division, his entire world had been turned upside down.

What had once been a career of dealing with criminals and terrorists who were a danger to the country was now a responsibility for beings he couldn't see without assistance. He'd had to trust his leading operatives' word about their very existence until recently when the technology had allowed him to see specters for the first time.

Now he spent his days dealing with the invisible, filing reports about unexplained disturbances within a four-state radius. With every passing week, the division was growing, and so was the pressure. The team had increased from five to over two hundred in a matter of months, and resources were being funneled into ensuring mortals could connect with specters without the need for conduits.

"Why me?" had once been his question of the day, but as the division had grown, SSA Hopkins had seen the opportunity to become a major lynchpin in this country's history.

If what he had been told just now was correct, he had discovered the missing piece of the puzzle that would move them forward and cement the next step in the SIA's development.

The door opened before he reached it. An agent waited patiently for him to pass and offered him a pair of SI goggles. These he took without acknowledgment before finding his seat among the gathered agents and clearing his throat.

This particular boardroom had never seen such an odd collection of individuals. Aside from his two main field operatives and a pair of trainee agents, there were two women sitting side by side at the table, and a young woman taking notes on a yellow legal pad.

One of these women caught his eye. Her red hair reached her shoulders, and she was dressed as though she had fallen straight out of a 1900s steampunk TV show. She wore sunglasses indoors, which he found unsettling, but he had been forewarned that she was sensitive about these and refused to take them off if she were to answer questions.

The other woman wore a black cloak with her hood down. She was younger than the first woman, with entrancing eyes, and when she met his gaze, she glanced nervously away.

When he turned back to study the first woman, who was introduced by the assistant taking minutes as Genevieve King, the stare she gave him over the top of her sunglasses was unfaltering. The power he usually held that made new initiates shrink before him clearly didn't work on her.

How interesting, Hopkins mused, a slight curl of a smile at his lips. *This could be a fun challenge.*

<hr>

"So, it seems like some things went down in New Jersey last night…"

Jennie stared at the man at the head of the table, who was the definition of a government type if she ever saw one. The man's face told tales of a thousand stressful meetings, desperate fieldwork, and years spent fighting for justice guided by the hands of those above him.

Not necessarily always in the right direction.

The agent, one SSA Hopkins, placed a pair of goggles on his face and read from the document in front of him.

"Two trainee agents were sent out to investigate a mild disturbance, which quickly became a hostage situation. Trainee Agent Clive Bannon was taken by a cult known as 'The Shadows.' Agent Bannon got his dumb ass captured and became ritual fodder for the offending cult, intended to commit homicide with the sole intention of practicing black magic. Said cult then managed to kill one of their own and create a spectral disturbance using the blood that was spilled."

Hopkins glared at the assembly. "Am I correct so far?"

There was a smirk from Genevieve, and the others gave grudging nods.

Hopkins continued. "While Agent Bannon was busy getting trussed up like a turkey, Agent Hansen was guided into the forest by a group of the spectral phenomena we call wisps before a chance meeting brought him into contact with Genevieve King."

"Actually, I go by Jennie," Jennie interrupted. "And it wasn't chance. Jack was in a hole, and I was guided to him."

If Hopkins was annoyed, his face didn't show it. "Jennie King," he corrected. "Agent Hansen decided to ignore protocol and allow a civilian to accompany him to the scene of a crime in progress. On the way back to Batsto, Agent Hansen encountered a defector from the cult who led them back to the village and gave them further intel on the events unfolding throughout the night. From this, the three of you fought your way into the church in order to disrupt the ritual ceremony and were able to save Agent Bannon's life at the cost of an innocent civilian."

He paused and scanned the room. "Is that all correct so far?"

Jack and Clive nodded but remained silent.

Hopkins said as he laced his fingers on top of the document, "This is where your report loses me." His eyes found Jennie's again. "Miss King, I believe you are well-informed enough to fill in the blanks?"

Jennie had been waiting for this question. While they traveled back to Washington and rode in relative silence, she had turned over the events in her head again and again, trying to work out the best way to describe them to civilians. She knew she would be tested. She knew she would have to demonstrate her powers at some point, but initiating those around her into what she was capable of would always be something she approached with caution.

The last thing she wanted was to become a fugitive fleeing from a government division who were interested in running experiments on her, no matter how much she wanted to figure out exactly what her genetic makeup was and how she had acquired her talents.

Yeah. Like they would ever catch me.

Jennie straightened in her chair and directed her words at Hopkins while the others watched her intently. "Of course, I am more than happy to elaborate on my side of the tale, Senior Special Agent. However, in order to do so, I must first understand what level your knowledge of the spectral world stretches to. Understanding a lot of what I tell you relies heavily on your awareness of it."

Hopkins gave a small chuckle. "Miss King, you realize you are sitting in the central hub of the Spectral Intelligence Agency, a select secret division of the US government. Our agents are trained in the fields of spectral research, development, and reconnaissance. I assure you, this facility has the *latest* intel regarding the spectral world. We seek to bridge the gap between the mortal and spectral worlds and eradicate the threats so that we may all reside in peace on this planet."

"Cute," Jennie enthused, her patronizing tone enough to earn a scowl from Hopkins. "How long have you been up and running?"

"Bordering on twelve months," Hopkins replied.

"So, still a relatively young division?" Jennie commented.

Hopkins growled. "I assure you we work with great speed and diligence on these matters. We are even working closely with our overseas counterparts to ensure that a global initiative is launched and that peace remains at the forefront of all operatives' agendas."

Jennie nodded. "Okay. In that case, I assume you've been in touch with the paranormal court and its associates in the United Kingdom?"

Hopkins, Daggro, and even Rhone were slightly taken aback.

"The paranormal court are associates of ours." Hopkins worked to regain his composure. "In fact, it is thanks to the paranormal court that we obtained the intelligence needed to form this division." He leaned forward once more. "Though, tell me, Miss King, how is it you know about the court?"

Jennie debated telling the truth or bending it. Over the years, she had always operated in secrecy, utilizing the innocence of others to remain in the shadows.

Now, however, she knew she had to play a different game. If she was to make the most of her current situation and form ties with the SIA, she would need to think about the long game. If she started their relationship by lying, she might never have the opportunity to earn their trust again.

"I'm a former associate of the court," she replied, deciding to feed him the truth in bites. "I've worked with them in the past."

"So, you're a conduit?" Agent Daggro asked before she could help herself.

"In a sense," Jennie replied.

"What does that mean?" Hopkins nudged.

Jennie shrugged. "Let's just say, if conduits were meat, the ones you know would be hamburgers, and I'd be a twelve-ounce sirloin steak."

A moment of silence ensued before Hopkins let out a laugh, the sound like a spluttering gas mower. The laughter grew until the other agents joined in, and soon every federal agent was chuckling.

"You sure think a lot of yourself, Miss King," Hopkins replied at last.

"I know what I am," Jennie answered without emotion. "You asked the question, I gave the answer. Do you think I would be alive to tell my story if I wasn't extraordinary?"

"How extraordinary are we talking?" Hopkins asked.

This time, it was Jack who replied. "Sir, there is no doubt in my mind that Jennie is a veteran of this game. Had it not been for her protection in the woods, I would still be out there, stumbling around in the dark." He paused. "Well, no. Both Bannon and I would be dead. Not only did she lead me where we needed to go, but she also fought a pack of spectral wolves nearly singlehandedly and freed me from the clutches of a power I would have thought it impossible to escape."

"Nearly singlehandedly?" Hopkins picked up. "You're saying there was help against these…" He glanced down at the report. "What in the name of Christ are 'Yokai?'"

"Spirit animals," Jennie replied flatly. "Rare occurrences found only in forests where humanity has had very little contact with nature. To be honest, I certainly didn't expect to find any in the heart of New Jersey, but it seems that people can look after an area and preserve the natural beauty it holds."

Unsure if that was an insult, Hopkins asked Jennie to elaborate. Jennie explained what she had seen in the forest, detailing her encounter with the wolves and how she had vanquished them in order to save Baxter and free their spirits.

"And Baxter is?" Hopkins asked.

"My specter," Jennie replied as if she'd just been asked what day it was.

Hopkins' disbelief was visible on his face. "You have a personal specter?"

"It's not like that." Jennie turned to the chair where Baxter sat. "At least, not anymore. Personal specters were tied to my previous role, but I'm pleased to say that this one came along with me voluntarily. Baxter's power is most of the reason we're alive to tell the tale today."

Hopkins' attention moved to the empty chair. "You're telling me there's an uninvited specter here in this room?"

Jennie nodded with a smirk on her face. "I guess your security protocol isn't quite as tight as you thought, eh? You might want to fix that before you carry on advertising yourself as the Spectral *Intelligence* Agency."

Flustered and growing red, Hopkins placed the SI goggles on his face and pounded his fist on the table as Baxter gave him a wave.

"No one bothered to check the spectral plane?" he exclaimed in disbelief. "No one?"

To his surprise, it was Jack who answered. "Sir, Baxter is an asset to the team. He falls on the loyal side of the spectral scale, and was very useful in helping capture the Shadows."

Daggro and Rhone also put on SI goggles and examined Baxter closely. Rhone'd had no idea he was sitting next to a specter and leaned away as if repulsed by what he was seeing.

Hopkins massaged the sides of his head. "Okay, Miss King. I think it's time you describe to us exactly what is going on here. Who are you? Why are you here? What happened in that church tonight?"

"Happy to," Jennie replied. "But before I do, I'm going to ask you all to open your minds a little wider than you thought possible. What I'm about to tell you is going to sound like fiction, but I assure you, it's not even close to the things I've witnessed in my life."

Jennie told them everything she could remember about the previous night. Of the power of the ritual, the formation of the *sturmgeist*, and the battle that had raged in the storm contained within the spectral world. She told them about some of her abilities and the weapons she carried, but she didn't go into the full extent of her powers or the truth about her age.

As she spoke, the agents maintained a respectful silence, with Hopkins scribbling notes and the assistant doing her best to record everything that was said. The agents kept their SI goggles on and occasionally glanced at Baxter throughout her story.

When Jennie finally finished her tale, the room was silent. She was used to that, of course, having shocked many mortals over the years with the information she harbored about the spectral world. But she had thought that for a government-led agency, they might be a little more clued in than they apparently were.

"A storm, you say?" Hopkins leaned back in his chair and wiped his glasses with a cloth. "Within whatever abomination they conjured, there was a storm?"

Clive confirmed her story. "You should have seen it, sir. Darkness took the church. People were lifted off their feet and spun around in the air as if pulled by a tornado."

"Why have we never heard of *sturmgeists*?" Hopkins asked, directing his question at Rhone and Daggro.

"I don't know," Rhone replied. "Out of all the intelligence we've been given, there has been no such mention. No Yokai either, I might add."

"There's a lot you won't know about the spectral world," Jennie told them. "How long have humans been searching the oceans, and still we don't know half of what's down in the deep? The spectral world and the mortal world have been separated, so why would you know all there is to know?"

Hopkins eyed her curiously. "You speak like someone who has lived a life of study, yet you can't be more than thirty years of age."

"Ouch!" Jennie pouted. "Most say I'm twenty-five. Twenty-one if they're trying to get in my knickers."

"How old are you?" Hopkins asked.

Jennie leaned over and signaled toward a small selection of papers beneath Hopkin's initial document. "Don't you have that information in there?"

She smiled, knowing they wouldn't have a drop of information on her real identity.

Hopkins shook his head, his face curdling. "Nothing. Not one iota of information on a Genevieve King. No date of birth, no place of residence, no occupation, no family history. Nothing. Zilch. Nada. Do you know what that tells me?"

"That your data analysts are shit?" Jennie asked sweetly.

"That you're an alien, Miss King." Before Jennie could make a joke, he added, "And no, I don't mean an extraterrestrial from outer space. I mean you're a ghost in the machine. Somehow you have managed to erase your identity from the system. You don't exist. Does that sound correct?"

Jennie nodded. "I suppose you could put it that way."

"Even our cross-continental associates couldn't pull you from the mortal system. Nothing on the electoral register, no birth certificate, nothing."

Jennie pointed at the papers. "If that's the case, what's all that under there?" She smirked, already knowing the answer.

Hopkins' demeanor shifted. "Well, after a call to our contacts at the paranormal court, we managed to find something on you. Turns out that Genevieve King isn't what you're known by, is it?"

Jennie nodded. "I told you that."

"Nor is it Jennie King," Hopkins continued. "Does the name 'Rogue' ring a bell?"

Now Jennie was smiling. "A cutesy nickname given to me by my associates. Honestly, there's no truth in the title."

"Miss King, I'm going to ask you this one more time, and I need you to give me a straight answer. What we choose to do with you and your…associate depends on your veracity."

Jennie dropped the smirk. "Go ahead."

"How old are you?"

"Don't you know it's rude to ask a girl her age?"

Hopkins stared intently at her.

"One hundred and thirty-eight years young," Jennie replied.

There were audible gasps in the room.

"Impossible," Daggro breathed.

Hopkins regrouped, then asked, "Miss King, what is your purpose on US soil?"

Now it was Jennie's turn to lace her fingers and lean forward. "My purpose is to help you, Agent Hopkins. My purpose is to help all of you. To share my firsthand experience and knowledge to further your progress and give you the support I know you've been lacking from the paranormal court."

"Hold on," Rhone interjected, flicking through his papers. "It says here that you're associated with the paranormal court?"

"A clerical error, clearly," Jennie replied. "That's a story for another time. Just know I'm here to help you."

"Why should we trust you?" Hopkins asked. "You don't owe us anything."

Jennie met his confused stare with a look of disdain. "Because *you* owe *me*. I saved your agents' asses last night. I rescued two of your men and brought a cult dabbling in black magic to justice. I can open your eyes to a whole new realm you wouldn't believe exists, way past your puny goggles and toy spectral guns."

Hopkins raised his eyebrows, intrigued. He turned to the other agents, then back to Jennie. "Suppose we're interested. Where do we start?"

"Slowly," Jennie told him. "You can start by showing me around your facility, and I'll start by telling you all the things you're doing wrong."

Hopkins considered that for a moment. Daggro clenched her teeth, clearly not liking the way this woman was talking to her boss.

Eventually, Hopkins replied. "Miss King, would you mind stepping outside? I think my colleagues and I need a moment of discussion."

"Please," Jennie replied. "Call me Rogue."

CHAPTER SEVENTEEN

<u>Washington DC, USA</u>

Jennie, Baxter, and Ruby were shown to a small break room equipped with a water fountain and vending machines stocked with high-protein bars. Jennie helped herself to water and sat down.

Ruby took a nearby seat, occasionally glancing at Jennie as if she were about to say something before thinking better of it. Baxter paced around the room.

Jennie already knew what the verdict would be. The agents would call her back in and ask for a demonstration of her powers. If Jack told them about her vanishing trick, she would no doubt have to add credit to his story before they took either of them seriously. Even though she *had* saved the day, they would need to rule out any possibility that she was some crackpot magician armed with a bag of illusions.

"What?" Jennie snapped after Ruby once again made a move to talk and then retreated into her shell.

Ruby considered her words carefully, pulling back slightly in fear as she spoke. "Are you really able to communicate with ghosts? All that stuff in there, that was true?"

Jennie sighed. She understood her trepidation. Looking at her now, she felt sorry for the girl. Jennie thought back to where she had been at age eighteen, which she considered "the innocent years" before she was initiated into the paranormal court and her world had changed.

She couldn't even imagine that innocence now.

"Why would I lie?"

Ruby shrugged. "People lie under pressure. People say anything to make you believe."

"You're a smart kid," Jennie replied. "Hold onto that. You're right not to trust people. It'll get you far." She leaned toward Ruby. "You want an extra bit of advice? Ignore that first part and learn to trust people. It'll get you farther than that first part."

Ruby let out a relieved laugh.

Jennie smiled. "Seriously, Ruby, if there's one thing I don't do, it's lie. I don't have all the answers, but this is who I am. You wanted to discover the spectral world, well, here it is. I'm the key you were looking for, not some hyped-up cult leader with an ego complex."

Ruby weighed Jennie's words and relaxed into her chair. There were dark bags beneath her eyes. "I'm so tired."

Jennie yawned. "I know the feeling." She closed her eyes and counted the seconds in her head. "Believe me, I know the feeling."

***

"You can't seriously believe her," Daggro spat. "This is… It's insane!"

The tension had ratcheted up the minute Jennie had left the room. Hopkins had even sent out the assistant, wanting the discussion off the record and between the immediate agents who were affected.

Daggro's ears pulsed red. "We're talking about a woman who believes she's over a century old. Need I say anything else?"

"I bet you're gonna," Rhone whispered under his breath.

"That's over a hundred years old, sir. She doesn't look a day over thirty. I've never heard of anything more preposterous in my life."

Hopkins remained tight-lipped, his mind working double-time to process what he had heard in that room.

"Sure, I can get on board with the fact that she's a conduit," Daggro continued, doing her best to reason through the facts. "She clearly has a spectral assistant, and that's pretty unique. But to claim that she's lived for a hundred and thirty-eight years? That would have her born in the late 1800s. That's just not possible."

"What if it is?" Rhone retorted. "Let's be honest; there are a lot of things we've heard tonight that many of us wouldn't have believed a year ago. Who's to say what the boundaries of this reality are? Need I remind you that we're talking about a world in which *specters* exist? We're talking about ghosts here. You can believe that souls escape bodies and remain in another realm which happens to co-exist with ours, but you can't believe a woman has lived beyond her years?"

Daggro practically shook as she replied, "We have evidence of specters. Tons of it. We've created technology to prove the existence of the spectral realm. We're building files on our encounters, and we've got conduits on our payroll, so we have an abundance of reasons to believe. Find me another example of a woman with hyper-mortality."

"So your argument is ruling out that it exists?" Rhone ran a hand over his face. "Hansen, Bannon, what are your thoughts?"

Bannon, a seasoned veteran of federal politics, spoke in a calm, reasoned voice. "I think, as unlikely as it is, we shouldn't rule it out. Based on what we've seen tonight, I'd go so far as to say we can trust her." He turned to Jack. "Wouldn't you agree?"

Jack cleared his throat, aware that all eyes were on him. His shoulder throbbed, reminding him that all that had happened that night was real.

"I trust every word that comes out of her mouth," he told them. "I don't understand it, nor do I believe there's an easy explanation, but that woman has done nothing but help us to get that cult in our custody before they could cause further damage."

Clive nodded.

"The real question," Hopkins stated, making his first contribution to the conversation since Jennie had left the room, "is whether or not we bring her on-side. The paranormal court didn't have a lot to say about Rogue, but I could tell they were biting their tongues. Whatever her connection is to the specters overseas, there's something they're not telling us."

"Maybe she pissed them off?" Rhone suggested.

"Maybe that's why she's here?" Clive added.

"Whatever it is, we proceed with caution," Hopkins continued. "If she is what she says she is, Rogue could be a powerful ally with the current Baltimore situation. Not only that, but she could also move us leaps and bounds ahead in terms of arming us for spectral combat."

"But, sir," Rhone countered. "I thought the main aim of the SIA was to prevent spectral conflict and resolve any nuisances before they grow too severe?"

"Don't be naive," Hopkins told him sharply. "You think the government is secretly piling millions into this research so that we can help some old woman in Idaho whose teapot has jumped off the table? We have to be armed for a full spectral war. It may not happen in our lifetime, but we need to be as prepared as we can for an enemy we've yet to fully understand. The President has ordered an accelerated program within the SIA, hence our efforts with new recruits."

Jack and Clive sat silently, knowing better than to interrupt their superior.

"With Rogue on our side, perhaps we can get answers to the long-unanswered questions we've had. It might benefit us to work with a mortal who has lived around specters her entire life rather than conduits who think they know what's going on."

Daggro scoffed. "If she is telling the truth, she's no mortal."

"She's got a working heart and breathes our oxygen, doesn't she?" Hopkins snapped.

"She's got a bigger heart than most of the agents in this division," Jack put in. "That's one thing I know for sure."

Jennie woke from her nap when she was called back into the boardroom. Judging by their reactions as she walked in, she knew it was a positive result.

"Show us what you can do, Rogue," Hopkins instructed. "Rhone will be your guide. Take it all in, share what you know, and you'll do well here." He took a long breath. "Lord knows we could use your help right now."

The sentiment was not reflected by everyone in the room, judging by the way Daggro stared daggers at Jennie as they left. Jennie felt the general atmosphere was one of optimism. Hopkins dismissed all present agents, and soon Rhone was leading Jennie down a corridor toward the living quarters of the SIA facility.

"You'll stay here," Rhone instructed, tapping a code into a panel on the door and watching it open. "I'll send around security to set you up with a retinal image for your lock, but otherwise, feel free to rest up.

"I thought we were going to take the tour?" Jennie asked, impressed by what she could see of the facility's amenities.

"All in good time." Rhone smiled. "It's been a long night for all of us. Rest up, and report to me at 18:00 hours. Lord knows we all need to recuperate."

"Really?" Jennie scoffed. "All of this evidence of life after death, and you're still going to say you believe in God?"

"What can I say?" Rhone told her. "You have your beliefs, and I have mine. Goodnight, Miss King."

Rhone left Jennie to her ablutions, and soon Jennie was tucked in bed and fast asleep. She dreamed of nothing and awoke when the irritating buzz of an alarm clock she definitely hadn't set blared in her ear.

"Why do I get the feeling they're watching me?" she muttered as she lifted herself from her bed. She found Baxter in the living area, slumped in the armchair, snoring gently with his mouth open.

"Rise and shine, ghostbag." Jennie latched onto him and pulled him up until he was wobbling on his feet. He overcorrected and landed in a push-up position before realizing what was happening.

Baxter rubbed his head. "There are nicer ways to wake someone up, you know?"

"I know." Jennie laughed. "This way is far more fun."

Baxter shook his head. "This day's been too long to deal with your idea of fun. Man, can you believe the last twenty-four hours? Who'd have thought a road trip to Washington could be so eventful?"

Jennie shrugged. "That's just a Tuesday for me." She scanned the living facility, eyes narrowed. "Hey, do you think they've got any booze here?"

"Booze?" Baxter scoffed. "Booze? In a government facility? You're kidding, right?"

Jennie shrugged. "All these agents must have something here to help them unwind."

"Isn't that what the shooting range is for?"

"I suppose." Jennie sighed. "What I wouldn't give right now for a Manhattan."

"We've only just left there." Baxter grinned as Jennie looked down her nose at him.

"Nice one," she said flatly. "Come on. It's almost six. We should go find Rhone and see what all this is about.

The building had seemed to be a modest size when they had first arrived. With a nondescript gray stone front, the HQ could have held any number of businesses.

An elevator had taken them into the basement levels of the building, where the facility stretched beneath the city like the roots of a tree. Now, Jennie was finally seeing the full magnitude of the operation they were running here.

"The facility is guarded by the latest security technology, with only a limited number of operatives cleared to access the full inner workings," Rhone informed her as he strode down the clinical white corridors. "Retinal scanning, voice recognition, and guards at all major entrances are employed in order to ensure that everything that we do here remains a secret."

Jennie turned her lip up, impressed. The facility looked to be the very definition of top-secret, complete with sour-faced agents wandering the halls, and steel doors with nothing more than small squares bearing Roman numerals on their fronts.

Occasionally the painful white of the corridors would be broken by a large green shrub in a pot, but that wasn't enough to make the place any warmer. Rhone showed her a series of break rooms, a number of offices with agents staring intently at computer screens, and a room where a number of specters were in deep conversation with a series of agents who were undoubtedly also conduits.

There were rooms fitted out as gyms, a firing range, and meeting rooms with digital boards and an array of equipment designed to streamline tactical planning of operations.

A set of stairs led them down to a near-identical copy of the floor above. The only difference from the first was the men and women in white lab coats interspersed with the SIA agents in their black uniforms, many of whom chewed over digital tablets as they scratched their heads and mumbled to themselves.

Rhone took Jennie and Baxter to a door labeled XXII and placed a thumb on the keypad. A robotic voice announced, "Agent Rhone requests access."

A human voice from inside the room mumbled, "Access granted."

The door hissed open on hydraulics, revealing a lab so clean that Jennie felt she was contaminating it just by being there. In the center of the room, a skinny old man fussed over something she couldn't see. His back was hunched, disguising his true height, but Jennie could tell that this man must have neared seven feet in his prime.

But that wasn't the most surprising thing. That was reserved for the obese lady specter sitting in a tall chair beside him. She looked bored, and she was swinging her legs beneath her like a child at dinnertime.

"Proctor!" Rhone declared, arms wide as he brought the others farther into the room. "Long time, no see."

"That never gets old," Proctor replied.

"I've got some visitors for you. Some people I think you'll like to meet."

"What're you…" His voice trailed off as he spun and saw Jennie, then he gasped. "You!"

He moved so fast that he took Jennie off-guard. She took a step back until she realized that he wasn't gunning for her; he was standing in front of Baxter, examining him with delight.

"You've brought me a new toy to play with?" Proctor asked, a manic smile on his face. "Good, good. The more, the merrier, I say. Tell me, specter, what's your name? What's your history? I want to know everything you can do."

Baxter and Jennie exchanged glances.

"I'm…Baxter?" His voice rose as though he was uncertain of what he was saying. "And I'm…a specter?"

Rhone now had his SI goggles on and began laughing.

"You can hear them?" Jennie questioned.

Rhone shook his head. "I've trained myself in the art of lip-reading. SI goggles are great, but we've yet to find an elegant solution to enable agents to hear specters." He motioned toward Proctor. "That's where this guy comes in."

Proctor tore himself away from Baxter and presented a feeble hand for Jennie to shake. "Nice to meet you, dear. My team is leading the research efforts investigating the limits of spectral technology." His face lit up as he talked. "Fascinating stuff. Truly fascinating. It's our duty to explore the frequencies the specters exist on, and to find methods and processes to bridge the gap between mortals and specters so we can widen the world's knowledge and test its boundaries."

"How big is your team?" Jennie asked.

"Half a dozen strong right now," Proctor replied. "Sourced from the most talented scientists experimenting in the world of paranormal physics."

Rhone leaned over to Jennie and spoke out of the side of his mouth. "Crackpots who happen to have a Ph.D."

Proctor's eyes widened in alarm. "Excuse me, *Agent*, but these are *scientists*. They might have earned an unhappy reputation out there in the wider world because for years, people thought paranormal science was hokum. It's only through progress and repeatedly testing theories that we've been able to shift the government's perspective and ensure the wider public is protected by what we've been doing. Society might not be ready for paranormal experimentation, but that's exactly what we're here for."

"What kinds of things are you working on?" Jennie asked in earnest, her curiosity aroused by the chair the spectral woman was sitting on, which was fitted with numerous pads that were each a couple of inches square. Wires led from the chair to a device nearby, whose screen displayed bursts of static that looked like white fireworks burning at various intensities.

"Sorry. Classified," Proctor snapped, moving to block the screen with his body.

Rhone let out a small laugh. "Proctor, I don't think you're being entirely fair with our associate here. If you knew what this woman is capable of, you might change your mind."

"Oh? You think you've found a higher grade of conduit?" He laughed. "Don't waste my time on fantasies."

Jennie latched onto Baxter and disappeared from the mortal realm.

The doctor's goggles showed him the spectral energy that appeared where Jennie was standing, but it wasn't until he removed the goggles and realized she was immaterial that he let out a gasp.

He stumbled back, hand fanning toward the table for support. "How is that possible?"

Jennie reappeared and tilted her head toward Proctor. "Don't judge a book by its cover. We've all got our secrets."

Proctor's mouth flapped open and closed. He clawed for his digital tablet and started tapping vigorously on the virtual keys. "Impossible. A human who has the abilities to...what? Turn spectral? Remove herself from the mortal realm? What is going on here?"

Jennie was about to fire off a sarcastic response when she noticed that there was a large dusty tome on a plinth nearby. Its cover was thick and made of cracked leather, its pages yellow and dog-eared.

"Is that what I think it is?" Jennie asked, moving closer. She noticed that several pages were missing, their jagged edges indicating they'd been torn out in a hurry.

Instinctively, Proctor moved in her path to block the book. He held his arms wide. "That's currently under scientific investigation. You are not cleared to interfere with—"

Jennie vanished before his eyes and walked straight through him. She came out on the other side and was just able to glimpse some of the words before Proctor slammed the book shut.

"That was the Shadows' ritual," Jennie stated. "Where did you find this book?"

This time it was Rhone who answered. "It was in one of the townhouses in Batsto, stored in a small chest in the corner of a room. Our best guess is that this was the material Meister Donavon used to study the ritual, but he chose to learn it by heart and leave the book in a safe space while they underwent the ceremony."

"There are more spells and rituals in there?" Jennie asked.

"Oh, yes," Rhone replied, folding his arms. "Pages upon pages. We've given the resource to Proctor to see if there's any kind of scientific explanation that he can give us to further understand what happened in the ritual."

"That, and every other experiment you want me to run." Proctor groaned. "You need to tell Hopkins that we need more staff. We're already working at full capacity."

"In time," Rhone answered simply. "Come on, Jennie. There's much more to see."

Jennie tore her eyes away from the book and followed Rhone out of the lab.

"Wait!" Proctor called when they reached the door. "I need to ask the woman more questions!"

"Later!" Rhone called back. When the door hissed shut behind him, he turned to Jennie. "Great guy. One of the smartest people in the world."

Jennie grinned. "But batshit crazy, yes?"

Rhone snorted. "You really know how to read people."

"I've been around for a while."

Rhone eyed Jennie. She caught his glance.

"I'm telling the truth, you know," Jennie assured him. "I'm going to be a fantastic asset to this agency."

Rhone nodded, smiling despite himself. "I know. I don't know why I believe you, but something tells me I should. We've not met anyone like you yet."

Jennie winked. "And you never will again."

They made their way back to the upper floor, and Rhone accompanied Jennie to a large cafeteria where agents were finishing up their dinners and beginning to filter out of the room.

Jennie studied those around her. She looked entirely out of place in her current attire. Not that it bothered her since she had never been one to fit in. She placed her tray on the table and got the veggie-fest started. "What happened to them?" she asked between bites.

"To who?" Rhone asked.

Jennie swallowed her mouthful. "The Shadows. What happens when the SIA arrest people found to be involved in spectral criminal activity?"

"We have our own detainment facility," Rhone replied. He spotted Jack and Clive leaving the food line and waved them over. "We have a very effective method of filtering out the whack jobs from the civilians caught up in something they shouldn't be. Many are given slaps on the wrist, a few are handed over to the local authorities to deal with as they see fit, and those who present a hazard to themselves and others come with us for further questioning."

"So, the Meister is here?" Jennie asked.

"Oh, come on," Jack growled, lowering his tray to the table. "I'm about to eat my dinner. Do we have to talk about him?"

Clive chuckled and took a seat beside him. "He has a point. At least let us wake up first."

"Wow, I guess you really needed that sleep," Jennie commented, impressed by Jack's energy considering the long night they'd all shared and the exhaustion from the events.

"Yeah, Hansen tends to get a little cranky when he's tired," Clive joked, prodding mashed potato with his fork. "Without his beauty sleep, he's impossible to work with."

"We've partnered on one mission," Jack countered. "Who was the one who got kidnapped and offered up for sacrifice?"

Clive looked incredulously at Jack. "Who was the one who ran away to play with the fairies?"

"They were *wisps*," Jack replied. "And it wasn't my fault. They have powers…"

"Enough bickering, agents," Rhone laughed. "You two are going to have to put all of this aside if you don't want to mess up your next assignment."

Jack's eyebrows raised. "You already have us assigned?"

"Of course," Rhone told him with a grin. "Ain't no rest for the wicked."

"What is it?" Clive asked.

Rhone wagged his finger. "That's not for me to tell you. Your briefing will be at 21:00 hours in conference room seven." Rhone stood up with his tray. "I trust you boys can take care of Jennie until then? I've got some duties to attend to myself before the briefing."

"The tour's over?" Jennie asked.

"For now," Rhone replied. "Now that you've got your bearings, you'll be able to make your way around the facility. Further introductions will come later. Let's not overwhelm you on your first day." He made to put his tray on a line of shelves when he suddenly turned back. "Oh, and don't try to go anywhere you shouldn't. Remember, our security is state-of-the-art. We'll find you quicker than you can say 'specter.'"

Rhone laughed at his own joke.

"Can't you just give us a small clue?" Hansen asked. "A little teaser?"

Rhone grinned and said one simple word: "Baltimore." Then he was gone.

"Baltimore?" Jennie repeated. "What's that supposed to mean?"

She gathered from the look on Jack's and Clive's faces that the word meant a lot more to them than it did to her.

"Baltimore," Clive breathed, "is the Agency's number one concern right now. Their top priority after developing resources to aid in the spectral fight."

Jennie leaned closer to Jack and Clive as they explained everything.

CHAPTER EIGHTEEN

The situation in Baltimore had evolved over many months, following a parallel growth with the SIA's involvement within the spectral intelligence arena.

It had started off as nothing more than a few minor disturbances. A handful of civilians were reported missing. A number of others had seen strange phenomena down at the docks. It had come down to the SIA to investigate the situation and find out what was going on in order to quell the excitement, but things hadn't gone as planned.

"SIA was considerably smaller than it is today. A few officers and agents were initiated into the SIA and worked closely with the Special Agent in Charge, Kurt Rogers."

"Solid name," Jennie commented, interrupting Clive. "Like something from a Burt Reynolds movie."

Clive ignored her and continued. "Rogers was trusting to begin with. Allowed to assign his own team, he chose recruits he had known for years and who he knew would follow his orders to the letter. He needed the best and the brightest, and that was what he got."

He sighed. "At the time, his assistant special agent in charge had been a colleague and friend by the name of Brendan Koa. He'd worked by Kurt's side for nearly two decades, and had studied and absorbed everything that was thrown at him during those first few months of the agency's operation."

Jennie nodded. "So how come Koa's not around now?"

"Brendan was the one who was sent to lead the team in Baltimore and represent the SIA in order to contain the disturbances," Clive told Jennie, taking a seat on the couch in her living quarters. "He was instructed to report back to the SIA and follow commands as they came."

Jennie tsked. "Let me guess, that didn't happen?"

"Bingo," Clive told her. "SAC Rogers reached out to Brendan again and again, but he got no response. An hour after Brendan was due to report back and they had been met with silence, Kurt sent another squad into the heart of Baltimore in order to establish a connection and discover where the team had gone."

Jennie shook her head when Clive told her gunfire had met them at the docks. The killers had pistols with silencers and took the team out one by one. The one survivor was an agent who had only been with the SIA for a week or so. She was allowed to return to Washington, but with the burden of carrying a note which would be hand-delivered to SAC Kurt Rogers.

"What did it say?" Jennie asked, the room pregnant with tension. Beside her, Baxter waited patiently for the rest of the tale.

"It said that Brendan was sorry, but he couldn't pass up the opportunity to be the leading expert on one of the greatest discoveries the world had ever seen. Brendan wanted to go down in history as the greatest leader in the world of spectral relations, and Kurt Rogers was standing in his way."

"His own friend," Jack muttered, shaking his head. It occurred to Jennie then that this might be the first time Jack had ever heard the tale, too.

"His best friend," Clive added. "He didn't have the guts to overthrow him, so he split off and went out on his own. They tried to hunt him down, even sent teams into Baltimore in the cold light of day, but they could find no sign or trace of him anywhere. The man had enough money and resources to disappear, and he was recruiting, too."

"Then what's the problem?" Jennie asked. "If he's gone and there's been no sign of him, why is this an issue?"

Clive told her that the disturbances had been reported to have started up again over the last few months. There had been reports of clusters of specters causing trouble, further civilian disappearances, and thefts of precious liquids, metals, and chemicals from high-security facilities.

The door hissed open, catching Clive mid-sentence. Rhone stood there, studying them all for a few moments. He'd obviously heard the topic of their discussion.

"They're out there somewhere," Rhone told them. "Brandon and his gang will be brought to justice. We've just got to be careful what we do. The last thing we need to do is underestimate our enemy and have a rebellion on our hands. They're vying for the number one spot in spectral intelligence, but they have neither the funding nor the federal backing we do."

Jennie processed all she had just heard, wondering how this situation had accelerated so fast. Only a month or two ago, the spectral world had been a well-kept secret among those in the know, and now she had discovered two American entities fighting over who would be the first to control the situation.

"Are you sure you should be telling us all this?" Jennie asked. "We're new associates, remember?"

Rhone didn't look concerned. "The SAC makes a point of people knowing the story when they are fully initiated into the SIA. Rogers would rather people know the story so they can be alert and prepared for the situation ahead. It also teaches a great lesson about not trusting anyone. No one is above betrayal in this world; they just need the right incentive."

"Well, how come Jack didn't know about it?" Baxter asked, forgetting for a moment that only one person could hear him.

"Well, how come Jack didn't know about it?" Jennie asked on his behalf.

"Agent Hansen has yet to complete training and meet SAC Rogers," Rhone answered. "The SAC has been…preoccupied with other matters this past couple of weeks. But don't worry, it'll happen." He checked his watch. "Now, follow me. It's time for your briefing."

Jennie's heart rate increased as she followed Rhone down the hall, eager to know what they'd been assigned by Hopkins.

Two hours later, Jennie was back on the road.

Hopkins had been thorough in his briefing. The assignment was a simple one on the surface. Led by Agent Rhone and Daggro, Jack, Clive, Jennie, Baxter, and—much to the distaste of Daggro after Jennie declared that she wouldn't take no for an answer and that she would be a vital asset to their team—Ruby. They were to investigate the Baltimore docks and see if they could sense or discover anything spectral that might lead to the discovery of where a missing couple had gone.

The mission, Hopkins told them, would be a good chance to sniff around and see if there was any connection to what they'd come to call Operation Casper—or, as Jennie called it, "The Case of the Disappearing Asshole."

Jennie followed Rhone's Dodge Charger in her Mustang—another negotiation she had managed with Hopkins—and soon the freeway yielded a scenic view of Baltimore from a distance.

Baxter sat quietly beside her, watching the world pass outside the window. "I never thought you'd allow yourself to become an agent for another faction," he told Jennie over the gentle tones of Beethoven's Fifth.

Jennie was taken aback. "Excuse me?"

"We're acting under orders from the SIA," Baxter pointed out. "You're essentially an untrained agent on their mission. What about our guys in New York? What about the king's court?"

Jennie laughed softly. "I understand your skepticism, Bax. You've not been in the game as long as I have. You've got to play with the long game in mind. You think I'm getting my ass whipped by some federal agents trying to prove something, you'd best guess again."

"Then what is this, Jennie? What are we doing here? We've already gotten distracted by cultists. Why are we setting off for Baltimore?"

"Oh, I get what this is." Jennie smirked and pressed harder on the gas to overtake a string of cars. "You're homesick."

Baxter turned to look at Jennie, a small smile on his face. "Is it that obvious?"

Jennie nodded, keeping her eyes on the road. "Please. You've never been out of New York, and now you've been dragged around to all kinds of places by a mortal—London, Washington, Baltimore. Who knows when you'll next be back in your safe little nest? Am I close?"

"Something like that," Baxter admitted. "It's just, New York is all I've ever known. I love it there. It's friendly. It's familiar."

"It *was* friendly," Jennie reminded him. "Don't forget the queen fucked all that up with her power grab."

"How could I forget?"

Jennie patted Baxter's shoulder. "Look, we've got some work to do yet. The SIA is in a position where they're just coming to grips with what specters can and can't do. They barely know anything about me, really, so why would they fully trust me? If I can earn their respect, then we've got them like putty in our hands. You heard Hopkins earlier today. They've got contacts inside the paranormal court. That means it's likely that they know *something* of our conflict with them. And even if they don't, you don't think Queen Victoria will have her guard up about us creating another organization?"

Baxter considered this, rubbing his palms gently together as he realized the implications. "I thought she was good with your deal?"

Jennie rolled her eyes. "Be reasonable, Baxter. Of course, she was cool with it *then*; she was under threat of exorcism by Yours Truly. Do you think that mentality is going to stay once she's back on the throne and the fear of a shrinking empire gets to her?"

"Damn." Baxter shook his head and returned his attention to the outside. Twinkling lights from houses blurred by like shooting stars. "Politics are complicated."

"You've got that right," Jennie agreed. "That's why you've got to play the long game. Get this right, and we will have made one small step for specters and one giant leap for the king's court."

"Neil Armstrong quote? Really?"

"Did you know—"

"Let me guess," Baxter interrupted. "You've met him too? Shook his hand?"

Jennie gave a coy giggle and bit her lip. "We went somewhat beyond a handshake."

It was Baxter's turn to roll his eyes.

Baltimore, Maryland, USA

It was a little past midnight when they pulled up behind the Dodge and exited the car.

The docks were almost silent. The only sounds came from the gentle lapping of water against the wood and the faint rumble of cars passing by on the freeway behind them. Sodium arcs illuminated sections of the docks, leaving other areas in darkness.

Jennie and Baxter approached the agents and stopped beside the car.

"It's a little more commercial than I'd envisioned it," Jennie remarked. "I was picturing storage containers, wooden beams, and bird shit."

Rhone laughed. "This area became a commercial district for Baltimore a few decades back. They took advantage of the waterside views and built it up with hotels, fountains, banks, and eateries, and now it's the latest place to be avoided, according to the local press."

They split into two teams and investigated around the waterside, each agent wearing a pair of SI goggles on their face, while Jennie walked alongside Ruby, who was disappointed because they hadn't issued her a pair.

"I mean, it's not like they don't have money leaking out the wazoo," Ruby pointed out huffily. "Did you see that place? It had everything you could've wanted."

Jennie gave her a strange look. "We must have been sleeping in different facilities. Mine was stripped bare. Besides, you're lucky to be out on this assignment. Don't get hung up on gadgets. That'll come, once they've seen your potential."

"What potential?" Ruby's head hung low. "I'm a traitor to a cult, and I have no special skills."

"You have bravery and honor," Jennie replied. "That'll take you a lot farther than you think you can go. Just believe in yourself and open your mind to the possibilities, and you'll go far. Trust me."

The docks were a couple of hundred meters long each. Arranged like the slanted prongs of a fork, the team scoured the edges near the water, taking their time scrutinizing marks on the decks. Eventually, they met back up with the agents in the center.

"Anything?" Rhone asked.

Jennie shook her head. "Nothing. You?"

Rhone grimaced. "I'd kinda put all my eggs into the basket that you'd find something. We found nothing. Nothing whatsoever to go on."

"How do people know that those missing were at the docks when they disappeared?" Jennie had chewed over this nugget of information before they'd arrived but had decided to give them the benefit of the doubt. "If they've disappeared, who's to say they were here in the first place?"

"Witnesses," Rhone replied. "The victims were here with friends. They claimed they heard a musical hum while they were sitting on the edge of the docks, then our victims all went to investigate. When they didn't return, their friends got worried. An hour or so later, they reported it to the cops."

"And the cops called you guys?" Ruby asked. "Why?"

"Well, when the cops came down to investigate, they heard the humming too. Spooked them badly. Even more so when one of their force said he saw the broad silhouette of a man holding a machete a short distance away. By the time he'd raised the alarm, the man had gone."

They searched the docks for another hour or so, checking every square foot along the way. Occasionally they'd run into a group of people out celebrating their evening and under the influence of a few drinks, and Jennie's stomach would remind her that she hadn't had anything to enjoy for several days now.

"I think you've got a problem," Baxter told her.

"It's not a problem," Jennie retorted. "We all have things we enjoy. Did you know there are over a thousand different mixtures of cocktails?"

"I did not," Baxter told her with a smile.

"Exactly. Yet, there are only a few varieties of cordials and hot drinks that people tend to enjoy. You may argue that cappuccinos and lattes and cortados are all different, but at the end of the day, they're just coffee and milk. Cocktails combine hundreds of different ingredients to create sensations that surprise your mouth."

Ruby glanced up at Jennie. "That sounds like so much fun."

"You've never tried a cocktail?"

Ruby raised an eyebrow. "I'm eighteen."

Jennie stared at her blankly.

"It's illegal to drink in the States until you're twenty-one."

Jennie slapped her forehead. "Right. I forgot how backward you guys are. Can't drink until twenty-one, but can power a moving death machine at the age of fifteen. Smart."

They reached the end of the dock and stared out across the vast black stretch of water that led to the Atlantic Ocean.

Ruby chuckled. "'Moving death machine?'"

"Cars," Jennie replied. "You can drive at fifteen and join the Army and own a gun at eighteen, but you can't so much as sniff a cold brewski until you're twenty-one. Sounds ludicrous to me."

Ruby nodded her agreement.

"Because letting minors use intoxicants is *so* smart," Baxter countered.

"Adulthood begins at eighteen in the UK," Jennie reminded him.

"Still," Baxter offered. "Could you enjoy a view like this with a head hazy from booze? There's something about water that's calming, isn't there?"

Jennie supposed there was. Whether it was the gentle hush of the waves lapping at the shore or the slight smell of salt in the air, the whole thing was peaceful.

Peaceful enough that they didn't notice the man standing twenty feet away on the docks behind them.

It wasn't until they heard the exclamations of the agents who turned around and saw the specter.

His grin was Cheshire Cat-wide, his hat shadowing his face. He had long arms, and a machete was gripped tightly in one fist.

"Oh, my God," Ruby whispered, fear lacing her voice.

"You can see him?" Jennie asked.

Ruby didn't reply, but her body language said she did.

The man pointed his machete at the girl, then started running toward the agents.

"Wait? Where did he go?" Ruby moved closer to Jennie.

So that's him, huh? Jennie thought, noting that she was dealing with a specter who had the ability to switch his corporeal form on and off. That was a rare gift among specters indeed, and one she'd only ever seen used for mischief. Specters with a strong moral conscience who could appear before mortals at will tended to hide their powers and go about their lives without taking advantage of it.

It was only specters with an agenda who played with mortals and appeared before them, either to scare them for kicks or to get them to follow them.

Which was exactly what they now did.

The specter ran straight at the agents and through them before they'd even registered what had happened. With the SI goggles being a new addition to the force, Jennie supposed they would never have watched a specter as their immaterial bodies passed through the agents' mortal ones.

Yet, neither had this specter ever known mortals who were able to see him and give chase no matter his form.

And chase him, they did.

CHAPTER NINETEEN

Baltimore, Maryland, USA

They ran as a group, sprinting as fast as they could after the specter.

The specter had never experienced a chase like this. He threw occasional glances over his shoulder, his eyes wide with alarm as he bolted away from the docks.

Fueled by their instincts, the SIA agents drew their weapons. Jennie noticed that each of them sported the gleaming silver SI pistols Jack had used in the woods. Had they been issued spectrally imbued bullets, too?

"Freeze!" Rhone shouted, causing a nearby group of partygoers to glance their way. "Federal agents. We will shoot."

Jennie already knew the specter wouldn't stop. Why would he? After years of being invisible to the public, why would he suddenly fear bullets that he believed would go straight through him without damage?

They reached the end of the docks, and the specter sprinted up a small flight of steps. Jennie broke free of the group. The only one who could keep up with her was Baxter, who she encouraged with a little bit of persuasion from her spectral powers.

The specter dashed along the side of a grandiose hotel. Jennie could hear the agents behind her, their feet slapping the sidewalk. Their efforts to entice the specter back increased as they saw his trajectory, and the next thing she knew, a gunshot sounded.

The bullet chipped the wall, missing the specter by inches. He gave a panicked grunt, then ducked his head and ran straight through the wall and into the hotel.

Jennie followed without hesitation, leaving the agents in shock outside as the brick melted around her. She emerged in a dark corridor, lit only by emergency lighting.

A series of panting gasps drew her attention farther down the corridor, where the specter was hunched over with hands on his knees.

Jennie trained her pistol on the specter. "Freeze, you slippery wanker."

The specter let out a cry of anguish, looking as if he was about to start running again. Jennie added, "One move and the only way you'll leave this building is if someone sweeps what's left of you into a bag."

The specter considered his options and placed his hands in the air. "Please don't shoot me. You don't understand."

"Oh, I understand very well," Jennie told him. "You've been luring victims away from the dock and taking them somewhere for your own private gain. The only thing I don't understand is why?"

The specter's head tilted to the side. His eyes were dark. Jennie was more than aware of the machete still in his hand.

As was Baxter, who shuffled uncomfortably behind her.

"You're new around here, aren't you?" the specter asked at last.

"New to this city?" Jennie asked. "Yes. New to this game? Definitely not."

"There are probably some things you should brush up on." The specter leered at Jennie. "Not everywhere is as safe as your precious England. You think you can survive in a place like this and threaten a specter without understanding his background, you're going to find yourself in trouble, ma'am."

Jennie took a step forward, adjusting her grip on her pistol. "Is that a threat?"

"No." The specter's demeanor had calmed. There was a quiet confidence in his words that put Jennie on edge. The only people she knew who would speak like this under the threat of gunfire were those who had powerful friends, people they believed would be their savior in times of crisis. "It's a warning."

"A warning is the same as a threat, douchebag," Baxter told him.

The specter replied with another dark grin.

"I'd like you to come with us," Jennie offered, although her tone suggested there wasn't another option. "We've got some questions. Those nice agents outside would be more than happy to give you a chance to clear your name and explain what is going on here. Come along quietly, and we can make this easy for you. If you choose to—"

"*Aaand* he's gone," Baxter declared.

While Jennie had been talking, the specter had taken a sudden sideways step and disappeared through the wall.

Jennie sighed. "Why do they never make it easy?"

Following in his footsteps, Jennie took a large sidestep and appeared in a brightly lit lobby. White marble floors reflected the LED lights, and a wide walnut reception counter made up the entirety of one side of the room.

The staff at the counter showed no indication of seeing Jennie or the specter, who had already sprinted halfway across the room and was about to fade through the far wall when Jennie latched onto him.

A long rope of spectral power surged through the air, and the moment it connected, she tugged as hard as she could.

The specter, stunned, came toward her feet-first. His arms flew out as his legs were whipped behind him, given him the momentary appearance of Superman before he crashed to the floor on his stomach.

He struggled and tried to fight Jennie, but it was fruitless.

Jennie flipped the specter onto his back so she could stand above him and aim her pistol at his face. All will to fight faded from him at that moment. He exhaled, and his entire body seemed to deflate.

"Now, that's better." Jennie smirked until Baxter tapped her on the shoulder and pointed toward the reception desk.

A female member of staff froze with a phone nestled between her shoulder and ear. She was looking straight at them.

Jennie realized that both she and the specter had made themselves available for mortals to view in their struggle.

With an awkward wave and a chuckle, Jennie focused on becoming spectral, and a second later, they both vanished from view, leaving the woman at the counter perplexed as she tried to explain to her colleague what she had just seen.

Washington DC, USA

Hopkins stared at the specter through the one-way glass. His arms were folded, and his goggles were tight on his face. The specter continued to look around, seeking a safe way to escape the interrogation room.

A door opened and closed behind him. Jennie appeared at his side. "Don't worry, he's not going anywhere."

Hopkins gave a curt nod and his stare intensified. The interrogation room they had built specifically for specters was new. Proctor had found a way to imbue the room with spectral energy that would prevent any specter from escaping, but the strength of the barrier had yet to be tested.

Surprisingly, every specter they'd had in this room had obeyed and complied so far. He sometimes wondered if the mere fact that they'd been able to capture specters had been enough to deter them from making stupid moves.

But he wasn't certain that this one wouldn't try.

"That was a hell of a capture," Rhone had praised back in Baltimore after Jennie had dragged the specter back with her. After a quick round of questions, Rhone had determined it was best to drag the specter back to HQ for further interrogation. Even under the threat of Jennie's powers, he had remained, for the most part, tight-lipped.

A buzzer sounded before Agent Daggro entered the room. She had her own set of goggles, although they did nothing to mask the stern look that appeared to permanently decorate her face.

Daggro held a small digital tablet, the glow of the screen lighting her features harshly. She took a seat without looking at the specter and scrolled down the page. Inside one ear was an earwig that transmitted messages from Hopkins' side of the mirror.

"Six missing person reports over twenty-three days. Two seventeen-year-old females from Butchers Hill, one sixteen-year-old male from Pigtown, a brother and sister from Franklin Square, and a twenty-year-old from Gay Street."

Daggro looked up from her tablet without moving her head and saw the specter trying not to laugh. "Something funny about that?"

The specter shook his head. "Nope."

Jennie touched a button below a mic on a long black arm. She repeated the specter's words to Daggro, even though she likely didn't need to, given his short response. As the only person in the group who was able to hear the specter, she had offered to repeat everything to Daggro to assist with the interrogation.

Daggro returned to her table. "Every eyewitness report has described a man appearing on the docks holding a machete. Is there any reason we shouldn't believe you were the perpetrator?"

The specter remained silent.

"I don't like to ask questions twice, Mr…" she scrolled up the screen again, "Ricket. Either you cooperate, or we find ways of making you talk."

"Like what?" Ricket grumbled. "What's a bunch of mortals going to do to me? Tear off my nails with tweezers? Stick a taser on my gonads?" He spat on the floor. "You've got nothing to go on, bitch."

Daggro gave a small grin and reached down to her ankle, where she drew her handgun. She placed it in front of her on the table. "Does this work?"

Ricket returned the grin. "Please. You think your bullshit mortal contraptions scare me?"

"The gun may be mortal, but I assure you the bullets it contains are not. We can test it, though, if you like?" She picked up the gun and aimed it at the specter's shoulder. "One quick finger flex, and you can say bye-bye to your shoulder."

Jennie leaned closer to Hopkins. "Has she ever shot a specter with one of those before?"

Hopkins shook his head. "They're fresh off the press. Looks like we're about to see it firsthand, though."

Jennie glanced to her side, where she knew the Big Bitch was hiding behind her own spectral cloaking. For years she'd had the technology, patented and kept secret. It had been given to her after a private negotiation between her and a mortal with higher intelligence than anyone she had ever met. What would the world be like once these blueprints were released? Secrets never remained hidden for long.

Hopkins looked down at her. "Know something we don't?"

Jennie fixed her eyes ahead. *I know lots of things you don't.*

Daggro leaned toward Ricket. His eyes betrayed his fear as the gun came closer to him. "What do you say? Are you ready to confess?"

The specter stared at her, determined to remain quiet and take his chances despite her warnings.

"Very well," Daggro told him.

Inside the small room, the report was loud. There was a small nozzle flash followed by a loud shout only Jennie and Baxter could hear, although the agents could *see* the specter's anguish.

Daggro's composure slipped when she saw the mess that the specter's shoulder was in. A large chunk was missing, revealing a spectral projection of flesh and bone beneath.

The specter covered the wound with his free hand and gritted his teeth. "You goddamn bitch!"

Jennie took great pleasure in relaying this to Daggro. "He thinks you're a bitch."

Daggro's eyes darted to the one-way mirror.

"Are you prepared to answer my questions now?" Daggro growled.

The specter looked at her in disbelief, occasionally glancing at the pistol still gripped in her hand. He grimaced as he tried to move his arm, then gave a resigned nod.

Daggro threw questions at Ricket for an hour while Jennie, Hopkins, and Baxter watched. Rhone, Jack, and Clive had been dismissed until questioning had been completed and were instructed to see that Ruby was okay after their trip to Baltimore.

Ricket told them a lot about the missing people but gave them nothing further to go on in terms of motives or reasoning. When questioned about his abilities, he made himself material for long enough that Daggro could remove her goggles and they could hold a conversation.

Daggro asked about Ricket's intent with the disappearing civilians, as well as any other information he had on spectral activity in Baltimore.

"Recruitment," Ricket replied simply. "We haven't kidnapped a single soul. They all came willingly."

When pushed further on the subject, Ricket added, "I don't know what happens after they're taken, okay? I'm a frontman. A recruiter. I scour the city for willing participants to follow me, and we take them in. Treat them right. Introduce them to the world."

"You keep referring to your operation as 'we.' Who is this 'we' you keep talking about?"

For the first time since he'd been shot, Ricket's mouth clamped shut. "Look, lady, I might tell you some stuff, but do you think I'm dumb enough to rat my bosses out? I'm no snitch, I tell you. Your bullets may be painful, but I'll recover and live to tell the tale. If I go back there having given you everything, you know what they'll do to me?"

"I imagine much the same as what we've done to you."

"Exactly," Ricket confirmed, leaning back in his chair. "If I tell you everything, I'm a snitch and in pain. If I remain loyal to my crew, I keep my integrity and I'm in pain."

"What if we offer you payment for your efforts?" Daggro reluctantly asked. "We're building a hell of an operation here. You could get in on the ground floor of something special."

Now it was Ricket's turn to lean toward Daggro. "I'm already in on the ground floor of something special. Nothing you say or offer is going to make me change my mind."

Daggro growled.

Jennie shuffled on her feet beside Hopkins. It was painful watching the interrogation, knowing that they were at a stalemate. She had worked with specters for decades and knew that this one had the upper hand. He was right. What possible device, contraption, or payment did they have to convince a specter to betray his kind and give them the information.

Specters were loyal to the bone in most cases, and they were creatures of habit. Without sufficient incentivizing, all they would have is a confession that Ricket had been involved in the disappearances.

That wasn't enough.

Jennie moved toward the window, and Hopkins placed a hand on her shoulder.

"Please leave it to the professionals," he told her, his tone so patronizing that it fueled Jennie instead of pacifying her.

"I am." She grinned as she latched onto Baxter and disappeared through the glass, proving in front of Hopkin's eyes that the spectrally imbued interrogation walls were definitely in need of further development.

She appeared beside the agent and rested one hand on her shoulder and the other on her hip.

"You?" the specter growled.

Daggro shook Jennie's hand off. "Please, Miss King. Leave the interrogation to the..." A tinny voice gave orders in her ear. She nodded reluctantly. "Roger that, sir."

Jennie skirted the table and stood behind Ricket. She placed her hands on his chair and leaned over his shoulder. "Mr. Ricket, I know this might all seem like fun and games to you—you know, mortals have invented contraptions to finally communicate with specters without the need of relying on the rare conduits of this world—but I should probably warn you that you might not be as safe here as you think."

"What are you going to do, drag me around the room? Beat me up a little bit?" Ricket grinned. "What's the worst you can do to me, bitch? No mortal can rough up a specter—"

Jennie's punch to the side of Ricket's head silenced him.

"That's better," she murmured. "Bet you've never seen a mortal do that before?"

Ricket glared at her but remained silent.

"Now, here's how this is going to go down." She climbed onto the table and sat in the center, folding her legs, much to the annoyance of Daggro, whose view was blocked. "You tell us what we need to know, and I'll ensure you don't get exorcized today."

"Exorcized?" Daggro blurted, despite herself. "Are you a priest now too?"

Jennie ignored her.

"You don't have the power to exorcize me," Ricket protested uncertainly. "Few have that power, and only those from the spectral world have the power to erase specters from life entirely."

Jennie shook her head and laughed. "Man, for a specter, you've really got a lot to brush up on. The first thing is, while you're right, and exorcism can be taught within the spectral realm, there are other…methods of its acquisition." She manipulated Baxter's energy enough to take her sword out of its sheath.

Daggro pushed her chair back and pointed her pistol at Jennie's back. "Miss King, I don't know where you got that from, but if you don't place down your weapon right now, this is going to turn ugly." She touched a spare finger to her ear. "Hopkins, call in backup. This bitch is going rogue."

Jennie glanced nonchalantly over her shoulder. "Relax. Where do you think the nickname came from?" She returned her attention to the specter. "This is the Saber of the Holy Divinity, a sword from legend with the power to exorcize any specter it touches."

Ricket stared at her. "I call bullshit."

"You could," Jennie told him. "Or you could accept that if you don't answer my questions, your death is inevitable."

The door crashed open behind them and half a dozen agents trained their pistols on Jennie.

"Looks like you'll die before I do." Ricket chuckled.

"I doubt that very much." In one swift maneuver, Jennie grabbed Ricket's shoulders and used him for support as she performed a hand-spring over his body and landed firmly behind him. She wrapped an arm around his throat as they faded. She held the sword an inch in front of his face to draw his attention to its shimmering blade and whispered into his ear.

"Where did you take your victims?"

"I'll never tell." He was shaking now.

Jennie grimaced and pulled him tighter. "Who are you working for?"

"You'll have to kill me."

The agents slowly moved closer, Daggro battling in a hissed conversation with Hopkins through her earpiece.

"Last chance, shitbag. Tell me what you know!"

"Miss King, release the prisoner and come out with your hands in the air," Daggro shouted, grim satisfaction on her face since she appeared to have won her argument. "We will not ask again."

"I've already asked you nicely," Jennie snapped at Daggro, "to call me 'Rogue.'"

At the mention of her name, Ricket's entire demeanor changed. His breath caught as the rumors and stories he'd heard about the infamous Rogue came to the forefront of his mind. "Rogue," he managed in a breathless whisper.

"Nice to meet you." She chuckled. "Even if it was short-lived."

She moved the blade closer to his neck. Suddenly he shouted, "Fine! Fine! I'm sorry. I'll tell you what you want to know. Just don't exorcize me, okay?"

Jennie stared at Daggro with a broad smile on her face. "You hear that, Agent? He's willing to cooperate. Now, the question is, are you?"

CHAPTER TWENTY

"That was a risky maneuver," Baxter grumbled as they waited in the common area outside the interrogation room. After Ricket had agreed to comply with their investigation, Daggro had demanded that Jennie be removed from the room so they could proceed with their protocols.

Given that Jennie had already moved beyond their typical rules and demonstrated her power over Ricket, she knew she didn't have to be present for them to get answers. Ricket was scared now, and that was all they needed.

"Sometimes you just need to show them who's boss," she replied quietly, craning her head around the doorway to see two guards standing on either side of the door under Daggro's command. "Go outside of the lines and set new boundaries."

"You really think a federal agency is going to like your demonstration of going rogue?" Baxter rubbed his head. "I mean, that might work for the Spectral Plane and other spectral organizations, but these are mortals you're dealing with. People with egos and jobs at risk."

"The worst they can do is kick us out of their facility," Jennie told him. "And even that would be difficult for them if I turn spectral. At the end of the day, I'm here to form connections, not to abide by their rules. They are newbies to the spectral world. They're humans who have just discovered intelligent life on Mars and are letting their egos guide them into thinking *they're* the intelligent species. The spectral world is dangerous, and they need to know what they're dealing with. I promise they've not encountered the things I've encountered."

Baxter grinned. "You mean, like wraiths and *sturmgeists*?"

Jennie gave him a knowing look. "I mean like *sturmgeists* on steroids and wraiths who could swallow cities whole."

Baxter's eyes widened.

"I'm exaggerating for dramatic effect," Jennie reassured him.

Baxter let out his breath.

"Kinda." Jennie winked. "Let's just wait and see what happens in there. We can read the room once they've gotten all the information they need."

Just then, Jack walked past the room and glanced inside. "Jennie? Aren't you supposed to be in there?" He eyed the guards, gave a curt nod to one of them, and shuffled inside.

"I was," Jennie explained once Jack had closed the door. "It was recommended that I take a short recess and leave the heavy work to the professionals."

Jack raised an eyebrow. "What did you do?"

"What do you mean?" Jennie smirked. "Why would you suggest I'd be anything but innocent?"

"Because over the last two days, I haven't seen you play by the rules once. Daggro hasn't shut up about how much she hates your guts."

"Good thing she hides it well," Jennie replied sarcastically. "I thought we'd be besties before the week was through."

Jack tapped some buttons on a nearby coffee machine and waited for the thick brown sludge to trickle into the eggshell-colored cup. He took a seat beside them.

"Haven't you got things you should be doing, rather than waiting here with me?" Jennie asked. "I bet a trainee agent like you has a lot they could be getting on with."

Jack chuckled. "You'd think. But since Agent Rhone is my supervisor, and he's been wrapped up in this whole Baltimore situation, my training has gone a little off-book. Clive is feeding me info, but his knowledge is still limited about most of what's going on around here."

"If anything, you're probably getting a better education learning on the job," Baxter offered.

Jack couldn't hear him.

"Oh." Jennie laughed, realizing that and telling Jack what Baxter had said.

"I suppose," Jack agreed. "Man, I keep forgetting you've got an imaginary friend who can hear me. Where is he right now?"

Jennie pointed to a nearby chair.

Jack waved.

Baxter waved back.

Jennie rolled her eyes. "Well, that was pointless."

The door to the interrogation room opened and Daggro came out. She looked tired. Bags clung to her eyes, and her hair had lost its military neatness. She glared at Jennie, then disappeared into the adjacent room, where Hopkins waited for her.

Jennie rested her head back against the chair and closed her eyes. "They really do a song and dance when they're pissed, huh?"

Jack laughed. "Can you blame them? Top dogs like her live off the fear of others. It's all they know to do."

"Well, you know what instills fear in dogs, right?"

Jack and Baxter shook their heads.

"A top lion."

Jennie chuckled at the mental image of her as a lion chasing two dogs that looked an awful lot like the agents around the HQ.

Jennie missed when Hopkins and Daggro exited the adjacent interrogation room. She also missed the spectral prisoner being removed from the main chamber.

She had drifted off to sleep without being aware of it. The first thing she knew of consciousness was Jack cautiously shaking her awake and saying, "Jennie, they've called you to the boardroom."

His worried expression spoke a thousand words, but Jennie had been through this before. She'd likely get a smack on the wrist, perhaps be removed from the HQ, at the worst. Maybe they'd make an effort to confiscate her weapons, but that would be it. What could they possibly do to someone who demonstrated her powers and ensured the job was done. They were lucky that she remained on the right side of the law.

Hopkins and Daggro stared at Jennie as she entered the boardroom. Rhone had taken a seat on the other side of Hopkins, and now they presented to her as though she were in a job interview situation.

Baxter followed closely behind until Hopkins stated, "Without the specter, Miss King. He's to wait outside."

Baxter froze, unsure whether to obey. None of the agents had their goggles on, so how would they even know?

Jennie nodded at Baxter and he slunk out of the room through the wall and waited obediently outside, where several agents trained their guns on him, the majority of whom wore SI goggles.

"What happened to 'Rogue?'"

"Informalities are reserved for those who remain on our side of the law," Hopkins replied, his lips barely moving. She could see his muscles were tense with the anger roiling beneath his skin. "Do you have *any* idea what impact your tricks might have had in there?"

Jennie concentrated on maintaining a calm demeanor. She answered the question as though she were a school kid pleading innocence over a minor piece of graffiti.

"As I understand it, I ensured that the specter obeyed and gave you the required answers to your questions. Did you not receive the information you desired?"

"We did," Hopkins ground out as though ashamed to admit that she had assisted them in some way. "But what the hell were you thinking?" He leaned over a piece of paper and placed his glasses on his face. As he listed each offense, his finger traced the page. "Interfering with an agent's interrogation practice, assaulting a witness, carrying unlicensed weaponry into SIA HQ without declaring it. Need I go on?"

Jennie tilted her head and motioned toward Hopkins' paper. "Excuse me for asking, but why do you continue to murder trees and unnecessarily print pages when your colleagues all use digital tablets for their work?"

Hopkins stared blankly at her.

Jennie pointed to the paper. "Your documents earlier were printed, too. Is that just for show? A prop to get your point across? If so, I suggest going green. The last thing you need on your plate is accusations of a new federal department going against the green agenda."

Hopkin's ears flushed red. "Miss King, I don't think you understand the seriousness of your current situation. You have broken the law on several instances with this current investigation, and your blasé attitude toward what you have done only further showcases that you are a liability to the SIA. Do you have anything to say to defend yourself, or are you going to insist on playing the fool in order to try to distract us from arresting you on the spot and reporting you to the authorities?"

It was Jennie's turn to give Hopkins a long stare. The room was deathly silent.

"Senior Special Agent Hopkins, with all due respect, no one in the world would be able to arrest me. In case you haven't noticed, I am a force for good. I've played the spectral game for over ten decades—"

Daggro clicked her tongue and rolled her eyes.

Jennie ignored her. "In that time, I have done nothing but work on the side of justice. Sure, my methods are sometimes unorthodox, but I assure you I have the experience to back up my decisions. Your department is still in its infancy, so I can forgive your naivete, but you are children compared to me. The spectral world is unlike anything you can imagine, and if you want someone to help you navigate the pitfalls and bring *specters* to justice, you're going to have to rely on me. I'm more than happy to show you the way, but I need a *little* bit of leniency when it comes to protocol."

Daggro's hands were clenched into fists on the table. In the presence of Hopkins, she did everything she could to remain calm and even. "Even if you were as old as you state you are, there is no excuse for barging into the middle of a federal investigation and thrusting your power in our faces. Yes, it's clear you have certain talents, but we have ours, too. We know what we're doing, and we get shit done. Don't question *our* abilities, Miss King."

"Let me ask you one simple question," Jennie offered. "Did you get the information from Ricket?"

Daggro unconsciously moved her hands to cover her tablet screen. "That has nothing to do with the current situation."

Jennie didn't relent. "Did you or did you not get the answers you were seeking?"

It was Rhone who replied, "We did."

Jennie leaned forward, bridging some of the chasm between her and her interrogators. "As far as I'm concerned, that settles the matter. Agent Hopkins, let me say for the record that I'm impressed with what you guys have going on here. Really, I am. Advances in spectral technology are wonders I've been waiting for for a long time. However, know that I am a walking embodiment of everything you are hoping to achieve. My main goal here is to connect with the US government and further what you are trying to do so my organization can work with you for the benefit of the US as a whole. Judging by your current short-sighted attitude, you are determined to become barriers that stand in my way. That's not something I take kindly to."

"Are you threatening us, Miss King?" Hopkins asked darkly. "We have almost two hundred agents in this building who would readily obey our commands and capture you. Do you want to take that risk?"

Jennie smiled at Hopkins. "Who is threatening who? Watch your tone, Agent. We're having a polite conversation here, and you're striking me as rude. I have several hundred specters who are ready and willing to obey my command in New York City. I have specters at my beck and call, Agent. Do *you* want to take that risk?"

Hopkins and Daggro sat back in their chairs and exchanged glances. Only Jennie saw the small twitch of a smile on Rhone's face.

"Bullshit," Daggro muttered.

Jennie wondered what her issue was. This went beyond skepticism. "Check your records, Agent Daggro. Several weeks ago, a disturbance took place in Times Square. A gaseous cloud covered the area. I caused that to cover a spectral battle, the likes of which this country has never seen."

Hopkins didn't need to check the records. "You're connected with the terrorist attack on NYC?"

"Terrorist attack?" Jennie retorted. "Get your head out of your arse, Agent. I saved every specter in the US from oppression by the paranormal court. I won't go into the details." She smiled at Daggro. "You're welcome, by the way. Since that event, things have changed somewhat over there."

Hopkins fell silent, processing everything he had just heard. Daggro stewed beside him, while Rhone simply watched Jennie closely, not wanting to disrupt Hopkins' thinking.

After a time, Hopkins sat back again in his chair and exhaled loudly. Jennie could see she had defeated him, if only for now.

"What do you want from us, Rogue? Clearly, you have your own agenda."

"I told you," Jennie repeated. "I work for the greater good. I want nothing more than justice for both mortals and specters, and I'm the best vehicle you and your team have for ensuring that everyone plays ball. If the mortal and spectral worlds unite, I'm going to be a part of that."

"You know I'm going to have to raise this with the special agent in charge?" Hopkins told her, his face refusing to soften. "This is not a matter I can take into my own hands."

For the first time since she'd known them, Daggro broke rank and turned to Hopkins with disgust. "I'm sorry, sir, but you can't seriously be considering letting this…"

"Rogue?" Jennie offered.

"*Clusterfuck* go free after everything she has pulled today?"

Hopkins quieted Daggro with a stare so intense that she shrank back in her chair. "The spectral world remains largely uncharted waters for us, Agent Daggro. If we were to explore new territory, would we not accept assistance from the locals?"

"I-I suppose," Daggro grumbled.

Hopkins nodded, satisfied with her acquiescence. "If we are to make a success of this agency, we need to recognize the opportunities available. I hate it as much as you do, but part of leading a team and developing it is knowing when to check your ego at the door and make a decision for the greater good."

At that, he turned his attention back to Jennie. "Miss King, I will raise the issues with my superior. I cannot make promises or guarantees, but I can bring your presence to his attention."

"Good," Jennie replied stern-faced. "In the meantime, I'm going to suggest something to you all."

"What's that?" Hopkins' frown returned.

Jennie knew she was already pushing his limits. "While we wait for a response, you're going to tell me everything Ricket told you and let me lead the charge in Baltimore."

Hopkins cast such an intense stare at Jennie that she thought she might have broken him.

Jennie didn't give him an opportunity to refuse. "You might also want Proctor to look at those interrogation chamber walls. Whatever tech is in there, it isn't working." An idea came to her. "In fact, I might know someone who'll be able to help you."

CHAPTER TWENTY-ONE

<u>Baltimore, Maryland, USA</u>

"So, let me get this straight," Baxter stated, watching the world blur past as they made their way along the 295. "The kids this specter kidnapped went along of their own free will, but we're going to capture them and release them from some imaginary prison?"

Jennie turned down the music. "Not exactly. When Ricket insisted the kids followed him of their own volition, he was lying. The rest of the stuff he told the agents, I believe."

"That there's a nearby church where the kids are being looked after by the priests?" Baxter asked.

"Right," Jennie replied.

"But it doesn't make sense," Baxter complained. "Why lure teenagers away and induct them into the church? How many kids do you know who are that religious these days?"

Jennie shook her head. "After seeing a real-life specter and following them to a church? I'm guessing they're more likely to believe in religious fables than most."

The city of Baltimore grew dark around them as evening began to settle in. Jennie followed Rhone's Dodge along the winding streets until they neared the docks. This time, instead of turning right, they turned left, and soon a quaint little Methodist church came into sight.

"This is where we're stopping?" Baxter asked. "It's a cute little city church. What damage is likely to be going on behind those doors?"

"I guess we're about to find out," Jennie replied.

She parked at the curb and climbed out of the car. Agent Rhone exited his vehicle, with Clive and Jack in tow.

"You know you're one lucky son-of-a-bitch, right?" Jack's smile lit his face as he crossed over and shook Jennie's hand.

"I'm assuming you were saving that for when you were far enough away from your owners that they wouldn't see?" Jennie poked her tongue between her teeth. "I'm sorry about all that back there, but sometimes you've got to smack a dog on the nose to show him who's boss."

Agent Rhone adjusted the goggles on his face. "Let's just hope it pays off. I haven't seen anything that brazen in all my time of service. Who knows how this is all going to go down with the SAC?"

"We'll just S-A-see, I guess," Jennie quipped.

Rhone laughed and turned to look at the church. "A sleepy little building, isn't it? Really think we're going to find those kids there?"

"I don't know," Jennie replied honestly.

"Given that their faces have been all over milk cartons and the news, I highly doubt it," Rhone replied as he fumbled in his pocket and pulled out a cigarette. "I guess we'll S-A-see, then."

He laughed again and shook his head. "Man, you're funny."

They stood in the shadow of the church and looked at its facade. None of the windows were smashed, there were posters advertising various services for attendees, and a large banner declared Jesus Christ is our savior.

"Really takes you back, doesn't it?" Rhone finished the last drag of his cigarette and flicked the remains onto the sidewalk. "Any time I'm around a building like this, I imagine the history inside. The years that devotees have spent inside, and the stories it could tell. Look at that architecture and those stained-glass windows. Isn't it beautiful?"

"It's all right, I suppose," Clive offered. "Just another building, really."

"No." Rhone laughed. "Jennie, you'll back me up, won't you? Don't you just get transported back in time in these places, especially given your age? You must be able to visualize how these places might once have been."

Jennie feigned offense and planted a hand on her chest. "Since when did it become okay to call me old? Just because I look young, does that mean I don't get the decency offered to the eighty- and ninety-year-olds of this world? You'd never make a comment like that to one of them, would you?"

Rhone looked embarrassed. "I didn't mean… I was only saying…"

It was Jennie's turn to laugh. "Gotcha! You really are too easy."

Given the late hour, the church was closed. The wrought iron gate was padlocked, and the church was surrounded by an iron fence.

"We need to find another way in," Rhone instructed.

"You guys do. I'm going in this way." Jennie passed through the gates and looked back at them through the bars. "Don't worry, I saved just enough of this for just such an occasion."

She drew the vial of acid from her pocket and placed a few drops inside the padlock's mechanism. After a few seconds, she kicked it gently with her boot and the padlock fell to the ground.

The gate whined as it swung open. Across the street, a couple of people turned their heads in their direction but kept walking.

"Close it behind you," Rhone told Jack.

They skirted the building, occasionally peering through the large windows. The inside of the church was dark, with no indication that there was anyone around.

They went around the back, then worked their way along the other side. There was no sign that anyone had taken up residence inside.

"There's only one way to know for certain," Rhone decided, twisting the door handle to the back door and giving a gentle nudge with his shoulder.

"It's locked," Jack guessed when it didn't open.

"No shit, Sherlock." Rhone reached into his pocket and withdrew a lock-pick kit. "These old places usually have ancient locks, which are fairly easy to pick for those with the skills."

"Or I could just go inside and investigate?" Jennie offered.

Rhone shook his head. "Nice try. We're to work together on this mission, Hopkins' orders. Besides, don't you think it might be a little more fun to work *with* us for a change?"

Jennie thought about that. "Not really. It's usually quicker if I go it alone and do it my way. Other people muddle my process and cause disruptions." She turned to Jack and Clive. "Isn't that right, fellas?"

Baxter shook a finger at Jennie. "Play nice, Jennie. Remember, you wanted these connections to grow. You're going to have to work with people sometime."

Jennie rolled her eyes and nodded.

After a few attempts and a number of curses, Rhone heard the satisfying click of the lock opening. He led them into the darkness and put his goggles on, advising the others to do the same. The agents each readied a pistol in one hand and a flashlight in the other and held them crossed in front of them to light the way.

The church was deathly silent. A steady chill ran through the building, as though it was generating its own cold. The temperature dropped several degrees as they made their way through a back room and out toward the main body of the church.

This church was much the same as the one in Batsto, which in Jennie's opinion made it much the same as every other church she had visited. Although Christianity was the inspiration for the most unique and beautiful pieces of stained glass, art, and architecture in the world, Jennie's long-ago conversation with the specter of Galileo Galilei about the historical control the church had exerted over artists had soured the beauty in her eyes.

The architectural interior of this church, however, left a lot to be desired.

I suppose if the main purpose is to pray and commune with the Lord, there's only so much you need in terms of utility.

The flashlights illuminated the bulk of the church in a faint glow from the concentrated beams, thick cones of light. They roamed over the church as the agents scanned for any signs of life, and only when Jack aimed his flashlight at a life-sized statue of Jesus Christ hanging on the cross and jumped did anyone make another sound.

"Easy, coward." Clive grinned. "The statues aren't going to come to life and grab you."

"I know," Jack growled. "Just took me by surprise, is all."

"*Shhh*," Rhone commanded. He shone his flashlight at himself and zipped his fingers across his lips. He pointed toward the front door, then switched off his flashlight and moved behind the nearest pillar.

Taking his cue, the others followed suit. Soon they could hear it, too—the faint beat of footsteps approaching the front door.

CHAPTER TWENTY-TWO

<u>Baltimore, Maryland, USA</u>

They each found a hiding spot and ducked. The first physical sign of someone approaching was the flickering glow of a lantern as it reached the front door. Leaning over the pew, Jennie could make out the faint silhouette of someone waiting at the door.

They know we're here, Jennie thought. *That's why they're waiting.*

She was certain that was true until they heard the faint jangling of keys, followed by the front door squealing as it was opened.

The figure entered.

The door closed.

The candle in the lantern did nothing to illuminate the figure who paused inside the door and swept the lantern over the church's interior. Clad entirely in a thick black cloak, the only part that gave any indication of their identity was the bare hand stretching through the sleeve to grab the lantern's handle.

The figure waited a few moments more before deciding that they were satisfied they were alone. Without a word, they skirted the right-hand side of the church and disappeared through a wooden door, then the team heard the faint sound of feet on stone steps.

When the sounds had ceased, the team rose from their hiding places.

"Who was that?" Clive asked.

"Why don't you go and ask them?" Rhone retorted. "Seriously, I bet they're waiting. Just go through and say hi."

"I don't see an upper floor to this place," Jack pointed out, straining his neck to peer at the high ceiling.

"That's because there isn't one," Jennie commented. She sighed. "How come it's always underground with these types of people? Never out on the surface where anyone can find them."

"I think you've just answered your own question," Rhone told her.

Jennie glared at him. "I was being facetious."

Rhone shrugged. "Fair enough. Well, since our companion has decided that downstairs is where the party is, I think we'd be remiss if we didn't follow her and find out what's going on."

The voice came out of nowhere. "They're preparing for the service."

They turned as one as Rhone switched his flashlight on, and found another cloaked figure standing immediately behind them. How they hadn't heard his footsteps Jennie didn't know.

The agents kept their guns aimed at the cloaked figure. Although his cloak did a great job of masking his physical features, judging by the sound of his voice and the size of his frame, he was young.

"You're trespassing," the boy told them, his voice devoid of emotion.

"We're with the SIA," Rhone informed him, showing the boy in the cloak his badge. "We're looking for a number of missing young people. We have reason to believe they might be here. I need you to lower your hood so we can see your face."

The request was fair, and Rhone remained calm.

"Trespassers are not allowed," the boy stated. "You must leave now."

Rhone shook his head. "We will not leave until we know that the young people are not here."

Great, talk to the kid in a language he'll understand, Jennie thought.

Rhone continued. "If you continue to deny our requests, you will be arrested for obstruction of a federal investigation. I'm going to ask one more time: lower your hood and show us your face."

A chill ran through the church. Whether due to her years of training or acute sensitivities toward spectral energies, Jennie was the only one who felt it. Her skin came out in gooseflesh.

The boy gave a small chuckle, the sound chilling them to the bone. "You should have listened, Officer. You will be removed."

What followed happened so fast that even Jennie was taken off-guard. One moment the flashlight illuminated the boy, the next, the light shut off. Rhone slapped the flashlight, hoping to reengage the battery somehow, but nothing happened. When they looked up, the boy's eyes shone a spectral blue in the dark. They became aware of a flurry of movement, and more eyes lit up in the dark, surrounding them.

"Quick, try your lights," Jennie called.

They did, but none of them worked. They aimed their guns in all directions, but being clustered in a group in the dark meant that there was a real possibility they might accidentally shoot one of their own.

It wasn't until the loud footsteps came from the far side of the church, followed by the glow of the lantern, that they all turned and watched the figure appear through the doorway.

Jennie waited patiently, calculating the odds of organizing an escape in her head. She could do it, she thought. Her reflexes were fast, and she believed she could take them down if needed, but the last thing she wanted to do was leave before she worked out what the hell was going on.

The figure approached, the light wobbling with each step, and more blue-eyed figures in cloaks came from the doorways around the church until their number had swelled to at least three dozen.

The figure stopped about fifteen feet from the group. Jennie could just make out the bright red lips of the person beneath the cloak.

Arms held wide, a familiar voice came from the hood of the cloak. "Ah, agents. I wondered if we'd see you again. I'm glad you decided to join us this evening."

The woman placed the lantern on the floor. She reached for her hood and slowly lowered it to reveal a pale face with ruby-red lips.

Jennie felt a surge of anger running through her as she glared at the woman she recognized from her whisperings into the Shadow leader's ear in the Batsto village.

"And what an evening it's going to be." Julia grinned.

CHAPTER TWENTY-THREE

Jennie stared at the woman in disbelief. She couldn't understand what was going on. How was this connected to the Shadows?

"You join us on a merry occasion," Julia told them. "For tonight, we shall be creating life where there was none before."

"Merry?" Jennie questioned. "Oh, yeah. I can tell from all the laughs and smiles of your henchmen."

"Henchmen?" Julia raised an eyebrow, that irritating smile playing at the corner of her lips. She really was breathtaking.

Jennie was no stranger to how a woman's attractiveness directly correlated to their influence over men, but even so, to have so many men following her into a situation like this seemed odd.

And it certainly didn't explain their glowing eyes.

"You of all people should know that henchmen are hired," Julia told her. "No coin has been exchanged in this transaction. These are loyal followers of the Shadows, men and women who understand the noble cause and will die to see His vision come to life."

"His?" Jennie glanced around the room for any sign of a power higher than the woman. Her eyes fixed on the statue of Jesus. "Oh. Right. Christians, are we? The Father, Son, and the Holy Ghost? I get it now."

"This has nothing to do with Christianity," Julia retorted. "Christianity doesn't tell of specters roaming the mortal plain. We bow to a new religion, one in which we can use specters for our own advancement."

Julia broke eye contact with Jennie and slowly walked down the long aisle of the church, her arms spread wide. Her followers didn't move an inch, obediently awaiting her orders.

"You saw it yourself several days ago," Julia declared. "The power granted through what some might consider black magic. The dark arts. Powers that have no explanation but yield incredible results.

"The power that was summoned was the proof I needed to believe in our purpose and tie myself to its destiny. With Meister Donavon leading the charge and finally committing to the final dark act, we made our reality come true. The pages of the grimoire were full of lost truths. All we needed was to break the barrier and cross over into the realm of the mystics. The Realm of Shadows."

Clive glared at the woman, his breath loud and rapid. Jennie imagined the thoughts running through his head as he relived his moments strapped to the pentagram, awaiting his murder.

"But your boyfriend is with us," Jack called out, venom in his words. "We have him in custody. Without him, you have no leverage. We even have your book of spells. Without them, you're nothing. This is nothing more than a pipe dream."

Jennie flashed back to her visit to Proctor's lab. "No," she told him quietly. "There were pages missing. The book wasn't whole."

Julia turned back to the group. "Bingo! Do you really think we *need* the Meister to perform our ceremonies? Ha! All this time, he was nothing more than a puppet for me. A conduit to be used until we could prove that the magic worked. Men are so easy to manipulate. Stroke the right body parts and they'll bend over backward to do anything you say. Donavon was no different. He made the perfect scapegoat to take the final risk before we could prove that what we wanted to achieve was possible."

Jennie took a step toward the woman, but the cloaked figures closed in on them and barred her way. She latched onto Baxter and turned spectral, intending to walk straight through them, but once again found her way barred.

Beneath the cloaks, spectral figures stood in the same locations as the mortals. They were like Russian nesting dolls, a specter nestled inside a mortal.

Jennie turned material and gave an understanding nod. "Possession? Really? You've found a way to command specters to do your bidding by trapping them inside mortals?"

Julia's grin broadened. She made her way back to the others. "Clever, isn't it? By channeling specters into the mortal bodies of my followers, I have created a group willing to bend to my every command. The mortal consciousness can only fight for so long against the spectral power as the two intertwine, and then there we are. The specters I've raised are bound to me, and now the mortals are, too. Even someone like you can't just apparate through my order."

"Your order?" Agent Rhone queried. "From what you've said so far, I wouldn't have thought you were the mastermind behind this. All this talk of 'His' and 'we.' Why don't you tell us who you're working for?"

"I could," the woman mused. "Or I could raise more specters and have them take you, Agents." She snapped her fingers, and immediately, they were gripped by the possessed humans.

Rhone, Jack, and Clive struggled against them, but after a glance from Jennie, they stopped.

"Good choice," the woman told them. "It's better just to accept your fate. Now, come along, gentlemen. It's time to show you what we can do."

They were marched toward the side door of the church that Julia had appeared from, and down a long flight of stone steps. The temperature dropped rapidly as they passed through stone passages that looked long-abandoned beneath the church's foundations.

Large rooms opened on either side through arches with no doors. They were brought to a standstill inside a large chamber, at the end of which was a tall stone obelisk with an arrangement of candles around its base.

That might have been bad enough for someone who hadn't lived around cemeteries, morgues, and the dead for years, but it got worse, even for Jennie, when the smell hit them.

Jennie's nose wrinkled. She knew that smell. She didn't like that smell. She knew what that smell meant.

Rhone let out a disgusted grunt as the lantern illuminated a pile of bodies in the corner of the room. Although they were cloaked and covered in their Shadow robes, it was clear from the dark stains beneath them that they were dead. Murdered and gone from this realm.

"Don't concern yourself with them, Agents." Julia laughed. "They're not dead. Not really."

It was then that the group understood what had been going on. This woman—this psychopathic woman—had murdered these men and women in order to summon their specters.

Specters that were now nestled comfortably in the bodies of the men and women who guided them roughly toward the obelisk.

"You're sick," Jack declared. "You killed all of these people, for what? Power?"

Annoyance flickered across Julia's face. "I told you, they're not dead. Their spirits have been released, and they are with us now, working together to achieve the impossible. It's not murder if they chose to die for a higher purpose."

Jennie had encountered fanatics and lunatics a thousand times in her life, but never before had she seen someone take things this far. Ordinarily, mortals caught wind of specters and found ways to manipulate the ghosts—soft methods guided by priests or those who claimed they were psychic. For a group of followers to offer themselves up for sacrifice for the sole purpose of being controlled by this woman was sickening.

"Let me ask you a question," Jennie interrupted, already putting her spectral feelers out into the room to try to read the frequencies of power around her.

Julia half-shrugged. "Sure, why not? May as well make use of your final breaths."

"You talk about a higher purpose. What are you referring to? What could all this be for, other than an ego trip to try to control what you don't understand?"

The woman flushed red, clearly offended by Jennie's statement. "Don't understand? Oh, I understand all this perfectly. We have been given a gift, my dear. The gift of an extra life. No longer do we need to live in fear of only living once when we know there's a backup in the great beyond. With this knowledge, we can stretch the boundaries of what is possible. Once specters are controlled, we can utilize them to end the world's suffering. Ship them into war and find new ways of battle, the likes of which the enemy has never seen.

Julia's eyes shone with madness. "Imagine an entire enemy fleet countered by our specters infecting their minds and bringing them under our control. An entire army converted to join our cause. The world will find peace for the first time in its history, and the best part? It'll all be because of us. It'll be because I found a way to make it happen. My name will go down in history as the witch who brought about world peace. Once I feed this method to Him, we will be ready to multiply. To spread out into the world and end all the wrongs we find."

Her eyes went glassy. "Imagine it. Just imagine it."

Jennie, Rhone, Jack, and Clive exchanged looks.

"You're joking, right?" Jennie asked, a sour expression on her face. "Your plan for world peace is to murder the living to channel their spirits into the enemy?"

"Why restrict ourselves to the mortal plane?" Julia asked as though it was the most obvious question in the world. "When we have two lives to pick from, and one of them gives us near-immortality, why spend our time playing in the realm where death is an inevitability?"

"And you're doing it all for 'Him?'" Jennie took a cautious step forward. "Who is he?"

The woman stared at Jennie as if debating whether or not to answer her question. "Since you'll be dead soon, I suppose it doesn't matter if I tell you." There was a manic look in her eyes. "He is the guiding one. The knowledge behind the operation. The mortal who can commune with the dead and tell us their truths. It is he who sowed the seeds that led the Shadows to the ass-end of New Jersey in order to find a quiet place far from our base where we could test the rituals. He is the one who knows our direction and speaks the language of war." She took a long breath and her smile returned, the dreamy smile of a schoolgirl remembering her first crush. "It is He who will soon unleash our specters on the world, once I've brought him the start of our army and confirmed his theory."

"I don't suppose this 'He' has a name?" Rhone asked. "Just asking for a friend."

The woman gave a dark chuckle. "The Umbra…"

At the mention of the name, all the cloaked figures dropped to their knees and placed their hands flat on the floor in a diamond shape. A chant of "Praise him, praise him," echoed around the chamber before they stood again.

"Am I dreaming?" Clive asked the others.

"This ain't no dream," Rhone replied. "If it was, that broad would be naked and sitting on my lap right now."

Jack and Clive struggled to contain their laughter.

Jennie, however, stared intently at Julia. She opened her mouth to ask another question, but before she could, the woman clapped her hands twice and held them out before her. "Shadows, bring me the prisoners. Let us grow our army and send a message to the SIA scum who think they've got what it takes to control us."

Rough hands gripped Jennie and the others. They struggled, but they were outnumbered by the Shadows. They were marched toward the obelisk, where they were forced to their knees. The agents' weapons were confiscated. Dark sacks were placed over their heads, but not before Jennie saw a sight she found disturbing.

Before the darkness enveloped her, she saw the woman draw a pair of SI goggles from the pocket of her cloak and place them on her face.

"Don't forget the pet specter," she ordered, her words now muffled through the sack. "We can channel him into one of our new recruits."

Jennie gritted her teeth as she heard Baxter struggling against their number. Although he was big, there were many more of them. He fired a couple of shots from his weapon before it was taken away and his pained grunts confirmed that he had been wrestled to the floor.

When he was silenced, Jennie heard the telltale sound of a blade being drawn from a sheath. She closed her eyes and took a few deep breaths, wracking her brain to find a way to break free and rid them of the Shadows.

CHAPTER TWENTY-FOUR

Their energy signatures were all around her, but Jennie knew it would be those who were possessed who would be doing the killing.

The woman had developed bloodlust. She could see it in her eyes. With all her eyewitnesses under her control, she had nothing to fear by slicing their throats. She had dozens of people she could use to confess to committing the crimes. What did she need to worry about?

The Shadows began to chant. Julia flicked through the loose pages and found the required incantation. Her voice dropped as she read the ancient Latin script and began the ceremony.

Jennie's hot breath filled the sack and began to make her sweat. Pulses of spectral energy came to her, and soon she discovered she had a reading of where the Shadows were around her. Each signature came back to her in varying strengths, acting almost like sonar does for a bat.

Two behind each of us. Sixteen, no, seventeen gathered in front of us, all of them sharing the same ability of possession with no other discernible traits. At least that's something.

Jennie's mind went back to the Batsto church and the *sturmgeist* they had unleashed inside it. She shuddered and was thankful there was no signature for that, as far as she could see.

As Julia walked around them in counterclockwise circles, Jennie thought through every eventuality. Beside her, the agents remained quiet, no doubt also matching her thinking as they tried to figure a way to escape. A few seconds later, Clive rose to his feet and tried to run from his captors, but with another snap of her fingers, the woman's men brought him down.

"Unde oriri potest mortuorum et vivorum incolunt, species suas conflator in liberalibus disciplinis," Julia continued undeterred.

Inspired by Clive's efforts but determined to be more tactful, Jennie began to work her hands toward her waist. She moved infinitesimally slowly, determined to not draw Julia's attention, and by the time her steps grew closer, Jennie's thumb was inside a pocket.

She blindly felt around for one of her vials, hoping to high Heaven that she was selecting the right one. With her vision impaired and the pressure on, she was ninety percent sure it was correct, but that ten percent imposed a lot of risk if it failed.

"Subire voluntatem patiuntur formantur," Julia chanted.

Jennie hoped that the possessed Shadows were unaware of her movements. If they were under Julia's control, would they have enough of their own consciousness to report her manipulations to their mistress?

Jennie pulled the vial free. *Apparently, they don't.*

Working as quietly and quickly as she could, Jennie twisted off the cap and gripped it tightly in her hand. She took a few steadying breaths, knowing she only had one shot to do this correctly.

Now or never, girl.

Jennie folded forward as if moving into a rapid bow, and brought her arms up in an arc behind her to launch the vial.

Liquid hurled through the air in all directions, falling like pretty raindrops on the floor. The minute the liquid made contact, it exploded into a thick cloud of blue smoke.

"Now!" Jennie shouted. "Run!"

Without hesitation, the agents, Jennie, and Baxter rose to their feet. They shrugged off their sacks and entered the smoke that had filled the chamber.

Rhone, Clive, and Jack involuntarily coughed, their bodies telling them the gas was toxic.

"What is this?" Rhone called. "I can't see anything."

Nearby, Julia screamed.

"It's okay," Jennie told them. "It's not toxic. It obstructs the view of mortals, although specters can still see perfectly."

Jack coughed. "If that's the case, now every possessed specter can see us, but we can't see them?"

"Yes," Jennie replied with belief in her plan. "But guess who else can't see what's going on?"

Jennie made her way toward Julia, who had backed herself into a corner of the room and was shouting, "Get them! Get them!" Jennie grabbed her collar, aware of the possessed Shadows who were already beginning to round up the agents again and make their way toward Jennie. She punched Julia square in the jaw.

The woman's eyes rolled back as her head hit the wall. She slid onto her ass and slumped, unconscious.

"Maybe that'll shut you up for a little while." Jennie ripped the pages from her hand, quickly rooted through her pocket, and stood up again.

A dozen possessed mortals were behind her. Jennie spun to face them, her hand hovering over her hips where her weapons were hidden. She thought about making this easy for herself by destroying them all, then realized it wasn't their fault that they had been caught up in Julia's stupid game. From what she could see, none of them were armed.

She called to the others, "Hey, guys, how are you all doing?"

"Golden," Baxter called back, his fist connecting with a Shadow's face and sending him to the floor. Several more attackers were clawing at him and wrestling to bring him down. A gunshot rang out, scaring Jennie into thinking Baxter had been shot, but the next second he confirmed, "I'm okay!"

The agents, however, were not having a good time. Unable to see anything even with their SI goggles, all they could do was try to blindly bat away anyone who came toward them. Trained in combat, they did a good job to begin with, but once Jack went down, the other two followed.

Jennie cracked her knuckles and took a defensive stance. She raised her fists in front of her and scrolled through her memory bank for all the various training sessions and fights she'd taken part in.

"Come at me, bitches," she urged.

The Shadows obeyed. Wrapped in their cloaks, it was almost impossible to see what she was aiming at, but Jennie made the best guesses she could. She sent a right jab into the chin of the first attacker, ducked her head sideways to avoid the fist of another, and then crouched and rose with an uppercut to a Shadow's ribcage.

The Shadow buckled and started to fall, allowing Jennie to strike with a powerful knee to the side of their head. The Shadow fell backward, blocking the others from making progress toward her.

A hand grabbed Jennie's arm. She twisted and grabbed the Shadow's arm, using his momentum to fling him over her before delivering a swift back kick into the chest of another.

Another gunshot rang out as she fought free from the corner and made her way toward Baxter. Jennie backhanded a Shadow and sent them into a wall before sweeping out another's legs and stamping on their chest.

"Bax! Still with us?"

A quick look confirmed that he was, but for how long, Jennie didn't know. Baxter was wrestling his gun away from three Shadows while several more attacked him from behind. The barrel pointed toward the exit, where small holes had been made in the wall.

"Yep," Baxter growled. "Just...trying to ensure...I have all my bits intact."

Jennie ran over to him, avoiding the attackers blocking her way. When she got to him, she leapt and drove a fist into the top of one Shadow's skull, before ducking and wrapping her arms around another's waist, driving him away from the scuffle. In her mind, she saw herself in the center of a rugby game, tackling an opposing scrum-half into the floor.

This maneuver afforded Baxter enough time to free his gun from the remaining specter and aim it at his face. Baxter growled as he pulled the trigger and watched the specter's head explode.

"No!" Jennie shouted. "Baxter! No shooting. They're just people!"

Baxter examined his gun, ignoring the Shadows clawing at his back. He looked down at the floor, where he could see that the mortal's head was still intact, while the specter who had been possessing him now writhed in pain.

Jennie witnessed this too, coming to a sudden realization. "Your gun is entirely spectral, unlike mine." Jennie grinned. "Baxter, take them all out."

Baxter nodded, his brow furrowing. He batted the Shadows away with one powerful sweep of his arm behind him, then took aim and began firing.

Pieces of the specters in the room exploded as the bullets connected.

With each shot, their group became weaker. The mortals stumbled as if the shot had affected them, but not a single drop of blood was spilled. Only the specter pulling the strings felt the pain, and soon they were all on the floor, holding their wounds.

"What's going on?" Rhone shouted into the gas. "Why can I hear people falling?"

"We've got this," Jennie reassured them. "It's almost over."

"Oh, thank fuck," Clive breathed.

Jennie checked on the woman who had started it all, glad to see that she was still out cold. She moved back to the center of the room and rifled through the torn pages she had collected, looking for a way to free the bodies from the specters.

A page popped out at her, with bold decorative Latin lettering at the top. Jennie was relatively rusty, but she could work out the gist. The spell was for possession and was the one Julia had used to channel the specters into the mortals.

Her nose wrinkled as she read the page, discovering vivid descriptions of the lengths the cult had gone to to create their army.

And on the back of the page, the reversal.

To reverse possession of the host,

Channel power through the ghost,
Thrice repeat this incantation,
To reverse the spectral desecration.

Jennie tried to understand what was being asked from the words. "Channel power through the ghost? What ghost?"

Baxter stood by her side and tried to read the page. When he realized it was in Latin, Jennie read it for him.

"Channel power through the ghost," Baxter mused. "Maybe it means just connect to them spectrally and pull them from the body? The specter is the source of power, right? Maybe it just needs something, or someone, to connect with each specter and pull them free?"

Jennie sighed. "It's worth a shot, I suppose."

"What is it?" Rhone asked. "What's happening?"

Jennie explained the paper and what she was about to attempt. "Find a place to sit comfortably. This might take a few minutes."

Jennie worked her way around the room, approaching each crawling specter and kneeling beside the body. Putting her full focus on each in turn, she latched onto them and repeated the mantra three times, delighted to see that the moment she stopped speaking, the specter began to leak out of the body as though it had melted and found a place to escape.

When it was entirely out of the body, both the specter and the mortal would gasp and sit up, confused and dazed. Jennie would reassure each mortal to remain calm until she was finished, given that they had awoken in a thick blue gas.

Eventually, Jennie had cleared the room. With specters and mortals separated, the place felt a lot more crowded, and each waited patiently for an explanation of what the hell had happened in that room.

After the final separation, Jennie drew a second vial from her pocket and smashed it into the center of the room. Immediately the blue fog started clearing, and all was visible once more.

Jennie stood in the center of the room and clapped for everyone's attention. "This may come as a shock to a lot of you, but you have been the victims of black magic rituals. You mortals were possessed, and you specters were forced to possess mortals against your will."

The members of the Shadows looked around in confusion, wondering where the second group was that Jennie was talking to. Some of the specters, on the other hand, argued back, anger on their faces.

"We asked for this!" one of them cried.

Another called. "None of this was against our will. We wanted what we got. We've attained immortality!"

One countered with, "I never signed up for this. I chose to become a specter, but not to be used as a tool to dominate a mortal. It was like I was a zombie, unaware of what was going on." He turned to Jennie. "I'm so sorry."

Jennie shook her head, trying to work out how to deal with them all. "Specters, I'm going to give you an option. The choice is in your hands. I know that becoming a specter can be overwhelming, and the reality of it can be nothing compared to your expectations. Therefore, you may choose to come along with me, Baxter, and the SIA because your arses are under arrest, or if you prefer, I can exorcize you, sending you into the eternal darkness." She drew her sword and presented it to the room. "The choice is yours."

At that, a group of three specters broke free and made a dash for the wall.

Jennie quickly latched onto them and pulled them back into the room, creating a ripple of gasps from the others of their kind.

"There's no escape. I gave you two options. That's what we're working with."

Jennie instructed the SIA agents to guard the entry and to keep the mortals contained. Rhone, Clive, and Jack recovered their weapons and waited patiently by the arch. For the next few minutes, she delivered on her promise, rallying all the specters toward her and allowing them to make their own minds up.

The first exorcism was intense. The specter, a middle-aged woman with a puffy face and a sad expression, begged Jennie to end it. She hated being part of what had occurred and decided she would rather be dead than not be allowed to enjoy the pleasures of mortality. Jennie confirmed several times that this was what she wanted before touching the blade to her flesh and turning away as the specter exploded in a ball of white light.

After that first exorcism, the remaining specters took her much more seriously. Of their number, five requested exorcism, while others stated they'd rather pay for what had happened. Before long, the specters waited patiently for Jennie to give them their orders.

Jennie was sure that several others had snuck out, but she wasn't too bothered. They wouldn't make much trouble in the short run.

Once the specters were corralled, Jennie joined Clive in checking the mortals. She was none too surprised to discover that, among their number, as they lowered the hoods of several mortals, they looked into the bright young faces of teenagers. Jennie confirmed that their names matched those given to her by Hopkins and Daggro and helped them to their feet. When everyone was identified and ready to leave the church, Jennie turned to the corner of the room where the woman had been unconscious.

"Oh, for fuck's sake," Jennie grunted, seeing the empty spot where the woman had been. She turned to the agents. "Where is she?"

They looked around the room.

Rhone's anger was clear. "No idea. No one has come in or out since the gas has cleared."

"She must've run before we cleared the room," Jennie speculated. She clenched her fists, angry that they had allowed the woman to escape.

"Come on," she told Rhone. "Let's get this lot back to base. We've got a lot to discuss with your boss."

CHAPTER TWENTY-FIVE

Washington DC, USA

Transporting the mortals and specters took some figuring. In the end, Rhone called HQ, who sent a bus to ferry the Shadows back to Washington.

Jennie drove ahead of the bus, with Rhone driving his Dodge at the rear. Baxter, Jack, and Clive were left to guard the Shadows and ensure that they arrived in Washington in one piece.

When SIA's HQ came into view, Jennie felt relief wash over her. It had been risky, and in off-loading the captives, she counted that they had lost a handful of the specters, who had simply slipped out of the back of the bus. However, all of the mortals remained.

They delivered the captives to a stunned Daggro, who immediately barked orders at a number of agents and arranged to have everyone put into separate rooms where they could be kept under watch until she had reported to Hopkins and figured out what their next steps would be.

Hopkins arrived a few hours later. He looked exhausted and surprised to see the others back so soon.

Daggro tried to grab him before anyone else could get to him. "Sir, can we speak in private, please? We've got an urgent matter to attend to."

Jennie guessed what that matter was. Daggro wanted him all to herself before anyone else could tell them what a great job they'd done.

With sick glee, Jennie spoke before Hopkins could answer, "Special Agent Tom Hopkins, we've found the missing teenagers and brought you a bucketload of mortals and specters to interrogate. You're welcome."

Hopkins stopped on the spot, stunned. "Excuse me?" He looked around as if seeing the room for the first time. Everywhere he looked down the corridors, agents stood guard at the doors. "Come with me," he told Jennie.

Instinctively, Rhone and Daggro followed. Jack and Clive waited, not wanting to push their luck further with their superior.

"Tell me everything," Hopkins instructed, bending an eager ear to listen to the events that had transpired that night.

Jennie told them all about the place that Ricket had sent them to. She described the encounter with the woman who had gone missing from Batsto village and her plan to grow an army of possessed mortals.

His face was difficult to read as Jennie listed the tactics she'd had to use to earn their freedom. He nodded as she detailed her use of her gaseous cloud and the Saber of the Holy Divinity. A growl escaped his lips when she mentioned that she had to put the agents at risk in order to take down the specters.

Daggro couldn't hold herself back at that point. "You see, sir? She's a danger to all of us here. She doesn't care about anything except herself. Putting agents in danger deliberately? That's the opposite of everything we've been taught. Do you really expect that the special agent is going to allow her to—"

Daggro stopped talking when Hopkins raised a finger in the air. He rubbed his tired eyes, then laced his fingers beneath his chin.

"Miss King, thank you for your service tonight," he told Jennie quietly.

Daggro looked aghast. "You have got to be kidding me?"

"*Agent Daggro, I highly suggest you check what you're saying to your superior,*" Hopkins roared, flashing into anger. "Another word out of line, and you'll find yourself disgraced and out on your ass, you got that?"

Daggro met his eyes and kept her lips zipped. It took a great effort to relax back into her chair, and she fixed her eyes on Jennie.

Hopkins continued as though he'd not been interrupted. "Miss King, I have just finished speaking to Special Agent in Charge Kurt Rogers. Let me tell you, he's a hard man to track down, and an even harder man to impress.

"I've told him about your situation. I've given him an overview of what you're capable of and the help you've given our team despite your...unorthodox ways."

"And?" Jennie asked. "What did he say?"

Hopkins took a deep breath. "He wants to meet you, Miss King."

Jennie's heart fluttered with excitement. Over the course of the last few days, there had been a few shaky moments where she believed she might not be able to earn the respect of the SIA necessary to work her way into their network. Now, she had the opportunity to meet the top dog and would possibly be able to achieve what she'd been after the whole time—a partnership with a mortal organization run by the US government. If she could seal this deal, she'd have achieved her first step toward growing the king's court and gaining independence from the paranormal court.

"It would be an honor," Jennie replied solemnly.

Surprise filled Hopkins face at the lack of Jennie's usual indifference. He gave a curt nod and shook her hand.

"If you think I'm a hard man to impress, wait until you've met him," Hopkins added. "He'll scrutinize you down to the bone and strip you bare until you've got nothing left to hide."

"Funny," Jennie remarked. "Sounds a little like my tactics."

Hopkins and Rhone laughed.

"Now, if you'll excuse me, Miss King, thanks to you, we've got a whole host of specters and civilians to interview to get to the bottom of what is going on over in Baltimore. You said that there was mention of another force? A…what did you call it?"

"An Umbra," Jennie answered.

"Umbra?" Hopkins mused. "What does that mean?"

"I don't know who it's referring to," Jennie told him. "But I can tell you that the 'umbra' is the darkest part of a shadow, the point at which an object has blocked all light from reaching it."

Hopkins shook his head in disbelief. "All this with shadows, huh? What is it with people playing with darkness? You'd think people would understand that light is right and darkness is wrong."

"I'd be careful how you phrase that, sir." Rhone grinned.

Realizing how it sounded, Hopkins stuttered. "I didn't… You know that's not what I…" He waved a hand. "Oh, forget it." He snapped his fingers. "Rhone, Daggro, shouldn't you be leading the interrogation of our witnesses? Seeing what you can glean from their testimony?"

"On it, sir," Rhone replied, jogging out of the room. Daggro followed him without a word.

After they were gone, Hopkins turned to Jennie once more. "I mean it, Miss King. I know I've put a lot of pressure on you over the last few days, but please understand that all this is new to us. I've met a number of conduits since taking this role. I've met a number of specters and been introduced to a world I couldn't have imagined, but I've never met anyone like you. Forgive me for my skepticism."

"Of course," Jennie agreed, taking his hand again. "You're just doing what you think is right for your operation. I get that. I'm just doing what's right, too. In those two worlds of ours, there's going to be a middle point we'll find soon enough."

Hopkins studied Jennie's eyes for a few seconds, then nodded. "Get some rest, Miss King. An appointment is being set up to meet with the SAC. I'll update you when further information is received."

Jennie thanked Hopkins and left the room.

When Jennie awoke in her chambers, she could hear someone shuffling around nearby.

Her instincts kicked in, and before she knew it, she was out of bed, gun in hand, creeping toward her bedroom door.

Something clinked and was followed by a soft, "Shhh."

Jennie teased the door open. It was dark, but she could make out two figures in the room, hunched over the coffee table.

Jennie slapped on the light and pointed her gun at the intruders. The one on the left immediately placed both hands in the air, while the other continued to fight to grasp several glass bottles in the crook of his arm.

"Surprise?" Jack announced uncertainly.

Clive frowned as a bottle began to slip out of his grip.

Jennie glanced at the table, surprised to see a number of bottles of spirits.

She grinned. "What are you doing?"

"What does it look like?" Jack asked as Clive put the rest of the bottles down noisily. "We wanted to get you a thank you for all you've done for us so far. You know, saving his life, helping us accelerate our learning without spending hours in a classroom. That kind of stuff."

Jennie laughed. "Should we have alcohol in here? Don't federal agencies frown on consumption of alcohol on their premises?"

"Ordinarily, yes," Clive answered. "However, since you're not an agent and Hopkins gave us clearance, we're all good."

Jack beamed.

Baxter, who had been snoozing silently in the corner, rose and lifted his head. "Whozzat?" he asked groggily.

Jennie chuckled.

"What do you say?" Jack asked. "Want to show us how to make one of those cocktails you were going on about the other day?"

Jennie went into teacher mode, using the glasses, measures, and spirits provided. Although they weren't entirely up to the standard she was used to, she was more than thankful for what they'd brought her.

Eventually, a pretty pink cocktail was poured in a tall glass. Jennie decorated the top with a cherry on a cocktail stick and an umbrella. She then popped a cherry in her mouth and tied the stalk into a knot using just her tongue.

Jack stared at her, a small sheen of sweat on his forehead. "Impressive."

"I'll say," Clive added.

"Who's going to take the first taste?" Jennie grinned and offered it to the gentlemen. "I'm guessing you're off-duty, correct? Considering you've both broken into a lady's quarters with the ultimate gift that doesn't involve grunting and getting sweaty in bed."

"Well," Clive admitted, "almost off-duty. There's one more thing we've got to do before we clock out."

"What's that?"

Jack answered for him. "Your meeting with Special Agent in Charge Kurt Rogers has been confirmed. He's coming to the facility at 17:00 today."

Jennie glanced at the clock on the wall. It read 08:14.

"Oh, good," Jennie enthused. "That gives me plenty of time to prepare." She raised the glass to her lips and downed it in one. The boys stared at her. "What? A little Dutch courage never hurt anyone." She winked and stuck her tongue out.

"Besides," she continued. "I need to have a word with your man down in the lab. See if we can work out a more elegant solution for spectral containment in your facility."

"Who do you have in mind?" Baxter questioned.

"An old friend," Jennie grinned. "Someone who specializes in the kind of science mortals don't teach."

"Alchemy?" Baxter asked, realizing who Jennie was suggesting.

"Absolutely. Now, gents, since your work is done, why don't you get one of these down you?"

Jack and Clive exchanged glances.

"I don't mind if I do," Jack told her.

CHAPTER TWENTY-SIX

Baltimore, Maryland, USA

"Ancient lore tells us of a state of manipulation—a thousand ways to dissect and arrange the fabric of everything that's known to be tied to reality. Tug on one of these threads, and the whole thing unravels like a knitted sweater caught on the thorns of a rose bush. Just keep pulling until everything breaks, and all that's left is the naked vulnerability of what we are."

Julia met the speaker's gaze, her eyes unblinking. Her mouth was cotton-dry. Two behemoths stood somewhere behind her. Although they didn't make a sound, the men's presence was not unfelt by her.

The speaker shifted in his chair. The shelves behind him held rows of books so heavy that the shelves bowed in the center, tomes thicker than encyclopedias, filled with fragile pages that a single rough movement could dissolve into dust. One such volume sat on his lap, the pages spread wide. He carefully flicked through while he spoke.

"In the beginning, there was only guesswork and superstition. The Mesopotamians were the first to conclude that something lay beyond our understanding. They had their gods, and they had their theories, but it would be thousands of years later before anyone got any real knowledge of the expanse of the world beyond our own. Life after death. A most beautiful thing."

Julia had heard it all a hundred times before, but that wouldn't stop her from listening again. His voice had a lyrical quality, each note an individual component that made up a symphony. It was an orchestra of wondrous information that filled her soul and plugged the gaps in her mind.

He was a being with a total understanding of all that was. A guiding light in the dark corridor of her pilgrimage to an understanding of what life is, was, and would ever be.

"The Mesopotamians had some of it right, of course. Though their civilization wouldn't survive to know that to be true. They believed that in the moments after death, a judgment is rendered. Each individual is tested by the god of morality, who dictates whether they will find their precious loved ones in death. It was the Mesopotamians who forged the belief in an underworld, long before the Greeks ever threw Hades down there to watch over the River Styx.

"Each following culture had their superstitions and their own stories. Egyptians were judged on their ability to name the forty-two gods and list the sins they did *not* commit—trivial matters, and a long list for those pure of heart—before having their heart weighed against a feather. Those who passed were committed to Sekhet-Aaru, and those who failed had their souls devoured by the Goddess Ammit.

"Some Mayans sacrificed dogs to accompany them into the afterlife to help them perform their final tasks. Others believed the dead lived in volcanoes. The Mayans were, in my opinion, the least sensible of the lot, and actually steered the progress of man far away from the straight and narrow toward today's conclusions.

"The Greeks judged men and sent them to the Underworld, or to live on Mount Olympus with the gods they fabricated, and thousands of years later, Christianity gave the world a book that told of Heaven and Hell and the wonders of each."

The man plunged his fingers into the thick of his beard and scratched his cheek. His dark eyes were sunken into his head, as though they were sorely tired of the exploration of text and in need of a rest—a rest he would never give them. "And that was where we began—books."

Julia bit her lip. This was the part she liked.

"Books!" The man swept his arm behind him, eyes lighting up with excitement. His raised voice caused Julia to jump and let out an excited squeal. "Thousands of books on the study of the dead. Recorded accounts of the paranormal, cults, the occult, rituals, spells —the trials and the tribulations of interacting with the paranormal."

He rose and strode over to the bookshelves and held his arms wide. "Thousands of books that I have studied over the years, and now… Now, we finally have our evidence. We finally have the truth of it all." His excitement dissipated from his body, but his eyes flamed. "We've finally proven it to be true. Julia, show me the evidence."

Julia smirked and gave a small nod. Her heart thumped so hard inside of her that she wondered that no one could hear it. "Yes, sir."

Julia bowed low. When she rose, she double-clapped her hands, and the door behind her opened wide. At least two dozen figures entered the room, their bodies shrouded in the folds of dark cloaks.

"Divine Umbra, please observe our recruits from Batsto, who serve our great purpose and have returned to the nest for further instruction."

Umbra advanced on the cloaked figures with a small smile on his lips. He reached into his pocket and drew out a dark pair of goggles that he placed on his face. At the touch of a button, the rims of each lens glowed bright green.

"They're possessed?" Umbra marveled. "I thought you had told me there were no more? That the enemy had captured them all and taken them to their HQ?"

"They have," Julia replied smugly. "But upon further inspection of the pages our puppet Donavon read from in order to kickstart the ritual in the village, it seems that the destruction of a *sturmgeist* is something that is not so easily done."

Umbra stalked around the cloaked figures, inspecting them each in turn. Occasionally he twisted a finger in a hood to glance at the face beneath before nodding and turning to the next. "The woman didn't destroy the *sturmgeist?*"

"Oh, no. She destroyed it, all right," Julia told him. "I don't know how, or what she is, but there is no question that the *sturmgeist* is gone."

Umbra pointed at the cloaked figures. "Then what is this? Speak frankly. I tire of guesswork."

Julia nodded eagerly. "They are the product of a spectral fracture." She withdrew a page from her pocket and showed it to Umbra. "In the rare cases when a specter reaches an energy level that is far greater than it was intended to have, the soul of the original specter may divide upon its exorcism. The fragments will accommodate any and all bodies that may be in its vicinity."

"Yet you managed to avoid it," Umbra pointed out. "How?"

Julia grinned. "That's the best part. Since I was so heavily involved in the sacrificial ritual, it appears that I've gained my own influence over the possessed. Isn't that right, boys and girls?"

Each cloaked figure nodded simultaneously. The two behemoths' hands flexed on the butts of their guns.

"Delicious," Umbra remarked, his starry eyes wide.

"Indeed," Julia confirmed. "After the dispelling of the Shadows in the village, many of the group were interrogated and set free to go about their lives. Yet, they couldn't quiet the voice inside that fought against their mortal souls and bound them to us."

Umbra roamed around the room and stopped in front of Julia. She unconsciously leaned toward him when he placed a hand on her shoulder. The musky scent of sweat and man clouded him, but rather than repelling her, it had the opposite effect.

"You have done well, Julia. Better than I could have asked for. With your assistance, we finally stand a chance at claiming our rightful place in the world. With an army of specters behind us, there's nothing to stop us from rising up and dominating everything, just as we were born to do!"

Umbra raised a fist in the air with a triumphant look on his face.

Julia and the behemoths followed suit, and at Julia's instruction, every cloaked figure in the room held their fist high.

Umbra laughed, the sound like a car backfiring. His teeth were chipped and yellow, with many missing. He took both of Julia's shoulders in his hands and stared into her eyes. "With this development, we may even be able to break free of *Her.*"

Despite herself, Julia's face fell. "Her? You can't be serious. She would never…"

"She is one of *them*, isn't she?" Umbra leered. "What we can do to one specter, we can do to them all. One does not supersede the others." He let out a final howling laugh and wrapped an arm around Julia's shoulder. With a powerful grip, he turned her around and marched out of the room beside her. "For the first time in history, humans will not just understand what happens beyond death, we will also be able to *control* it!"

Julia met his laughter and relaxed into his shoulder. Of all the men she'd had the misfortune to meet in the world, this was the only man she would bow before.

The only man who understood the cause and had given his life to execute it.

CHAPTER TWENTY-SEVEN

<u>Washington DC, USA</u>

It had been a long while since Jennie felt anything close to real nerves. Butterflies raged in her stomach, and her throat was desert-dry. Guided by Senior Special Agent Hopkins, the corridors seemed longer than they had before, the SIA agents a little more hostile.

But why should she be nervous? Jennie had done nothing wrong. Over the years, she had battled fearsome creatures, been on the brink of death, found herself alone and surrounded by poltergeists in dens far beneath the surface of the Earth, come to terms with the mortality of her parents, and dived headfirst into a world she could never have imagined.

So why was this so nerve-wracking?

She chewed this over in the heavy silence that accompanied their walk. Hopkins' hot and cold nature had turned cold again, and Jennie didn't feel much like thawing him out.

Her only conclusion was the weight of the situation. With her arrival on American soil, the firm ground on which she had planted her feet for the past century had crumbled beneath her. Her entire history had been rewritten upon the discovery of Queen Victoria's failure to keep her moral compass pointing north and employing specters to take her place on the throne. The world she had cloaked herself with had been pulled away, leaving her naked in the cold with the realization that there was no one else out there willing to do what was right to keep justice in the world.

There was no one else in the world with abilities like hers, and no one as keen to bring peace between mortals and specters.

That weight was hers alone to bear. As the one who stood between both worlds, it was up to her to shoulder the responsibility while she worked to build a network that could support her on her quest.

This was the next step. First impressions were important, and meeting with the SIA's Special Agent in Charge would be a big step in ensuring that she had the backing of the federal government as she eradicated the filth and transitioned the world into a new era of mortal and spectral relations.

Hopkins paused outside the door, his hand resting on the knob. There was a concerned look on his face, but he settled for a brief, "Good luck," before knocking and allowing Jennie entry.

The room they'd assigned Kurt Rogers was not dissimilar to every other boardroom in the facility, yet the atmosphere was vastly different. Jennie was aware of the power some leaders exuded. Certain individuals gave off a presence that felt almost physical, a power that could silence a room the moment they stepped inside.

Kurt Rogers was one of those people.

He was a handsome man, with a wide, chiseled jaw and deep-set eyes. His hair was dark and immaculately combed to the side, and his eyes were ice-blue. He sat upright, hands clasped before him, and his suit was without flaws. A red tie added color to his otherwise monochrome attire.

Behind Kurt Rogers stood a woman with a sharp glare and small rectangular bifocals. Her hair was parted and drawn back into a bun so tight nothing could penetrate it, and in her hand was a digital tablet. She tapped the screen and glanced at the woman who had just entered the room.

"Miss King," SAC Rogers greeted her, standing and offering a hand as Jennie approached. He had a firm grip, his hands padded with callouses. "Thank you for meeting with me today. This is my personal assistant, Ashleigh Callaghan." His voice was authoritative, yet there was kindness in his tone.

At the mention of her name, Ashleigh forced her eyes away from her tablet and shook Jennie's hand.

"Please, take a seat," Kurt Rogers offered.

Jennie took the chair adjacent to him and made herself comfortable. "The pleasure is all mine," she told him. "I've heard a lot about you."

SAC Roger's eyes widened slightly at this. "From who? Information about my status, my business, and my personal life is classified. Who gave you this information? I'll have them kissing the curb before the day is through!"

Jennie was taken aback. Roger's face turned red as a terrifying injection of anger contorted it. He slapped a hand on the table, and although Jennie jumped, she was surprised to see that Ashleigh didn't move a muscle.

Must be used to it.

Kurt's eyes bored into Jennie's.

Jennie met his gaze with a polite smile. "Apologies, Agent Rogers, but I'm no snitch. If you want that information, you should speak to your agents. All of that," she waved her hands, "is none of my business."

Rogers continued to stare at Jennie for a long moment, then finally sat back and relaxed. The red left his face instantly as he let out a chesty laugh. "My guys were right. It takes a lot to intimidate you. You hold your ground well."

He reached behind without looking, and Ashleigh passed the tablet into his hand. He flicked through a series of tabs on the screen.

"No confirmed birth certificate. Alleged age, one hundred and thirty-eight. Committed service to the paranormal court for an undefined number of years. Alias, 'Rogue.'"

"Only to my enemies," Jennie replied. "You can call me Jennie."

"With the greatest respect, Miss King, I'll reserve judgment on that."

"Smart."

Rogers continued, "Key figure in the dispersal of a cult and the resulting spectral outbreak in New Jersey, accompanied the SIA to Baltimore to intervene in a missing persons case and caught a key spectral witness, and played an important part in finding the missing persons and stopping the sacrificial possession plot of the group known as 'The Shadows,' led by an unknown male who goes by the name of 'Umbra.'"

Jennie grinned, thinking Rogers was finished. "That would make a good book, wouldn't it?"

Rogers ignored her and carried on reading. "Uses foul language often, has no care or respect for authority, has threatened a witness and the agents around her, constantly pulls weapons from places no one can see, and looks down her nose at the Spectral Intelligence Agency."

Agent Rogers' words had taken on a sharper edge. What had sounded like a list of achievements at first now sounded accusatory, and Jennie didn't like the road it was taking.

Still, she bit her tongue.

"Influencing fellow agents into a negative mindset about their mission, holding specters hostage, carrying unlicensed firearms, and controlling specters against their will."

Rogers shifted forward in his chair, put the tablet down on the table, and studied Jennie across it. "I think that about covers all the notes I have on you, Miss King. Now, tell me. Who the hell are you, and why are you turning my organization upside-down?"

A thousand retorts hovered on Jennie's lips, quick snaps that would put Rogers in his place. Statements to justify everything she'd done. Sarcastic responses that would make her feel good, but would undoubtedly turn the situation more frosty than she needed it to be.

Instead of those, Jennie settled for, "Special Agent, have you ever truly seen death?"

Rogers was taken aback. Although his eyes remained fixed on her, a slight change in his posture showed that he was genuinely contemplating the question. "Miss King, I've been around specters and their world for the best part of a year, now. I've seen death. I've seen specters born, and I've seen specters wandering through these halls."

Jennie nodded. "As I thought. With the greatest respect, I've *lived* around death my entire life. I understand that what you've got on that tablet seems impossible to you, and I'd be likely to agree, had I not lived a life beyond what anyone else has known. Unless you were raised with specters and lived between the worlds of the living and dead, you don't have the slightest clue what death truly is, or the forces you're trying to battle and contain."

"What are you trying to say?"

It was Jennie's turn to study the special agent in charge. Although he was difficult to read, she was sure she sensed intrigue behind those eyes—a deep-seated curiosity about what Jennie might be and the kinds of possibilities she offered.

Jennie took a deep breath. "I'm saying you need me. I'm saying I need you. You believe your greatest problems are missing persons and rogue ex-partners, but the world is wider than Baltimore. You've seen ants struggling to find food, but you're not looking for the drought that's changing the landscape. The situation is bigger than you know, and without that knowledge to arm you, your efforts are going to be in vain."

All eyes were on Jennie. Rogers contemplated her words, then sat back in his chair. "Assuming I believe you are who you say you are, why should I believe you'd be any more loyal to the SIA than you were to the paranormal court? Our British counterparts have provided us with tech, with information, and with support while this operation raises itself from the ground up. You abandoned your duty, and now you're here. Alone. Why should we trust you?"

There it was. The paranormal court already had a hand in with the SIA, and this was Jennie's chance to break the connection once and for all and cut the queen off from the US completely.

Jennie again deliberated the best approach. "Kurt... May I call you Kurt?"

"It's Special Agent in Charge Rogers to—"

Jennie didn't let him finish. "Kurt, let me ask you a question. Out of all of the dealings you've had with the paranormal court, how many of their own have they sent over to assist with the founding of this agency?"

Ashleigh looked from Rogers to Jennie, unable to believe her brazenness.

Rogers, meanwhile, smiled. "None."

Jennie nodded, her face solemn. "How many times have you asked?"

Rogers sighed. "I've lost count."

"I guessed as much," Jennie told him, allowing a hint of her anger to show in her tone. "Don't you think it's odd that an organization that has offered you a partnership is unwilling to send anyone to assist in the startup of this organization?"

Rogers shook his head. "They have priorities to take care of in Europe, but they're more than happy to communicate remotely."

Jennie leaned forward and laced her fingers on the table, looking through the dark lenses of her glasses at the classically handsome man before her. "Their reluctance has nothing to do with Europe. Well, maybe a little bit. The queen has admitted to me that she doesn't yet have the resources to exert any real influence in the United States, but they wouldn't have told you the real reason. That's something they wouldn't dare to admit to themselves, let alone to you and your men."

Rogers sat forward, meeting her in the middle of the table. Their hands were just inches from each other. A waft of his cologne teased Jennie's nostrils. "Then what's the real reason?" he asked.

Jennie smirked. "The real reason is me. You want to know who I am and what I've done? Then here it is. The uncensored, unfiltered story of Genevieve King. Or at least, as much as is relevant to furthering our partnership, despite how unbelievable it will sound to mortal ears."

With that, Jennie told Rogers the truth, the whole truth, and nothing but the truth.

CHAPTER TWENTY-EIGHT

The Plaza, New York City, USA

Lupe dived into the mini-fridge for the third time that evening. He ran his finger through the beads of condensation on the glass bottles as he hmmed and ahhed about which drink would satisfy his craving.

There was everything anyone could ask for. Beers, ciders, liquors, spirits, and juices. It was as though Jennie had expressly asked for one of everything, and the Plaza's staff had delivered. He couldn't imagine a hotel accommodating such a wide variety of drinks as standard.

Then again, he'd hardly ever been in the circumstances to experience luxury living. Lupe had been making the most of what was on offer since Jennie had promised to continue funding the penthouse suite in the world-renowned hotel for as long as they needed it, and he was beginning to enjoy this life.

Lupe selected a cold bottle of beer with a label in a foreign language. He cracked the top, listened to the satisfying hiss of the gas escaping, then sat in the armchair and stared out over the city.

He kicked off his shoes and rested his feet on the table in front of him. "Ah, this is the life."

"It might be all right for you, but having to look at your gnarled little toes is ruining the view for me." Carolyn recoiled, moving her hand to her nose. "Seriously, there's a five-star shower in here, and you choose not to use it?"

"I don't like the smell of the soap," Lupe told her.

Carolyn's face dropped. She turned to the table where Tanya was currently sitting at the table, with a small book with thick pages open in front of her. Beside her, Sandra pointed to the various words and repeated them back to Tanya, each word slightly hesitant as it left her mouth.

"I'm not getting stuck into another one of these conversations with you two." Tanya's nose wrinkled when the smell hit her a moment later. "On second thought, stick something over those mold-infested feet."

Lupe tore his eyes away from the blazing sunset and looked at his feet. The tops sprouted several hairs, and his nails needed care.

"Fine." He sat up and put his shoes back on. "You'd think that sitting at the top of the world, we could let ourselves settle in a little bit and enjoy being free."

"We can," Carolyn agreed. "Just not your feet."

"Agreed," Feng Mian added, making one of his rare contributions to the conversation.

Since Jennie had left for her expedition to Washington, the Spectral Plane had continued its metamorphosis into a much different operation than the one it had been weeks ago. Those who had battled in Times Square were still loyal to the Plane, and Lupe and Tanya had worked with the spectral residents of the city to ensure that animosity wasn't a pervasive element in the zeitgeist.

It would have been easy for the city to have fallen into another war in the absence of Jennie or a strong representative of the crown, but the group had spent a lot of time fostering a culture of kindness and civility for specters of all factions.

Not only that, but whatever had happened between Jennie and Queen Victoria in her private chambers had had a visible effect on the city. While wandering the streets, they had seen an increase in specters aligned with the paranormal court just going about their business. They'd seen neutral specters mingling with both groups, and they'd seen members of the Spectral Plane actively seeking to forge connections with their kin in the court.

Specters were specters, at the end of the day. That was the message that needed to be sent. No one faction was above them all.

Not that all animosity had been erased, of course. Over the course of the last few days, Lupe, Tanya, Sandra, Carolyn, and Feng Mian had been in their fair share of scraps. Alleys were a common place for specters to gang up on each other and cause problems, poltergeists continued to pop up across the city, and it was becoming clear that a certain group was hunting specters who had been subjugated to spectral entrapment for their cause.

Whatever that cause may be.

Lupe enjoyed his beer and soaked in the sunset. He thought back to how it had all been before Jennie had come into his life. How he'd had nothing and no one to call his own. No real friends, no family, no job, no life. And now. here he was, surrounded by people he cared about.

All except one.

"How much more time do you think she needs?" Lupe asked. He didn't need to clarify who he was talking about. They had all thought about Jennie at some point throughout the day.

"Who knows?" Carolyn replied. "She could storm the doors, go in there, and grab their chief by the collar, but would kicking ass really be a healthy start for a relationship?"

"I don't see why she needs them," Tanya commented, finally intrigued enough to join in. "With her powers, anyone would be stupid not to join her cause and follow her."

Sandra continued her reading, which she'd gotten good at quickly.

"Absolutely," Lupe agreed.

"She needs more than that," Feng Mian offered. "It is not as simple as *commanding* respect. A leader has to earn the devotion of their followers. Brute force can only get you so far. It can earn people's minds, but it will never earn their hearts."

"He's got a point," Carolyn conceded, rolling her eyes. "As always. If we hadn't come across Jennie in our own individual ways, we would never have fallen in behind her. Despite the pressure everyone else put on me to pick a side, she stepped back and gave me a free choice in the morgue. While others were pressuring me, she offered fair and honest guidance. If it hadn't been for her support, I'd have sworn allegiance to the paranormal court, and where would I be then?"

The others nodded thoughtfully. "Tanya," Carolyn continued, "Jennie was there to help you when you needed it. She knew your greatest dream was to meet specters and be able to view one in the flesh—"

"There's no flesh on specters," Lupe muttered.

Carolyn ignored him. "And that's what she delivered. She helped you at a time when she could have just helped herself. Despite everything that was going on, she stuck by your side and offered you hope."

Lupe raised his eyebrow, mind casting back to his first encounter with Jennie. "She cost me my specters. Shot at them with that oversized firearm she carries."

"Oh, the Big Bitch," Carolyn enthused.

Tanya gasped and covered Sandra's ears.

Lupe carried on, eyes deep in thought. "Then she hunted me down in the subway and attacked my specters, trying to steal them all away from me." He looked at the others. "Maybe I'm the exception to the rule."

Carolyn laughed disbelievingly. "She gave you *real* followers, not just those bound by oath. Let's be honest, you were on the brink of turning into a dick, and Jennie pulled you back. If it wasn't for her, you'd be grumbling in the dark, surrounded by a bunch of specters you didn't know what to do with. The influence of the crown would have continued to grow, and before you knew it, you'd have had a full-scale war on your hands you weren't equipped to win."

Lupe grinned. "I suppose you're right."

Carolyn nodded, then turned to Feng Mian. He stared placidly at her, not a flicker of emotion in his eyes.

"And Feng? Well, I don't know what Jennie did for you, but you're here, and that's all that matters."

Feng Mian grunted and turned to face out of the window.

"I'm sure she won't be much longer," Tanya told Carolyn soothingly, a hint of uncertainty in her voice despite her attempt to comfort the younger woman. "As long as we keep abreast of what's going on in New York in her stead, we've got nothing to worry about."

At that, Lupe glanced at the clock on the wall and sat up straight. "Speaking of. Carolyn, it's time."

Tanya looked at the clock to check. "Man, the days fly so fast."

"Can we come this time?" Sandra asked.

"Not today, honey," Tanya replied before giving Sandra a quick peck on the forehead. "We've got to stay here and work on your reading."

Sandra gave a sheepish nod, then returned to her page.

Carolyn strolled down the street and scratched her head. "She realizes that Sandra is not her kid, right? I mean, Sandra is dead. Several hundred years dead. If anything, she could be her great-great-great-great-great-great-great..."

They turned right at a busy corner, Lupe shrouded in his cloak with Carolyn and Feng Mian on either side. While he had to duck and weave around people, the others floated right on through.

"Great-great-great-great-great—"

"We get it," Lupe snapped, alarming a young boy holding his mother's hand as they crossed the road. He lowered his voice and spoke without moving his lips. "She's old. We get it."

"It's cute," Feng Mian offered.

"I'm not saying it isn't cute," Carolyn agreed. "I'm saying the girl has superpowers. Like, she's stronger than any other specter I've ever met."

Lupe smirked. "You mean, in the five minutes you've lived as a specter?"

Carolyn ignored him. "She's a cocktail of power. She can perform exorcisms, and she has the ability to make mortals see the spectral world. I mean, what else can she do?"

A car horn blared at several New Yorkers jaywalking at a half-run. Nearby, out-of-tune karaoke spilled out of an Irish bar.

Lupe guided them along the street, then took a shortcut through a back alley. During his time working with the Spectral Plane, he had finally begun to come to grips with the layout of the city.

"We just don't know," Carolyn continued, not caring that no one had asked her to. "We may never know, not while Tanya treats her like the daughter she never had. It was cute at first, but now I'm starting to worry."

Lupe paused suddenly down the alleyway. He turned on Carolyn so quickly that for a moment, she forgot he couldn't physically touch her.

"Listen to me," Lupe told her. "Tanya's not hurting anyone. Sure, the girl might be a few centuries older than all of us, but that doesn't mean she's not still a little girl mentally. She was entrapped in rock for that entire time. What opportunities has she had to learn or integrate with the modern world? We can't just use her as a jack-in-the-box of power. She's a person with real thoughts and real feelings, and she needs to adjust."

Carolyn looked down at the little man and met his gaze. His breathing was heavy, small puffs of condensation filtering through his lips.

"I get it," Carolyn assured him. "It's just, Tanya hasn't joined us for any of these rounds in days. I'm worried about her. She's getting too protective of Sandra."

"Someone needs to be a mother to that girl and keep her on our side," Lupe argued. "Without a positive force in her life, she could be out in the wild with *them*, and where would we be? She's safe with us, and that's all that matters. You're a woman. Where are *your* maternal instincts?"

Carolyn glanced down at the ground, unable to meet Lupe's eyes any longer. A beat of silence passed between them before she said, "We thought about it, you know. Me and Cody spoke about kids. A lot. He came from a large family with five siblings, and I was an only child. We'd only been together for two years, but it was something I could tell he wanted. I wasn't so sure."

Lupe softened at that. Staring into Carolyn's shimmering eyes was enough to take some of the wind out of his sails. "Why not?"

Carolyn gave a half-smile. "Because how could I ever be sure? I didn't grow up around children, and I never had children present in my life. Why would I think I could handle that? He had all these expectations and visions of how it could be, and it was overwhelming." She chuckled. "I suppose that might be why I started dog-walking. It was a way to practice and step up to the responsibility of real children, taking care of people's fluffy companions."

Lupe kicked his shoe through the dirt of the alley. "I'm sorry. Sometimes it's hard to remember that specters have a history. It's easier to see you guys as nothing more than the people I know you as."

"I can understand that," Carolyn told him. "For the record, it's hard to forget the life I used to have."

Lupe gave an understanding nod, then turned and continued down the alleyway. Before he reached its mouth, he turned over his shoulder and added, "For the record, I reckon you would've made a great mother."

Carolyn sniffled, smiled, then followed.

***

The specters were waiting for them at Forty-First Street. The moment they saw Lupe and the others heading their way, they snapped to attention, cutting short whatever conversation they were involved in.

One woman and two men. While the two musclebound men were plain terrifying, the woman was also disconcerting to look at. She was clearly recovering from an injury that had disfigured her face. What Lupe and the others didn't know was that several weeks ago, Jennie had blasted the woman's head to bits with the Big Bitch. While her eyes, mouth, and nose were mostly operable, they were all slightly off-center. Her attitude, however, had been righted much faster than her facial features.

"Any luck?" Lupe asked, his hands deep in his pockets. He asked casually, as if querying what the weather was like, or who won the latest baseball game.

The woman, Belinda Carragon, gave a haunting grin and nodded. Beside her, the two grunts stood like silent sentinels.

"They led us straight to their nest," Belinda reported with glee. When her allegiance with the crown had gotten her into trouble with Jennie, she had joined the handful of specters who had realigned their loyalty and taken oaths to the Spectral Plane. "We followed them for days, hiding from view. They thought they were sneaky, but they were nothing compared to us."

Lupe wondered how three huge mammoths of specters could ever consider themselves as "sneaky."

"Where is it?" Carolyn asked before she could help herself.

Belinda gave a sly grin, her face growing dark. "A little way south of here. Down in Chinatown."

Although no one paid attention, Feng Mian's eyebrows twitched.

CHAPTER TWENTY-NINE

<u>Washington DC, USA</u>

"The facility is yours?" Baxter gasped. "The *whole* facility?"

Jennie beamed as they walked down the corridor together. Whereas before she had felt like an intruder in the SIA, now she felt liberated. The world was her oyster, a smorgasbord she could eat from whenever she wanted.

Well, within reason. There were some conditions.

"That's right, Bax," Jennie replied. "We were granted full access to pretty much every room in this place. Full access to the weapons store, full access to the training rooms, full access to the gym, and free access to any and all agents I wish to take with me on my missions."

Baxter let out a stunned laugh. "I can't believe it."

"Well, believe it, pal. Rogue has got some influence around here."

Jennie approached the nearest door, placed her thumb on a small black pad, and leaned closer to the retinal scanner. A blink of red light confirmed her identity and the electric door swung open, revealing Proctor's laboratory.

Where before Proctor had been in control of his experiments, to the point that he was clearly annoyed at Rhone and Jennie's intrusion, now his annoyance was aimed at something else entirely.

The once-immaculate lab was in an absolute state. Flasks were scattered on all surfaces, plumes of vapor clouded the air, and electrical equipment beeped and buzzed.

Proctor groaned and protested as he followed the small man around the lab, cleaning up his mess. "If you would just *explain* to me the process by which you're… I mean, that *shouldn't* go into th— What are you doing? No. *No.* Oh, come on, how is it possible to move so fast when you're… *This is my lab!*"

Jennie watched Proctor's dance with his new lab companion with a certain amount of smug glee. It wasn't until Proctor moved away from his new colleague and accidentally dropped a flask on the floor that he realized that he even had guests.

"Oh, good. It's you." He stomped over to Jennie, fury on his face. His hair stood up in all directions, and his eyes were laced with bolts of red. "This is *your* doing, is it not?"

Jennie chuckled. "It is."

"How *dare* you?" Proctor stood only a couple of feet away from her now. His fists were clenched as he studied her, clearly debating the wisdom of attacking her, given the powers he knew she possessed. "*I* am the head researcher of this facility. I decide on my staff, and I decide what projects are approved. Tell your little friend to cool his fervor and get in line before I report his disobedience to my superior."

"Would that be Special Agent in Charge Kurt Rogers?" Jennie feigned fear, a hand going theatrically to her mouth.

Proctor's face twisted into a smile. "The one and only."

Jennie let all pretense drop. "Can it, Proc. It's on his orders that I'm here. I've been granted full access to HQ on account of my updated status with the agency. If you want to go to your superior, go ahead. However, I think you'll find that you'll be wasting his time on nonsense, and if there's one thing the chief operating head of this agency doesn't have, it's time to spare for a whiny scientist who can't tuck his ego between his legs and accept support when it's offered."

She pointed at the research assistant, who was busying himself with weighing cellophane bags of ingredients that looked to have been brought from home. "That man is a legend. He's been in this business a hundred times longer than you have, and he's got solutions to the issues with your inventions. You need to work with him and ensure that things are in functioning order around here."

Proctor turned a fierce shade of crimson. His mouth flapped open and closed a couple of times before he managed a weak, "My inven… There is *nothing* wrong with my—"

Jennie cut his protest off. "Spectral interrogation chambers one can simply melt through? Spectral Intelligence goggles that don't enable the wearer to *hear* the specter? Come on, lad. Even I can see those need work."

She cocked her head toward the scurrying research assistant and called, "Isn't that right, Hendrick?"

At the mention of his name, the ancient man turned his bald dome around and gave her a painful smile. The folds around his neck and face screwed into harsh lines, but there was kindness in his eyes. "Right as always, Genevieve. Right as always."

Chinatown, New York, USA

Chinatown was bustling with activity.

The late-night market was in full swing. Hundreds of stalls lined the already cramped streets, spilling a variety of mysterious scents into the air. People meandered along at a painfully slow pace, making Lupe wish he had Jennie's ability to turn spectral and simply flow through the crowd.

"How are we supposed to find them in all this?" Lupe asked, grunting as a shoulder bumped him. He hated environments like this. Being considerably shorter than most New Yorkers, crowds did not serve him well at all. Memories of getting lost while out with his parents flooded back, and as hard as he tried to push it all back down, it did little to soothe him.

Belinda had gotten some distance in front of him. She heard his question and turned to look for him, discovering him only after a number of people had passed through her. "There you are. I keep forgetting you're not one of us."

"Not sure if that's a compliment," Lupe told her as they set off again.

Belinda led them right into the heart of Chinatown, where a celebration was taking place in an open square. Performers blew fire into the air from their mouths, and a large red dragon operated by five people, judging by the number of legs beneath, circled around the platform where the firebreathers stood.

"Up there?" Lupe pointed to the roofs around them, where specters could be seen looking down and watching the entertainment, invisible to the mortal world but not to a conduit's eye.

Belinda shook her head, then continued walking.

Lupe skirted the edges of the crowd, managing to somehow squeeze through dozens upon dozens of bodies. When they reached the street on the other side, Belinda took a sharp right and stopped outside a dark wooden door.

"In there?" Lupe asked.

Belinda nodded, placing a finger on her lips.

Carolyn stopped beside Lupe and gave an acknowledging nod. Feng Mian appeared tense, his jaw a little tighter than usual.

"Everything okay?" Lupe asked.

Feng Mian was silent for a moment. "Dangerous people occupy this area. I pray we are not being led into a snake pit."

Lupe chewed this over. If you thought about it, the entirety of New York was occupied by dangerous people. Most of the world hid secretive people whose moral compass had broken and now pointed permanently to hell. But did that mean you didn't push forward and try to scrape out the filth when you had the chance?

Belinda was halfway through the door when Lupe hissed, "Wait. Not a specter, remember?"

Belinda rolled her eyes and came back into the street. "Fine. I think there's a back entrance around here somewhere."

Luckily, there was. A narrow alley gained them access to the rear of the building. A small metal door waited for them, but Lupe could not open it.

"Wait here," Carolyn told him. She melted through the door, and a moment later, Lupe heard a small click. The door swung slowly open, revealing a room bathed in shadow.

They explored the house by dividing and conquering. While the specters melted through the rooms, Lupe went through a small kitchen and into a living room, stripped bare of any form of American culture.

Chinese tapestries covered the walls, incense candles were burned to stubs on a small table that took up the center of the room, with several small cushions surrounding it.

There were photographs and drawings of family members, all of whom Lupe assumed would be out enjoying the celebrations that night. They had picked a perfect time to raid the house.

Or so Lupe thought.

The telltale click of a shotgun being pumped came from behind. Lupe slowly raised his hands in the air as he heard the soft footsteps of the man approaching.

"You are trespassing." The man's voice held a faint hint of his Chinese descent. "What do you want?"

Lupe paused in his tracks. "If I told you, you wouldn't believe me."

"Try me."

Lupe's throat had gone dry. Without turning, he wouldn't be able to tell if his attacker was a specter or a mortal. Either way, there was a fifty-fifty chance his brain matter might decorate this man's walls.

"I'm hunting specters," Lupe told him, resigning himself to the truth. What other option was there? "Ghosts. I hate to tell you this, but your house is full of them. Somewhere around here are bad guys who live in the afterlife and are on the verge of being a real problem to New York's spectral relations."

He expected a laugh in response. A snort of derision, at least. Anything from a man who he had just informed about the world of ghosts. Lupe knew how ridiculous it sounded.

Out of the corner of his eye, Lupe saw Carolyn emerge at the top of the stairs, tucked around the corner and just out of the man's line of sight. Her eyes widened before she disappeared back through the door, hopefully to summon the others for help.

Instead, he was met with stony silence. Cold metal touched the back of his neck. "That doesn't sound ridiculous to me," the man crooned. "In fact, those specters you seek have employed me as a guardian to keep them safe, away from prying eyes like yours. You are the ones who have been following them, aren't you?"

Great, Belinda. Some subtlety you have with your work. They figured you out right away. Played you and me for fucking fools.

"Do you think I'd be stupid enough to stalk a specter?" Lupe asked.

"I think you're stupid enough to enter my home without permission," the man replied softly.

"Would you have let me in if I'd have knocked?"

"No."

"Well, there you are, then."

The barrel pressed more firmly into the nape of his neck. Lupe closed his eyes and took a steadying breath, thinking that really this could be his time. One twitch of the finger, and it was all over. Maybe he'd come back as a specter, or maybe he'd choose the abyss. Considering he had spent considerable time around specters, he realized now he hadn't ever considered the possibility that he could join them and walk among their ranks.

The possibility of an afterlife brought a surge of confidence back. He puffed out his chest and slowed his beating heart.

"They're not here, are they?" Lupe asked.

"Who?"

"The specters we followed. The ones who have been disrupting the peace. Attacking other specters and disabling them for days at a time for no real reason."

"Oh, there's a reason." The man coughed. "There's always a reason behind malice. You think because the Spectral Plane miraculously battled off the crown that it's all over? That the world can be sunshine and rainbows? What about all the other specters who are stepped on? All the ones who are ignored? All the specters who choose not to— *If you take ONE step closer, I will shoot. Do NOT tempt me.*"

His voice went up several notches. Lupe braved turning his head enough to see that Belinda and her thugs were creeping up on the man. They were only feet away from being able to seize the gun and disarm him, but now they froze.

"What are you?" Lupe asked.

"Same as you, I guess," the man replied. "A mortal with powers. Confused. Uncertain. That was until a group of specters showed me my place. Lit the darkness of my life with reason and understanding. You know we're a rare breed, don't you?"

"Becoming less rare by the second," Lupe muttered. He had always thought he might be the only conduit. There was a small part of him that wished that was true. It made him feel special and unique. Now he found that there was another just a few miles from where he had grown up and battled his own confusion.

"How about this?" Lupe kept his hands in the air and turned painfully slowly. He revolved until he was looking into the face of his attacker—a man, not much taller than him, with a white goatee, deep lines set into his forehead, and dark eyes.

The shotgun rested between his eyes. "We've got a lot in common. You can see and talk to specters, and I can do the same. Inside your house are five specters, all sworn to serve the Spectral Plane—"

"Scum," the man interjected, spitting as though it were an involuntary reflex.

"All sworn to *me*," Lupe continued, watching the man's face for any significant changes in attitude or demeanor. "Whatever the other specters are promising you, we can work out a new deal. Come to our side, and you'll be less likely to end up committing homicide and going to jail. We could use someone like you. Someone with your abilities would do well with us."

The man's eyes flickered back and forth. A slight tremble reverberated down to the end of the shotgun's barrel. "I can't."

"Why not?" Lupe asked, emboldened by the response.

The man hesitated. A small bead of sweat trickled down his forehead. "They have my wife."

"Your wife?" Carolyn asked before she could stop herself.

Lupe closed his eyes in annoyance, once more expecting the sound of the bullet as the man fired from fear.

Carolyn continued undeterred, "How can specters kidnap your wife?"

"You don't understand." The man's hands were trembling now. "My wife. She's… She's…"

"Dead?" Feng Mian asked softly.

The man swiveled his head, hunting for the source of the voice. His eyes were wide as he moved the shotgun away from Lupe, aiming it all around him as he spun.

When he spotted Feng Mian in the doorway on the far side of the room, he gasped and pulled the trigger as a series of fireworks exploded simultaneously outside.

Lupe threw himself to the floor with his hands over his ears. The specters darted forward, each of them doing their best to materialize in time to wrestle the gun away. Another shot went off, shattering the ceiling and sending down a shower of debris. A pipe burst and water joined the splinters of wood raining down on them.

Lupe used the moment of distraction to raise himself to his feet and dive at the man's legs. His shoulders connected with the man's knees, causing him to buckle and fall to the floor. His grip loosened on the gun, which was wet from the spraying pipe.

The specters relinquished the gun.

Lupe sat on top of him, desperately pinning his arms to his sides. The man looked up from the floor, his eyes wet with tears. Feng Mian had moved closer now, the bullet which had aimed in his direction doing nothing more than blowing a hole in the wall behind him.

Feng Mian stopped inches short of the man and knelt, his eyes glimmering with tears. His words were whispers. "My mother is dead?"

CHAPTER THIRTY

<u>Chinatown, New York, USA</u>

"This is my father, Feng Li," Feng Mian seethed.

The man studied Feng Mian with disbelieving eyes. "No! It's not possible. You…you…"

"Is Mom dead?" Feng Mian asked more firmly than before.

But as simple an answer as it would have been to give, the man neither confirmed nor denied the statement. His face melted from wonder to sadness, then to anger before he wrestled himself to his feet and stormed over to his son.

His fist swung, meeting nothing but air. Feng Mian stood passively, allowing his father to vent his anger. A left hook. A right hook. One after the other, until his father grunted with rage, picked up a small analog clock with a yin and yang picture behind the hands, and threw it across the room.

Cogs, springs, and various other components littered onto the floor after it hit the wall. The hissing of the pipe continued behind them.

"You've got a lot of nerve coming back here," Feng Mian's father growled.

Feng Mian cupped his hand around his father's throat. Although he wasn't material enough to inflict pain or constrict the airways, his father reacted to the spectral chill by raising himself onto his toes. His skin prickled as the icy feel of Feng Mian's hand pulsed through his body.

"Is. She. Dead?"

Feng Mian's father didn't blink as he nodded.

"Did you—" Feng couldn't finish the sentence.

Lupe watched beside the other specters, unable to understand what was going on. In all the weeks he had known Feng Mian, the specter had hardly shown a drop of emotion. Now they'd stumbled across his father, and the anger emanating between them both was palpable.

His father took a deep breath. "I…"

"Did you murder her?" Feng Mian shot, his voice stern and authoritative.

His father's lip curled into a sneer. "She wouldn't let it go. She was going to tell them. She was going to tell the police. I couldn't allow that. I couldn't. You must understand."

"Understand?" Feng Mian echoed, his words leaking through his lips like gas through a faulty pipe. "I understand nothing of this. You taught us honor. You taught us loyalty. You spoke of family and love and the bond of blood, yet you cut us down like branches in an orchard. You are shame embodied."

Hatred seethed between Feng Mian and his father. Lupe couldn't understand what the hell was going on. This was not how he had expected the night to go.

"What do you want from me?" Feng Mian's father asked reluctantly. "I did what I had to do."

"No," Feng Mian countered. "You didn't. You did what you *wanted* to do, and we paid the price." He took a step back. "Tell us where she is. We will find her. We will free her."

Relief flooded his father's face. "Oh, thank you, son. Thank you. Please, I need her back. There are a thousand things I wish to say to her. A thousand things to apologize for. I never meant to—"

"*Where is she?*"

Lupe imagined he saw a dark cloud forming above Feng Mian's head, a shadow over the room. Outside, fireworks continued to explode, followed by cheery "oohs!" and rounds of applause.

"Come. I'll show you." His father turned to the specters. "I'll show all of you."

Lupe hid the shotgun in the folds of his coat as they followed Feng Mian's father out into the streets.

The Manhattan Bridge was a thoroughfare through the heart of Chinatown. Along its edge, a pedestrian footpath overlooked a series of rundown apartments, shops, and offices that had become targets for New York's juvenile graffiti artists over the years.

At the top of a five-story apartment building, the words "1800VIOLENCE" were scrawled in crude black paint. Beneath that in the same primal script was, "1800MALPRACTICE," followed by a series of colorful tags by artists.

These Lupe studied by the bright glow of headlights as they walked along the bridge in the brisk night. The celebrations and fireworks were behind them, and in front of them, the city opened up again. On the left-hand side a little farther on from the graffiti-adorned buildings, a block of high-rise apartments at least forty stories tall pierced the skyline like an abandoned dragon's tooth from ages long past.

Feng Mian's father stopped on the bridge and pointed at the building. "There. Straight up to the top. There you'll find the Dragon."

"The Dragon?" Lupe asked. "Who's the Dragon?"

"I don't know," Feng Mian's father replied. "No one does, not really. All I know is that she is on the top of that tower, and I don't have the ability to fight the guards."

"Oh, you just know the whole thing is packed with them," Carolyn whined. "I've seen *The Raid* movies. Every damn floor will have at least sixty men ready to kick ass. Trained in Ninjutsu or Muay-Thai." She sighed. "Any of you guys got a history in martial arts?"

Feng Mian's father smiled. "My son does." His smile faded when he saw Feng Mian's molten stare. "Again, I'm sorry."

Feng Mian returned his studious gaze to the apartment building. "There's no way we're getting in there as we are. We'd need intel, and someone on our side who can sneak us in. We need to disguise ourselves to infiltrate the security, or we'll get nowhere." He turned to Lupe. "We need backup."

Lupe let out a long breath. "I was hoping it wouldn't come to that."

Carolyn chuckled and clapped her hands. "Oh, goody. We're reuniting the gang?"

Feng Mian's father raised an eyebrow. "The gang?"

"Let's just say we know a few guys who would be well-suited to a mission just like this," Lupe informed him. He took one more look at the tower. Lights dotted windows up its length. At the top floor apartment, a silhouette passed in front of the window, then disappeared. "Don't worry, Dragon. We'll be back."

As they turned to leave, Feng Mian's father spoke up. "Can I come with you? Please?"

Feng Mian paused and cast an angry glance at his father. "Why should I take you with me?"

His father bowed his head. "I don't know what'll happen if I'm left alone and they find out about this. They've got other humans working with them, too. They'll probably kill me."

"Good," Feng Mian stated flatly. "Then perhaps you will know how it feels."

Lupe and Carolyn exchanged glances. Belinda and her men remained silent.

Feng Mian turned to face his father, nostrils flared wide. "You may come. You may not talk. You will listen to us and obey our orders, and you will cause no problems. Got it?"

His father gave a small nod.

Feng Mian took a step closer and showed his father the meaning of honor. "No matter what you did, family is important. You taught me that. I will not sink to your level. Ever."

· · ·

Washington DC, USA

Over the course of the next few days, Jennie familiarized herself with the SIA headquarters. As with all new premises, the longer she spent there, the smaller it felt. It was a sensation she had experienced many times before and had come to expect.

Her first visit to Buckingham Palace had been much the same. As the large front doors opened up to reveal the grandiose entrance hall, she had felt like a mouse. A tiny version of herself stared in open wonder at the chandeliers, the chintzy decor, the immaculate red carpets. When the door closed behind her, it had made her feel as though the place had swallowed her whole.

Each step was a discovery, each new room a new page in her adventure. Summoned by the paranormal queen, Jennie had been inducted into the world of royalty over the course of weeks as her training and her work for the paranormal court had begun.

Yet, as the weeks turned into months and the months turned into years, the world around her had shrunk. The chambers that had seemed like enormous caverns of wealth before had begun to feel like the norm. The corridors were reduced in length, and the ceilings pressed down on her.

Now just four days into her new role with the SIA, which had much less glitz and glamor than the palace, headquarters had begun to take on the same reductive quality.

Not that Jennie veered off-course. During that time, Jennie had worked day and night to ensure she put her mark on the SIA compound.

Special Agent in Charge Kurt Rogers remained on-site throughout this period, regularly meeting with Jennie to check on her progress. She roamed the halls and had begun to learn each agent's name. She spent time in the labs with Hendrick and Proctor, discovering the abilities of his team as they worked to solve some of the problems the SIA had been having with their equipment.

She had her own quarters, but they were hardly inhabited. Since Hendrick's arrival at the SIA, he had provided her with elixirs that kept her fueled and provided the benefits of sleep, but in the form of liquid stimulation.

Occasionally, she would catch Hendrick clocking out of his duties, and she would spend an hour or two catching up and talking about old times. Hendrick sure had some stories to tell, and Jennie relished returning the favor by regaling him with her deeds.

During this time, SIA agents were sent to monitor the Baltimore area and report any occurrences or strange goings-on that might in some way be linked to the Umbra. Setting up intelligence within the city center was a gamble, given that they were all aware of the influence of Brendan Koa and his group on the city.

Not that they had seen hide nor hair of him. Over the past year, Agent Rogers had done what he could to keep track of his activity but didn't have adequate resources to track him around the clock. Now it seemed that Koa was gone. In the wind. Three days into their stakeout in Baltimore, the agents reported back nothing that could be linked in any way to Koa.

"Impossible," Rogers mused in one of his evening catch-ups with Jennie. "Simply impossible. How can a man vanish without a trace?"

"Easily," Jennie replied. "A snake just needs to know how to lose itself in the undergrowth."

On the fifth day of Jennie's work with the SIA, the first real improvements came to the organization. Proctor's team had been working on three major developments: SI goggles with the capacity for audio function, wall paneling that repelled specters and ensured that nothing could pass in or out of the room, and tasers that had the capacity to shock and stun specters when shot from close range.

"It's taken some work," Proctor told them excitedly, presenting the tech to a panel composed of Jennie, Hopkins, Rhone, and Daggro. SAC Rogers had been unable to attend due to other priorities involving meeting with central federal divisions. "But we got there."

He unclasped a metallic briefcase and revealed a pair of goggles that looked nearly identical to the previous pairs they had manufactured for their staff.

"SI goggles?" Hopkins sneered. "Proctor, I have three pairs of those in my bag. Tell me you're not wasting my time."

"Not at all." Proctor beamed. Over the past few days, he had hardly slept, and the bags beneath his eyes were like heavy, wet sacks.

Jennie might have wondered if he had been drinking Hendrick's potions if she hadn't been present when Hendrick first suggested he take them to assist in his work. Proctor had slapped the vial out of the pudgy man's hand and it had soared across the room, smashing on the floor as a thin heated vapor rose lazily into the air behind it.

"These are SI goggles 2.0," Proctor clarified. When Hendrick moved forward to take them from the case, Proctor slapped his hand away, then changed his expression and smiled at his superiors.

Proctor held up the goggles and rotated them in the air. They were, in fact, near-identical. The only real difference was a small black nodule on the side of the lenses.

"Press this button here to activate audio mode." Proctor demonstrated by tapping a button. "A small antenna pops out here, and then just shimmy the goggles onto your face and ensure that the strap covers your ears."

"Smart." Rhone nodded.

"Oh, it's more than smart," Proctor declared. "You see, it's all about being able to tune into the right frequencies. We experimented with a variety of metals, both elemental and compound, in order to achieve the finest transmission of audio through the rod. It was then a case of studying and understanding the frequencies emitted by specters and applying that knowledge to fine-tune the goggles. Now, here's where it gets interesting."

"Can you show us that it works?" Hopkins interjected dryly.

Proctor nodded. "Of course."

He handed the goggles to Hopkins. Clearly not yet ready to trust Proctor's work, Hopkins handed them to Daggro, who had been noticeably absent from headquarters over the last few days.

Daggro begrudgingly pulled the strap over her head. She lowered the goggles to her eyes and pressed the power button.

"Don't we need a specter here to prove these work?" Daggro

grunted.

"Of course!" Proctor proclaimed, realizing how stupid he had been. "Rogue, isn't your friend with you?"

Jennie turned to Baxter, who was sitting beside her. "Well, yes. He's right here."

Daggro huffed. "Fat lot of good these do."

Proctor whirled to Hendrick. "You said these were ready."

"They are." Hendrick rolled his eyes and waddled over to Daggro. From where she sat at the table, all Jennie could see was Hendrick's head and upper torso casually bobbing along as though he were on a raft out on the open sea.

When he eventually made it to Daggro, she recoiled. He moved behind her, raised his hand, and slapped the back of her head.

Daggro's face was so contorted with rage that her eyes couldn't open anymore.

"Loose connection," Hendrick muttered. "Sometimes it just needs a quick jolt. Should be in working order now."

Daggro tore her eyes open and was set to whirl on Hendrick when she glanced past Jennie and stopped with her eyes fixed on the place where Baxter was sitting.

"There." Hendrick pointed at Baxter. "Visible now?"

Daggro nodded.

"Baxter, say something," Jennie encouraged.

The room held its collective breath. Even Hopkins was more alert.

Baxter considered his words. "Agent Daggro?"

Daggro stared blankly.

"Well?" Jennie pressed.

"I don't think she can hear me." Baxter leaned closer. "Agent Daggro, can you repeat the word 'pumpernickel?'"

Again, Daggro didn't reply.

Emboldened by this, Baxter continued. "In that case, Agent Daggro, I want you to know that you are the most despicable person I have ever met. Your manners are atrocious, you couldn't care less about Jennie's integration into this organization, and you can't get your ego out of your ass. If you could hear me right now, I'd love to say how much of a colossal bitch you are, and how I can't wait for the day you die and choose to become a specter, so I can finally smack you upside your head with the back of my hand. I now live for nothing more than the sweet satisfaction of teaching you decency and morals so that you may in some way become a normal human being. Which you wouldn't be. Because you'd be dead."

He sat back in his chair, hands laced on his stomach. A small smile played on his lips.

"Anything?" Hopkins asked, his own SI goggles 1.0 on his face.

Daggro's face did something strange. Over the course of the next few seconds, her cheeks bloomed with crimson, the color spreading to the rest of her face like giant drops of ink on paper. Her eyes narrowed, and Baxter and Jennie understood that she had absolutely heard him. She'd heard every last word.

"What did he say?" Hopkins urged.

When Daggro spoke, it was between clenched teeth. Her knuckles grew white from clasping her hands so tightly. "He said… He said that it was great to finally get a chance to talk to me, rather than us just passing each other like two ships in the night."

Baxter grinned awkwardly, while Jennie stifled a laugh behind her hand.

Hopkins thanked Proctor and Hendrick—particularly Hendrick—for their work on the tech, and asked about updates for the rest.

Proctor proceeded to showcase a series of tiles that had been manufactured to prevent a phenomenon that he had decided to call "spectral leakage."

At that, Jennie had to hold herself back from offering a joke to the room in which she would go on to describe spectral defecation and urination.

Proctor allowed Baxter to demonstrate that not only could the tiles not be penetrated by specters, but they would also repel them, thanks to an additional component worked into the base compound.

Baxter discovered this to be true when his hand met the material. His whole body tensed as he was pushed a foot back from the others, and this time Daggro smiled.

Hopkins then gave instructions to Rhone to ensure that these tiles, once manufactured in bulk, be installed in every interrogation room and cell across the facility.

The final demonstration was underwhelming. Although they had found a way to imbue the tiles with specter repellent, the tasers left a lot to be desired. They were an early prototype, but after they shot the prongs toward a tentative Baxter, they merely melted straight through him and landed impotently on the floor.

"Two out of three ain't bad," Rhone offered.

Hopkins nodded. "This is good. With the right resources and the right oversight and guidance, we'll be leaps and bounds ahead of the UK before we know it."

Rhone raised his head. "With all due respect, sir, isn't the paranormal court our ally? Shouldn't we share this information with them?"

Hopkins ran a hand through his hair, disturbing the neat grooves. "The paranormal court has gone radio-silent. We've tried several times to contact them, but there's been no response."

"Why?" Daggro asked with genuine concern in her voice for a change. "Any indication as to the reason?"

"None," Hopkins stated. "We have our suspicions, of course, but no solid evidence. All I can say is that we keep operating and working on strengthening our independence, and we should be fine. They may have opened the door for us, but we're not relying on them to house and feed us, too. We are Americans. We fought for freedom, and freedom we shall have."

Although no one would say it aloud, Jennie had a sense that she knew what the reason for their silence was. It didn't seem to be a coincidence that the moment Jennie insinuated herself with the SIA, the paranormal court had fallen off the radar.

This suspicion was confirmed when Hopkins' eyes met her own, his silence saying a thousand words.

Please don't do anything stupid, Jennie thought as she wondered what was going on in the queen's head. *We had a deal, girl. Don't go backing out now. It won't end well for you, I promise you that.*

CHAPTER THIRTY-ONE

The Plaza, New York, USA

Preparations took a little longer than planned.

There was no easy way to amass the right specters. That was still a problem that needed figuring out. While specters had the capacity to dial their frequencies into modern society's mobile phones, the frequencies varied from specter to specter.

Specters in the know would often practice connecting via spectral frequencies in the same way mortals would exchange phone numbers. However, specters could accidentally tap into the frequencies of others on rare occasions. These moments would often be met with mirth and the exchange of pleasantries before the specters tried once again to reach their desired contact.

This meant that a specter could only connect with one specter at a time. There was no mass communication system in place, at least in New York, through which Lupe could put a call out to his required specters. He had to rely on the good old-fashioned method of word of mouth.

Over the course of the week, specters came from across the city. They hovered around the Plaza and inhabited its many rooms, unbeknownst to the mortal occupiers. Lupe continued his preparations as more specters came together, sending specters out to watch the apartment block and keep an eye on the activity inside.

One core advantage they did have was in the form of Angus and Mona, two of the Obake who had accompanied Jennie and her crew from England. These he had employed to follow and take out specters as they left the building, then take their shape in order to infiltrate and collect insider knowledge.

Their first foray had been twenty-four hours ago. The pair had yet to return.

There was no time to worry about that now, though. As the sun began to descend once more above Central Park, Lupe found himself in the middle of yet another heated discussion with Tanya.

"No. I won't tell you again." Tanya's voice was soft, yet firm.

"Why not?" Lupe asked. "How are we supposed to find out all she can do if we don't put her out on the job?"

Tanya glanced down at Sandra, who was busy practicing her letters on a large sheet of white paper. So far, she had spelled her own name, as well as a variety of three-letter words; dog, cat, pig, bug, and cow. "She's only a child, Lupe. What do you think you're going to do with her? Barge in and use her as a human shield? These people are animals. They're murderers. They're criminals, and they wouldn't be above hurting her and taking her for themselves."

Lupe rubbed his temples. "She exorcised Worthington single-handedly. She sent a bunch of specters into the beyond and ended the battle that was being waged in the center of Times Square. I think she can handle an apartment block, backed up by a hundred of our best fighters."

Tanya violently shook her head. "No. She could die."

Lupe bit his tongue. Ever since Tanya had adopted Sandra and chosen to be her guardian, they had allowed her to play the mother. To look after Sandra and induct her into the world. They had tiptoed around her and let her grow close enough to believe she was her mother, but that needed to stop.

"She's already dead!" The other specters currently talking in Jennie's apartment stopped their chatter and turned their heads,

Carolyn, Feng Mian, and his father among them. "She died *hundreds* of years ago. The worst they could do is exorcise her, and unless I'm mistaken, it takes a powerful-ass specter to exorcise another specter." He turned to the others for reassurance.

"He's right," Carolyn agreed, cautiously walking toward Tanya. "Look, it's great that you want to protect her and teach her and be there for her, but Sandra is one of us. She's a specter. She has less to fear from being shot at than you do."

Tanya's eyes lowered to the young girl, who had taken to squiggling in red pen along the right-hand side of the page.

"If anything, they need to fear *her*," Lupe asserted more calmly. "She has the ability to exorcise, and she can control it. She's the greatest weapon we've got."

"She's not a weapon," Tanya combatted, feeling like she was losing the fight. "She's a girl."

"A spectral girl," Carolyn reiterated. "Tanya, we can find a balance. She needs the mortal side you offer—the nurturing, reassuring, teacher side. But she also needs to come to grips with her powers. She's been stuck inside ever since the day we left for London. She needs to spread her wings and realize what she's capable of."

Sandra picked up a black pen and scratched its tip on the paper, drawing dark circles on various locations of her creation.

Tanya chewed her lip, her brow furrowed. There was sadness in her eyes as she glanced at Sandra and tousled her hair. It was only when she turned from Sandra to the drawing that her expression changed.

"What's that?" she asked.

Sandra continued scribbling, the excess ink so wet on the page that it looked as if it were about to tear through at any moment. "The Shadows," she replied.

Tanya exchanged glances with Lupe, then leaned closer to the image. Sandra finished her drawing and passed it roughly to her surrogate mother. The exchange was so quick that it caught Tanya off-guard. She caught the paper in her hands and felt the damp black ink on her palms.

Lupe and Carolyn gathered closer as the paper shook in Tanya's hands.

On the page, Sandra had drawn a crude Chinese red dragon, stretching and coiling in bold strokes of red. In its mouth were large white fangs, and it had blazing yellow eyes.

Or, at least, it used to have.

Where the eyes should have been were black whirlpools of ink. All along the dragon's back were thick black lines, as though the dragon was being chased by its own shadow.

"Sandra?" Tanya asked uncertainly. "What is this, sweetie?"

Sandra looked up with baby-doll eyes, her expression passive. She shrugged. "The Dragon's Shadow."

Lupe opened his mouth to ask another question when his phone began vibrating on the table. He pulled himself away, picked up the handset, and saw the caller ID on the screen.

"It's Jennie," Lupe told them.

Washington DC, USA

Jennie hung up the phone and felt the added weight on her soul.

Things could never stay quiet; that was something she'd learned over the years. You could spend a lifetime putting out fires, and there'd always be someone to start another.

The call with Lupe had been satisfying in one sense. It was nice to reconnect and talk with the others and discover they were okay. She was comfortable, knowing she had left New York to the Spectral Plane. They would do whatever it took to maintain peace where possible, which gave Jennie time to continue building her relationship with the SIA and working out what the hell was happening in Baltimore.

After the display of tech from Proctor and Hendrick, Jennie had stayed to sit in on further updates from Hopkins. As it transpired, Baltimore was becoming a hotbed of spectral activity. In the last few days, reports of inexplicable disturbances in mortal residences had risen, and their intelligence had shown that more mortals were going missing across the city. Although there was no pattern to the disappearances, Jennie and the SIA felt that there was no coincidence in the sudden increase in cases. Based on what Jennie had seen on her last visit to Baltimore, it would do them well to scour the city and act fast in order to try to bring peace once more.

The problem was knowing where to start.

Much worse than that was the strange feeling that churned Jennie's gut after her conversation with Lupe. He had described Sandra's drawing and sent a photo of it to her phone. The dragon was surprisingly detailed for a young girl to have drawn. The shadows that danced across its body and inhabited its eyes seemed more like a living force than an absence of light.

Shadows.

Jennie shook her head to clear her thoughts.

Toward the end of the SIA intelligence briefing, Jennie had made the bold suggestion that she should take a small team of SIA agents and search the city. Since most of her previous missions involved getting her hands dirty, she had found she was beginning to itch to leave the facility and go on the hunt.

Despite Daggro's low-level grumbling every time Jennie spoke, her request was granted, and now Rhone led Jennie and Baxter through the corridors toward the agents' briefing room so she could meet the troops and get everything in line for the mission ahead.

Rhone paused outside the door and scratched his cheek. "Word of warning. These guys are tough to please. First impressions are everything. Think you got what it takes?"

Jennie smirked. "This isn't my first rodeo."

Rhone smirked. "A Texas gal, are we?"

Jennie laughed. "Do I sound Texan to you?"

Rhone chuckled, then turned. Before he could even bend for the retinal scanner, Jennie latched onto Baxter and melted through the door.

Five agents in black SIA uniforms were sitting on chairs around the room. They were in the middle of good-naturedly ribbing an agent who sat at the edge of the room and batted away their words as though they were nothing.

"It took me six months of training to get a place in this unit," a woman with cropped blonde hair bragged. "Six months of rigorous fitness tests, intelligence training, and working with the new equipment." She shook her head and laughed. "How long you been here, rookie?"

"About four weeks," Jack Hansen replied. "Look, it's not my fault. Some people got it, some people don't. I've got it, okay?" He smiled along with the others, used to the shit talk that was a constant part of life in a unit.

A man with biceps that looked like they wanted to tear out of his sleeves and introduce themselves turned his chair around and straddled it backward. "Whose dick did you have to suck? Was it Rhone's? I bet it was Rhone's."

"Nah, Daggro's!" another woman with her hair pulled back in a tight ponytail exclaimed. "Gotta be Daggro's. When was the last time you think she got laid? No wonder she's so uptight all the time."

Clive Bannon waved their exuberance down with a chuckle. "C'mon, guys. They'll be here any minute. You know these walls aren't soundproof, don't you?"

"Or specter-proof." The agents all turned in alarm when Jennie materialized in the middle of the room.

The three agents unused to Jennie's abilities scrambled for their guns. Before they could shoot her, the door opened and Rhone stepped into the room.

Rhone fanned his hands. "Calm down, agents. This woman is not a threat, no matter how risky she chooses for her entrances to be." He stopped by her side. "This is Jennie King. She'll be running point on the operation you're about to embark on." He pointed to each agent in turn, starting with the ponytailed woman.

"Jennie, this is Natalia Chernov, a sniper with a rifle and equipped with a dagger for a tongue." He turned to the ripped man. "This is David Leroy. Don't let his physique fool you. His bulk doesn't slow him down. He's incredibly fast."

David grinned. "They call me 'the Rolling Stone.'"

"Why?" Jennie asked.

"Because when I get rolling downhill, I don't stop."

Natalia rolled her eyes. Despite the Russian influence of her surname, her accent was all American. "Please stop. No one has ever called you that. Stop trying to make it a thing."

"And this," Rhone continued, trying to keep the introductions on track. "This is Sade Burnwell. She's been with the SIA almost as long as Rogers has. She'll be able to show you the ropes and keep this motley crew in order."

Sade saluted. "I've got your back." She blew a bubble with her gum and popped it with a loud crack.

"You not going to introduce the noobs?" Natalia chuckled.

"No need for introductions," Jennie told them. "Jack and Clive have already worked by my side, haven't you, boys? We took down an entire cult in New Jersey, and they helped me bring down a *sturmgeist*."

Jack smirked triumphantly at Natalia, whose face had dropped.

"What's a *sturmgeist*?" she asked.

"Technically, that's classified." Rhone shot Jennie a look. "Why don't I leave you folks to get acquainted? Jennie, look after them. They're good fodder."

"Fodder?" David's eyebrow raised.

"He means we're dispensable," Natalia replied. "Bullet bait. Sacks of flesh to do his bidding. That about right, Rhone?"

Rhone grinned and left the room without another word.

Jack shuffled in his chair. "What you got for us, boss?"

Jennie raised a finger. "Let's get this clear from the start. I am no one's boss here. I am not employed by the SIA. I am, however, the lucky leader of you guys for the next few days while we do a little bit of exploration and see what we can dig up. You will find that I work differently from the SIA. My methods will be unorthodox compared to what you are used to. Agents Hansen and Bannon know this well."

Jack nodded eagerly, while Clive winked at Natalia.

"Usc this as your chance to spread your wings and expand your knowledge about the spectral world," Jennie continued. "I'm not sure what types of assignments you've been given so far, but I can assure you, you still have no idea what the spectral world holds. When I'm done with you guys, you'll know a little more. Not a lot, but a little. Got it?"

Natalia caught David's eye, a look of disbelief on her face. "She's not serious, right? You're saying that all that training we did over the last half a year was wasted effort?"

David's face grew stern. He folded his arms and sat back in his chair. "What's the point in training and protocol if it's all going to go out the window? Who are you to tell us what we can and can't do?"

Jennie fixed David with a stare. "I'm the woman the head of this agency has agreed is going to guide you into this new era." A small grin grew on her face. She liked a challenge. "Your training has not been wasted. What you know will be useful, but there is always more to learn."

Jennie turned to the small black box Rhone had left at her earlier request. She thumped the box on the table, opened it, and threw a pair of goggles to each agent in turn. "Brand-new kit. Hot off the press."

Natalia scoffed. "New? We've had SI goggles for almost a week now. Girl, you need to get the latest info before you try to show off."

"Shut up and put them on," Jennie told her.

Natalia's smile faded. She didn't like that one bit.

David chuckled when they placed the goggles on their heads. "You know, for someone who's supposed to be down with specters, it's funny that you don't realize there's one behind you."

"Oh, Baxter?" Jennie asked with feigned surprise. "He's a good friend of mine. It's actually because of him that I was able to become spectral and appear in the room. Watch."

They didn't blink as Jennie latched onto Baxter with a string of spectral energy that glowed white-hot in their lenses. As she turned spectral, Jennie's color changed and became a ghostly white to match.

"Nice," Sade muttered.

"Okay, I admit that's impressive," Natalia muttered. "But again, what's so great about these goggles? They do exactly the same as our last pair. Maybe the vision is a bit clearer, but there's nothing else I can see."

"What about this?" David reached to the side and tugged out the small antenna.

"Baxter," Jennie urged. "Say hi to our new friends."

Baxter glanced at Jennie, a little off-balance from being put on the spot. "Hey?"

As the sound transferred into their ears, Natalia and David let out surprised gasps. Clive grinned broadly, and Jack stood up. "Baxter? I can hear you."

"Yeah." Baxter rubbed the back of his neck. "Pretty cool, huh?"

Sade's grin stretched from ear to ear, but she sat back coolly in her chair and stroked her chin. "Okay, I like this. Jennie, you have our attention."

CHAPTER THIRTY-TWO

<u>Baltimore, Maryland, USA</u>

They took two cars. Jennie and Baxter took the Mustang, with Jack and Clive in the back, while Sade drove her Dodge, ferrying Natalia and David with her.

"Man, their faces," Jack mused, resting his elbow against the window as the car ate up the road. "Unbelievable. Those three are all ex-FBI agents. They're used to shocking situations. I don't think their jaws have dropped like that since... Well, Clive probably knows better than me."

Jennie glanced in her rearview mirror toward where Clive was sitting quietly.

His expression was contemplative, his eyebrows knitted together when he was pulled from his thoughts. "I don't know them well. The FBI is a big organization. We crossed paths a few times, but that's about it. Good people, as far as I know."

Jack seemed a little disappointed that Clive hadn't continued his assessment of the others. "Still, it was funny to watch."

"They been giving you a hard time?" Jennie asked.

"No more than I expected." Jack leaned between Jennie's and Baxter's headrests. Since receiving the SI goggles 2.0, he hadn't taken them off, making sure to include Baxter in every conversation. "It's normal for the team to want to get a measure of the character of new recruits. It's not their fault I'm one of the freshest on the force and have already been inducted into the big leagues."

"You earned it," Clive assured him. "Thanks to your help at Batsto, you probably already have more firsthand experience with specters than a number of the seasoned recruits."

Jack's lip curled into a smile. "Thanks, that means a lot."

"Same goes for you, Chief," Jennie told Clive. "Both of you have shown you're made of solid stuff. It was a special request of mine to have you both on the team. You're more capable than you think."

Jack's smile remained. Clive's face looked pained, as though he wasn't used to taking compliments and didn't know how to process them.

"What about Ruby?" Jack asked. "Ruby was there from the start. Why didn't you pick her for the team?"

Jennie was silent for a moment. She had considered putting Ruby into the action, but it just didn't seem right. Although she had shown courage and bravery by rejecting Meister Donavon's ritual and granting Clive time to escape, she was only a kid. The coming missions would require much more experience if they were to make heads or tails of them.

"She's too young," Jennie told them, deciding to be honest. "Besides, during my talk with Rogers, I managed to negotiate and get her an analyst place with the agency."

"Oh?" Jack encouraged.

Jennie didn't sate his curiosity. "Don't worry, chaps. You'll see her again, I'm sure. I'm sure her knowledge of the Shadows will be useful in the days ahead."

Baxter, who had been studying an image on the screen of Jennie's phone, glanced up. "Do you really think the two are connected?"

Jennie hit the outer lane and overtook a Chevrolet, packed tight with luggage and two small children in the back. A red-faced mother was screaming something at the father as he white-knuckled the steering wheel and engaged in a staring match with the road.

"I don't know," Jennie admitted. "It's something to be cautious about. We don't know the full extent of Sandra's abilities. Why would she have added all that detail if it meant nothing?"

"Creativity?" Baxter shrugged, though the uncertainty was clear in his words.

"I don't think so. I think we just need to be cautious. The US is a big place, and New York is but a small percentage of that. We can't rule out any possibilities at this point."

Jack and Clive checked out the drawing on Jennie's phone as they closed the distance between Washington and Baltimore. That triggered questions about Jennie's activity in New York.

Jennie refused to divulge any real information; she did speak fondly about her friends there.

"Why didn't you bring them here with you?" Clive asked as he handed the phone back to Baxter.

"Because New York needs them right now," Jennie replied.

She refused to go into more information than that.

It was around an hour later that they arrived in Baltimore. The SIA had rented an empty business unit in Butcher's Hill for their agents to use as a base of operations.

The unit took up one floor of a twelve-story high-rise. The building stuck out like a literal sore thumb, and it had clearly been some time since there had been any kind of renovation work done there.

At first, Jennie wasn't sure they were in the right place. They put jackets on to cover the "SIA" patches on their uniforms and exited the cars into the brisk morning air.

They were greeted at the door by a man wearing a maroon cardigan with a white-collared shirt beneath, and a pair of slacks. To Jennie, he looked like a run-of-the-mill father who had prepared for his first parent-teacher meeting and was ready to ask about little Tommy's progress in the third grade.

When he led them to the fifth floor, Jennie realized the mistake she had made. All the agents were out of uniform and deep undercover. The office was filled with aged desks stacked with paperwork. Charts lined the walls with sales projections and targets, as well as the occasional inspiration poster telling their staff to "Keep their heads high, for only in looking at the sky, can we aim for the stars."

It was only when Jennie looked at the computer screens that she saw the nature of the business was vastly different from the facade. Anyone able to look in through the large glass-paneled windows would see nothing more than a small corporation holding onto its dollars, while inside, the agents were busy combing articles, hacking phones, and putting calls in to their people in the field.

"Mrs. King?" A solid woman in black slacks and a blue shirt that was two sizes too small came to greet them.

"Actually, it's 'Miss,'" Jennie replied, taking her hand and shaking it.

"Apologies, Miss King. I'm Hannah Drampton, supervisory special agent of the outreach efforts here in Baltimore." She scanned the agents up and down. "Nice to finally meet you."

Jennie beamed. "Likewise."

Agent Drampton eyed her suspiciously. "You have no idea who I am, do you?"

Jennie shook her head. "Not a clue."

Drampton laughed. "I like your honesty. Come, let me give you the latest on what's been going down in Baltimore."

Chinatown, New York, USA

The Spectral Plane approached the apartment block from the west, moving into the trailing light from the setting sun. If anyone was to look their way, the light would be far more likely to dazzle the viewers and block the sight of any and all specters, but that wasn't the only precaution they took.

They waited a mile away, gathering on the rooftops where they could see the Dragon's apartment block like a needle pointing into the sky. Behind it, the sky was bruised and fading into darkness. Soon they saw the speckle of lights flickering on across the floors, including the top floor.

The Spectral Plane had taken to calling it the "Dragon's Den."

Angus was the one to coin the name. He had returned with Paige not long after first light with as much intel as they could gather. The pair of them detailed the security inside, listing the floors where security was heaviest, the places where residents lived in the building, what kinds of weapons the mortals and the specters carried—because there were mortals involved in there, too—and much more.

When it came to a description of the Dragon, however, the pair had nothing to share.

"We couldn't get close enough," Angus admitted, a frown on his face. "We tried. We really did. He stays at the top of the tower and doesn't leave. Everyone else does his bidding."

Carolyn laughed. "Sounds like Jabba the Hut."

Only a handful of specters understood. Many were too old at the time of their deaths to have seen the *Star Wars* saga. Tanya had brought a few of her best mortals from the original Spectral Plane, and they understood, but they did not laugh.

So they had drawn up maps. They had debated and planned and talked, then debated some more. By late afternoon, they had gathered a hundred specters together and took to the streets, and all that was left was for the light to fade.

"You ready for this?" Lupe asked Tanya, the wind blowing his cloak.

Tanya took a deep breath. "I guess I don't have too much choice." She placed a hand on Sandra's shoulder and waited.

This is the hardest part, Lupe thought. *The wait. Action is easy since adrenaline keeps you going, but this part...*

Twenty minutes later, the sun had set. Lupe called to the Spectral Plane and they took to the streets, dividing into small groups so they could surround the place.

It was time to take it by storm.

Baltimore, Maryland, USA

Drampton pointed to the image of a black-painted semi-truck with a large metallic grill, projected onto the wall. "Agents on the northern side of the Harbor Tunnel have clocked a number of trucks and vans making frequent rounds throughout the day."

"It may be nothing, but DMV checks have come back. They're unregistered vehicles, and they're making a regular appearance as far as tracking shows. Usually late at night or early in the morning, when traffic is quiet."

"How many of them are there?" Jennie asked, folding her arms and squinting at the image.

"Around half a dozen trucks, maybe a dozen or so vans."

"I bet the Harbor Tunnel loves them," Natalia commented. "The amount of change they must be handing over to get through the toll."

"That was our trigger," Drampton informed them, adjusting her pants before pressing a clicker to change the image. The next image was a long-distance shot of a man leaning his elbow out of the toll booth, and a driver in the cabin of the black semi-truck. The driver lifted his shades and held up a small plastic card to the toll booth attendant.

"ID pass?" David suggested.

"Definitely not," Drampton replied. "As far as we can find out, all Harbor Tunnel toll booth employees are instructed to accept nothing except cash or card transactions. There's no policy or intel anywhere that suggests any kind of pass."

Jack asked if ex-employees were exempt from the toll.

Drampton shook her head. "Not to our knowledge. Even so, the employees don't carry ID cards. They have lanyards with metallic fobs to log into the register when they need to. Other than that, it's as simple as sitting back and collecting cash."

Jennie ran a hand through her hair. "So, something is going on there?"

"I suppose that might just be. It could be to do with Umbra. It could be nothing more than part of a trade deal that hasn't been cleared with the proper authorities or listed as a perk on their website. Either way, it's worth a look."

Jennie asked what time the semis had been seen most often. Drampton gave her a detailed sheet of all sightings over the past three days, as well as an average of when the optimum time to spot them would be.

"Evening?" Jennie moaned, reading the list. "Well, that cuts right into my favorite time of day."

"You're a night owl?" David asked with a wink.

"*Carpe noctem*," Jennie told him. "*Carpe noctem*."

CHAPTER THIRTY-THREE

<u>**Chinatown, New York, USA**</u>

The front of the building was vaguely lit by an aged security light. The plastic shade was coated in years of dust and muted the light, leaving the three men standing out front and smoking cigarettes in an almost fantastical haze.

"Targets acquired." Lupe looked through the window of the sedan parked roughly thirty meters away, thinking they had done well to get as close as they had without raising the alarm.

"They're mortals," Tanya muttered.

Carolyn chuckled. "I know I've been dead for the smallest amount of time, but I already find it weird when a mortal refers to other mortals as mortals, you know?"

Lupe slowly shook his head, gaze fixed on the three. "I'm afraid I didn't get a word of that."

Carolyn rolled her eyes at Lupe. "Why call them mortals? Just call them people. You're mortals, too."

"Is now really the time for this?" Tanya asked. Beside her, Sandra remained tucked out of the way. All around the perimeter, they could just make out the shape of the other specters waiting for their cue.

"Remember," Feng Mian whispered, "subtlety is the key."

Lupe grunted his agreement. The men raised cigarettes to their lips and let out soft plumes of smoke into the night.

"Gotcha. Tanya, it's time."

Tanya closed her eyes and steeled herself. "Is this really the best way?"

"They're hot-blooded men. Of course, it is."

Tanya shook her head. "In an era where women are fighting for equality. Men are so dumb."

She checked her reflection in the sedan's window and stroked a lock of hair out of her face. "Look after her," she instructed Lupe before emerging from behind the car.

It was all of five seconds before the men noticed Tanya. They turned, elbowing and nudging each other excitedly, their eyes widening like a hungry dog's.

The man on the right raised his cigarette to his lips. The lit end burned bright orange as he studied Tanya. When he spoke, the cigarette danced between his lips. "Hey, hot stuff. Ain't seen you around before."

The other two whistled as she approached. She stopped just short of where they were, causing them to push back on their heels in surprise. She wondered if they were used to just cat-calling and watching the women they harassed run past in fear.

"You gents locals?" Tanya asked. "I'm a little lost."

"You're a lot lost to find your way to this place," one of the men told her, stroking the thin goatee and several chins defining his face. "You know this area is full of poor people, right? Hardly suitable for your type."

His eyes lingered on the flush of her exposed chest under her blood-red cloak.

"My type? And what type would that be?" Tanya retorted, a coy smile on her lips.

"Go back to Manhattan, Princess. You ain't got no business here," the first man replied.

Tanya cringed inside, but she pressed on with the plan. "How do you know I'm not a whore?"

The man stuck out his bottom lip as he thought about that. "Let's just say you ain't the typical caliber of whore we get around these parts. You don't see too many women wearing designer clothing walking the streets."

"Word of advice?" Goatee offered. "Scram. You don't want to be around these parts, especially at night."

I can't believe it, Tanya thought. *Scumbags with a conscience.*

Tanya decided to change tack. "Tell you the truth, guys, I *am* lost. I'm looking for the Rockwood Music Hall. I've got a date meeting me there. You guys know which way north is?"

The three men stared at the sky, trying to work out how best to direct her. While the first man muttered something about the North Star, Goatee spoke a line of verse about the sun rising and setting. The third man remained oddly silent.

"Over that way," the first man told her, pointing past the building. "Other side of this block."

"Would you mind showing me?" Tanya blinked at the men. "If it's really so dangerous around here, I'd hate to have something happen to me on the way."

The first man exchanged a look with the other two that Tanya didn't miss. He wrapped an arm around her shoulder and led her around the side of the building.

The light grew fainter as they went around the building. When they reached the other side, the man pointed at an alley between two buildings. "That's your way. Careful, though. Bad things happen to pretty women in the dark."

"Would you mind walking with me?" Tanya asked. "At least a little bit of the way. You seem so nice."

"I suppose," the man replied. Although he kept his calm demeanor, Tanya could see the flicker of excitement in his eyes. She had seen it in thousands of men over the years—the triggering of the hormones that could turn even the gentlest of men into a predatory beast in the right circumstances.

But Tanya had nothing to worry about. The minute she faded into the darkness, she quietly slipped a hand into the folds of her cloak and drew a .44 Magnum. It had been a gift from her late father before he passed.

"That stuff we were saying back there?" he continued. "We didn't mean no offense by it."

Tanya dropped back a step. She could hear him, but she couldn't see his face anymore. Only the panting of his breath and the gentle woosh of his clothes against his skin gave away his position.

"You're a pretty lady is all we were saying. Very pretty. Prettier than anything we've seen come this way."

"Charmed," Tanya muttered, preparing herself for his inevitable advances.

He didn't make her wait long. "I mean, I know it's probably a no, but I was always taught that if you don't ask, you don't get. So, I was thinking you could do me a quick favor before you go. One good turn deserves another."

The man let out an audible sigh when he felt something hard poke into his ribs. "You bitch."

"Call the others," Tanya ordered, forcing the pistol into the man's side. "Don't make it sound urgent. Just draw them near."

The man growled, then called the pair over. Soon the men he'd identified as Club and Rango—clearly codenames, Tanya gleaned— appeared in the light around the corner.

"Call them over here," Tanya added. "Tell them I've fallen and hurt my ankle."

He did so. Meanwhile, Tanya made small grunts and wheezes of pain.

Goatee, who Tanya assumed to be Club, trotted obediently into the darkness. Rango waited by the edge of the building.

The moment Club reached them, Tanya raised the Magnum and hit him between the eyes with the butt. There was a sickening crunch as he gave a small yelp and folded to the ground.

The first man made a move to attack Tanya, but threw his hands in the air when she quickly trained the gun on his chest. When she turned back to Rango, he was gone.

"Shit," she muttered.

"Oh, no!" The man sneered. "You're in trouble. Rango's quick. He'll have the alarm raised in seconds. Soon this place will be flooded with backup. You wait."

Unsure of what to do, Tanya froze at the idea she'd already fucked it all up. She'd raised the alarm before they'd even entered the building.

A shadow signaled the appearance of backup from the front doors. Tanya shrank further into the darkness, ready to run.

To her surprise, Rango appeared again, only this time, Lupe was behind him with a gun pressed to his back.

"Over here," Tanya hissed.

Lupe marched Rango toward Tanya, and between them, they forced the guards to their knees.

Lupe grinned. "Nice to see you alive."

"Thanks," Tanya muttered. She turned to the two on their knees. "Now, shitbags, give us the code to the front door. We want in."

The first man's laughter was cut short when Tanya's knee connected with his mouth. He spat out the tooth she'd knocked out but said nothing.

Rango remained tight-lipped, too. Even when Lupe thumbed the safety catch, he didn't utter a word.

"Search their pockets," Lupe suggested.

A moment later, Tanya withdrew a keycard from the inside of her man's pocket. "Bingo."

"You'll never get him," the man growled, his voice slurred by his daze. "No matter how far you think you'll get, it won't be far enough. He has fighters on every floor."

"Oh, I think we'll manage just fine," Tanya told him. "We've got our own fighters."

With that, she smashed him in the face with the gun.

Lupe followed suit, leaving all three men to enjoy their impromptu nap in the alley.

The first three flights of stairs were unguarded, exactly as Angus and Paige had described.

With access into the building for Lupe and Tanya and their men and women sorted, it was now down to the specters to blaze the trail.

Although the pair of Obake had managed to gather intel, it wasn't as detailed as they'd have liked. They had the locations of some of the players along the way, fighters and gunmen on particular floors who never left their posts, but they didn't have an accurate headcount of how many mortals and how many specters were involved.

The specters invaded the entirety of the lower floor, leaking in like rats through sewer pipes. While some took the stairs, others melted through the walls and searched the area before climbing onto furniture and dissolving through the ceilings.

This was their plan. The mortals trailed up the steps, prepared and ready to take on whatever and whoever they came across when the specters raised the alarm.

That alarm came on floor number four, as expected.

A handful of spectral gunmen spotted the specters climbing the stairs and went into an instant attack. Those at the front of the line lost limbs and chunks of their body as the spectral bullets rained into them. For Lupe, the specters, and Tanya, who was connected with Sandra, the sound was deafening. Lupe ducked, even though he was well aware that the bullets wouldn't hurt him one bit.

The gunshots were muted when the specters who had floated through the ceilings found the shooters' legs and tripped them. They pawed and grabbed them, overpowering them like the hungry souls that inhabited the River Styx until the attackers were neutralized.

The peace didn't last long.

The sounds of gunshots raised the alarm above. Soon, specters were descending through the ceilings and appearing from all angles. Chinese warriors armed with an array of guns, knives, and swords got to work on the Spectral Plane. They fought with grace and attacked with calm determination.

Although their numbers were depleted slowly, for every warrior who appeared, two Spectral Plane specters were incapacitated.

"Fuck," Lupe grunted. He was backed up against the wall, watching the display above. There was little he could do at this moment other than watch while specters took on specters. "This got out of hand quickly."

Guns fired. Specters moaned in pain. Swords sang.

Lupe turned to Tanya, who was watching with a horrified expression. This was the first spectral fight she had ever seen, and it wasn't pretty.

"Tanya…" Lupe's eyes danced to Sandra, who looked the least scared out of all of them.

Tanya followed his eyes and realized what he was about to suggest. "No. No, you can't."

"They need her," Lupe retaliated. "*We* need her."

Sandra turned her head to Tanya. "It's okay, Mommy. It's okay."

Tanya hesitated a moment longer, her hand clasping Sandra's tightly. With a tear rolling down her cheek, she let go of Sandra's hand and watched as the young girl walked up the stairs, pacing herself as if there was nothing else to do but relax and take her time.

Lupe saw Belinda at the top of the stairs, battling a spectral warrior whose eye was shimmering with silver blood. She used her bulk to slam him out of the way, then used her momentum to charge into the others, knocking them all to the floor.

A short distance away from her, Angus and Paige fought, shifting into perfect replicas of their attackers to confuse them. They gained the upper hand and moved away from their enemies' weapons, giving the Spectral Plane specters room to shoot.

A little farther from them was Feng Mian. For a man who remained stoic for the majority of his waking death, the man could move. He blocked punches, twisted limbs, and sent enemies to the floor. It was mesmerizing to watch.

But still not as mesmerizing as watching the little girl.

As Sandra scaled the stairs, her form glowed brighter. Light emanated from her and reached out to the specters surrounding her.

Her bare feet padded gently on each step, and waves of power poured from her in gentle pulses. Those who had been injured healed rapidly, their wounds and cuts and breaks knitting and realigning as they rose off the floor and got back to their feet.

Sandra reached the top of the stairs and placed a hand on the rail. Her eyes were pure white, and as each member of the Spectral Plane recovered, another warrior went down. She bolstered their number, yet somehow miraculously concentrated her power away from the enemy warriors, who could hardly believe what was happening.

Soon the floor was cleared, and the Spectral Plane regrouped on the open concrete landing. Footsteps rang from above as the next wave of fighters came, but this time the specters were ready.

"Take formation," Feng Mian commanded, his voice booming louder than they'd ever heard it before.

The specters huddled together, too many to fit on the landing, so some took the stairs. They readied themselves, their hands on their weapons and their eyes narrowed.

When Lupe saw their next attackers, his heart dropped.

Coming down the stairs were mortal men with assault rifles and grim smiles. Undeterred by the specters they could not see, they strode with confidence, the barrels of their rifles aimed at Lupe, Tanya, and the other Spectral Plane mortals.

"Well, well, well," the first gunman remarked with a wolfish grin on his face. "What have we got here?"

Lupe didn't have a chance to reply before the first shot was fired.

CHAPTER THIRTY-FOUR

Chinatown, New York, USA

A high-pitched whine rang in Tanya's ears. She had seen the bright flash from the muzzle of the gun before it fired, but now she could hardly see.

"Lupe!" Her voice might have been loud, but she couldn't hear herself speak. More gunshots were fired, and all Tanya could do was clap her hands to her ears. She fell on her ass behind a large potted fern and waited for it all to be over, holding onto hope and praying that she wouldn't be mowed down in the crossfire.

An arm draped over her shoulders, and someone hugged her in a protective cocoon. It wasn't enough to stop a bullet, but it was definitely a comfort at that moment. Hot tears fell from her face although she was unaware of it.

"It's going to be okay," a voice whispered in her ear. Desperate. Convincing. "It's going to be okay."

Tanya knew that voice. She turned her head, and through blurry eyes saw Lupe just inches away from her. His eyes wide and terrified, but even now, a small smile of comfort was on his face.

"How?" was all Tanya could manage.

Lupe pointed toward the stairs. Tanya raised her head to see a man with a wispy beard and a feral grimace training his pistol on the dead soldiers on the floor.

Feng Li was thunderous, with one QSZ-92 pistol in each hand. He waited a moment longer, then glanced up the next set of stairs before running down to Lupe and checking that he and Tanya were okay.

"I'm fine," Lupe answered, grunting as he pushed himself to his feet. He glanced at the pistols. "Where did those come from?"

"A gift from the Chinese army," Feng Li replied. "Not a great time to get into it, don't you think?" He passed assault rifles to Lupe, Tanya, and several of her men before placing a fresh magazine into his own. "We must hurry. Those shots will be like alarm bells to the upper floors. They're coming. I can sense it."

The specters waited obediently for their next command. Lupe gave the word, and they worked their way to the next floor. Their nerves kicked into gear as they climbed the stairs. All was quiet above, which made it worse. They could handle knowing where their enemy was coming from. It was the silence that put them on edge.

"Wait here," Feng Li instructed, holding them back with one arm.

"Father!" Feng Mian broke free from the specters and approached his father. "Why are you doing this? For years, you've hidden from your responsibility, and now you try to lead the charge?"

Feng Li's face softened. "I no longer fear death, son. I have seen the other side. You and your mother are there. I may not be able to make up for what I did in your lifetime, but I can at least find some way to repent." He smiled. "These mortals are your friends, are they not?"

Feng Mian nodded. "They are."

"Then I will do what I can to protect them," Feng Li told him. "When they had the chance to kill me, they chose mercy. That was honorable, and more than I deserved."

Feng Li ran up the stairs. The sudden movement was enough to spark the specters into action again. They continued up the stairs, finding resistance one floor from the top of the building.

Gunshots were the first sign that anyone was there. They saw Feng Li ahead, cautiously peering around the corner and ducking at the first sound. Bullets ricocheted off the wall, bombarding them at an alarming pace.

Lupe had only ever heard that sound in films. Feng Li dashed down the stairs and confirmed his theory.

"AK47s," he yelled, given that whoever was firing above was unrelenting. He held up both hands with one finger lowered. "Nine."

As suddenly as it had started, the deafening noise stopped. It almost made Lupe wonder if his eardrums had burst, listening now to the silence which followed the gunfire.

"We know you're down there," a gruff voice shouted. "Give it up. Go home. This is the only warning you will receive."

The Spectral Plane waited for their orders. A painful silence followed. Lupe pulled Feng Li closer. "Are they mortals or specters?"

"I didn't take stock," Li replied. "They were shooting at me."

"But you managed to count them?" Lupe stated.

He shrugged. "It's a gift."

Feng Mian rolled his eyes. "If you had to say, which would you go with?"

Feng Li considered this. People mumbled on the floor above them. "I don't know."

Lupe screwed his fists tight. He waved Angus over to them. "You said the upper floor was guarded. Did you know by who?"

Angus shook his head. "We never got to the upper floors. Didn't you see how many there were below? We didn't want to chance it."

Lupe said, "Well, you're going to chance it now."

Angus looked at him questioningly. "How?"

Lupe glanced at the ceiling above. "If someone gives you a boost, do you think you could go through the ceiling and get a look at them from behind?"

Angus shrugged one shoulder. "Let's find out, shall we?"

Paige dashed over to him, seeing what was going on. "You can't. What if they shoot you?"

Angus shrugged. "Hey, if they blast my head off, at least I can transfigure my body into something that should make up for it until it grows back. You'd still love a headless Arnold Schwarzenegger, right?"

Paige kissed his cheek. "Climb on my shoulders."

As Angus walked behind Paige, her body shifted until she stood at least seven feet tall. He climbed up on her shoulders, and his head disappeared through the ceiling.

Lupe waited with bated breath, half-expecting to hear gunfire any second.

"Mortals," Angus confirmed as he lowered himself down. "Nine of them, all in dark-red cloaks. They're lined up a couple of feet in front of the door. It's like they're guarding a treasure chest."

Lupe turned to Tanya, who was shrouded in her own red cape. "Friends of yours?"

Tanya stared blankly back.

"There's only one way to take them out," Feng Li muttered, aware that time was not on their side.

"Yeah, just melt through another room into the main apartment," Carolyn offered.

Feng Mian shook his head. "They may have backup inside. It could be a massacre."

"With Sandra on our side, they can't do anything," Carolyn countered. "We can heal fast enough."

"What about the mortals?" Feng Mian glanced at the Spectral Plane mortals who lined the stairs. Although their faces were hidden within their cloaks, their fear was apparent. Nothing had prepared them for this.

Tanya sighed. "Man, if only we had Jennie with us."

"We don't need Jennie," Lupe replied. "We just need to be smart. This time, it'll be the mortals who get the jump on the bad guys."

Lupe gathered Tanya, Feng Li, and the remaining mortals closer. When they were gathered at the bottom of the stairs, he summoned Sandra toward them.

"Think you can make us invisible?" he asked.

Tanya opened her mouth, but Lupe silenced her with a glare.

Sandra smiled at Lupe uncertainly. "I don't know. I've only ever done one before."

"Will you try?" he asked with a smile.

Sandra turned to Tanya for permission.

Tanya gave her a long stare, then nodded.

Sandra beamed. "I can try."

It was a strange sensation, turning immaterial. Although Lupe had seen Jennie turn spectral a hundred times, and although he was a conduit who could see specters at all times, he never imagined what it would feel like.

It wasn't unpleasant. To Lupe, it felt as though a wash of tepid water was flushing through his body, the same way it felt to drink a cold shake on a hot summer's day. His hands disappeared in front of his eyes, turning a ghostly blue, and when he turned to the others, he saw that all of them, besides Feng Mian, who had already been spectral, had undergone the same transition.

"Woah," Lupe muttered. "This is wild."

Feng Li grunted in confirmation.

When they were all certain they had vanished from mortal sight, they worked their way upstairs. They each marked a guard standing just a foot in front of their faces. They'd left the assault rifles behind, having discovered that Sandra's powers didn't extend to their weapons.

Angus had been right; the sight of the men in cloaks was unsettling. They stood as still as statues, flanking a man with a Neanderthal face whose eyes never left the staircase.

Feng Li took the man in the center while Lupe and Tanya took either side. The remaining mortals readied themselves, their fists prepared to smash into the faces of their enemies.

Lupe held up three fingers and counted down.

Three.

Two.

One.

"I wouldn't recommend that if I were you."

Li's eyes widened as the Neanderthal grinned with a mouth full of silver teeth. The eyes of the mortals beneath the cloaks suddenly blazed with a white glow, appearing like car headlights through a tunnel.

Sandra shut off her connection and everyone became material again. They all moved quickly to take their guards out. Lupe punched his guard in the nose before hooking his leg around the man's ankle and giving him a sharp shove. The man went down and landed with a painful *oomph*.

Gunshots sounded to his left and right. Two of the cultists were faster than the Spectral Plane, and his people fell under a rain of bullets. The remaining Spectral Plane mortals moved as if their lives depended on it—which they very much did—and managed to take down their attackers before working on those to either side of them. They attacked hard, the threat of death enough to remove any inhibitions they had about fighting.

It all happened so quickly and in such a furious mess that it was difficult to work out what was going on. After a few frantic seconds, the only guard remaining was the Neanderthal.

It was at that moment Lupe noticed the knife sticking out of Feng Li's chest.

The Neanderthal grinned and stepped back, arms widening as if inviting death to him. Lupe obliged by confiscating a dead cultist's gun and aiming it at his chest. He pulled the trigger and felt a grim satisfaction as the light was extinguished from his eyes.

"Feng Li!" Tanya knelt by Feng Li's side, his head cradled in her arms. It was too late. The man was gone.

She looked at Lupe for help, as if he could somehow snap his fingers and bring him back to life. He knew what she was thinking: that Feng Mian would be distraught at the loss of his father, whom he had only recently reconnected with.

Sure enough, Feng Mian made his way up the stairs, face characteristically stoic. Tanya and Lupe stepped aside as he knelt at the crown of his father's head and bowed so low his forehead touched Feng Li's.

He closed his eyes and muttered something incoherent in another language. When he opened them, his father's spirit rose into a seated position. He pawed frantically at his stomach, face tense and grim as if he still felt the pain from the knife.

But the pain was gone.

"Welcome to the afterlife," Feng Mian told him solemnly. "Now you know how it feels to die."

A pained expression fell across Feng Li's face. "I do, son. I can never apologize enough, but I can spend the rest of my days trying. I understand if I cannot earn your forgiveness."

Feng Mian cocked his head to the side. "Kneel."

His father did so cautiously, as though he was rediscovering his limbs, testing their limits and scared to make a wrong move.

When they were facing each other, Feng Mian placed his palm on Feng Li's forehead. He closed his eyes and said something Lupe couldn't understand.

Feng Li, however, did. "Thank you," he told his son, tears brimming in his eyes. "I will."

Feng Mian stood and helped his father to his feet. "Honor and family—that is what we fight for."

Feng Li pawed his eye with the back of his hand. "Let's go find your mother."

Before they could storm the door, more specters rose from their fallen bodies. The Spectral Planes fighters were the first to rise, and Lupe was filled with a sense of foreboding. Surely, now that the guards were dead, their spirits would rise, too?

While Tanya reconnected to Sandra and inducted her fallen friends into specterdom, Lupe, Carolyn, Feng Mian, and Feng Li hovered over the body of the Neanderthal as he awoke and pushed himself to his feet. They held him at gunpoint and left a group of specters to keep watch over him. He didn't speak, nor did he show any remorse. He just glared and grinned.

The fallen guards did not rise, which was strange indeed. Determined now to get to the bottom of this, Lupe left a force of specters to watch over the fallen as they connected once more with Sandra and made their way to the topmost apartment.

The Dragon's Den was decidedly underwhelming. Based on the description of the room, Lupe had expected a veritable palace of wonder with golds and reds and expensive ornaments lining the walls. Throws and pillows and tapestries. Incense and music, and maybe even a few glamorous women doting on fat men sitting upon puffy thrones.

Only one part of all that turned out to be true.

The room was filled with a nicotine-scented haze. There were no candles, no lights. Only the faint milky glow of the moon and stars coming through the windows cast any light whatsoever.

The man wasn't hard to miss, however. Passing through a small corridor, they could hear his breathing before they saw his face.

He sat in an armchair that bowed under his weight. The top of his head was as smooth as buttermilk, and his breathing was labored. He wore a sash that was reminiscent of Buddha but gave him none of the prestige or respect.

He pressed an oxygen mask to his mouth, its wires trailing to a large canister of gas beside him. Tubes and cables were plugged into various veins over his body, and the only real movement came from a thin, frail woman who sat on a stool beside him and attempted to pass soup between his thick, blubbery lips. Rivulets of vegetable juice rolled across his layers of fat and found homes between the folds.

Lupe approached slowly, afraid any sudden movements might startle the man. The woman paid no attention to the intruders, continuing to ladle soup into his mouth between breaths. Tanya, Sandra, and Carolyn followed him.

Lupe made it to the center of the room without incident. Without so much as a sideways glance, the woman wiped a stained napkin across the man's chin before taking the bowl away and exiting the room.

Lupe waited a few moments before finally speaking. "Are you the one they call 'the Dragon?'"

The man ran a thick tongue across his lips so slowly it appeared as though a slug had emerged from his mouth. He smacked his lips and made eye contact with Lupe.

"There's a mysticism to death, isn't there?" His words were slow, his voice so deep that they hardly sounded like words. "A poetry to the nuances of the mysterious. We all fight our entire lives to live, but what is it all for? We delay the inevitable so that we can have one last moment of pain and regret. Life is not for everyone, is it?"

Lupe detected the note of rhetoric in that final question and chose to stick to his own agenda instead of answering. "Your reign is over. Whatever madness you have been plotting to impose upon the citizens of New York is done. We will have none of your tyranny anymore."

The Dragon turned his gaze to Tanya, studying her with hungry eyes. "You don't even know what's begun, do you?"

Although his eyes bored into Tanya's, she remained silent. The Dragon let out a chuckle that quickly turned into a wheeze. His cheeks protruded and flamed red, and the slug of his tongue danced on his lips once more. His hand pawed toward the gas canister, but it was only when the woman reappeared and passed him his mask that he was able to take deep breaths that slowly cleared.

"Why don't you tell us?" Lupe encouraged. "If we're so naive, why don't you enlighten us, O mighty Dragon?"

The Dragon let his head fall against the chair back. He gasped at the ceiling for a few seconds before returning his gaze to Lupe. "The world is twisted in strange, unknown ways. Life and death are connected to each other, with only a few degrees of separation. You may not have heard of us until recently, but my friend, I have heard of you."

Tanya spoke up at last. "You don't know us. You sit in your tower and command your men to do your bidding, but we've already taken them down. We're already here, and you are at our mercy. So why don't you quit playing the big man and get to the point?"

The Dragon nodded slowly. "I suppose that's only fair. Did you know, Mr. Sanchez, that a network of conduits has existed in New York for the best part of a decade? A cluster of incredibly gifted people working toward understanding the spectral world?"

Lupe flinched at the mention of his surname. He hadn't mentioned it to the Dragon, so how did he know?

"It has been slow work," the Dragon wheezed. "For mortals to understand the spectral world is no easy task. We've had glimpses and hints for years, but it's only in recent months that we have seen the progress we needed to take our understanding to the next level."

The Dragon snapped his fingers, and the woman scuttled back into the room.

This time she dragged a small table on wheels. On it was a laptop. She placed the laptop in the center of the room and flipped open the lid. Bright artificial light stung their eyes, a sudden contrast in the dark.

The Dragon grinned. "Look."

Lupe advanced, careful to tread slowly for fear this might be a trap. He imagined the laptop exploding and triggering a reaction with the oxygen tank. He foresaw the woman raising a needle-like knife from her pocket and sticking it into his heart. He saw a number of different scenarios, yet his curiosity was too strong to ignore.

For weeks he had been aware of specters upsetting the balance in New York City. He had sent specters to investigate the disappearances of mortals and the strings that tied the specters to the cases. In the aftermath of Times Square, their attention had been divided by the cleanup, but he was almost certain something larger was at play here.

The screen confirmed his theory.

"What do you think, Mr. Sanchez?" the Dragon asked before taking another deep inhalation of oxygen. "Impressive, isn't it?"

Lupe scanned the page, unable to quite believe what he was seeing. "Tanya? You might want to see this."

Tanya joined Lupe's side. "What is it?"

The screen was filled with boxes of text. Lupe had seen similar interfaces years ago, in the days when chat forums were first springing up on the internet and social media was yet to be invented. There were hundreds of responses and comments, anonymous users discussing the same topic and sharing images and files.

"A cult," Tanya ground out. "This is definitely a cult."

"One you came across in your days of paranormal hunting?" Lupe asked, softly enough that he hoped it was out of earshot of the Dragon.

"Maybe?" Tanya moved closer to the screen. "There's always a lot of internet chatter. Do you know how many cults there are in the world?"

Lupe scrolled through the page. Buzzwords leaped out and caught his eye. Phrases like, "beyond the grave," "ritual," "murder," "at last, we know," and "from the shadows."

And then he found it—the link at the top that had started it all. The original post underneath a headline reading, *Recruiting for The Shadows: Controlling the Dead.*

"Shit," Lupe breathed. "Look at this."

He pointed to a large post that described a ritual discovered in the US, a method and means that had been used to animate the dead and combine spectral spirits with mortal vessels.

It was dated just days ago.

The Dragon beamed once more, a sickening banana slice of a mouth. "You wanted to stop it? It's far too late, my friends. What is now public shall remain public forever. The knowledge of the dead is spreading across the world, and the ritual is being attempted. I can tell you it works. I've seen it firsthand."

Lupe suddenly realized why the guards' specters hadn't yet risen from their corpses, and how they had reacted so quickly to the Spectral Plane's attack.

His theory was confirmed when he heard fighting resume outside the apartment. The specters who had inhabited the mortal bodies couldn't be so easily killed by bullets, fists, or knives.

"Like the many-headed hydra, the Shadows will only grow until all the world is covered in darkness." The Dragon took a lungful of oxygen. "The game has begun. Your move."

Lupe and Tanya emerged from the apartment a little past two AM and breathed the chilly air. It hadn't been easy, but the enemies had been removed. Sandra had exorcised the opposing specters, and they had found the specters held hostage in one of the filth-stained rooms of the apartment.

Feng Mian had been ecstatic, as far as he could show excitement.

If only the reunion with his mother had been enough to erase the troubling information they'd received from the Dragon in the gasping moments before his final breath. The moment his lungs gave up and the oxygen was not enough to keep him going.

"What now?" Tanya asked, surprised by how loud her voice sounded in the quiet of the night.

Lupe stared ahead into the city. "I don't know."

Tanya sighed. "It isn't over, is it?"

Lupe shook his head. He clutched the Dragon's laptop in the crook of his arm. "No. No, it's not. I have a funny feeling it's only just begun."

CHAPTER THIRTY-FIVE

Baltimore, Maryland, USA

Natalia, David, and Clive camped out a short distance away from the entrance to the Harbor Tunnel, watching as the traffic passed by.

With the world fallen into darkness, it was easy to remain invisible, but difficult to discern the cars between the flares of their headlights. The roads were two-lane, and the lights reflected off the metal, creating a dazzling multi-star effect that rivaled the night sky.

They waited on the hill for two hours before they found what they were looking for. Three dark trucks drove to the toll booths. They watched the exchange between the drivers and the attendants through binoculars. No cash was exchanged. They showed a pass card and exchanged a friendly salute.

Clive dialed the number. "Black Hawk, this is Silver Crow, the suspects are on their way."

On the other side of the tunnel, almost a mile away, Jennie received the message and started her engine. Traffic had been coming through at a regular pace, and she had begun to wonder if they would ever find what they were looking for.

Jennie turned down Five's greatest hits collection, as much as it pained her to stop midway through their mega-mix, and watched the tunnel entrance. It would be only a few minutes until the semis arrived.

Sure enough, right as Jennie was counting down her internal clock, she saw them. Like silent ships in the night, they drove on, and Jennie followed.

They took the 895 for a long while, cruising along the road as if they were in no hurry to get anywhere at all. Baxter, Jack, and Sade were sitting silently in the back of the car, as though any noise might suddenly alert their targets that they were being followed.

"I've been in a hundred graves and mausoleums, and I don't think I've ever been anywhere so quiet," Jennie remarked, looking in her rearview at the passengers.

"That's because your mausoleums and graves are inhabited by the lively dead." Baxter shuddered, remembering the sweep of smoky black cloaks from the wraiths in London.

"The dead don't stay dead," Jennie replied.

"So, what happens to them?" Sade shifted in her seat, suddenly interested. The goggles were bulky on her face. "If the dead don't stay dead, surely we should be overrun by specters today?"

"Okay, well, maybe I'm not being entirely factual," Jennie conceded. "If no one ever finally died, then the world would be smothered in specters. Everywhere we looked, there'd be dozens of specters walking into each other. Think about it—thousands of years of human existence, thousands of years of dying and burials. It'd be ridiculous."

"So, what happens?" Sade repeated. "How does it work?"

"I can give you the answer to one but not the other," Baxter told her, half-turning his head. He explained to Sade the two options all specters had a right to choose—to exist as a specter, or to dissolve into the great abyss.

"Of course, sometimes that choice is made for you." Baxter glanced at Jennie. "Some possess the power to exorcise specters and remove them from the world entirely. Priests, powerful specters, and..."

"And those in possession of ancient relics imbued with power,"

Jennie finished without taking her eyes off the road. She could feel the saber at her side, yet it was still cloaked from view.

"There's no coming back from the abyss?" Sade asked.

"Afraid not." Baxter turned completely in his chair. "At least, not that I've ever been made aware of in my time as a specter."

Sade tilted her head at Baxter. "How long is that?"

"A hundred or so years," he replied.

Sade let out a small scoff of disbelief and shook her head. "Amazing."

After another ten minutes, the trucks finally turned off the highway. One by one, they banked up the offramp and slowly navigated into a built-up residential area.

Chain link fences bordered children's parks. Neat paths from the sidewalk led to small houses nestled so closely together, it was as though they were whispering to one another.

Jennie began to wonder where they were being led. Was the answer to their riddle really in this neighborhood?

Her question was swiftly answered when the small convoy took a right at a wide road, then another right, then looped back on themselves down a parallel road. Jennie quickly realized they were heading back toward the highway.

"Back the way they came?" Jennie muttered.

Whatever the trucks' business, they clearly weren't confused. They slipped back onto the highway and trailed down the 895 once more toward the Harbor Tunnel.

"You think they're just trying to take advantage of their free passes?" Baxter suggested. "Y'know, up and down, up and down, just performing circuits on the track?"

"It doesn't match their times." Jennie fished out the paper Drampton had given her and passed it to Baxter. "See?"

"They're taking the slip road," Jack told them, pointing over Jennie's shoulder.

She slapped his hand away. "I have eyes, Agent Hansen."

Jack laughed.

The trucks took the off-ramp, and soon the landscape around them changed.

Instead of houses and residential neighborhoods, they entered an industrial quarter where the road was concrete. Aside from a few stubborn weeds, the world was hard and gray. They passed large factories and abandoned outlets, as well as enormous vacant parking lots.

They drove for a few more miles until the dark, inky waters of the bay came back into view. As they neared their apparent destination, Jennie switched off her headlights and followed for the final mile as silently as a specter.

The trucks pulled up outside a large, plain factory that looked as though it hadn't seen use in over a decade. The windows were shattered, weeds skirted the building, and ivy had begun munching the brickwork.

The only sign of occupation was a small spotlight above a peeling red door.

Jennie pulled the car around the corner away from the light and switched off the engine. From the faint glow of the spotlight, they watched as a couple of dozen men and women hopped out of their vehicles and gathered in front of the door. A woman who was smaller than the rest of them, called instructions and elicited a raucous laugh from the others. They nodded and dispersed to their vehicles once more as she knocked three times on the door and let herself in.

"What do you think they're up to?" Baxter asked.

Jack tsked. "Abandoned factory? Suspicious black vehicles? Rowdy men and women operating in the dark? I'd say that's a recipe for something outside the law, wouldn't you, Agent Burnwell?"

Sade grinned. "I'd have to agree, Agent Hansen."

They watched while the men and women unloaded their vehicles, rolling up the doors at the back before hauling out large unlabeled boxes. The huge rolling door on the side of the building opened and they dumped the boxes inside, handling them quickly while throwing occasional glances over their shoulders.

After twenty minutes of unloading, the watchers thought the

trucks were empty. Then people were dragged out of the back of the semis.

Jennie couldn't make an accurate guess of their ages because of the sacks over their heads, but she worked out that they were teenagers by the way they moved. The ten captives were dragged toward the dark, cavernous space and forced to move in single file, tied together by a length of rope around their waists. Heavy hands guided them to the building, where they were rapidly marched inside.

"Who are they?" Baxter wondered out loud.

No one replied. They were all eagerly watching, taking note of every individual working together to shepherd their victims into the building. A few moments later, after the last captive disappeared inside, the garage door was pulled shut. Single drivers in each vehicle engaged the engines and drove them away from the front of the building.

The world fell deadly silent.

"You think that's enough evidence for something criminal?" Baxter asked.

Jennie chewed her lip. "Those teenagers didn't kidnap themselves. We have to get them out of there."

Sade wasn't so sure. "The only problem is, without knowing what's going on inside, we can't know for sure if we'd put those kids at more risk by storming the place. This is above our pay grade."

Jennie's brow knitted together. "Call the others and give them our location. Tell them to approach with caution, no headlights, minimal noise. You'll meet them, and you can watch over the building between you and let me know if anyone else is approaching."

"Wait," Sade told her. "You're not thinking of going in there, are you?"

Jennie smirked. "What good is having superpowers if I don't put them to good use?"

Whatever operation was going on inside, their lookouts weren't very thorough. Even in her spectral form, Jennie was surprised to not see anyone in the rafters or any kind of closed-circuit video feed capturing what was going on outside.

"Remember, Bax. This is just reconnaissance, okay? We're not to draw guns and go all-out in there unless it's vital. Let's try to be sneaky and subtle for a change, shall we?"

Baxter leaned back on his heels, giving Jennie an incredulous look. "You realize the irony of what you're saying, don't you?"

Jennie grinned. "I do."

In the spirit of keeping things quiet, Jennie skirted the building and stopped when they reached the back. A long stretch of grimy and busted windows showed no activity inside. Jennie chose this place to melt through the wall and start her exploration.

The building was huge, and the layout was confusing. Emergency lights illuminated the rooms just enough to see by. Small offices opened into large production areas, then blended back into small meeting spaces. Long corridors snaked between.

Every time Jennie entered a new room, she prepared for an ambush.

"I've never seen you so jittery," Baxter whispered. "Are you okay?"

"It's not jitters, it's preparation." Jennie placed a hand on her chest and took a steadying breath. "Though I feel a lot is at stake here. If this is just a common drug bust, we'll have wasted our time."

"*Common* drug bust? How many of those have you encountered in your life?"

Jennie searched her brain. "1,562…and a half."

"Oddly specific," Baxter remarked. "What's the half?"

"I found a stash of cocaine around the back of a newsagent's on Canvey Island. I was sorely tempted to try it."

Baxter stared at Jennie. "You're not serious?"

She rolled her eyes. "Of course not. Do you think I'd do something so stupid? I handed it over to the authorities and got on with my day. Also, you realize I'm not Einstein or Hawking, yes? How am I supposed to know how many drug busts I've been a part of? More than I should have, to be honest. It's nothing to want to keep score of."

"Let me guess, you've met Einstein and Hawking?"

"Einstein, no. He was a hard one to lock down. Hawking, however… Well, we passed each other on the street a few times. I think he had his own problems to deal with. Head so far in space that he hardly ever looked at the ground."

"Wow." Baxter nodded, impressed. "I'm surprised you didn't tell me you'd played chess with one of them or challenged them to a game of riddles."

"Please, I haven't got a story about *every* famous person or celebrity."

Baxter raised his eyebrows accusingly.

Jennie chuckled softly. "Well, maybe most." She walked down the dark corridor toward the next bend. "Besides, everyone knows that it was Tolkien who loved riddles. Einstein and Hawking hated them. Thought them derivative."

"Is that true?"

Jennie didn't answer.

After hunting through a handful of rooms to get a lay of the factory, it was clear that whoever had entered this place was either already gone or hiding. They found their way to the loading bay they had seen the boxes transferred into and were surprised to find the boxes were stacked precariously in the corner of a large warehouse, while any trace of human activity was gone.

Moonlight streamed through a thin window high above the ground. Occasionally a cloud would pass across and the light would pulse.

Jennie traced a finger along the lid of one of the boxes. "I'm telling you, people will swear to the opposite, but the world is ready for an apocalypse. You don't realize how many people are in lairs beneath the ground, hiding and living secret lives away from the rest of civilization."

Baxter scanned the floor as if he was about to find some kind of trap door. "You think they're underground?"

"It's either that, or they fled out the back without us realizing."

Jennie studied the box, its six sides made from thick wooden panels. There were no markings on the outside to indicate what was inside.

"Just stick your head inside," Baxter suggested. "You're spectral now, remember?"

Jennie lowered her glasses a fraction and stared at Baxter. "Science 101, sight needs light. If I stick my head in there, I'm going to see nothing but darkness."

She disconnected from Baxter and picked up the box. It was heavier than she'd thought it would be, but she managed to place it on the floor without too much of an effort. She grabbed a crowbar from the corner of the room where it rested among a pile of tools and jammed it in the lips of the lid.

The box protested with a small creak. Long nails were pried from the wood. The lid came off, and Jennie lowered it gently to the floor.

She gasped.

Baxter came closer, looming over Jennie's shoulder to see inside the box. "What is it?"

Even with limited lighting, Jennie could make out the strange shapes—rows and rows of cylinders with dark tops, all unbranded and unmarked. She lifted a cylinder out, her eyes struggling to understand what she was looking at.

The cylinder was top-and-tailed with black and no longer than a larger stick of deodorant, but it was the contents that held the fascination for Jennie and Baxter. Cold, clear glass allowed them both to see the thick silver liquid inside rolling and shifting with each minute movement of Jennie's hand. It looked like liquid metal sloshing around with the consistency of soup.

The whole effect was mesmerizing. As Jennie watched, small pulses of light came from the contents. A strange feeling began to churn in her stomach, familiar yet indescribable.

"I've never seen anything like it," Jennie eventually replied. She put the cylinder back and picked up another, then another. "They're all the same."

"It looks like melted aluminum," Baxter offered, eyes fixed on the liquid metal inside.

Jennie's shoulders dropped. Her head slumped as if she had just been told that the tickets to her favorite show had been sold out. "Really?"

"What?"

"*Aloo-mi-num?*" Jennie retorted. "*Aloo-mi-num?*"

Baxter shrugged. "What's the problem?"

"It's *al-u-min-ee-um*. There's an 'ium' in there. Like barium, sodium, vibranium."

"That last one isn't real," Baxter argued.

Jennie scoffed. "Tell that to Stan Lee."

Baxter placed his hands on his hips. Outside of their whispers, there was no other sound around. Not even the gentle hush of passing traffic or a steady breeze floating through the rafters. "Are you really going to give me another lesson on language?" He looked wearied by the suggestion.

Jennie raised her hands defensively. "All I'm saying is that you guys stole our language. It's not my fault you butcher the Queen's English."

Baxter straightened his back and puffed out his chest. "In 1808, Sir Humphrey Davy discovered a metal alloy that he initially named alumium. In 1812, he updated that name to aluminum, and proudly took ownership of his invention. It was a short while after that the 'ium' was added to conform to the other elements."

Jennie looked set to celebrate, but Baxter continued before she had the chance. "However! In 1828, the year of the publication of the *original Webster's Dictionary*, the book lists it as 'aluminum' and introduces the name on a global scale."

Jennie pouted. "Hold on. You—"

"*In 1925!*" Baxter's voice raised above Jennie's, talking over her and quieting her once more. She folded her arms with a bemused look on her face. "The American Chemical Society decide to retain the original spelling, 'aluminum.'"

He gave a curt nod and let the final sentence hang there.

Jennie's straight lips curled into a grin. "You've been studying."

Baxter smiled. "I have."

"You know I hate it when I'm proven wrong," Jennie told him.

Baxter smiled back. "Does it happen much?"

"Hardly ever."

Baxter held Jennie's gaze, trying his best to contain his widening smile but failing.

"Don't make a habit of it," Jennie told him before the sudden sound of footsteps caught them off-guard.

Jennie threw the lid back onto the top of the box, not stopping to make sure it fit properly. They just had time to duck out of sight before a woman in a zipped-up leather jacket and dark Levis appeared around the corner. She held a flashlight in her hand and searched the room with its beam.

Jennie's mind cast back to a situation in the 1950s, where helicopter lights had searched the scene and dogs had barked furiously while they tried to track her down. The misunderstanding was soon sorted by a small amount of persuasion and a large amount of money.

The beam of light passed over the top of the box, and for a half-second, Jennie thought they'd gotten away with it.

The beam came back and fixed on the skewed lid. The woman muttered a soft, "What the…" before approaching. In the silhouette of her figure, Jennie thought she saw a gun in a holster around her waist.

Baxter leaned sideways until he was millimeters from Jennie's ear. "Your choice, boss. Take her down and start the siege or duck back out and regroup with the others?"

Jennie had been thinking exactly the same thing. The only advantage they had on their side was that they were spectral and this woman was mortal.

Or so they thought.

The woman circled the box, standing just a few feet away from them now. Glass clinked as she played with the cylinders. Now convinced something was awry, she drew her gun and began scanning the room.

Which would have been fine if she hadn't lowered a pair of goggles to her face.

And if those lenses hadn't lit up with green light.

Jennie grabbed Baxter's hand and pulled him through the wall.

CHAPTER THIRTY-SIX

<u>Baltimore, Maryland, USA</u>

"SI goggles?" Jack asked after Jennie and Baxter had told them what they'd seen. "How is that possible?"

They were gathered around the car. Natalia, David, and Clive had arrived at some point while Jennie and Baxter were in the building. Now the rear doors stood open like bat wings, with Natalia taking the spare seat in the back, and Clive and David leaning against the doors.

"Could be any number of things," Sade replied. "First among them being that there's an SIA mole delivering information behind our backs."

"Could they not be another branch of the SIA?" Baxter offered.

Sade shook her head. "Impossible. SAC Rogers would have told us before we set out. If neither Drampton nor Rhone has mentioned anything about a Baltimore facility, I don't believe there is one."

"Then how have they managed to get their hands on SIA tech?" Jack wondered aloud.

Jennie had been considering that very thought. Not only had all the men and women they'd seen not been in the facility, but they had SIA tech. That suggested a place of hiding and a covert set of operations.

She closed her eyes as she remembered the last time she had seen a pair of SIA goggles on a mortal. Memories of the Baltimore church came flooding back—a woman with red lips and a dark cloak.

"The bitch from the Shadows," Jennie breathed. "Julia. It has to be something to do with her. She's the only other person I've seen who used goggles. It must be her."

"How did she get her hands on those goggles?" Natalia asked.

Jack sighed. "She stole them from Clive."

Clive's jaw clenched.

Sade's eyes narrowed in thought. "What about those cylinders? What on Earth do you think they were?"

Jennie had no good answer for that. The liquid metal was something she'd never before seen in her life, at least not at those chilly temperatures. It was the wrong density for mercury, and it looked *active* somehow. She imagined that liquid metal would need to be kept above a painful temperature to maintain its state, but this was different.

"I don't know," she admitted. "But whatever's going on in there, I'm going to say we need more than just us. We're going to need backup. Judging by the heat that woman was packing, these guys are serious business."

Backup arrived twenty minutes later.

The cars arrived like a silent fleet of ships, maneuvering toward a meeting point Jennie had identified that was farther away from the facility.

There was no point in arousing suspicion if they could help it.

Led by Jennie, they divided into teams. Her team went around to take the back door, while she sent the others to the front where they would remain out of sight until Jennie gave them the command to storm the building.

Around the back, the paint-flecked door was the only obstacle between them and entry. An agent with nimble fingers was sent forward to pick the lock, and not a minute later, the door opened wide.

Jennie took point and guided them in. Each agent wore their SI goggles. Jennie's team was blessed with the 2.0s, given that they had yet to make their way to the undercover Baltimore agents.

Jennie was able to navigate the halls with relative ease, thanks to her earlier scouting effort. As they approached the door that would lead onto the factory floor, and consequently onto the main loading bay filled with boxes, she held up a fist to the agents, then pressed her ear against the door.

Definite movement on the other side. Voices talking softly.

Jennie cautiously stuck her head through the door just far enough that she could see what was going on.

Two men stood among the conveyor belts and machines, their hands on deadly-looking rifles Jennie couldn't identify from afar. The woman Jennie had seen was with them. All of them wore SI goggles.

Jennie scanned the room for additional entrances or threats.

Satisfied, she pulled herself back through the door and detailed the situation to Sade and the others. She instructed one unit to take the corridor that led to the left, and another the hall that led to the right. There she had spotted shattered windows where agents could survey the scene and offer long-range protection if needed.

She sent a third unit up a flight of stairs farther back along the corridor. If her memory served her correctly, that would lead to a balcony above from which the agents could pick off any enemies attempting to get the drop on them.

When everyone was in their positions, Jennie passed through the door.

It was time to begin.

"You sure you're not just crazy?" a gruff man asked the woman with a note of laughter in his voice. "Not afraid of the dark, are you, sweetheart?"

The woman glared at the man. He wore a dark v-neck t-shirt that exposed his muscular chest. His head was shaven, but his face was not.

"Fuck off. Someone was here. Why else would that box's lid be askew?"

"'Askew?'" The second man's voice was softer than the first man's. He wore a baseball cap so low over his brow that it touched his goggles. His frame was skinnier, reminding Jennie of a mongoose or ferret.

"Not on straight," Muscles shot back.

"Oh. Why didn't you just say that, then?" Ferret retorted. "Using fancy words when you could just say it how it is."

The woman looked incredulously at Ferret, unable to understand what she was hearing. "Someone was here. I swear it."

Muscles swept his eyes around the room once more. "Well, whoever it was is gone now, aren't they? What's the phrase? No sense crying over spilled milk."

Jennie kept herself low and snuck closer, ducking behind a large metal pillar. They couldn't have been more than twenty feet away now.

"No sense… What are you talking about? You think they're going to like knowing someone saw the goods?" The woman moved closer to Muscles, and even under his impressive stature, she didn't shrink. She approached as if he were just another man and she a woman who could knock him down with a single blow. "You heard them say the words, didn't you? *Top-fucking-secret*. Someone's been in here, which means that someone is now out *there* with the knowledge that something is happening. We've got to tell them."

Muscles squared up to her, looking down with dark eyes. "Or maybe someone knocked the box on the way in? Maybe the box was already open? Maybe you're fabricating stories in your head? Do you think the boss wants to be disturbed with fictional nonsense? No. He's busy plotting the next phase of our future. What's the point in putting us in charge to protect the loot, if we're going to bump him on the first hurdle?"

Weirdly, Jennie felt a twang of sympathy for the woman. Although she couldn't be a hundred percent certain, she was right. Just because Muscles was speaking down to her, it didn't mean that she was wrong.

Jennie stepped out from behind the pillar and disconnected from Baxter. The three of them heard Jennie cock the hammers of her pistol and the Big Bitch before they knew someone was there.

Their eyes widened at the sight of her. Not with the innocent fear of civilians who had never stared into the barrel of a gun before, but with the disinterested twitch of criminals who were used to danger.

"Impressive guns," Muscles remarked.

"I could say the same to you," Jennie replied. She had the pistol trained at the woman's head and the Big Bitch aimed at Muscles' heart. Ferret was out of her line of fire, but Jennie knew he was the least dangerous of the lot. "Make a noise, and I'll make a louder one. Reach for your guns, you'll lose your hands. Try anything sneaky, and I've got forty armed agents surrounding this facility, ready to open fire and turn you guys into Swiss cheese. Understand?"

Although they didn't show fear, their eyes began hunting in the darkness for the supposed agents.

"Bullshit," Muscles growled.

"Maybe," Jennie replied. "But is it worth the risk?" She took a step closer, turning her attention to the woman. "You. What's your name?"

The woman sneered. "Fuck you."

"A little unorthodox, but who am I to question? Okay, Fuck You, I'm going to give you a couple of options. It's up to you to choose the right one if you want to live. You got that?"

She remained silent.

"Good," Jennie continued as though her question had been answered. "Option number one, you come along with me and tell me what you know about this place. I've noticed a couple of things that don't quite make sense to me, which is unusual, given that I know a *lot* of things. You can also show me where the rest of your fellows are hiding, and give me precise information on how many there are, what to expect, and what the hell this entire operation is about."

Jennie looked at Fuck You expectantly.

The woman raised an eyebrow. "Or?"

"Or?" Jennie repeated.

"You said there were a couple of options. What's number two?"

Jennie's face went from confusion to mirthful understanding. "Oh! I did, that's right. Sorry, I misspoke. What I meant to say was that you have one option, and that is it. Now, tell me what you know."

Muscles chuckled darkly, hands moving to his waist. Jennie waved the Big Bitch at him again. "Hands where I can see them, Tank. This baby can blow a hole in you so wide you'll be shitting out your chest."

He raised his hands. "You have no idea what you're dealing with, do you? We don't fear death. We know what's beyond it. The next level. Go ahead, try us."

With that, he plunged his hand to his waist and drew a silver revolver. He fired so quickly that Jennie hardly had time to latch onto Baxter and move out of the bullet's path before it sped past her.

At the shot, Baxter leaped from behind the pillar. The bullet drove through his forearm, leaving behind a small ghostly hole.

He roared in pain. "Son of a bitch!"

Jennie's eyes widened as she glanced at the gun and realized that the bullets were imbued with spectral energy. Without a moment's hesitation, she holstered her weapons, dipped both hands into two of the pockets at her waist, and withdrew two vials. A black liquid sloshed around inside, and these she threw into the center of the trio. She latched onto Baxter as a black cloud seeped into the air.

The trio wheezed and shouted, their voices echoing around the empty factory floor until they trailed off as they were knocked unconscious. Jennie covered her mouth with the crook of her elbow and waited for the inky gas to clear before becoming material again.

The gas soon subsided, and Jennie approached the trio. She drew a thin coil of wire from one of her pockets and bound their hands behind their backs before waving for the SIA agents over to join her on the floor.

The agents worked methodically, sweeping the floor for any sign of further intrusion. Certain that the sound of Muscles' gunshot would raise an alarm with the enemy, they kept their rifles at their eyes, prepared for any eventuality.

No one came.

"Scour the area," Jennie instructed Sade, who it had quickly become clear was the most experienced out of her troop of agents. "Search for trapdoors, trick walls, and anything else that might show us where they came from."

Sade nodded and relayed the commands to the agents while Jennie walked over to Baxter and checked that he was okay.

"I've been through worse," Baxter assured Jennie, holding his forearm to his eye and looking at her through the hole.

Jennie grimaced. "Still…Can you use it?"

Baxter lowered his arm and tried to lift his wrench. Jennie could see the knots of tendons and ligaments struggling to lift the weight. Baxter hissed with pain.

"I'll take that as a no."

Baxter gave a weak laugh. "At least I've still got one arm. It's enough to work this." He waved his pistol in the air.

Jennie wrapped her arms around Baxter, surprising both herself and him with the sudden display of affection.

Baxter blushed, as far as specters could blush. "What's that for?"

Jennie lowered her eyes. "I don't know. I guess I was afraid for a moment. I'm not used to having people around who it would make a difference to me if I lost. I need you, Bax."

Baxter grinned and placed a large hand on her shoulder. "You don't need me. You're Jennie-fucking-King. You know, *Rogue?*"

Jennie met his eyes and returned his smile. "I don't know. Rogue wouldn't give a shit if anyone lived or died as long as justice was served." She went quiet, falling into thought. "You're the first person in a long time I've grown close to. I wouldn't want to see anything happen to you. I've had a hundred Worthingtons. I've never had a Baxter before."

Baxter nodded, his own eyes growing glassy. "I'm not going anywhere, Jennie."

Someone called for Jennie across the room. She turned her head, and just as she started walking, heard Baxter mutter, "Even if I wanted to, you'd latch onto me and pull me back."

She shot a look over her shoulder.

Baxter winked.

The call had come from David, who stood by a rack of steel shelves that divided a section of the room. Carved into the floor by his feet were four concentric circles. Each circle contained a further three circles, with symbols spaced equidistant from each other inside.

"A puzzle," Jennie murmured, kneeling closer to the art and tracing the smooth grooves of the circles. She tested her theory, putting pressure on them and discovering that each rotated. "That star indicates the top point. Each panel needs to be lined up in the right order to open the door."

"How do we know the right order?" David asked as Natalia, Sade, Jack, and Clive joined them. "There must be a hundred possibilities."

"At least," Jack agreed.

Jennie took a closer look. Each circle contained a crucifix, an eye, and a crescent moon. She noticed that each groove glowed strangely with a faint pulse of light.

"I wonder…" Jennie mused. She traced a finger along the groove and inspected it. The faint glow stained her fingertip, the liquid residue still wet.

Without a word, Jennie rose and walked briskly over to the box of silver cylinders. She took one delicately from the crate and brought it back to the puzzle.

Bending back down, she found the lid and unscrewed the top. A strange scent came from the liquid, reminding her of freshly packed earth and blown-out birthday candles. Her stomach spoke to her, protesting something she couldn't quite understand. One hand moved unconsciously to her gut. She'd almost swear she heard a scream.

The agents watched while Jennie held the cylinder over the puzzle and poured a small amount into each groove.

The liquid occupied the spaces between, illuminating each circular groove in seconds. The icons lit up brightly, but it was only when Jennie noticed a few glow brighter than the others that the combination appeared.

She twisted the circles, and the concrete panels ground against each other. At the top came the eye, followed by the moon, then crucifix, then the eye once more.

When the final piece was in place, the puzzle gave a loud click, and the entire circle rose out of the ground a few inches, revealing a hole large enough to place a hand inside to grip.

Jennie exchanged glances with the agents, who all trained their guns at the puzzle. She lifted the lid, and a warm rush of air greeted her. The hole dropped straight down, and there was a short ladder fixed to its sides.

CHAPTER THIRTY-SEVEN

<u>Baltimore, Maryland, USA</u>

It took some time to filter a healthy number of agents down through the tunnel. Jennie confirmed the coast was clear down below, marveling at the corridor that opened up at the bottom of the long rung ladder, and soon two dozen agents were lined up and ready.

At Jennie's instruction, a handful of agents swapped their rifles for their SI pistols. She commanded a unit to remain above ground to keep watch over the hole and the facility. Jennie didn't want their escape to be blocked should they need to use it.

Not that it would be a problem for her. But now she had mortals to worry about, too.

The corridors reminded Jennie of a hospital. There was a strange clinical smell, and the walls were painted in a white which had faded over the years. Strip lights lit the way as they approached the first set of doors on either side of the walls.

Jennie placed a finger on her lips and stood next to the door on her left. She signaled for Baxter to do the same to the other room. They pressed their ears against the door for a few seconds.

Silence.

Jennie counted down from three on her fingers, and when she was holding nothing but a fist, she and Baxter quickly passed through the doors with their guns aimed in front of them.

Two bedrooms, empty and vacant. A cot sat in the corner of Jennie's room, the sheets disturbed and the bed unmade. A small washroom lay off the main wall, with a smattering of miscellaneous items scattered around.

Jennie exited the room. Baxter reported the same when he returned from across the hall.

They advanced down the corridor and cleared the next set of rooms, then the next, then the next. The bedrooms had all been vacated. After the fifth set of rooms, the corridor split into a crossroads, and all Jennie could see to her left, right, and in front were more doors.

"Is this some kind of fancy underground hotel?" Natalia whispered.

"Not one that I'd want to collect loyalty points at," Jack replied.

Jennie left four agents at the intersection and took the rest of them with her along the corridor straight in front. Her father had once told her, "If in doubt, and you've got no way of picking the best option, just make a decision. What difference will it make?"

When they reached another intersection after another five pairs of doors, Jennie left four agents standing guard and kept walking until they hit yet another intersection ten minutes later.

"What the hell is this place?" Clive grunted. "It's like a labyrinth."

"That's it," Jennie exclaimed in an urgent whisper. She looked back at her team, aware that almost half of her agents were now stationed back along the corridor. "The facility is *trying* to separate us. If we keep leaving people guarding, we're going to have no one left. It's designed to confuse and ensure that no one can storm it."

"You're saying that this is all planned?" Natalia asked, uncertain. "That these are just prop bedrooms to make us think there are more people than there are and that their small number can attack us?"

"I don't like this," David grumbled, training his eyes to the far reaches of the corridor, where the squares shrank into nothing but darkness.

"It would make perfect sense," Sade conceded. "Why else would this place be so quiet after the ruckus we made above? It's too coincidental. We need to go back and—"

She was interrupted by gunshots popping back the way they had come. Men and women shouted. They could just make out the agents falling to the floor before the lights at the far end shut off and engulfed them in darkness.

The agents at the intersection behind them began firing back at an enemy Jennie could not see. One fell down. Then another.

"Prepare yourselves," Jennie shouted, running toward the action, determined to protect her people.

Another down.

Jennie was halfway down the corridor with the agents running behind her when the final agent she'd left on guard went down and the lights in that strip of corridor extinguished.

"Shit!"

The lights at the intersection they had just left went out, too. They were trapped in an island of light, with darkness on either side and no visual of their enemy.

"In here, quick," Sade hissed, holding a door wide.

"And here," Natalia urged.

The agents split between them, cramming into the bedrooms. Jennie and Baxter melted into another bedroom and waited in silence.

Footsteps came down the corridor, slow and deliberate, echoing through the halls. A crash came as a door was thrown open, and without even checking who was inside, shots sprayed the wall.

"Damn," Jennie cursed. "These guys mean business."

Baxter looked down at an imaginary watch on his wrist and tapped it.

"You're right," she agreed, steeling herself.

Another crash, and another rain of bullets. They needed to move and fast.

Jennie stuck enough of her face through the wall to be able to see what was going on without drawing attention to herself.

They all wore tight black clothing, and each of them had a dark mask covering the lower half of their faces. Armed with rifles, they looked set to wipe out anyone and everyone who intruded on their facility.

Around their necks were more pairs of SI goggles.

At least they're not on their faces.

Ensuring she was sufficiently latched onto Baxter, Jennie passed through the wall and took a position in front of the shooters. They were about to kick open the next empty door—then all they would have were agents—when Jennie appeared in front of them, catching them off-guard.

"Looking for something?" She smirked and unloaded her guns into them.

The men on either side went down in a spray of blood. The rest fired at Jennie, who had already become immaterial and disappeared before their eyes.

They scrambled for their goggles, urgently trying to get them on their faces. By the time they did, Baxter was standing in the spot where Jennie had been. He pointed behind them, and they turned and saw Jennie once again as she fired and took two more down.

This time, they tracked her as she turned immaterial and melted through the wall. A trail of bullets followed her, but unlike Jennie, their bullets couldn't easily make their way through solid surfaces.

"Porcupine!" one of them shouted. The attackers obediently formed a circle, standing back to back so they had a three-sixty view as a group.

Not that it mattered, much. Jennie came through another door just long enough to fire her pistol and the Big Bitch and take two more down. She sprinted and dove across the corridor, bullets missing her by inches before passing through the other side.

The SIA agents in the room were shocked to see Jennie appear as a spectral vision through the wall. She came out into the room next door, then repeated her duck-and-dive maneuver and took out two more of the enemy.

They died quickly enough. Two by two, they went down as they tried to find Jennie before she shot them until all that was left was one.

He ran, pulling a device from his pocket. The corridor lights went out, and all that was left was darkness. He made it as far as the intersection before Jennie, who had been expectantly waiting around the corner for such a move, turned material and wrestled him to the ground. She landed on his back and pressed the gun against the back of his head.

"Don't fucking think about it, arsehole," Jennie growled.

She patted down his sides until she felt the device. She took it from him, ensuring she also nabbed his gun, and pulled him to his feet.

He strained in Jennie's grasp. He was fast and strong. Before she knew it, he had worked himself free, and his fist connected with her face. "What are you?" he grunted, his breath coming in sharp bursts.

Jennie tapped a number of buttons on the device, hoping for the best, and the lights above them came on.

The brightness was painful after the darkness. The man had his fist poised, ready for another blow. He soon lowered it at the sight of the agents who emerged from the rooms.

Jennie rubbed her cheek, feeling the heat on her skin as blood rushed to its surface. She regained her posture, drew her own fist back, and planted a right hook on the man's jaw.

He grunted and spat blood.

"We're even," Jennie told him, raising her chin. She examined the man closely. His amber eyes flared with anger. There was a rash of stubble spilling over the top of his mask. A strange chemical smell came from his mouth. "Now, why don't you tell us who you are and what the fuck is going on in this facility?"

The top of his cheeks rose in a satisfied grin. "You mean, you don't already know?"

Jennie shook her head. "Reception was closed, darling. We had to break in. Why don't you go ahead and tell us before I shoot you in the kneecaps and *make* you talk?"

The man stared at her. There was a movement in his mouth. She heard the faint crack of something which reminded her of biting Tic-Tacs.

Her eyes widened when he choked. "No!" She lunged at him, ripping down the mask, but it was already too late.

His eyes stared vacantly at hers as his face flushed red. He dropped to his knees before collapsing to the floor, dead in a matter of seconds.

Baxter stood next to Jennie, staring at the dead man. "How… What just happened?" he asked.

Sade joined them. "Cyanide pills. They can be shaped like teeth to provide agents and informers with a way to kill themselves to escape interrogation. Work the tooth free and bite into the cap, and the poison hits your system in seconds."

Jennie's eyes fixed on the man. There had only been a handful of times when she had been around people who needed to equip themselves with a master off-switch. Those situations tended not to have the brightest outcomes.

"The stakes have been raised," Jennie stated, looking down the corridor. "They know we're here."

"We're in the right place, then?" Sade asked.

Jennie nodded her confirmation. "We just need to work out the floor plan and get out of this goddamn labyrinth." She turned to the others. "Keep your eyes open. Stick together. That was but a taste of what is to come."

CHAPTER THIRTY-EIGHT

<u>Baltimore, Maryland, USA</u>

Brendan Koa watched them on the CCTV footage with a smirk on his face.

"Years ago, we wouldn't have been able to enjoy any of that." When he spoke, his voice was a deep, rumbling bass in the back of his throat. "Even ten years ago, technology was infantile compared to what we have today. We used to have to watch CCTV in black and white, making do with jittery screens and cut footage when connections failed. The cameras were big boxy things that couldn't be missed. But now…"

He chuckled as one of his men collapsed dead to the floor in front of the intruders. In his fingers, he rolled an object that looked like an LED bulb, but it contained technology to house a camera system that was almost completely undetectable. "Look how far we've come."

With barely any effort, Brendan pinched the device in his fingers. Tiny shards of glass pierced his thumb and forefinger, but he didn't notice the pain. He sprinkled the debris onto the floor and spun his chair toward the man and woman standing on the other side of his immaculate mahogany desk.

"It's impressive," Cole Kipman agreed, his words slightly muffled by the scarf covering his mouth.

"Impressive isn't the half of it," Brendan snapped. "It's like I'm there in the room, watching from the walls as they try to take over our base."

Julia looked nervously from Cole to Brendan. "With the greatest respect, sir, you seem pretty relaxed, considering SIA agents are working their way into the facility."

Brendan ignored her comment and pulled a handle on the desk to reveal a drawer filled to the brim with gold and purple wrapped candies. He rifled his hands through them, causing the wrappers to crinkle loudly, and selected one. He twisted the wrapper and threw the chocolate into his mouth, closing his eyes as he let the sweet flavors wash over his tongue and delight his taste buds.

He swallowed with a loud gulp and pushed himself up from the desk, standing only inches away from the screen. He was of medium height and had the figure of a man who had worked out all of his life but had begun to slow down in his later years. The definition of his muscles had softened.

A small patch of facial hair rimmed his lips, and a thick purple scar ran down his cheek. It was a permanent reminder of an encounter in 'Nam when he'd been ambushed, and only his lightning-fast reactions had allowed him to wrestle the knife away from the enemy.

"The best part about the internet is the accessibility," Brendan answered at last. "Remote locations, accessibility, and speed. If you know the right ways to play with a machine, you can have it do almost anything at all. They're not to be trusted, really." He chewed his lip. "Not to be trusted."

The leader of the intruders turned around on the screen. Julia let out a slight gasp as Brendan paused the feed and zoomed in on her face.

"Is that her?" he asked.

"Yes, sir," Julia confirmed,

Brendan nodded slowly, eyes narrowing as he scrutinized the

woman. She was attractive and certainly didn't care for the uniform. While the rest of the invaders sported the three-letter logo that made him want to punch a hole in the wall, she wore tight clothing that looked to have come straight out of a steampunk movie.

"Interesting," he mused.

They watched her for a few more moments until she vanished from the camera feed. When she was gone, he pressed a button on the remote, and the feed jumped back in ten-second intervals. He stopped at the moment Jennie appeared before his men and watched the moment she vanished from sight.

He waited for her to reappear, then jumped back to the time stamp and watched it all over again.

He grinned. "Fascinating."

"The woman's a freak," Cole complained. "Comes out of nowhere and slaughters our men. Give me the command, and I'll have her exterminated."

"No need to worry about that," Brendan told him, his words slow and measured. "Powers like that need to be studied. They need to be *understood*." He turned to Cole. "Bring her to me."

"She's dangerous," Julia warned him. "Her power knows no bounds."

"Everyone has limits, my dear," Brendan told her. "And everyone has their price." He watched Jennie on the feed again and smiled. "Wait until she sees the magic we've uncovered here."

Jennie felt like she was in a modern-day catacomb, searching far under the ground and running around an elaborate maze of traps and enemies where every step could mean death.

They took formation, guarding their front and back as one of their number, a young agent by the name of Conroy, sketched a map on his phone screen to keep track of where they had and hadn't been. Eventually, they found a part of the labyrinth where the corridor ended and a steel door accessed by a pin combination stood as the barrier.

Jennie strode up to the door with a sense of confidence that could only be earned from years of walking through walls and existing around specters. She latched onto Baxter, faded from sight, and—

Walked straight into the door.

What the hell?

There was a faint white glow around the edges of the door. Although the barrier was metal, a shimmering white pulse thrummed across its face.

Jennie checked that her connection with Baxter was tight.

Which it was.

She then tried to put her hand through the door.

But she could not.

"What is it?" Baxter asked.

"I can't get through." Jennie studied every inch of the door, aware of that faint shimmering glow. She put both hands on the door and pushed, feeling resistance where there should be none. "Something's off here."

"Is there a problem?" Sade asked, breaking from the group and joining Jennie and Baxter. With her goggles on her face, she looked like a strange alien insect.

"I can't pass through," Jennie replied. "This has never happened before."

"Haven't you been working on spectrally-imbued wall panels with Proctor?" Jack came closer now, running a hand across the door's smooth surface. He could see the faint pulse of light through his goggles.

Jennie whirled. "Who told you about that? That's top-secret information."

Jack looked incredulously at Jennie. "You did. After those daiquiris a couple of nights ago."

"Oh." Jennie's face colored.

"You said, 'what happens at SIA HQ, stays at SIA HQ.'"

Jennie chuckled. "I suppose that's not the worst secret to get out. But why would they be here?"

Natalia lowered her weapon and narrowed her eyes at the door.

"They already have SI goggles and some strange liquid metal. I'm guessing there's a mole in the agency, and the little shit has passed on our secrets."

The agents shuffled uncomfortably. Honor and respect were key among federal agents, especially those within the SIA. No one would want to be revealed to be a mole.

"Let's get solid evidence before we start pointing fingers," Jennie cautioned them. "Anyone here good with tech?"

A couple of agents were about to raise their hands when Jennie smirked. "Come on, Bax. Let's do this."

Jennie cupped the keypad with her palm and closed her eyes. She channeled Baxter's energy and sent a small pulse of power surging through the pad.

The panel sparked inside and shorted out. With a loud click, the door lock released.

Jennie reached for the handle, pulled, and stuck her head around the corner. She could see only darkness.

They filed through, careful to make as little noise as possible. Right now, Jennie wished she had a few of her specters from New York. With them on her side, she'd be able to navigate anything the humans might throw at her. They'd still get hurt by the spectral bullets, but they wouldn't die.

The only light they'd had was the green glow from the SI goggles, and they'd turned them off the moment they walked into the room. The sound of their soft steps carried a long way. Jennie, as blind as she was right now, could tell they were in a large room.

She kept close to the wall as the door closed behind them, feeling around for the switch that would illuminate their situation. "Porcupine," she whispered, hoping her comrades would understand her reference.

The agents fanned out around her, covering every inch of the room.

Jennie's hand rested on a switch. She only hoped she wouldn't accidentally trigger an emergency alarm that would draw more attention to them.

It couldn't do any more harm. We're clearly in the dragon's lair.

Jennie waited for the soft clicking of the SIA agents readying their weapons, then flicked the switch.

Overhead strip lights flickered into action, a hum of electricity shooting around the room. The light was overwhelming, momentarily stunning them all.

They had stumbled into a workshop. Desks were covered in papers, tools, and a variety of objects that caused the hair on the back of Jennie's neck to stand on end.

Pistols, rifles, goggles, gloves, shirts, batons—dozens and dozens of objects that could cause great harm to a human. Computers stood on the desks, and at each end were a number of the small cylinders of the liquid metal they had seen on the surface.

A loud clap drew the attention of Jennie and the agents. She looked upward at a man who was standing on a metal walkway above them. He clapped another two times, then rested his hands on the rail.

"That was quite a show you put on back there," the man declared. He wore the same clothing as the men they had taken down in the corridors, only his was blood-red. Two katanas were crossed on his back. "We really thought we were protected and no one would be able to work their way through our defenses, but we've heard a lot about you, Rogue. Or should I say, Genevieve King?"

Jennie felt a chill running down her spine. Did she know this man? How did he know her? She was pretty sure that the only people who knew both her alias and her real identity were located in New York or were with the SIA.

Unless there really is a mole.

"Call me what you want," Jennie called back. "It won't mean all that much when you're dead, will it?"

The man chuckled darkly. "Miss King, I thought of all people, you'd know that death doesn't scare us. It's the next level in human evolution, a world beyond the mortal realm where pain is only temporary and the possibilities are nearly limitless."

Jennie eyed the man, her hand poised ready to grab the Big Bitch if she needed it. She knew it wouldn't be long before things erupted.

Nothing stayed this quiet for long.

"What do you want?" Jennie asked, to the delight of the man on the walkway.

"What do you think?" he answered. "You are in possession of a great number of mysteries and abilities that we have never encountered before. We may be leagues ahead of the SIA in the development of our spectral imbuement, but you? You're the missing piece, aren't you?"

"I've been called a lot of things in my time," Jennie replied. "The missing piece wasn't one of them." She paused, glancing back at the workshop and the array of instruments and equipment lying around. "What do you mean by spectral imbuement?"

The man began to stride along the walkway, his hand never leaving the rail. "Oh, surely even you are not that dense. Your colleagues are carrying spectrally imbued firearms right now, are they not? Those goggles…SI goggles Mark 1.0, am I right?"

Jennie growled. "Mark 2.0."

The man nodded. "Impressive. Nice to see that Proctor is making a mark in Washington. Not the speediest guy, is he?"

Jennie grew tired of the man's cocky facade. Her mind worked at her next steps, knowing that this man would be the perfect person to interrogate. But given that the last enemy they'd tried to capture had killed himself, she didn't hold much hope that the same cyanide tooth wasn't lodged in his gums.

What would happen when all hell broke loose? He would run, sure enough. Others would come. She could feel them, ready and waiting to strike. "Why don't you show us some of your latest tech, then? But before that, you can tell us who you are. I don't like to be at a disadvantage."

"Yet I love seeing you at one." The man smirked. "But, hey, since you asked, let's give you a show. Gentlemen! The lady has requested a demonstration."

He clapped twice and the lights went down, plunging them back into darkness.

The agents reached for flashlights and shone them at the walkway. They thumbed their SI goggles and the lenses went green. Wide funnels of light illuminated the enemy as they sprinted toward them.

Jennie stepped back in alarm. Almost all of them were specters.

CHAPTER THIRTY-NINE

<u>Baltimore, Maryland, USA</u>

Jennie grunted as she drew her pistols and started firing at the horde. "I knew I felt something strange."

Baxter was beside her with his pistol and wrench at the ready. The specters could do little to the mortals, so they went for the one they could attack. The attacking specters had no weapons but simply ran at the team with the intention of pouncing on Jennie.

There was no way of telling exact numbers, given their limited view. The specters rushed them from all angles, outnumbering the agents by at least ten to one.

The SIA agents kicked into gear, sending a hail of spectrally imbued bullets their way. The first row of specters went down, limbs disappearing as silver blood laced the air. The next row fell before the specters had registered what was happening. A few from the third row dropped before the rest crashed into Jennie and Baxter.

"Cover Jennie!" Sade screamed above the ruckus.

The agents fired at the specters around Jennie, taking down the ones that posed the greatest threat.

Jennie was prepared.

An overwhelming surge of spectral energy flowed around the room. She could feel each of the specters' separate frequencies, and it was these she homed in on, foregoing her Big Bitch and pistol and choosing instead to rely on her innate powers. She had been born with and had no explanation for them, except that she had been put on this planet to create balance and deliver justice on both the mortal and spectral planes.

Jennie latched onto the specters, taking the first row, then the next. Threads of energy surged toward her. The specters gasped and held their chests, frozen in their tracks while the SIA agents sprayed them with bullets to incapacitate the threat.

The light grew stronger around Jennie. She stretched her arms wide, feeling the power coiling through every fiber of her body. She tensed, fingers curled at the end of her outstretched hands as she controlled her gift and held the specters in place.

More came to join the throng. With every additional specter, Jennie felt her power stretched further. She could hold a great number of specters, that she had learned. But she had never been tested to her absolute limit before.

A rain of shots fired, and Jennie heard a scream.

She opened her eyes and saw the muzzle flash of a gun. It lit the room long enough to let her spy the mortals coming for the SIA agents.

They were surrounded.

The SIA agents stopped shooting at the specters around Jennie and turned to face the oncoming threat, determined to preserve themselves. Jennie closed her eyes, unable to hold them open anymore, given the amount of concentration she was using to hold the specters at bay. Somewhere in the chaos, she heard voices shouting commands. Sade yelled at the agents to protect Jennie.

"Bax, tell them to go," Jennie managed through gritted teeth, loud enough for Baxter to hear.

"No," he argued. "We're not leaving you, Jennie."

Jennie had no time to argue. "Take. Them. And. Get. Out. Of. Here."

She squinted through the blinding light at Baxter hovering nearby, torn between his need to protect Jennie and his instinct to obey her.

Jennie flicked her hand at Baxter, filtering through the dozens of frequencies to single out his connection to her, and shoved him toward the agents. He flew as though he had been physically thrown.

All Jennie knew was exertion. Specters crowded around her. The shouts of the SIA agents faded as they followed Baxter's instructions. More shots were fired, and their voices faded; Jennie had no idea whether they were alive or dead.

"Take her! Take her!" the man's voice called from above like a puppet master controlling his toys.

Jennie drew the spectral energy toward her, feeling for any specific frequencies that could help her in this situation. The majority of the specters were unremarkable, but there was something nearby—she could feel it. Something…

Power. Strength. A wellspring of energy.

The connection drew her to a specter in the middle of the horde, a woman of great strength. The only specter who was able to inch her way closer to Jennie while the others were held at bay. Jennie opened her eyes, struggling to see her, but she could *feel* her all the same.

Jennie drew the specter's energy and felt it inflate her muscles. She drew her arm back and punched the nearest specter, sending it flying back. A left hook and the next one followed it. She gained momentum, her arms pinwheeling as she cleared the area in her determination to get the fuckers away from her.

Another gone, then another. One more after that. Jennie could feel the strength swelling within her. The woman she had latched onto froze, drained of her own power.

Determined to make a break for it, Jennie picked up the nearest specter and hurled him at the walkway. The specter passed through the man and the walkway.

The man wasn't bothered one bit that Jennie had taken out his specters, which Jennie didn't understand until she saw the mortals wading through the incapacitated specters to surround her.

Jennie turned material, reached for her guns, and fired six shots in quick succession. She turned immaterial before they could fire, but realized at that moment that it wasn't the bullets she had to hide from.

One man grabbed her left arm and another man grabbed the right. Jennie turned and couldn't believe what she was seeing.

Each man wore a pair of gloves that glowed with the same green light the SI goggles gave off. Although she was immaterial, they held her as though she were in the same realm they were.

"Get the fuck off me!" Jennie shouted, trying to find the tank woman to latch onto once more.

But it was too late.

Enemies shrouded in dark clothing began pummeling her. Their fists connected with her spectral body, then her mortal body, then her spectral body again as she tried to trick her way out of the situation.

A punch to her chin.

One to her ribs.

Another to her temple.

Jennie saw blinding white light as pain blossomed in her vision.

The specters faded into darkness, and the enemy disappeared, too.

Jennie was out cold before she hit the floor.

The Plaza, New York, USA

Lupe threw the phone at the armchair. "She's not picking up."

Carolyn watched the city out of the window. Central Park was a display of earthy colors. Dog-walkers strolled the streets, and taxis blared their horns. "Of course not. It's daytime. You know she only comes out at night." She spread her arms wide and bared her teeth. "She's like Dracula."

"I'm sure she'd appreciate that sentiment," Tanya replied.

"She's probably just busy," Carolyn added. "You know what she's like, always doing something or other. Leave her a message, and she'll call back."

Lupe had a strange feeling in his stomach. He had tried to call a number of times since their interaction with the Dragon. He assumed the information about the Shadows' rituals spreading online was something Jennie would be interested in. Surely she would've picked up by now, or called back.

Lupe didn't have the heart to tell the others the call was going straight to voicemail, which could mean one of three things: Jennie was in an area without signal, her phone battery had died, or she had destroyed the phone and run off.

He didn't think Jennie would do that to them, but what did he really know about her? Sure, they'd been on some adventures together, but did he know her deep down?

"I'm sure it's nothing," Lupe assured them, trying to hide the uncertainty in his voice. "Like you say, she's probably just busy. It's not like we've got to worry about her bleeding out on a table or being caught."

"Yeah, she's *Rogue*." Carolyn said "Rogue" in a tone that left no doubt Jennie was a superhero in her eyes. "She's our modern-day Wonder Woman."

Tanya laughed. "You know she was fictional, right?"

Sandra lifted her head and sleepily looked at the pair. "Who's Wonder Woman?"

Tanya brushed the hair from Sandra's face. "Never you mind, sweetie. Go back to sleep."

Meanwhile, Feng Mian and his parents were sitting in the corner of the room, talking in whispers with a laptop open in front of them.

Baltimore, Maryland, USA

It had been years since Jennie had slept this deeply. Decades. Maybe even a century.

Darkness swallowed her. No dreams came. She was unaware in a void, an empty, hungry belly at the bottom of an endless pit. She didn't feel herself being lifted and carried away and was undisturbed by the rumble of the vehicle's engine.

The voices muttering nearby did not disturb her slumber. The guards kept it down nevertheless, in case the mighty Rogue rose to consciousness and took them by surprise.

It wasn't unpleasant. Jennie sank into the darkness, allowing herself to bathe in its comfort. Something tugged at her consciousness. Danger. Her people. Jennie fought to break free and became aware of muted voices. A small dot appeared in the darkness, a light at the end of the tunnel to lead her out.

She reached for the light, driven by the need to fight to return to her body. The light grew wider, impossibly slowly, as though it were on a conveyor belt moving away from her. Jennie felt herself running through a viscous liquid, desperately seeking the light.

"Hush, she's stirring."

An unfamiliar voice. The words slid past Jennie's ears like moth wings. She tried to lift her head, unsure why it felt so heavy. Jennie found she couldn't move her arms or legs, either.

There were footsteps nearby, then a click and painful, stinging light flooded her vision. Jennie knew the setup. She'd been on the other side of it countless times. A lamp aimed at her face. Her accuser hidden in the shadows beyond.

So this is how it feels?

Jennie screwed her eyes shut. Her mouth was cotton dry. She smacked her lips together and was surprised when the chilled edge of a glass was pushed against her mouth. Water touched her lips. She gulped it down greedily.

"Better?" That same voice—a deep croak, confident and measured.

Jennie shook her head to clear it. When she spoke, her words were short and to the point. "Tell me who you are and what the fuck you want before this gets messy."

Silence.

The man shifted behind the light. She made out his frame as she blinked, holding her eyes open for a couple of seconds before she was forced to close them again.

The man laughed with genuine amusement. "Even after all that, you still think you have the upper hand? I'm impressed, Genevieve. I really am. You don't have any clue what you're faced with, do you? If you did, you'd probably be showing me those famous British manners of yours."

Before Jennie could respond, several things happened at once.

Another light flashed in her face, causing a fresh jolt of pain in her eyes. At the same time, an airhorn sounded in her ear. Then another, short sharp blasts that tore at her eardrums. Then another, until her vision was flooded with white.

Then came the rocking sensation. The chair, which had been sturdy on the floor, began to rock around as though Jennie were sailing in a ship on the ocean. She had no idea how the contraption worked, but she knew its primary goal.

To disorient and confuse her.

After a few seconds of this, all activity ceased. Jennie swallowed, feeling bile rise in her throat. Even just the short burst of sensory overload was enough to drain what little energy she had.

"Better?" the man asked, malice lacing his words.

Jennie tried to find him, unable to see his silhouette through the after-burn of light on her eyes. "What do you want from me?"

"Oh no, my dear. You mistake our motives." The man's voice came from behind her. "It's not what we want from *you*. It's what *you'll* want from us."

He switched the lamp off and the overheads in the room came on. Jennie blinked rapidly, struggling to recalibrate. When she did, all she could do was gasp.

CHAPTER FORTY

Unknown Location, USA

Jennie gazed at the panel of screens lining the entire wall.

At first, she'd thought they were showing various news channels, but now she realized they were showing live feeds of places around central Baltimore.

Two across and three down showed the docks and footage of the water, as well as civilians going about their day. Four from the right and seven down showed a front view of the church where Jennie had been reunited with her good buddy Julia and her possessed army.

One screen displayed the facility Jennie had at one point assumed was abandoned. Another showed the inside of the building, multiple angles of the cargo bay where the boxes of silver liquid had since been moved. Another showed the corridors and the labyrinth she and the SIA agents had gotten entangled in.

Another showed a looped replay of the fight that had transpired with the spectral horde and ended with the capture of Jennie. Right now, it pulsed with white light as the feed was disrupted. Jennie could just about identify herself among the circle of specters.

Jennie couldn't believe her eyes. "You've got the whole city bugged?"

"Of course," the man told her, the smile on his face clear in his tone. "When you're playing a game with high stakes such as this, you need to be aware of every possible angle. For months we heard and saw nothing, believing that maybe we would be left in peace to do what we needed to do. But then I got a phone call, the first warning that you had come, and soon the SIA would be coming to Baltimore."

The man moved into Jennie's peripheral vision. She tried to turn her head but found she couldn't move it. She could only look up and down.

"You see, you were the trigger, Genevieve. Without you getting involved in matters that didn't concern you, we'd have had no warning. We were monitoring Baltimore's activity, and we caught every damn moment of your so-called invasion."

Jennie's chest tightened. How was all this possible? "Who is it? Who's the mole?"

As she spoke, feeling began returning to her arms and legs. She tested her restraints as subtly as she could, flexing and tensing her muscles to free herself from her bonds. She felt around the room and could sense no specters to latch onto. For the first time in more years than she could count, Jennie was totally, unequivocally alone.

The man erupted into laughter. Spittle flew in front of the screens. "A mole! My dear, you really do underestimate our reach. A mole would be nothing more than a bug you could squish with your pinky. We've put in far more protection than that to ensure that our sources remain open and we get all the information we want. Our partner is very involved in ensuring that our projects go ahead. Very involved indeed."

A door opened and closed. Another set of footsteps. The man faded from her vision and reappeared a moment later with two glasses of red wine.

"You're a drinker of red, aren't you?" He held the glass beneath her nose. The deep fruity scent of fermented grapes invaded her senses. "I hear that red wine is really an older woman's drink. You're, what? A hundred and ten, now? One-twenty?"

Jennie's jaw clenched. It seemed impossible for a man to know so much about her without her knowing who on this planet he might be.

"What do you want from me?" Jennie asked again.

The man sipped from his wine. "I want you to join me, Genevieve. You are in possession of a certain set of gifts that would prove fruitful in my endeavors. I'd like to know you better, down to your very genes. To study and investigate what makes you so unique. How you are in possession of your abilities. Immortality. Spectral manipulation. The powers would be great assets to our cause."

"Why should I trust you?" Jennie growled. "I can't trust anyone whose face I cannot see."

The man slowly walked into her field of vision. "I suppose you're right."

He was older than she had anticipated. In his fifties, at least, with a rash of gray stubble. His eyes were keen, and he had kept himself in shape.

Jennie would know his type anywhere. *Ex-military.*

"You're Brendan Koa, aren't you?" Jennie asked.

Brendan flinched, taken aback by the sudden use of his name.

Jennie grinned. "I, too, know more than you think."

"I expected nothing less," Brendan conceded, regaining his composure. "I shouldn't be surprised by what you know, I suppose."

"That's right," Jennie replied. Her wrists grew slick with sweat as she tensed her arms and tried to work free of the restraints. While Brendan's men couldn't take her guns, she couldn't access them at the moment, either. Their power was bound to Jennie's specters in the same ways Jennie was, becoming invisible and fading from sight the minute her connection to specters faded. It wasn't all bad news, however. The guards had clearly been too distracted to have taken the vials hidden in her pockets.

If only she could get to them.

Brendan dragged a wheeled chair from the side of the room and sat in front of Jennie. "Now that we know a little bit about each other, why don't we make a deal?"

Jennie's lip curled. "I don't make deals with criminals."

"Criminals?" Brendan scoffed. "My dear, criminals are law-breakers who deal in mortal affairs. We're existing in a realm of the law that hasn't even been discussed yet, one that no one has even brought up in the federal courts. Nothing here is illegal, so we are not criminals."

"Then what is it you're doing?" Jennie cocked an eyebrow. "If you want me to join you, tell me what you're doing. I don't get this. From what I gather, you're fighting to become the leading spectral organization ahead of the SIA. Your buddy Kurt told me all about you, Koa. About your split. About your ego. About all you want to accomplish."

"That was a long time ago," Brendan told her. "Things have changed significantly since then."

"How?"

Brendan rose from the chair and dug a key from his pocket. He moved to the side of the chair, and a moment later, a lock clicked.

Jennie's hands, legs, and head were free now. She tentatively sat up, massaging her wrists. She rolled her neck around and turned to see Brendan standing beside a man she recognized as the puppet master of her capture.

"You!" Jennie leapt forward, fighting the weakness in her leg muscles. She stumbled, then gained her footing and dived at the man.

He caught her before she fell, missing his body by inches. She couldn't believe it. Had they put something into her system to weaken her?

"Don't be mad at Cole." Brendan chuckled, not concerned in the slightest by her sudden outburst. "For all you know, he might have done you the biggest favor in your long, long life."

Cole helped Jennie to her feet, then stepped back. He laced his fingers behind his back and obediently stood at ease.

"Come, Genevieve. Let me show you what we've got going on here. You might find you like what you see."

Brendan held the door open for Jennie. She passed him and went out of the room. Before the door shut behind them, Jennie heard Brendan whisper, "Make sure no specters get near her on the tour, got that?"

Jennie was guided down yet another ominous corridor.

"To say we've been working hard barely covers it. The year has been a grindstone on which we've whetted our blades in the spectral arena." Brendan opened a door to his left. A sign on the front read NO ACCESS, but that didn't seem to bother him.

"The spectral kingdom is the hidden wonder of the Earth. For years we've been looking at space and into the depths of the ocean for the things we might have missed, but they've been in front of our noses all the time."

Brendan grabbed a pair of SI goggles that were hanging from a bracket on the wall and placed them on his face. He took a second pair and offered them to Jennie. When she looked at him, confused, he laughed and put them back. He winked and smirked. "Just kidding. You don't need them, do you?"

Jennie remained silent and followed Brendan onto a metal walkway in the rafters of a building that looked somewhat familiar.

At least forty feet below her were rows of desks and benches with people stationed at each one. She recognized the various devices they were working on, the computers, and the layout of the place. Over on the far wall, she could see the doors the agents had escaped from.

If they'd escaped.

"What is all this?" Jennie asked. "An underground research lab? This was empty not too long ago."

Koa smirked. "Oh, Genevieve, you've been out for hours. I cleared the space when I found out about your invasion. I've got to protect my staff, you know. But here is where the most important work in the city takes place. Come. Let me show you more."

Brendan led Jennie down some stairs and introduced her to various members of the staff. Table by table, Brendan asked the researchers what they were working on, giving Jennie the chance to ask questions if she wanted.

At one table a man busied himself with a riot shield that had been disassembled. Each component glowed with that strange pulsing white light.

On another, a woman worked on a pair of handcuffs, examining them under a microscope with such scrutiny that the rim of the lens left an impression around her eye.

It wasn't until she got to the fifth table that Jennie had the chance to pose the question she'd been dying to ask ever since she had first seen the strange canister with her own eyes. "What is that? I've never seen anything like it before."

"Of course not," Brendan told her, a swell of pride in his chest. "That's new, a concoction of our creation."

He picked up a canister and held it to the ceiling. The overhead light refracted through the substance, spilling an array of colors. The liquid swirled, disturbed by the sudden movement.

Jennie noted the researcher eyeing them warily.

"This is the secret sauce," Koa told her. "The key to creating an array of tools that can cross the borders of mortality and work on specters. Before, all we could do was unlock the ability for mortals to see and communicate with them, but now we have the ability to hold them to account, too. No longer will specters be able to hold mortals for ransom. To break and disturb and frighten and terrify." He turned to the researcher, asking the question as though launching into a high school pop quiz. "What's the one thing most people on this planet are afraid of?"

"Er, death, sir."

"Exactly." A greedy expression painted his face as he stared at the canister again, rotating it in the light. "Death. Mortals fear what we don't know. What we don't understand. Anything that cannot be explained by science is something that gnaws at our intellectual brains and gives us cause for upset."

He continued in a faraway voice. "The worst part of combat was the unknown. Marching into enemy territory and not know what you'd face. Sure, you'd have intel, you'd do your research. But who knew if the enemy was one step ahead? Who knew if the ground you were treading was laced with mines? Who knew where the snipers were hiding when they could fire from over a mile away? The only way to win in this life is to have the upper hand, and this is our ticket to that."

"May I see that?" Jennie held out a hand for the canister.

Brendan paused, looking as though he was struggling to part with the object. "Sure."

The canister was cool to the touch, just as Jennie remembered. The minute her fingers connected, there was a dull ache in her stomach, a curdling she couldn't quite explain. The liquid swam and sloshed, moving as if by its own volition. As if it were *alive*.

"You talk about the paranormal world as though it's preparing to launch an attack on the mortal world." Jennie's words were soft, her eyes fixed on the canister. The liquid was mesmerizing. "For thousands of years, the two have co-existed. There's no need to prepare a full-scale attack."

Brendan extended his hand, and Jennie gave the canister back. His face grew troubled. "You misunderstand me, Genevieve. Maybe because you've spent your whole life in the company of specters, there's less fear within you. Maybe because the paranormal court has cared for you and watched over you since you were a small girl, you have more trust than we do.

"I'm not preparing for war. I'm not igniting anything in this world, just saying that mortals need protection. If there's technology to assist mortals with communicating and physically touching the dead, who's to say the technology couldn't be reversed? Who's to say that specters wouldn't want their mortality back? To be able to live and eat and drink and touch and love and breathe the same air that we do?"

Jennie scoffed. "Clearly we've been hanging around with different specters."

Brendan tilted his head with a pitying look in his eye. "Understand this from our perspective. We want to prepare, not attack. We want to develop good relations. Sure, it would be amazing to be the dominant force in spectral relations, but more than anything, I want our country to remain safe." He placed the canister back on the table.

The researcher picked it up, unscrewed the lid, and poured a small amount on a loaded M16. The liquid moved across the rifle, swallowing it whole. All that was left was a brilliant white replica of the gun for a moment, then the gun reappeared in its original state with a faint, pulsing glow passing across it.

"Beautiful, isn't it?"

Jennie refused to answer, reluctant to admit it was beautiful to watch.

"Come," he told her. "There's more to show you."

Brendan took Jennie out of the workroom and down a long corridor. She was surprised to note that this corridor, while mostly the same as the ones she had been lost in with the SIA agents, had large windows to allow passersby to see into the rooms.

The rooms were of modest size, able to comfortably fit twenty people. Each one was filled with men and women in dark cloaks gathered in a circle around a man or woman in the same dark outfit Cole wore.

Room after room was full. Class was clearly in session, although they couldn't hear the seminars.

"New recruits." Brendan smiled proudly. "Men and women who are desperate to discover the afterlife and see what we've got going on here."

Jennie couldn't believe the number of rooms that had been filled. For the first time, she began to feel afraid.

She caught glimpses of the classes as they went past. Projected on the wall was the anatomy of weapons and a description of the spectral imbuement process. Some screens showed illustrations of various specters, and Jennie was surprised to note that they were almost all accurate.

Brendan led her to the end of the corridor, where a large red door stood closed. "This is where some of our best work happens."

There came a scream. Faint, but a scream nonetheless. Jennie's ear cocked toward the sound, but Brendan showed no indication that he had heard.

Brendan opened the door for Jennie. "After you."

Jennie eyed him, listening for any more sounds of distress, and when she heard none, she followed Brendan's lead.

Contrary to the previous workshop, this room was as small as the seminar rooms. The lights were off, but they could see by the funneled glow of a projector showing a series of stats, lines, and beeps on the right-hand wall.

Two men in white lab coats busied themselves with an array of tubes, flasks, glasses, and instruments on the tables. On the far wall, dozens of tubes of different-colored liquids were displayed, with small labels identifying them. A large yellow triangle with a hazard warning was posted on the wall.

"Good morning, sir," the men greeted cheerily. "Come to see the latest?"

"Have there been many developments?" Brendan asked, a note of hope in his voice.

"Afraid not, sir. We're still trying to nail down the detection sequence. We can't initialize bootup until we're certain that we can capture the entirety of the body. Suction can cause quite a mess if not precisely utilized.

"Suction?" Jennie asked.

It was then that she saw the strange contraption on the workbench. The device was a large metallic cube with a wide-mouthed hose protruding from its front. There were a series of knobs and switches on its side, and on the table next to it...

"Holy water?" Jennie reached forward and picked up the glass. "*Holy. Water?*"

The researchers flinched, approaching Jennie now as if she were holding a bomb.

"Please put the glass down," one of them asked in a trembling voice.

Jennie looked at Brendan. He wore the same careful expression as his men.

Jennie placed the glass down. "What use have scientists for holy water?"

The researchers remained tight-lipped, determinedly returning to their work and trying to pretend they weren't in the room with them.

"Thank you, gentlemen," Brendan told them, ushering Jennie toward the door.

When they were out in the corridor with the door closed behind them, Jennie asked the question again.

Brendan sighed. "You know as well as I do that the normal scientific methods aren't enough to further our work here. Are you telling me you don't know what use holy water can have against specters?"

"I know perfectly well," Jennie retorted. "That's why I'm concerned. Exorcism isn't something you should take lightly. It's the ultimate kill switch."

Brendan gave an understanding nod. "I know. This is where our preparedness comes into play." He walked off without further comment, leaving Jennie to follow.

She could have run then. Could have tried to fight her way out of the compound. But she had to admit that her curiosity was piqued. She had the chance to discover what was going on in Brendan's facility, and she wasn't about to pass that up.

Brendan was right. Intelligence *was* the key.

He guided Jennie back to his office, the wall of screens still illuminating the room in a headache-y glow. He closed the door behind her and allowed her to sit in a chair free of restraints.

"Observe." Brendan moved over to a keyboard on a small shelf by the wall. He typed in commands, selected options, and soon the entire screen coalesced into one giant image.

A montage of horrors met Jennie's eyes, footage from spectral cameras that captured the activity of poltergeists, rogue specters, and beings much worse than *sturmgeists*. Situations in which mortals awoke in the middle of the night and were frightened into comatose states. Disruption at public events where poltergeists swept across the crowd and threw objects into the air to start riots. A museum where it looked as though a dinosaur skeleton had collapsed when really the specters could be seen toppling the structure.

Haunting after haunting, disruption after disruption—a comprehensive display of mischief and evil by the specters of the world.

"How did you acquire all this footage?" Jennie asked, aghast.

"You see?" Brendan asked, his face lit by the ghostly glow from the screen. "Protection. That device my men are working on? It's one of many forms of protection from the darkness that lies in the spectral world. A vacuum of sorts, laced with holy water. Enough to pull in a poltergeist and exorcise them in a heartbeat. Problem gone. Call us the exterminators of the filth of the spectral world."

Brendan's hands gripped Jennie's shoulders from behind. He leaned toward her ear, his voice soft and seductive. "For years you have fought the darkness alone, relying on ignorant mortals to help you accomplish your goals. You dream of a world purged of evil, a place where justice can rule supreme. You don't have to do it alone. You know that, don't you?"

Jennie considered his words. For over a hundred years, she had been the only one of her kind. The only person alive who could tread the line between the spectral and the mortal realms.

There had been times when she had a friend. Times when she wasn't alone. The queen could only give her so much, and each personal specter grew tired of her after a while. She had gotten used to being alone, isolated, one of a kind. Weighed down by the burden of her gift and her desire to help others.

But what if she didn't need to bear that burden alone any longer?

"The SIA," Jennie asked. "What about them?"

"The SIA doesn't know what they're doing," Brendan dismissed. "Come on, Jennie. We've both been operating for the same amount of time. Rogers and I parted with the same knowledge, but look at what I've accomplished. How many more steps ahead do I need to be before we're recognized as the dominant force on the mortal side?"

A thought came to Jennie. "Who's 'we?' Who are you?"

Brendan gave a small entertained snort. "You know who we are, Jennie. You've dealt with us already, just on a much smaller scale. We're the Shadows."

A jolt of discomfort ran down Jennie's spine. "Which would make you the Umbra?"

Brendan chuckled. "That's right. The darkest part of the shadow."

CHAPTER FORTY-ONE

<u>Baltimore, Maryland, USA</u>

Baxter's heart thumped wildly. Well, technically, it didn't.

Phantom palpitations were a hazard of specterdom, and Baxter was glad as hell he wasn't actually at risk of it pounding out of his chest.

The cars drove almost silently along the roads, a convoy of pedestrian hatchbacks and SUVs and a pickup truck or two. All were fitted with silenced mufflers. All had been chosen to avoid detection as the SIA gathered their full forces to invade the facility and reclaim their secret weapon—the woman who had given them a fresh injection of hope in their race to understand the spectral. A woman with a golden heart and the courage of the fiercest lion.

Jennie.

Baxter had never felt more isolated and alone. Sure, Natalia, David, Sade, Jack, and Clive were on his side, but there would always be something lacking in the connection between mortal and specter. Communicating with mortals sporting SI goggles made Baxter feel as though he were being ogled through the glass like fish in a tank or a polar bear at the zoo. There was a physicality that was missing. They were there, but were they really?

Oh, the irony.

The agents were as silent as their cars. An unspeakable tension pervaded the interiors as they homed in on the facility, at least two hundred agents and a handful of specters from their compound.

The journey from Washington to Baltimore had taken an hour or so for the other agents. Baxter and the others had waited with Drampton, tapping their feet until backup arrived.

They veered onto the off-ramp and began their final approach to the industrial park. The agents straightened in their seats, ready for anything. Leading the way, Sade cut her lights and crawled toward the facility.

Sade put the car into park when the building came into sight, but they were a safe distance away. The other cars gathered around them like dark clouds. They waited.

A few minutes later, a voice muttered in the agents' ears. Sade turned to Baxter. "Two bogeys near the compound. The rest of the area is secure."

"How can you tell?" Baxter asked.

Sade nodded out of the window at a black van not far from their convoy. A satellite dish sat on the top of it.

"Heat detection, sonar, and every other detector you can think of," Sade told him. "They know what they're doing. Trust me."

Baxter nodded. "I don't know why you couldn't have fashioned an earpiece for me."

Sade grinned. "And waste another few hours developing tech when we need to find your buddy?"

"She's your buddy, too," Baxter protested.

"I suppose." She clamped her tongue between her teeth and turned the engine back on.

The convoy swarmed the facility like ants around a fallen piece of candy. Baxter's phantom heart dropped when he saw the semi parked in front of the garage door. There appeared to be no one inside.

"I thought you said it was clear?"

"It was. I mean, it should be," Sade whispered. Her hand reached for the molded grip of her pistol. The agents followed suit. She eased open her car door and aimed her gun toward the cabin of the semi.

Baxter was at Sade's side, his own pistol poised and ready. Agents exited their cars all around them and advanced on the truck. If anyone were to jump out on them, they'd be in instant trouble.

He spotted Rhone and Daggro speeding toward them, eager to reach the head of the pack.

Sade approached the truck's door. She signaled for Baxter to take point. He broke ahead and cautiously melted through the door.

The cabin was empty. A small hula dancer ornament sat on the dashboard. There was a faint smell of vanilla mixed with pine. Several cigarette stubs littered a small ashtray.

Baxter exited and shook his head at Sade. She nodded toward the rear.

Baxter went ahead with the agents not far behind. He paused at the door and waited until the agents arced around the back. When they were in place, he took a steadying breath, aware once more of his phantom thumping heart, and was about to pass through the doors when they opened.

A hundred agents prepared to shoot. Baxter took a step back, unable to hold off the beaming smile that pulled at his cheeks.

"Easy now," Lupe called, hands held defensively in front of him. "You called for backup, didn't you?"

He shoved the door wider, revealing a truck filled to the brim with specters.

Unknown Location, USA

Jennie sat on the couch and looked around the room.

It was nice, a wide space that felt almost homey. It was a complete juxtaposition to the cold, raw, industrial feel of the whole facility. This room had clearly been decorated for her.

A large TV was mounted to the wall. Three plush couches were centered around a glass coffee table. In one corner was a fully-stocked bar, complete with every liquor and juice she could ever want. The room off to the right was a bedroom with a four-poster bed that looked fit to sleep eight. There was an en suite bathroom with a jacuzzi spa and a power shower, and another room off the living area with gym equipment that would keep Jennie in shape and ready for action.

If she hadn't known she was underground in Baltimore, she would think she was at home in her cozy little apartment beneath the Savoy. The absence of windows was not unsettling, given her acclimatization to living underground, but as she sipped her mojito and thought over her conversation with Brendan, she was very aware that she wasn't at home.

His words had seemed genuine. There was authenticity behind his motives. A world purged of darkness. A world free from evil.

Jennie had spent over a century fighting the darkness. Most of that time, she had been alone in her fight, used as nothing more than a weapon by a queen who had betrayed her trust and used immoral means to retain her throne. A queen she thought had seen her as a daughter, but who hadn't trusted her enough to tell the truth. A queen who had destroyed her own kin and relegated them to the crypts to live among the wraiths, then disappeared and left her throne guarded by maniacal specters with the single goal of holding the throne, no matter what it took.

It was lonely work. It was tiring work. Here she was being presented with a chance to put all that behind her. To work with the Shadows to realize a dream she'd had since she was a little girl.

A world purged of evil.

But if that was the case, if Brendan truly wanted to get Jennie on his side, why would he lock her in this prison? Because a prison it was. As comfortable and homey as everything had been made, the door was locked, and she was not allowed to leave. The truth was that he had turned the key and shut her inside. With no specter to latch onto and thus no way to melt through the door or walls, which were presumably already imbued with spectral protection anyway, she was at his mercy.

But am I? Wouldn't you do the same if you were trying to make someone change their mind? If you had the chance to convert someone you feared. You wouldn't just let them walk free, would you? You'd put them somewhere where they could think. Give them a chance to consider the information they'd been presented with.

The truth was that Jennie didn't know which way was up. The situation with the queen had shaken her world, and the normalcy she had lived for years had shattered and broken around her. The only thing she knew was that justice ruled all, and the world deserved to be at peace. What she didn't know was which way would achieve her results with the least amount of casualties.

No matter what happened now, the truth of the paranormal world was leaking out like air from a pricked balloon. If the SIA and the Shadows knew, it wouldn't be long before the world did. No secret this big could remain quiet forever.

Although it had had a fair run, hadn't it?

One mojito.

One martini.

One cosmopolitan.

A cocktail of her own creation.

Jennie's head grew dizzy as she pounded the drinks, hoping to find some clarity in the mushy mess. She lay down on the couch, closed her eyes, and let her subconscious do its work.

Baltimore, Maryland, USA

Lupe, Tanya, Carolyn, Feng Mian, and Sandra hopped out of the back of the truck.

Baxter embraced each of them, impressed to see how quickly they'd come. "You don't wait around, do you?"

Lupe smiled. "Let's just say that we already had a few Spectral Plane with us, and we were eagerly awaiting a call."

"Why? What happened in NYC?" Baxter asked, his voice laced with concern.

Lupe exchanged glances with the others. "That's a story for another time. We've got a Rogue to rescue."

The rest of the specters spilled out of the back of the semi-truck. The SIA agents stared in wonder as they flooded out, around fifty of them altogether, viewed through their SI goggles, although only those who had worked directly with Jennie sported the 2.0s and could hear the conversation.

Rhone smiled at the pack. Daggro's sneer remained on her face, but even she had traded her trademark growl for something akin to an impressed stare.

"You say you can lead us to where we need to go?" Rhone asked Sade and Baxter.

They nodded. Sade answered. "Of course. The main problem will be funneling through the tunnel, but there's room enough at the bottom for us all to gather. The specters will need to take point and check the coast is clear." She turned to Lupe. "Can your guys handle that?"

Lupe laughed. "Can my... Clearly you know nothing about the Spectral Plane."

Sade looked at him blankly. "No. I don't."

They filtered inside the building, agents trained with their rifles and pistols. This time they broke through the door at the front, kicking it in and readying themselves for return fire. Knowing what lay inside, they were certain the enemy would be in position and ready to attack.

The main facility was clear. Even the boxes filled with the strange liquid were gone. As they snaked their way toward the entrance to the underground compound, a feeling of apprehension pricked Baxter.

Why weren't they armed and ready? Weren't they expecting a rescue operation?

The specters assumed their positions, and at the instruction of Lupe, jumped down the hidden entrance, not even bothering to use the ladder. They took turns, waiting a few seconds and disappearing like lemmings. The only specter to stay behind was Sandra, who remained at Tanya's side. A small thread of energy attached them together.

"After you," Baxter offered.

Tanya didn't argue, but she did pause for a moment in apprehension. Sandra tugged her hand, and she too disappeared a moment later. Baxter knelt next to the hole and cocked an ear until he heard a soft, "All clear" from below.

He gave a thumbs-up to Rhone, Daggro, and Sade, and jumped down too.

The labyrinth of corridors wasn't any less confusing, and the lights were now off. Illuminated by dozens of flashlights, they managed to find their way, though there were several occasions where they hit dead-ends or realized they had turned themselves about.

The whole time Baxter and the specters listened for any sign of the enemy. He wondered again how they had been alerted to their presence the first time they'd entered the facility. There hadn't been any sign of cameras, which were usually in the corners of the room.

His eyes were drawn to the ceiling when a glint of light caught his attention. He stopped the specters behind him and pointed at a small black dot. It was no larger than a pinhead, but something had definitely just flashed there.

Rhone called an agent over and placed a foot in his cupped hands. The agent hoisted Rhone high enough for him to inspect the object. With careful fingers, he pried it from the ceiling, pulling out the wires that trailed behind it.

"A camera," he told them when his feet touched the floor. He rolled it in his palm, showing them what looked to be an LED bulb. "They're watching."

"Shit," Baxter cursed. "That was how they knew we were coming." He took the camera from Rhone and moved it closer to his eye. "Damn, that's an impressive piece of gear. It's not just a camera. There's also a transmitter/receiver, a mic, and I think infrared technology as well." He smiled like a child examining a Rubik's Cube. "How is technology this microscopic even possible? To think, the first commercial video cameras came about in the 1930s. Big blocky things. Basic. Black and white. These days, we have this. It's beautiful."

Rhone gave Baxter a strange look. "Sure, the tech is impressive, but we've got more important things to worry about." He glanced at the ceiling again. "How many of them do you think are rigged around here?"

"Hard to say," Baxter replied, his eyes not leaving the tiny camera. A goofy smile appeared on his face as his tech-fueled brain began to swirl with questions. "Could be a hundred, maybe more. If they're this tiny, how will we ever know?"

"It means they're watching us," Daggro growled, her lips pinned back in her signature sneer. "They're probably listening to every word we say. Why don't we quit the geek-out and get our asses back to the job at hand? Aren't we supposed to be rescuing Ginny?"

Tanya gave Daggro an incredulous look. "You mean, Jennie."

"Oh? Do I?" Daggro scoffed. "My mistake."

When they reached the door to the room where Jennie had been taken, Baxter paused and cocked his ears. The other side was silent, but then again, it had been silent before too. What kind of trickery could there be to catch them off-guard this time around?

"Ready?" he asked Carolyn, Feng Mian, and the others. He made a mental note to ask Feng Mian about the two older specters flanking his sides, who bore an alarmingly close resemblance to him.

They melted through the door like a wave seeps through a slatted fence. The agents waited patiently on the other side.

The room was dark. Baxter skirted the walls until he found the light switch. He flicked it several times, but nothing happened. He wondered if the fuse had blown.

Shit.

The room was silent. With no light or any sounds, he had his first glimpse of the abyss. Was this what ultimate death was like? To float forever in an eternal pool of nothingness?

When he melted back through the door, the agents readied themselves.

"Get your flashlights ready," Baxter commanded. "There's no light. No indication of the enemy. We'll need to move fast."

On Rhone's count of three, the agents charged the workroom. Their footsteps covered any chance of hearing the enemy, but they were poised ready to shoot attackers. They found positions, covering every part of the room.

Their flashlights danced around like the floodlights above a circus tent, the agents building a picture of what was before them as the beams of light illuminated the room.

They covered the walkways, the floor, the walls, and the ceiling until the whole room was lit by the hundred or so agents.

But no one came.

As the echo of their footsteps faded, they were met with further silence.

"Spread out and search the place," Rhone instructed, heading for a metal staircase leading to the walkway above. Lupe commanded half the specters to go with the SIA agents, while the other half searched the doors leading off the large room.

Twenty minutes later, the group reassembled. Both Rhone's faction and Lupe's faction returned empty-handed.

There was no sign of Jennie or her captors.

CHAPTER FORTY-TWO

Unknown Location, Baltimore, USA

Jennie started when a key was inserted into the lock, unable to remember when she'd fallen asleep. Her muscles protested as she sat up. She pawed her eyes and rubbed her neck.

The lock clicked, then there was a soft knock on the door.

"Is that really necessary?" Jennie called, her voice dry and raspy. "You've got a key. You could come in whenever you wanted."

"Take it as a sign of our hospitality that I haven't," a woman called back. "May I come in?"

Jennie recognized that voice but couldn't place it. "If I say no?"

"Then you'll be alone longer. People go crazy when they're alone for too long."

Jennie wasn't impressed by the woman's reply. *Girl, you think I haven't spent over half my life alone?*

Another knock. "Well?"

"Fine," Jennie conceded. "Come in."

The door opened and revealed a woman with bright red lips and a dark cloak. For the first time since Jennie had known her, Julia's hood was down, revealing a smooth curtain of dark hair.

Jennie's lip curled. "I think I've changed my mind."

The woman held out her hands, a note of genuine fear on her face as she took a tentative step into the room. "I can understand that. The times our paths have crossed have not been without their bumps."

"Bumps?" Jennie shook her head. "That's one way to describe it." The destructive whirlwind as the *sturmgeist* devoured the little Batsto church flashed through her mind. For a second, she was back there, fighting with all she had to contain the beast.

The woman watched her apprehensively.

"What do you want?" Jennie asked.

The woman's eyes danced around the room. They settled on one of the couches. "May I take a seat?"

"That depends."

"On?"

"Whether a black eye would ruin that pretty face of yours."

Julia took a deep breath and proceeded forward, her face determined. She took a seat across from Jennie. The farthest one, but it was still a bold move on her part.

"We haven't been properly introduced," the woman began. "My name's Julia."

Jennie's jaw clenched. She remained silent, eyes boring into Julia's. "No need to introduce yourself. I know who you are."

Julia cast her eyes around the room, uncertain how to broach what she had to say. Jennie couldn't help but notice Julia pinching her left ring finger and rubbing it unconsciously. There was a pale line where a ring might once have been.

Julia met Jennie's eyes. "I want you to know something. Despite our previous encounters, I'm not a monster. There are two sides to every story. Everything we've done, everything we've achieved, has been in the name of advancing science. We are unlocking ancient knowledge lost for millennia."

Jennie folded her arms and stared at Julia, unblinking.

Julia looked down at her knees. "A revolution is coming, Jennie. We have to be prepared. There are always casualties in war, but I assure you, we're the good guys."

"How can you *possibly* be the good guys?" Jennie snapped. "You risked the lives of dozens of innocents. You *murdered* mortals so you could, what? Test the limits of spectral possession? You abandoned your lover in an SIA cell without a second thought."

Julia's eyes sparkled. "Meister Donavon was an unfortunate casualty. He was a fantastic lover."

Jennie snorted. "He was a pawn."

"Progression demands sacrifice," Julia countered. "Those mortals we parted from their earthly bodies aren't dead. They're in this compound, willing volunteers ready to serve the Shadows. They asked for what I gave them. They were prepared to serve a greater purpose."

"Cult mentality," Jennie scoffed. "Sounds about right, doesn't it? The same mentality that had dozens of innocents playing accomplices as you were about to murder an SIA agent."

At this, Julia flushed. "That was an unfortunate misunderstanding. Desperation can often make people blind. Fear drove us to remove those hunting us. We didn't know it would go so deep."

Jennie shook her head. "Stop this 'we' shit. *You* led that ritual. *You* made it happen. Donavon might have thought he was in control, but you pulled his strings, gripped his mind through his libido, and made him think he owned it all." Jennie took a long breath. "How long have you been working for him?"

"For who?"

"Don't play innocent," Jennie told her. "Koa. How long?"

Julia stared at the wall, where an ornate mahogany bookcase held a collection of books centered around the theme of specters. There were books there that would have made Tanya drool in the days before she had encountered Jennie. "Not long. Not really. We didn't meet until he heard about the events in Batsto and reached out to me online."

Her eyes turned misty with admiration. "It's unbelievable to think how close we'd been this entire time. I had thought I was alone in my quest, he was just a state away, working on the same riddles I was working on. Only, I was the one to unlock them for him. To show him proof that the texts and the words in the scriptures were true. He loves me for that. He's rewarded me with rank inside his organization."

Jennie wrinkled her nose in distaste. "Great. Princess of a shitty little compound in Baltimore, and all it cost was an innocent life."

Julia's eyes met Jennie's. A small smile flickered, then died on her lips. "I know what you think, Jennie, but I mean it when I say we're the good guys. We stay in the shadows so we're not limited by law. We can test, we can probe, we can make progress. We want nothing more than to understand the spectral world enough to enact real change. To help the people and create an agency ready to tackle spectral issues. The paranormal court can take you so far, but true protection needs growth, and for that, we need you."

There it was.

Jennie silently rose to her feet and crossed to the bar. She pulled out a cocktail shaker and set bottles of white rum, gin, and vodka on the counter.

She unscrewed the lid of the vodka but hesitated before pouring it into the shaker. She shook her head, then took a swig straight from the bottle.

She swilled the burning liquid but did not swallow it. She took the rum next and added that to the vodka. Next was the gin. Finally, cheeks protruding and mouth almost bursting, she found a bottle of lime juice and added a measure of that, too.

She washed her mouth with the cocktail, then swallowed it loudly. Her body shuddered, and she turned her attention back to Julia. "Take me to Koa. We've got some talking to do."

Baltimore, Maryland, USA

The agents and the Spectral Plane explored the compound for another hour, combing every inch of the main research space. It yielded very little in the way of results. They searched cupboards, drawers, and under desks, anyplace that might shed light on where the hell everyone had gone. They were stumped.

"Not a single trace of evidence," Rhone muttered, face creased in confusion. "This is unheard of."

Daggro folded her arms. "They clearly knew what they were doing, unlike your hero, Rogue. I mean, wandering straight into an ambush. That's what happens when your ego leads you instead of logic and sense."

Baxter overhead this and squared up to Daggro. Standing at least a foot taller than the agent, he looked down his nose with eyes narrowed. "Watch your mouth, lady. You don't know what you're talking about."

"I know that we shouldn't be in this mess," Daggro growled, unfazed by the giant. "I know that if Rogers and Hopkins had listened to me, we wouldn't be wandering around an empty facility with possibly the world's greatest asset to spectral-mortal relations captured by the enemy."

Rhone glanced wearily at Baxter and Daggro.

"Jennie knows what she's doing," Baxter argued. "I'd follow her to the ends of the Earth. You haven't seen the shit I've seen her do. You've barely seen her power. She'll be fine, okay? Just fine."

Daggro laughed derisively. "Sure. I've spent over thirty years in this business. People change their minds and switch allegiance. Even the best agents get killed. I'm not going to keep my head in the clouds, swimming in optimism that the hot mess will roll up smelling of alcohol to save the day."

"Daggro, that's enough," Rhone warned. It wasn't only Baxter who was flushed with anger. Jack, Clive, Sade, Natalia, and David all looked her way, intense stares on their faces.

Daggro blew air between her lips. "What do I care? They're subordinates. We have a hierarchy for a reason."

"It's not them you should worry about," Rhone uttered softly, nodding at Lupe and Tanya, who were staring daggers at the agent.

Daggro shook off their stares. "Let's get the fuck outta here. There's nothing to be gained by staying any longer."

By the time they emerged into the open air, the sun was low in the sky. Streaks of blood-red painted the clouds and soft, cool air woke their systems.

"Where to now?" Baxter asked, blinking against the sunset.

Rhone and Sade were at his side. Daggro had already taken her unit over to their cars.

Lupe led the Spectral Plane from the facility.

"How do you track the untrackable?" Rhone answered with a sigh. "They left no map, no clues, and no indication of where they might have gone. They could have gone anywhere."

"What about camera feeds?" Tanya suggested, joining them with Sandra. "Won't there be anything to monitor the traffic around the industrial park?"

Rhone shook his head. "Already looked into that. There are no cameras on the streets here, so we wouldn't know if they even went overground when they left."

"What about the surrounding area?" Carolyn offered. "Bridges? Tunnels? Tolls?"

Again, Rhone shook his head. "We've got all that covered, but without knowing the exact vehicles they made their exit in, we can't narrow it down."

Baxter's eyes lit up. "The semis. The vehicles transporting cargo to the compound. They must have been coming from somewhere."

He explained what Drampton and the others had told him when they'd arrived at the Baltimore HQ.

"They must be smarter than that," Carolyn stated when he had finished. "They'd know we can trace the semis back to wherever they came from, right?"

Rhone stroked his chin, eyes heavy with thought. "Maybe, but it's something at least. Any lead is worth investigating." He turned to the remaining agents. "Head out to Baltimore HQ. Stagger your arrival. The last thing we want is to draw the attention of the locals."

The agents dispersed, heading back toward their cars. As Baxter was about to join the SIA once more, Lupe called from behind, "Hold on. We're not SIA, whatever that is, remember? We need directions."

Baxter turned from Rhone to Lupe with a grin. "I call shotgun!"

. . .

Unknown Location, USA

Brendan was sitting at his desk with his chin resting on top of laced fingers. A knowing look was on his face. "Ah, Genevieve. Please. Take a seat."

Jennie's stomach turned over. She realized she hadn't eaten for a long time, and she was hungry. She left Julia at the door beside Cole, who waited obediently in silence.

Jennie's stomach growled as she took her seat.

"Everything okay?" Brendan asked.

"Just a little peckish," Jennie replied.

Brendan snapped his fingers, and Julia exited the room. Behind him, the screens continued to show feeds of various locations around Baltimore. Jennie couldn't help but notice the array of agents queued up outside the facility beside a semi-truck. Baxter stood by the door, talking to the others. They looked set to storm the building.

Jennie smirked, nodding at the screen. "You've got visitors."

Brendan remained unconcerned, his eyes fixed on Jennie. A moment later, Julia returned with a plate of fruit, cheese, and crackers.

"I'm lactose-intolerant," Jennie stated flatly.

"We both know that's not true," Brendan told her. "Eat up. You need your strength."

Jennie stared at him a moment longer before her appetite got the better of her. She reached for a few grapes and a square of cheese, and before she knew it, she had devoured the entire plate.

Jennie sat back in her chair and exhaled, her hands resting on her stomach.

"Good thing those weren't poisoned, eh?" Brendan chuckled. "You're very trusting of strangers."

Jennie gave him a scornful look. "Please. After all those speeches you've given me, I'm going to assume that you don't want to kill me. You said it yourself; I'm valuable to you. You wouldn't kill me if I killed your best men and held you at gunpoint."

Brendan grinned widely. "Now we understand each other."

"Play your hand," Jennie ordered. "Lay it out flat on the table. What are you offering?"

Brendan held her gaze for a moment, then reached into his desk drawers and withdrew a thin stack of paper, perfectly flat, crisp and clean. Neat black print covered them. "It's all in here, Genevieve—the terms and conditions of our partnership."

Jennie glanced at the contract. "What makes you think I'd hold myself to this if I'd sign?"

"You're a woman of honor. A woman of your word." He pushed them toward Jennie. "Here are all the particulars. We'll allow you some time to digest this."

He rose from the table and crossed to the door.

Before he closed it behind him, Jennie called him back. "One thing before you go?"

"Yes?" he asked.

Jennie pointed the pen at him. "If you call me 'Genevieve' one more time, I'm going to take this pen and stab you in the eye."

Brendan laughed. "Understood."

Jennie was left alone in the room, only the faint electrical hum of the screens keeping her company. Her eyes were drawn to the screen with the semi-truck, but the street was now empty. She grinned, safe in the knowledge that her people were coming to get her. They'd be here soon. She knew it.

Jennie glanced at the papers, then rose from her chair. She wandered the room, keen to occupy the time until her rescue. It seemed Brendan's trust only extended so far, given that the room was pretty much stripped of any and all objects. A large potted plant took up the corner of the room, and the desk in the center was the only furniture. She tried the drawers and found them empty except for a single photo of two men in uniform, decorated with badges and standing side by side.

She examined the photo, looking at the unmistakable faces of Rogers and Koa. An inseparable team at one point, now sworn enemies. How could a relationship sour so suddenly?

The answer's simple, dumbass. It's the same reason you and Victoria aren't close anymore—power. The nuclear bomb to end all relationships. One might reach for it, and the other might give it. Either way, the imbalance causes an implosion.

Jennie flipped the photo over. On the back in an untidy scrawl of blue ink were the words, *Get reading, Genevieve. We haven't got all day.*

Jennie chuckled. Koa was a smart man, of that she was sure. Her eyes darted once more to the screen, the feeling of discomfort in her stomach again. Something she hadn't experienced in years, as though undigested food was causing her trouble, and there was nothing she could do about it.

She returned to her chair and flicked through the pages. A lot of the stack was nothing more than text, but she soon came across diagrams and illustrations that piqued her curiosity.

A contract of data research. Permission to use Jennie as a human guinea pig, and in return, she would be given anything she wanted. A key stake within the organization, a chance to oversee the development of tech, the opportunity to give her the answers to questions she had desperately sought for years.

What am I made of? Where have I come from? Who am I?

A non-disclosure agreement, an employment contract, and a personal waiver all rolled into one. The pages listed procedures Jennie had never heard of, promises of an understanding of her origins, the possibility of creating others like her.

Other mortals capable of treading the two worlds.

A chance not to be alone on the planet anymore, the only one of her kind. To assist in what could be the next stage of human evolution.

Jennie scoffed at the papers, uncertain what to make of all of the procedures and medical mumbo-jumbo.

Yet, the more she read, the more she became intrigued. A hundred and thirty-some years of unsolved riddles. The opportunity to unlock it all.

Would it be wise to throw all of that away?

Jennie flicked through the final documents and paused, the pages of the stack bending at the corners as her hand began to shake.

Jennie's breath caught in her chest when she read the header on the page. Her eyes scanned down, the words causing her heart to pound.

The Life and History of Genevieve King.

CHAPTER FORTY-THREE

<u>Baltimore, Maryland, USA</u>

"That doesn't make any sense," Rhone complained, leaning over Drampton's computer and looking at the information on the screen.

The screen was divided into four. Grayscale images of large black semi-trucks driving along the open highway were pictured in each. The vehicles were staggered at five-hour intervals.

"The camera never lies," Drampton refuted, offended. "Agent Rhone, you should know better than that."

The cameras followed the trucks to the edge of the city. Drampton's jurisdiction only allowed her to track the feeds so far. They managed to track the journey as far as the outskirts of the state, where the trucks turned into an intersection that would lead them down the 95 or the 295.

Both roads led to Washington.

"Why would they go that way?" Baxter asked. "If these guys are who you think they are, shouldn't they be avoiding Washington altogether?"

"Some people are just stupid," Daggro growled.

"They're clearly smart enough to avoid our detection," Rhone retorted. "Don't forget, they just lured us into an empty facility and left no trace behind."

"We've got to follow them," Lupe urged, his eyes fixed to the screen.

Daggro chuckled. "Who invited the eighth dwarf?"

Lupe stared daggers at her.

"He's right," Rhone told Daggro. "We have no choice. We've got to figure out where they're going. If they're in Washington, that gives us an advantage. At least there, we're closer to home base."

"Which makes even less sense," Baxter grumbled, screwing his fists into his eyes. "It's too dangerous for them to be doing *anything* in Washington."

"Hey, we're only assuming," Drampton told him. "For all you know, they could be splitting off and taking the 32 to Columbia. They could even hop off at 197 and head to Waldorf. The only thing we know for certain is that they're leaving the city." She gave Rhone a look. "These might not even be your guys."

"Either way," Baxter countered, "it's the best we've got." He glanced down at the timing records of the vehicles. "When's the next one due?"

"Twenty minutes," Drampton replied. "You better get your asses in gear."

<u>Unknown Location, USA</u>

It wasn't possible for someone to know this much about her.

The pages were filled with Jennie's history. They had her birth date, her years of service, the surface details of her major operations over the years. Her parents' names, her places of residence during her formative years, and a full list of the specters she had partnered with over the years.

She read names she hadn't considered in some time. Her eyes were drawn to Cartwright Alexander, Winnifred Rombirk, Victor Yarris, and worst of all, Worthington Conrad.

Her eyes devoured the paper, absorbing the words in a frenzy.

Jennie hadn't known that this much information had been collected on her.

A header reading Indoctrination covered the formal aspects of her induction into the paranormal court. The next section covered the repercussions of Jennie's actions over the years, verbal warnings written on paper, slaps on the wrist—things that had been learning curves for Jennie as she acclimatized to the spectral world.

Impossible.

That was the word that kept flying around her head. Impossible. There was only one way someone could have gotten this information on Jennie. One organization who knew more of her truth than anyone else. One person who would have had access to this information, the woman who had molded Jennie and made her into the weapon she was today. One woman and one woman only.

There, on the final page of the report, was a photocopied scrawl of Victoria's signature.

Jennie grew hot. Her eyes narrowed, and her mouth suddenly became too small for her teeth. Her fists clenched and she slammed them on the desk, causing a small cactus to topple and roll onto the floor, spilling dirt across the carpet.

There were more pages.

With trembling fingers, Jennie flipped the page and was presented with an envelope. The paper was yellow and crisp. She turned it over to see her name printed on the back and tore it open.

The letter read,

Dearest Genevieve,

After careful reflection upon our conversation during your last visit to my palace, it is with regret that I wish to inform you of a change of heart that struck me late last night in my quarters, a thought so sudden and desperate that I had no choice but to listen and act upon it immediately.

The United States of America will remain under the rule of the paranormal court. I cannot allow a divide to upset the global aims we are hoping to achieve, and therefore I have put into motion a series of events that will ensure the United States of America remains an allied party.

The paranormal court has always stood for the protection and welfare of specters the world over. It is our aim to unite the world and remain the only force that protects spectral rights and balances the ever-tricky relationship between mortals and specters.

Therefore, the paranormal court is proud to officially announce its partnership with the Shadows. Mr. Brendan Koa is to act as the American ambassador. It is my hope that you will gracefully subjugate yourself to his party and act as an ally rather than a traitor.

I have gifted Mr. Koa with all our intel. He is quite the admirable ally, and has already accelerated our technological advances to bring mortal and spectral relations closer.

I understand this might be difficult for you to process, and I do hope time will allow you to see this is my way of making up for my...sabbatical. After decades of neglecting my duty, I believe it's best to grasp this bull by the horns and ensure that the war we all fear does not come to pass.

It's best this way, Genevieve. You've always been a rogue. You wouldn't want to hold the weight of the spectral world on your shoulders. Believe me, as someone who has done so for over a century, it can get tiresome.

Your Queen,
Victoria

"She cares about you, you know?"

Jennie hadn't heard Brendan re-enter the room, her mind had been focused on the abomination she had just read. Victoria believed she was doing the right thing.

Koa rubbed his hands together as he walked across the room. "Her Majesty is a marvelous woman. She was willing to hand over everything to us. To trust us and connect with us as partners. It came down to us and the SIA, and your queen chose the Shadows. I think that sends a pretty powerful message."

Jennie's hands moved to her stomach. She felt sick.

"We've been communicating for some time," Brendan continued. "Months. We were lucky, really, that she would hear of our work and reach out to us. Well, her team did. Every week they'd send us reports of tech that would help us in our quest, and every week we'd impress them with the leaps we'd made in spectral technology.

He smiled at Jennie. "But there was never anything to explain *you*, Genevieve, or how you work."

Jennie cringed at the mention of her name. She wondered if her feeling of discomfort came from just how similar Brendan sometimes sounded to Victoria. Few people on the planet used her full name, and each mention was like a cheese grater to the flesh.

Jennie growled. "She's not my queen anymore."

Brendan gave a soft chuckle. "She's everyone's queen, but that doesn't mean there isn't a place for a king.

Jennie looked up at Brendan, taking her eyes away from the paper for the first time. "What?"

"While Victoria rules the paranormal court, there's a spot vacant for the mortal side of affairs. The 'mortal court,' if you will. I'm not entirely happy with the name, but in time, I'm sure we'll find an adequate solution. A powerhouse of monarchs working side by side, using the impossible to unite the world and lead it under one force."

Jennie's lip curled. "You're insane."

"Am I?" Brendan's eyes flashed. "To believe we can build something better? Have you *seen* the world? There's war, poverty, famine, genocide, and riots, and that's just the big stuff. We could end it all. We could wipe out misery and suffering and replace it with a unified world where specters and mortals are united under our order."

Jennie's mind worked frantically to connect the dots. The ritual in Batsto, the possessed mortals in the church, the advancement of technology designed to catch specters.

"You're using the rituals to possess mortals and bring them under your control so you can act as their leader." A fact, not a question

"Not just me." Brendan grinned, a shark-like quality to his expression. "Those I love and trust will be granted flocks." He gave a derisive laugh. "I can't possibly manage 3.75 billion people."

"There are 7.5 billion people on Earth," Jennie argued. "Where are the other…"

Jennie lowered her head, unable to believe what she was hearing. It all made perfect sense. Grotesque, disgusting, perfect sense.

Jennie's words were toneless. "The ritual demands the sacrifice of half of the population so that specters may be funneled into mortal vessels."

Brendan's eyes took on a sad quality, the look a father might give his child when he tells him his dog has to be put to sleep.

"A necessary evil," Brendan replied.

Jennie looked at Koa aghast. "Why not just take the current spectral population and, what, 'funnel' them into people? You realize you're talking about genocide, something you just listed as an evil of the world."

"It was something I considered." Brendan scratched his cheek, a thoughtful look in his eye. "But the preexisting specters are not mine to command. They already serve a mistress, and her name is—"

"Victoria," Jennie finished.

Brendan worked his way over to Jennie and sat on the desk beside her. She could smell his cologne, a strange smell that reminded her of antiques and rotting flowers. "I realize this is a lot to process, Genevieve. There was no easy way to indoctrinate you into this new world. But you have a choice, now. Everything listed in that contract, I will honor. I will dig deep and find your ancestry. I will decode your genetic makeup and discover what makes you unique. I will give you a position within our order and allow you to guide the world into its new day. Victoria is right; you wouldn't do well at the top. You're a workhorse at heart, a cog that functions better as part of the machine. Do you really want to shoulder the responsibility for the fate of the world?"

Jennie's eyes were drawn to the contract. Brendan reached down and flipped over to the final page, where a line reading, *I, Genevieve King, do hereby commit my body and soul to the Shadows according to the terms and conditions laid out in this agreement* took up the top of the white space, with a line beneath for Jennie's signature.

Brendan presented Jennie with a pen. "It's up to you, Genevieve. What's it going to be?"

Jennie took the pen from Brendan and held it in her quivering hand. A mixture of rage and annoyance burned through her blood, but it was also mixed with something she wasn't proud to admit.

Temptation.

She had loved the queen once. Had viewed her as a surrogate mother. Victoria had given her a chance to be something, a chance to make a difference. Sure, the scandal Jennie had uncovered had been a giant blip in that relationship, but maybe it was something that could be recovered.

As badly as Jennie hated to admit it, the loss of her parents had been a big hit. There had always been a part of her that had hoped that they would live on. And the older Jennie got, the more it didn't make sense why her parents grew older and she didn't.

She could discover the truth.

That was the dangling hook, something Jennie had secretly always dreamed of, but not allowed herself to truly want.

An image flashed into Jennie's head of her taking a seat beside Brendan, restoring her relationship with the queen. A paranormal court fit for specters. Fit to rule and lead and…

Dominate.

It all came back to that, the word Brendan had uttered time and time again.

The image in her mind changed, morphing into a scene of violence and desolation. The pile of bodies found in the Baltimore church, only larger, the empty husks freeing specters to possess bodies of mortals and bring them under the Shadows' control. It could be done. *Had* been done. Julia had proven that to be true.

That sickening feeling returned. Jennie doubled over, wanting to know what the problem was. When had she last felt this ill? When had her stomach been this upset?

Jennie hovered the pen over the dotted line. She could feel Brendan's eyes burning into her, his breath held in anticipation.

"I don't want the responsibility," Jennie told him, pressing pen to paper and scribbling on the clean page. "But if I don't take it, the world falls to arseholes like you!"

Jennie moved so suddenly it was as though a viper had possessed her body. She took the pen and punched it into Brendan's chest as hard as she could, embedding the point an inch or so before it was stopped.

Damn, the fucker is wearing protective gear. He *knew.*

Jennie didn't allow Brendan time to react. She smashed her fist into his jaw and sent him rolling backward over the table. The screens flickered and wobbled precariously on their mounts.

Jennie rose to her feet, unsurprised to see a knife in Brendan's hand. A snake like him would have a weapon prepared for this moment, although even with all he knew about Jennie, he still underestimated her.

Jennie shoved the desk over, toppling its contents onto Brendan. The signature page with the black scrawl read Fuck you.

Jennie fled for the open door. The pain in her stomach intensified, but not enough to slow her down.

She was a fighter, after all.

CHAPTER FORTY-FOUR

Unknown Location, USA

Jennie didn't bother looking back. She had learned over the years that looking back only delayed progress.

Cole and Julia were outside the room. Jennie passed them in a blur and took a right, not knowing how or why she had chosen that direction, only knowing she needed to make decisions and get out of there. She was holding onto the truth of it all, a bombshell of epic proportions that would affect both the mortal and spectral worlds.

She needed to ensure that the information didn't die with her.

Jennie heard the unmistakable sound of pistols being cocked before a shout followed her down the corridor. "No! We need her. Capture her and bring her to me."

An alarm sounded, a violent, ear-piercing noise that grated on Jennie. Red lights rotated on the walls as doors opened and the corridors began to fill with Shadows.

Cloaked figures hunted Jennie, beagles chasing the fox.

Jennie took a hard right and ran down a corridor lined with steel doors hidden behind access panels that Brendan hadn't bothered to show her. Again she heard muted screams and wondered what in the name of all that is mighty was going on.

Jennie slowed her pace as a handful of cloaked figures ran toward her at a T-junction. She couldn't see their faces, but their bodies betrayed their intent. The walls around Jennie shimmered and she knew escaping wouldn't be as simple as melting through them and hiding from the others.

Besides, there were no specters to latch onto.

Brendan had known what he was doing. He did well to hide them from her, knowing that the source of her power was the very thing he was trying to control.

One of the Shadows fired a taser at Jennie. She took a sharp side-step and avoided its prongs, aware of the thrumming shock that ran down its coiled wires.

Another followed with their taser, then another. Jennie dodged them all, but only just.

Knowing she needed to break past the Shadows, Jennie took a running jump and used the wall to launch herself at them. Her legs wrapped around one Shadow's neck, and she clamped her thighs tight as she brought him to the ground.

Her feet touched the floor milliseconds ahead of his head. She softened her impact by bending her knees and using her momentum to drop into a roll. She slapped the ground, pushed herself to her feet, and ran past them, additional footsteps coming toward her from the corridor she left behind.

Her stomach twinged with pain. Something inside pushed her to go left.

Jennie ran along a corridor she had never seen before. The entire right wall was paneled with thick glass. As she tore away from her enemies, she afforded a glance at the city outside. She didn't recognize where she was. It disoriented her since she'd been certain they were underground. The cityscape baffled her. How could she be above the surface? It didn't make sense.

A bullet ricocheted off the wall to her left, the Shadow before her a monstrous thing who clearly couldn't manage his aim during his slow, lumbering run.

"He said no shooting!" Jennie shouted at the man.

If the man heard, he paid no attention. The barrel of the gun stared at her like a dark, unblinking eye.

Fuck.

Jennie could do nothing but run toward the hulk. Something caught her attention out of the corner of her eye. She dove to the floor and rolled as a bullet whistled by her, finding its place in the chest of one of the Shadows chasing her. Jennie rose to her feet and lunged for the framed picture on the wall. She tore the abstract painting of swirling colors, which she supposed might have been calming in another situation, from the wall.

Hulk hesitated, pausing as he lined up his next shot to consider the wisdom of firing in close quarters when he might accidentally hit another of his team.

That moment of hesitancy was all Jennie needed.

She hurled the picture like a frisbee. Before he had a chance to dodge, the razor-sharp wooden edge caught him in the face and slashed his cheek an inch below his eye.

He dropped the gun, his hands instinctively flying to his face. Jennie closed the gap, grabbed his pistol, and slipped past the screaming giant.

Jennie felt the comforting weight of the pistol in her hand. A near-full chamber of bullets, if experience had told her anything. *That's something, at least.*

"She's got a gun!"

Jennie turned the corner just as they opened fire. The bullets sprayed and chipped the walls as she dived beneath them, going for the elevator to her right. Its flashing sign indicated it was waiting on her floor.

Jennie made her decision. She punched the button and jumped inside when the doors opened. They closed slowly, despite her urgent pressing of the Door Close button. She had hit the next floor up, not knowing why. It was only after the elevator started moving that she began to question herself.

You've never steered yourself wrong before. Trust your instincts, girl.

Jennie's stomach churned as the elevator went up.

"Eurgh." She clasped her stomach, bile rising in her throat. "What the hell is wrong with me? I've not felt this shitty since Gordon Ramsey tried his new recipe for chicken and leek pie in '82." She rolled her eyes. "Every chef has to start somewhere, I suppose."

The elevator dinged, and the doors began to slide open. Jennie took a steadying breath and held her gun in front of her.

The corridor was empty. Tentatively, she stepped out of the elevator. There was a chill in the air. Silence pressed on her. The alarm did not ring up here, but the lights continued to flash.

A warning to anyone that danger was nearby and her name was Rogue.

Jennie turned through a door to her right and found herself in another corridor where the external wall was made of glass paneling. She allowed herself a moment to stop and look out over the city, hoping to spot a landmark that would tell her what part of Baltimore she was in.

She was at least twelve floors up. A labyrinth of residential and commercial buildings unfolded below. Not too far away, she saw a river winding its way through the city.

There was something in the distance before the stretch of river, something almost anyone would be able to name on sight, but which plunged her mind into utter confusion.

The White House, standing like a solitary soldier on the skyline.

"I'm in Washington?" Jennie couldn't make sense of it. When had she arrived back here? How was this possible? To be above the ground in the same city where her search had started, looking over the beating heart of the USA.

A door opened and closed somewhere nearby. Jennie moved back and tucked herself into the recess of a doorway, hand searching frantically for a knob as footsteps grew louder, reverberating through the corridor.

She found the handle and thanked her lucky stars when the door opened, swallowing her like a hungry mouth and allowing her to escape.

Jennie eased the door shut and waited. The footsteps grew louder, pausing outside her door. There was a heart-pounding moment of silence before the footsteps continued on their way and faded into the distance.

Jennie rested her head against the door and breathed a sigh of relief. She closed her eyes and caught her breath, trying to think of her best way out of the building. Shadows were everywhere, and they would likely be congregated on the lower floors. The only possible exits would no doubt be blocked as they hunted her through the building.

She was trapped, but she wasn't going to freeze until they had her in their grasp

"Think, Jennie, think!"

She had a gun; that was something, but one gun wouldn't be enough to force her way out of the building. Who knew how many men Brendan had working for him? Who knew what other technology he had to contain her if she tried to barge out the front door?

A song came to her then, a tune that seemed completely ironic in its upbeat tempo and message. She altered the lyrics, grinning as she sang a line from one of her favorite songs to have hit over the last decade.

Aloe Blacc's voice sang in her head. Jennie tunefully mumbled, "*I need specters, specters. Specters is what I need...*"

Something hard clanged to the floor. Jennie turned sharply, holding her weapon in front of her, finger ready to tense on the trigger if needed.

A solitary woman in a lab coat stared at her, frozen in place. A pair of SI goggles was strapped to her face, and the item she had dropped was a canister of the silver liquid Jennie had seen all over the facility. The glass had shattered, and the liquid pooled on the floor, spreading into a larger puddle as each second went by.

Jennie took a step toward the woman, unblinking as she stared at the researcher, whose hand was moving infinitesimally slowly toward a large red button.

"Move that hand any farther and I'll be forced to turn it into soup," Jennie remarked, her low voice echoing around the large room.

The woman froze, a single tear tracing down her cheek. Her lips wobbled. "Puh-please…"

"I don't want to hurt you," Jennie told her. "I just want to get out of here. You haven't harmed me in any way, so don't give me cause to do something I don't want to do. Do you know who I am?"

The woman nodded.

"Then you know what I'm capable of?"

Another nod.

"Step away from the button," Jennie instructed.

The woman obeyed, taking a couple of cautious steps toward Jennie. She glanced at the liquid.

Jennie indicated her white coat with the barrel of her gun. "You're a researcher, aren't you?"

Nod.

"Tell me straight, because every other fucker in this facility is talking in riddles and my patience for it has run out. What is that stuff? How is it made? What does it do?"

The woman's eyes never left Jennie's. She uttered one word so softly through trembling lips that Jennie had to lean forward to hear it.

"Specters."

A powerful surge of pain lanced through Jennie's gut, as hot as if a dragon were breathing fire inside of her. She collapsed to her knees, fighting to keep the researcher at gunpoint. She stared at the liquid through misty eyes, then she saw what lay behind the woman.

Jennie had been so focused on maintaining the woman's obedience that she hadn't even glanced at the wall behind. One-way glass casing stretched a hundred feet to her left, creating a tank spanning the entire wall. Inside the glass were hundreds of specters piled together in a space far too small for their number.

There were women, children, men, and the elderly—specters from every era of the timeline. They huddled together, many lying curled up on the floor in pain. Tubes protruded from the ceiling at intervals, and Jennie saw with alarm that threads of spectral energy were pouring out of the specters and traveling along the tubing to fill containers at their end. Neat rows of filled canisters were stored beside the empty ones, ready and awaiting shipment to the floors down below.

"You're draining them?" Jennie blurted in sick disgust. "You're draining specters and using the energy to power your weapons? To power your tech?"

Jennie's eyes were drawn to the silver puddle on the floor. At that moment, she realized what was wrong with her stomach. It recognized the presence of spectral power, but it was spoiled, like milk left out.

The energy that would usually power Jennie was poisoning her system, causing whatever gift had been given to her to sour in its altered presence.

Jennie raised her head and gazed through the glass at the suffering specters, each looking as pained as she was.

Dear God, Brendan. What the hell have you done?

CHAPTER FORTY-FIVE

<u>Washington DC, USA</u>

They chased the sun toward Washington, following the semis like bloodhounds.

It was a difficult job. The roads into the city were choked with traffic, and on two occasions, they lost visual on the vehicles. It was only dogged determination and their training that kept them on the trail.

The agents leapfrogged as they followed the semis through the city, turning wherever the trucks turned, pausing whenever they paused, until at last, they pulled into a parking lot for larger vehicles.

The two SIA cars continued past the lot, finding spaces to park a block farther down.

Baxter exited the moment they stopped. All of them moved quickly, ensuring they wouldn't lose sight of their targets again. The mortals remained seated, leaving Baxter, Carolyn, and Feng Mian to pursue their suspects. Tanya, Lupe, and Sandra waited in one car, while Rhone, Sade, Jack, and Clive remained in the other.

Feng Mian had convinced his parents to stay back with the rest of the Spectral Plane and the Baltimore agents to continue the search for Jennie there. The SIA agents were awaiting the order to ship the specters from Baltimore should they need them in Washington.

They approached the high wall surrounding the lot and passed through it.

The vehicles were still there, something Baxter had been afraid would not be true. The little voice in his head had gotten louder, telling him they'd arrive and find that their suspects had known they'd been following them and thrown them off the scent. None of this made any sense anyway, being in Washington when they had been active in Baltimore not too long ago.

Baxter grunted and pointed. "There."

Carolyn and Feng Mian followed his finger to where two gruff-looking men had hopped down from the cabin and were drawing up the rear gate of the semi to reveal a stack of wooden crates identical to the ones they'd seen in the other facility.

"It's them," Baxter stated. "We've got them." He half-turned to Carolyn, afraid to take his eyes off the men. "Go tell the others to call for backup. We've found them."

"How do we *know* it's them?" Carolyn asked. "We don't know what's in those boxes. What if it's just deliveries for a store or something?"

Baxter considered this. It seemed unlikely the crates were for any good purpose. The building they were unloading the crates into was an abandoned warehouse. Graffiti decorated the sides, and rotten boards half-covered the shattered windows near the building's roof. "It's them, all right. Go tell the others."

Carolyn hesitated, then, seeing the stern expression on Baxter's face, slid away from them and disappeared to inform the waiting agents.

Jennie had once drunk curdled milk.

That night had been awful. Her stomach had felt as though a rubber band was squeezing it tight. Insects gnawed on her digestive system, trying to break free. Jennie had tossed and turned in bed, muttering pained sentiments to the ghosts of those she had lost but could see in the shadows of her room.

This feeling was so similar, Jennie began to wonder if Koa had poisoned her. Then it became clear. This wasn't her pain. It belonged to the specters trapped in the glass tank.

Free them, King. You can't leave them here. Free them.

But how?

The pain was almost too much to bear. Weak from her disconnection from spectral energy, she reached for the liquid on the floor, connecting instinctively with the remains of the specters pooled within. She could feel their pain, their heartache, and their loss, a puddle of misery with a sentient voice—a constant echo shouting in her head from all the voices within.

Help us!

Noooo!

Please, no more. No more.

Jennie's eyes narrowed, her vision blurred with hot tears. The researcher remained frozen, afraid to the core to move.

That was something, at least.

"Move," Jennie told her, growling the words.

The woman stared at her.

"*Get out!*" Jennie screamed, startling the woman into movement.

A mixture of fear and relief colored her face as she stumbled into action and ran for the door. Would she go and seek help? Alert the others to Jennie's location?

Maybe, but that wouldn't matter. Soon Jennie would be free.

So would all these specters.

The pistol's grip was slippery in her sweat-glistening palm. Her stomach tried to pull her attention, but she fought it. She had been through worse than this, hadn't she? She was Jennie-fucking-King. A survivor. A miracle. The hand of Justice.

She wouldn't allow misery such as this to continue for those who had passed.

She aimed and fired, and the glass that had been imbued with spectral energy drained from these very specters shattered into dagger-sharp rain.

The specters rose, startled by the sudden cessation of the draining. The ones on the floor made an effort to push themselves to a position where they could see her.

Jennie's eyes landed on a boy no more than seventeen years of age with a backward-facing cap and a missing arm. Jennie smiled.

The boy smiled back.

Then something amazing happened.

Spectral energy crashed into Jennie like a tsunami as the room was flooded with the energy that had been contained by the glass, unable to find its way to her. The pain and sorrow from the canister's liquid were overwhelmed by the surge of clean, pure spectral energy that leaked from the mass of specters.

Jennie felt her strength returning.

How long had she been without spectral energy? How long had she been cut off from the thing that fueled her and gave her the power to go on? Jennie soaked up the energy, feeling like adrenaline, caffeine, and all that was good and holy was flooding her system. Waking her up. Erasing the fatigue and providing her the strength she needed.

The specters were shaky on their feet. They looked at Jennie in wonder.

"Who are you?" the boy asked.

The overwhelming majority already knew the answer. It was a rare specter who hadn't heard the legend of Rogue, and they couldn't believe she was standing in front of them.

"That doesn't matter right now," Jennie told him, her skin glowing with spectral energy. She tossed the Shadows' pistol on the floor and drew the Big Bitch and her own pistol when they appeared at her hips. She was thankful for the gift she had been given all those years ago. "What matters is that we get you free."

"There are too many of them," one specter replied. "We'll never make it out the front door. Their tech is too advanced. We're trapped in here. Trapped like animals."

A murmur of agreement swept across the specters.

Jennie looked down at the glass on the floor, and an idea popped into her head. "We're not going to go out the front door."

"What?" the skeptical specter replied. "Then how are we getting out?"

"Follow me," Jennie instructed. She ignored the confused protests and grabbed a canister of spectral essence. Turning on her heel, she walked over and opened the door, glancing each way along the corridor to check that the coast was clear before closing it again when she saw no Shadows.

Jennie aimed her pistol at the glass, standing at a slight angle to account for the ricochet, and fired.

A chip appeared in the glass, the fracture behind it a jagged spider-web. The bullet bounced back, embedding itself in a table.

Jennie sighed. *Bulletproof glass. Is there anything they haven't thought of?*

She heard a ding as the elevator arrived on her floor. The specters waited in terrified silence as the doors slid open and they heard the footsteps of the Shadows in the corridor.

"Here goes nothing," Jennie whispered, aware that there was only one chance to make this happen. The glass pulsed with the twisted spectral energy. If she wanted to break through the window, it would need to all be gone.

Jennie added the Big Bitch to her pistol and opened fire.

The sound was a thunderclap. Jennie screamed with frustration as she worked the triggers. Tiny flecks of glass sprayed, each bullet spreading the spiderweb.

The pistol created the dents, while the Big Bitch thwacked against the remaining glass. The panel continued to splinter, holding fast, turning into a fractal artwork that seemed like it would never collapse. Jennie knew the truth, of course. Bulletproof glass wasn't really bulletproof, but it took a hell of a lot of force to break it.

Jennie fired again and again until her pistol clicked empty. The Big Bitch kept firing, but it wouldn't go forever. Shouts and hollers from both specters and Shadows could be heard, but Jennie didn't slow down.

There was a figure in her peripheral vision, then a muzzle flash. Jennie latched onto a specter—any specter—but the spectrally imbued bullet ripped into her non-firing arm.

Another bullet, this one embedding in her hip. Heat and pain coursed through her body, but she continued firing, knowing this was her last chance. She bit her lip to distract herself from the pain, spitting silver blood when a third bullet hit her in the meat of her thigh.

Jennie dropped to one knee. That one had gotten her. The glass held on by fragments, as though it was working against her, a part of the Shadows that wanted nothing more than to keep her contained.

Jennie weakened. She gasped for air and gritted her teeth against the pain.

A voice shouted to her left, "Final warning. Drop your weapon, or the next one goes in your head."

Jennie coughed, the iron taste of blood on her tongue. She turned her head left and saw the throng of Shadows in the corridor awaiting her capture. Cole took point, his gun aimed at her skull.

"No," Jennie told him slowly, her voice carrying through the corridor. The sudden silence was deafening. "No, you won't."

"Try me," Cole challenged.

Holding Cole's gaze, Jennie raised her right arm to aim the Big Bitch at the glass and pulled the trigger. This time, the glass shattered. Every last shard fell in a shower of diamond sparkles, the setting sun captured by the tiny flakes.

Jennie blew Cole a kiss. "Tell Brendan I'll be back."

Cole pulled the trigger, but Jennie was faster. With her strength replenished, she dived through the open space where the window had just been.

Cold air hit her face and numbed her body. As she fell, she rotated until she faced the blood-orange sky. A small smile appeared as specter after specter followed her, plummeting toward the ground while the Shadows had no chance to pull them back.

The boy who had asked who Jennie was sped toward her with his arms pinned by his sides, aiming to close the gap between them.

The ground came up to meet Jennie. She focused her energy on slowing her descent and hit it at a run, the impact jarring her injuries and setting off a fresh wave of pain. She glanced around and chose a direction at random. "Come on," she called to the specters. "We have to get out of here."

The specters surrounded Jennie as she led them away from the building.

She became aware of gunfire from above as the Shadows gathered at the window and shot at them. Worse, they deployed the devices Brendan had been so proud to show off. Flashes of light coming from those strange boxes with the funnels stunned her eyes. Specters screamed as the stragglers at the back of the group were instantly exorcised.

"Fuck you," Jennie screamed as the twisted energy overwhelmed her. She was scooped into someone's arms but was unable to identify the face as her vision grew blurry.

CHAPTER FORTY-SIX

Washington DC, USA

The two men had disappeared some time ago, leaving the semi-truck emptied of its cargo. They hadn't come back out through the old steel door, and Baxter was left outside the abandoned factory, wondering what the hell was going on.

"What do you think?" he asked Feng Mian. "She in there?"

Feng Mian remained silent, his eyes fixed on the building.

The agents waiting in the vehicles joined them a few minutes later. A few minutes after that, there was a surprise arrival that shocked the rest of the agents.

Special Agent in Charge Kurt Rogers exited the sleek black Viper that pulled up, looking more intimidating than usual with his office wear replaced by the sleek black armored plates of SIA tac-gear. Daggro dragged her feet behind him as he approached Baxter and Rhone with SI goggles already on his face. "This is it?"

Baxter nodded. "They went inside. It has to be them. There's no way it's anyone else."

Rogers snarled, "Right on our doorstep. Fuckers."

"What do you need from us, sir?" Rhone stood straighter in

Rogers' presence. "We're ready to breach the moment the cavalry arrives."

"ETA?" Rogers barked.

"Thirty minutes, traffic dependent," Rhone replied.

Rogers growled, "Serves us right for sending our troops across state lines. Koa is sly. He drew us there to divide our forces." There was a note of unwilling admiration in his voice.

Rogers scanned the building, his upper lip curled in impatience. "We go now. Who knows what they'll do with thirty minutes to prepare?" He moved his hand to a small radio on his chest and pressed the button. "Bring them around."

Three armored personnel carriers screeched around the corner. Black windows hid the interior. They parked, and agents armed with M4 carbines climbed out of the vehicles. Baxter hoped their ammunition had been spectrally imbued.

Rogers ushered the tac teams toward the door and paused outside. Baxter couldn't help but admire the old man. Even in his later years, he was prepared to deal with the problem and lead his men. While many would have retired years ago, glued to their stuffy offices and issuing remote commands, Rogers was involved.

For Rogers, this was personal. He nodded at his men and stepped back. They placed two parcels of C-4 at the base of the door and made a space. Rogers counted down from three with his fingers, and the trigger was pulled by the agent controlling the explosion.

The door was blown free, along with the brickwork surrounding it.

The agents waited for the smoke to clear, their weapons aimed at the door and the windows above. When nothing jumped out at them, Rogers waved the agents in, and they filed through the hole they had made.

Baxter knew something was wrong the moment they entered. The old factory was far too dilapidated to house any kind of operation. Cobwebs ruffled lazily against old beams. Dust mote swirled in the fading beams of sunlight coming through holes in the roof. The only sign of life inside was the footprints of the men embedded in the layer of dust on the floor.

Leading to nowhere.

They were gone.

The agents inspected every inch of the place. The crates that had been unloaded were examined and found to be empty.

Rogers released a frustrated cry. The sound bounced around the room and back at him. "Son of a bitch," he growled. "It was a goddamn diversion."

"Over here," one agent called, waving the special agent in charge over.

He was standing by a circle the size of a manhole cover in the place the men's footprints stopped.

"A puzzle?" Rogers asked.

Baxter and Sade exchanged glances.

Rogers caught their look. "You've seen this before?"

"In the warehouse in Baltimore, sir," Sade answered. "A lock we were only able to open due to the silver substance we found in the canisters. It revealed the combination to us and allowed us access."

"Smart man," Rogers mumbled. "Did you take a sample of that liquid?"

Sade's eyes moved to the floor. "No, sir."

Rogers knelt beside the puzzle and tested some of the rings. They rotated easily enough, but there was no way to figure out the combination. After a few attempts, he gave up and rose to his feet.

"Must be an underground tunnel leading somewhere." He turned and barked instructions to Daggro. "I want a spectral forensics team in this building pronto. We're working night and day to open this lock." He also ordered infrared scans and blueprints of the pipes and any tunnel systems below the city that might yield clues as to where the men had gone, as well as a group of agents to keep a constant watch over the building.

Finally, Rogers addressed Baxter, Sade, and Lupe and his group. "You're coming to HQ with me. I have a lot of questions, and I think you might have the answers."

"What the fuck is going on?" Rogers barked the minute the door to his office closed behind them. Anger colored his face, and deep grooves decorated his forehead. He slumped in his chair and faced them in turn.

"What do you mean, sir?" Rhone asked, his voice level in contrast to Rogers' bellow.

"What do you mean, 'what do I mean?' One week with Jennie King, and the entire agency turns itself on its head. I've got cults spreading throughout my city, spectral possession becoming a daily occurrence, poltergeists, *sturmgeists*, whatever-the-fuck-else-you-can-name-geists, and now my intelligence team has been outwitted not once but *twice* by an organization who is hiding behind technology we do not possess? I ask again, what the *fuck* is going on?"

A heavy silence met his question.

"Well?"

"We don't know, sir," Rhone answered apologetically. "We're working on it."

Rogers' eyes bore into his.

Baxter cleared his throat, raising a hand. "If I may, sir. Jennie is missing. That is the key issue here. With Jennie in their possession, there's no telling what they could get up to."

"Why should that concern me?" Rogers growled. "Even after everything we've given her, she's running her own operation. Jennie King has lived up to her alias already, taking *my* agents into situations without permission, bringing her own cavalry to join us *without* permission, and now she's God-knows-where in the hands of a lunatic who could bend her to his will if he wishes."

"We don't know who she's with," Lupe replied. "We only know she's gone."

Rogers leaned forward in his chair, elbows resting on the table. "I'm sorry, whoever you are, but if I wanted the opinion of a short-stack flipper from the big city, I'd ask for it."

Daggro held back a laugh.

Lupe narrowed his eyes at her. "I'd expected a more professional attitude from a federal agent."

"Who the hell are you, anyway?" Rogers barked. "Why are you here?"

Lupe took the lead and introduced himself, Carolyn, Tanya, Sandra, and Feng Mian. He told them about his connection with the Spectral Plane, and at the mention of their name, Rogers' anger dropped a degree. He knew about the Spectral Plane. Jennie had told him all about them during her initial meeting with him.

When Lupe had finished, he gave Rogers a considering look. "I understand that all of this will be new to you, and federal types like you like to be in control. But that's not the game we're playing here. You aren't equipped for this fight. Jennie is. Jennie has been playing this game decades longer than you."

"Jennie led the Battle of New York," Tanya told Rogers, drawing his attention. "Without her, the crown would have taken control, forcing the specters of the city to hand over their freedom."

"She confronted Queen Victoria in London," Carolyn added. "She discovered the truth behind the queen's lies and forced her to release her grip on the US. She took on the friggin' *queen* for this country."

Rogers' eyebrows raised at that. "Jennie mentioned a disagreement with the queen. I chose not to believe it."

"Well, believe it," Carolyn told him, adding a quick, "Sir, every word of it is true. We were there."

"What we're saying is that you need Jennie," Tanya continued. "She should be your priority right now. The walls of the spectral world are about to crack, and we need her here to help ensure that doesn't happen."

"What do you mean?" Rogers asked.

Before Lupe could respond, all SIA radios in the room blared with an urgent message. "Fiver-niner, we've received reports of gunshots in the downtown area. MPDC are on their way. Civilians report shattered glass and civilians firing at an empty lawn."

"Empty lawn?" Daggro muttered.

Rogers' eyes moved to Rhone's. He didn't need to say a word for them to understand.

Sade drove the SUV, with Lupe, Tanya, and the specters in the back. They sped through the city with the lights flashing, following the path of the police car in front while it parted traffic with its sirens.

Pedestrians stared in curiosity as the convoy of seven cars blurred past on the way to their destination.

Gunshots rang in the distance, growing louder with each mile. Baxter's eyes were fixed on the road in front, determination on his face.

God, Jennie. Be okay, please. Be okay.

If she was left alone without her specters, did she become just like everyone else? Baxter didn't know what would happen if Jennie got shot when she was in her mortal state. He silenced the thought. Jennie King was the invincible Rogue. That was what he had to hold onto.

The cars screeched around the corner, leaving hot tire tracks on the asphalt. Night was rapidly approaching, but there was enough light to see the figures dressed in black standing in the shattered window.

The Shadows reacted immediately to the sight of the police cars and the agent cruisers, and the cars were peppered with bullets.

"Get your heads down!" Sade shouted, hoping the bulletproof windscreen would hold. The screen shattered but stayed in place. However, her vision was obscured by a thousand tiny cracks. She slowed the car and swung it toward a nearby building, out of sight of their attackers.

The other cars followed suit. The cops and SIA agents exited the vehicles and used them as cover to return fire and mute the enemy.

Baxter sprinted toward a parked car. When he reached it, he ducked into its shadow.

"Bad day to get shot at," Lupe panted, dropping beside him.

A spectral body slammed into the car.

Carolyn's eyes were fixed on their attackers through the car's windscreen. "Isn't every day a bad day to get shot at?"

"Not if you're suicidal," Lupe answered.

Carolyn stared at him as though he'd just told her he shot a puppy. "You're kidding, right?"

Lupe shrugged.

"Where's Feng Mian?" Baxter asked.

Before anyone answered, Feng Mian casually got out of the vehicle they had been crammed into and strode across the road. He held one hand in the direction of the attackers, a faint blue shield protecting his body as he walked.

"Why couldn't I have gotten *that* power?" Carolyn asked.

"Consider yourself lucky," Baxter replied. "At least you got something unique."

Carolyn waved her fingers as though controlling an invisible marionette. "I can use spectral telekinesis. Wow, big whoop."

Baxter raised his eyebrows.

"What?" Carolyn scoffed.

"Don't you think that's something that could be quite useful at this moment?" he asked.

"Oh, yeah!" Carolyn's face lit up. She came around to the front of the car and looked at the window from which the assailants were shooting. Remaining out of sight, she clenched her hands and concentrated on repeating whatever the hell it was she had done on that fateful day at Buckingham Palace.

"Come on," she murmured. Her tongue darted between her lips, her face contorting in concentration. "Come *on...*"

After a minute of trying, nothing happened.

"Maybe you need to get closer?" Lupe suggested. "Maybe it's not a long-distance power."

"You saw me do it, though, didn't you?" Carolyn asked, doubt in her eyes. "You saw me do it before?"

Lupe nodded. "I did. Now make it happen again."

Carolyn's face became resolute. She left the protection of the car and ran to grab Feng Mian's wrist. "Cover me, my friend. I need to get closer, and I don't like the idea of tasting spectral bullets."

Feng Mian and Carolyn ran ahead. Baxter trailed behind them, keeping his enormous bulk behind Feng Mian's shield. Lupe's mouth flapped a few times before he sprinted after them, trying to regain the ground he had lost with his hesitation.

They made their way toward the building and stopped when they reached its safety.

"You can hide but you can't run!" a hate-riddled voice shouted from above. Chips of brickwork sprayed as bullets thunked around them.

"Let's wipe that shit-eating grin off his face," Carolyn stated, giving Feng Mian a gentle nudge he didn't need.

Baxter remained behind the shield as they narrowed the gap to the building. They crossed a neatly kept lawn, complete with a clean gravel path and benches. The men above continued shooting. Occasionally a body fell when one of the cops or SIA agents hit their mark, but there was still a good number of Shadows up there.

"Why aren't they fleeing?" Baxter wondered aloud.

"They're dumb?" Carolyn offered.

Feng Mian's shield flashed with each bullet strike. He remained silent as he focused his power on defending them, aware that one slip could mean death for Lupe.

When they were almost directly below the attackers, Feng paused and muttered, "Now, girl."

Carolyn's brow creased. She focused her attention on the cloaked figures and sent her energy toward them. Her fingers bent as though she were grasping an imaginary baseball. She clenched her hands, her face flushing with color.

Something happened, then. A rattling above, and a cry of alarm as a pistol was torn free of an attacker's hand. It streamed toward her, finding its way comfortably into her palm. She yelped in surprise at its speed and dropped it to the ground, then focused again.

Another gun, a rifle this time, plummeted toward them, then another pistol. Another pistol. A rifle. Before long, the Shadows were almost pulled through the window as they did their best to hold onto their weapons and fight Carolyn's power.

Carolyn's teeth gritted. A growl rumbled out of her throat, and with a final surge of concentration, she threw her hands to the ground, ripping every last firearm from the cluster of fuckers above.

The guns landed on the neat lawn, leaving muddy indents as they struck. The men above shouted in alarm and ran from sight, disappearing from the shattered window and heading into the building.

Rhone's voice called from behind, commanding and barking orders.

The SIA agents swarmed toward the building. They smashed through the doors without hesitation and went in for the raid.

Baxter turned back to find Lupe's head poking out from behind the wall. He waved him over. "Get your ass over here. We've got to block them before they escape."

Lupe caught up with them, and they headed inside.

CHAPTER FORTY-SEVEN

Washington DC, USA

They cut off the Shadows on the stairs on the second floor. With nowhere else to go, the cloaked gang sprinted toward them, somehow hoping they'd be able to reach the back entrance and run before the agents caught them.

As pleased as the agents were that they'd caught the cultists who had been firing at them, there was something bothering Baxter.

There were only twenty-three of them in total. That was all. It wasn't nearly enough.

Baxter had followed the SIA agents as they worked their way through the building. At least this time around, the enemy hadn't had the time to erase their work. The computers were open to the last thing their owners had been working on. The workshops were littered with a variety of strange devices, as well as the canisters of the metallic liquid.

But there was no sign of Jennie.

"Over here, sir." An agent ushered Rhone to a door where a strange light from within illuminated the left side of his face.

There had been a fight in this room. Plants were overturned, the desk had been thrown, and there was paper scattered all over the floor.

"CCTV," Rhone muttered, ignoring the mess in favor of the screens. "My God!"

Dozens of live feeds of the world outside. Baltimore, Washington. In the bottom right corner, there was even a camera aimed at the doors of the SIA HQ. On the screen right now were a couple of black-clad agents Rhone recognized tapping in the key code to gain access. "They've been watching us the entire time."

One of the agents picked up a sheet of paper from the floor. He brushed away a muddy footprint and pointed at the words on the bottom. "I guess we don't have to try too hard to work out who's behind all of this."

Rhone snatched the paper away and held it closer to his face. Baxter stood beside him and read the neat cursive of Brendan Koa's signature.

Baxter's eyes were drawn to a piece of paper on the floor that read *The Life and History of Genevieve King.*

"This can't be possible." Baxter fell to his knees and began scooping all the pages toward him. He collected the untidy pile, trying his best to assemble them in order. That became the least of his priorities when he saw what the pages contained.

Detailed information regarding medical procedures. Illustrations of possible theories. Line after line detailing the conditions which would be met by Jennie if she joined the Order of the Shadows.

"They're trying to replicate Jennie," Baxter gasped. "They're trying to identify her makeup and see if it can be cloned. Manipulated. Put on a production line. Koa's a monster."

Rhone put a hand to his head. "He might not be the biggest monster."

"What do you mean?"

"If Jennie has signed, she's not the woman we thought she was."

Baxter's face darkened. "How can you even suggest that she would do such a thing?"

Rhone sighed. He looked weary. "We have to remain open to all possibilities. At this point, all that we know is that this cult exists. Koa is at the head of it all, and he has Jennie. Whether that's willingly or unwillingly, we don't know yet. We have to be open to the assumption that Jennie has signed the contract. That she's considered it and might be with them. You said she'd be strong enough to escape. Where is she now?"

Baxter's brow furrowed. "I don't know."

"He's offering her everything on a plate, Baxter." Rhone sighed. "Wouldn't you be tempted?"

Baxter considered that, not liking the discomfort he felt. Sure, he'd consider it. The whole thing would be incredibly tempting. But to go against everything she'd ever stood for wasn't the Jennie he knew.

Before Baxter had a chance to answer, an agent went over the plant pot, where a small sheet of filthy paper was hidden beneath. He examined it, then passed it to Rhone. "I don't think you need to worry, sir."

Baxter and Rhone both grinned at Jennie's scrawl. The words "Fuck you" were written in black ink on the signature line.

Baxter let out a chuckle. "I knew it. I knew it."

Rhone's smile slipped into a mask of concern. "Well, if that's the case, where the hell is she?"

The smell of earth was thick and fragrant.

"Stand back, stand back, you filthy half-wits. Allow her some space to breathe." The woman's aged voice cracked around the edges as she spoke.

Jennie heard her through a veil of darkness. She was aware of others around her, shuffling and moving. Pain throbbed all over her body.

Cold hands with thin insect-like fingers pressed against her chest. The woman began to mutter something incoherent in an ancient tongue Jennie couldn't identify. Warmth began to spread through her veins, moving like liquid metal through her body. It wasn't uncomfortable, just warm.

Liquid metal?

Jennie opened her eyes, and her first thought was that she had been buried. The earthen roof was low, giving her only a couple of feet of headroom. She wasn't sure where she was, but the flickering of a candle told her she was underground.

Jennie propped herself up on her elbows and winced.

"Ah, I see. It's good to see the old ways still hold true." The woman's face split into a painful grin as she held Jennie's eyes. She was old, perhaps eighty or ninety. Her gray hair hung in thin strands above a gray scalp. Her cheeks were gaunt, and if the woman hadn't been a specter, Jennie imagined her shawl would have been the color of November rain clouds. "I'm glad you're awake."

"Where..." Jennie coughed. "Where am I?"

"You're safe, dear. That's all that matters right now. Safe in a place where they can't find you. You breathe deep. Susannah will take care of you, yes, she will."

The faces of specters appeared in the darkness behind Susannah. With a sudden agility that defied her advanced age, she jerked her head around and bellowed, "Out! Out, I said! Does privacy mean nothing to you urchins?"

When she turned back to Jennie, her face was sickly-sweet. A smile on thin lips. A twinkle behind dead eyes. She placed her one hand on Jennie's forehead and one on her chest and began to chant again.

Jennie didn't protest. Didn't feel the need to. Instead, she closed her eyes and let the energy pour into her, feeling the pain subside slowly, draining like a lanced boil.

"There we go."

Jennie relaxed, allowing the energy to flow through her, letting her mind work while her body rested. Flashbacks came to her then. Muzzle flashes and men in dark cloaks. Specters caged behind glass and pain.

They had shot her in spectral form, and now she was...what? What state was she in?

Jennie opened her eyes, surprised to see her connection to the specters had gone and she was fully material. Bloodstains drew attention to where the bullets had pierced, embedding themselves in her flesh.

But why couldn't she feel them anymore?

As if to answer her question, Susannah's hands slowly glided toward Jennie's thigh. A deep groove showed where the bullet had bitten into her. Susannah joined her hands together and gave them a rub, then placed her palms over the hole in Jennie's thigh and began to chant again.

The strangest sensation passed through Jennie's muscle, as though an insect was crawling around in the hole. It wasn't unpleasant. In fact, it tickled like hell.

"Keep still," Susannah muttered when Jennie began to fidget.

Jennie watched with wonder as the metal casing of the bullet appeared at the surface of her wound. It continued its inexplicable trajectory, gliding into Susannah's hands. She clapped them shut and discarded the bullet, then went to work on the next wound.

Each extraction was a marvel to behold, but that wasn't where the wonders stopped. It wasn't until bullet number three appeared that Jennie glanced at the other two wounds, astonished to see that they'd both healed. The skin had knitted itself closed, and there was no sign of the injury, not even a scar.

"Gotcha." Susannah gave a gap-toothed grin as she clutched the final bullet. "I've still got it."

"What did you just do?" Jennie asked. "I've seen a lot of crazy shit in my time, but this is new." Her eyes narrowed. "Who are you really?"

"I told you, Rogue. My name's Susannah." She chucked the shell at the small opening in the tiny chamber where more specters' heads had appeared. "Most people would just say thank you, you know."

"You're not like the other specters, are you?"

Susannah shook her head, sorrow in her eyes. "No, I'm not. You know, you're just as wise as they say you are. I've always wondered what it would be like to meet the great and powerful Rogue."

Jennie knew what Susannah was doing. It was an obtuse attempt to steer the conversation in a different direction, but Jennie would not be deterred. "You just fixed my wounds. My *mortal* wounds. Tell me what you are? I'm afraid I haven't met any of your kind before."

Susannah sighed, that smile appearing again. "You have me all wrong. I'm not so different from you or the others. It was only in life that my gifts were seen as a threat. They were the reason I was burned alive. Strapped to a stake and set on fire."

Jennie nodded. "You're a witch." It wasn't a question.

Susannah's head cocked to the side. "That's quite an accusation."

"Is it true?" Jennie asked.

"That depends on your definition."

Jennie's muscles protested as she sat upright. "A mortal with inexplicable powers."

"Ah." Susannah shrugged as if she'd just won the fight. "In that case, don't you think you're more of a witch than I've ever been?"

Jennie laughed. "I suppose you're right."

Susannah pressed Jennie to the bed and covered her with the blanket. "Enough now, dear. Get some more rest."

"One more question," Jennie begged.

Susannah raised an eyebrow.

"A quick one," Jennie assured.

"Very well."

"Where are we?"

"Beneath the place that began it all, Rogue. The true birthplace of the United States and the landmark of our forefathers. This is the forgotten realm beneath the Washington Monument."

The world beneath the Washington Monument was cramped.

After a few hours, the boy with the backward cap and only one arm had run into her chamber and woken her up. His face was a mask of excitement and gratitude. Before she'd even opened her eyes, he flung his arm around her, hugging her tightly and repeating, "Thank you" in her ear.

He introduced himself as Timmy Noble. The kid had been among the first casualties in Koa's scheme to create a global army of possessed mortals. Timmy had been in the wrong place at the wrong time, snatched from the streets at night and handed over to the Shadows to test their rituals.

"It was awful," he told Jennie, sitting at her bedside. "One minute I was happy, listening to my beats and thinking about taking the last Crunchie bar in the fridge. The next thing I knew…" His eyes glistened with tears.

"It's okay," Jennie assured him. "You're safe now."

Timmy helped Jennie to unsteady feet and showed her around the tunnels. The place was packed with specters, who all thanked Jennie and praised her as she walked by.

Eventually, Jennie was led into a chamber that allowed her the chance to extend to her full height. The floor dropped, looking like an empty swimming pool, devoid of any tiles or porcelain, left with only its muddy bowl.

"They really didn't think of installing any amenities in this place, did they?" Jennie quipped.

Susannah broke from the crowd. "That wasn't the point of these tunnels. These were thoroughfares over the years for the innocent to travel and hide. Now, they're our safe place, at least until we figure out what comes next."

"What do you mean?" Jennie asked.

Specters were gathered around the pair, listening to the conversation with clouds of concern hanging over their heads.

"You've already seen what's going on up there," Susannah told Jennie. "You know the threat we're facing. You're not the only one who has managed to free specters from the clutches of the Shadows."

Jennie interjected. "Hold on. I emptied that place of specters."

Susannah shook her head. "Sadly, no. You freed one group, but there are more going missing every day. Our friends here have lost loved ones and friends, and with each hour, we hear of more troubles across the cities. We need your help to bring them to justice. To stop this darkness before the Shadows cover the sun."

Jennie sighed. Every time she felt she'd gotten one step closer to defeating this cult, another problem sprang up. The bastards should have called themselves Hydra instead of the Order of the Shadows.

"You talk as though there are others helping you," Jennie commented. "How are specters helping to free specters when the very people we're trying to close down are amassing weapons designed to capture them?"

Susannah turned her head toward the entrance of the large chamber, where a woman and two men stood side by side, arms folded. They were all athletically built, with a variety of firearms strapped to their bodies. The man in the center held what looked like an M1941 Johnson rifle over his shoulder. All of them looked as though they had just hopped straight out of a steampunk movie.

Not only that, they were all mortals.

Jennie looked at her clothes, then at the others.

"Nice corset." The woman grinned.

The man on the right rolled his eyes. "I knew you ladies would jump straight to fashion."

The man in the middle remained silent but smiled nonetheless.

Jennie studied the three of them, then turned back to Susannah. "What is this?"

"The help you need, Rogue. Three mortals with extraordinary gifts. Three additional allies to help you take down the Shadows."

CHAPTER FORTY-EIGHT

Buckingham Palace, London, England

Queen Victoria sat alone in the throne room, her hands gripping the arms of her throne so tightly that her knuckles paled.

A dark cloud surrounded her. If emotions were weather, she would be a hurricane that had fucked a tsunami and pissed out a monsoon.

The phone she had just held to her ear lay in pieces on the floor.

A knock startled her from her thoughts.

Victoria couldn't bring herself to answer. She didn't trust herself to not rage and hurt whoever was on the other side of that door. The news was bad; worse than she could have imagined, and now she would once again have to pick up the pieces.

"You *promised* me she'd sign!" Victoria had shouted into the phone. "You promised me that all the information I sent would be enough to tie her down. I provide the history, you provide the technical innovation. That was the deal!"

The worst part of Koa's response wasn't even the content of his words. It was the collected coolness he had answered her with that bothered her most. While others cowered before her wrath, Koa replied as though he were telling a doting wife that he was running a few hours late at the office and he'd have dinner when he got home.

Maybe if she went over and met him in person, he'd understand why it was worth bowing before her might? Maybe that would shake him up and make him realize what was at stake here.

It had been a risk. A calculated risk, but a risk, nonetheless. Victoria had known what she was doing when she was feeding both factions information. Despite her promise to Jennie, she found that she couldn't relinquish control of her kingdom. Yasmine and Porter had done well to establish US-UK relations, and she could not sit around and see them become an independent spectral state.

Jennie was a small blip on the road to her total rule, one she would have to remove. She had thought about simply killing her, but she wasn't as heartless as that. Maybe, she wondered, there would be a way to get her to buy back in. Let her discover her ancestry to pull her back into the fold. Become one of her own again, a member of the paranormal court.

Keep your friends close, and your enemies closer.

Another knock on the door, followed by a tentative, "Your Majesty?"

There was nothing for it. Jennie had made a nuisance of herself for far too long. Gotten involved in international matters that didn't concern her. Foiled the plans of the paranormal court not once, but twice now. One could only stand so much disruption and torment before the exterminators were called in, reinforcements were summoned, and nuisances were eradicated from the planet.

Spectral technology was hitting its stride. UK mortal forces were beginning to be indoctrinated into spectral combat. Soon enough, she wouldn't need Genevieve King to rule the planet anymore.

Another knock. No hesitation this time as the door opened. Oliver Clark's head appeared around the corner. "Is everything well, Your Majesty? There were reports of raised voices."

Victoria shook in her chair. She tried to breathe, and it was several seconds before she managed to mutter the four words she'd never wanted to say. She had no other option if she was to protect the legacy of her kingdom.

The words leaked from her tight lips and carried across the room to Clark.

"Genevieve King must die."

CHAPTER FORTY-NINE

<u>Dartmoor, Devonshire, England</u>

Raymond Uttleton, known to his friends as Ray, his enemies as "Ratty," and to his closest friend Zach Burton as "R-Dawg," spent more time on his computer these days than he did in the real world.

His mother regretted the purchase, now unable to pull him away from his monitor no matter what the incentive. Dinner, family, friends, even visits from his estranged father were met with indifference as he scrolled and mashed his greasy fingers on the keyboard, totally immersed in the digital world.

"Staring at that screen all day will make your eyes square," his mother had warned, realizing the habit her son was developing.

That had been over a year ago. Were his eyes square? No. No, they weren't.

Still, it wasn't difficult to see why Ray had become so obsessed. There was little to do out on the ass-end of the moors besides roaming the babbling brooks. He couldn't be bothered to wander through pat-laced wolds looking for sleeping cows to tip. Dartmoor had been one of the last places in England to acquire the wonder that was the internet, and it had been another few years before his mother had agreed to fork out the monthly cost and installation fee to connect them.

"I can spend more time with Dad," Ray had argued. "He's had internet for years. We can Skype."

His mother's lip had curled at that. Still, she couldn't refuse her son's plea to connect with his father, so she'd reluctantly agreed.

Ray had taken to the internet like a moth to a flame, discovering its secrets while his mother worked long hours to build her cleaning business.

At the age of sixteen, two years after he had traded any possibility of a real-world social life for online anonymity, Ray discovered something that changed his life entirely.

"It's called the dark web." Zach's face was lit by his dual twenty-four-inch monitors, his fingers stained with Doritos dust. "You can search for *anything*. Look."

That preceded a night filled with searches for everything the two sixteen-year-old boys could imagine. They barely scratched the surface, discovering the places to buy illegal firearms, drugs, women, and an endless amount of pornography that had the pair watching wide-eyed long into the night.

For weeks after, every night was filled with exploration. Ray and Zach pushed their daring with the dark web to its limits. They found themselves in an auction for military-grade rocket launchers, they browsed mail-order brides. Then Ray found something that caught his attention on one of the conspiracy sites.

"The Paranormal Truth?" Ray's face was inches from the screen. The background was black, with vertical lines of green lettering that looked like code from afar. "Dude! This is a whole page about ghosts!"

Zach blew air between his lips. Flecks of Dorito flew toward R-Dawg. "Puh-lease. You're kidding me, right? Ghosts? They've got some weird-ass shit on that site, but ghosts? I think you should probably get some sleep."

Ray only half-listened, his focus taken up by soaking in all the information the site was giving him. There were detailed descriptions about a world of specters, accompanied by blurry photographs of white orbs and strange ghostly shapes behind smiling families.

The article ended with a mention of an organization called the Order of the Shadows.

Zach lay on Ray's bed, tossing chips into the air and catching them in his mouth. Outside, the first rays of dawn were beginning to creep into the sky. "Your mum will be home soon."

Ray glanced at the window. Zach was right; she'd be returning from her night shift at Tatterton's Elementary School for Boys. When she realized he'd been up all night again, she'd start shouting at Ray through the thin wood of his locked door.

"You should get going," he told Zach.

Zach took his advice, leaving Ray to his reading. A strange feeling churned in Ray's gut as a memory came back to him. He had been only twelve at the time, still reeling from his parents' divorce when he had run away.

That night he had hopped out of his window and onto the rear extension, precariously finding his footing in a tangle of ivy. On reaching the ground, he'd shouldered his backpack and sprinted across the moor without paying attention to his direction.

The night was thick with fog, and cows appeared out of the mist like ghostly ships in the dark. Eventually, he'd exhausted himself, and logic had kicked in. He was lost in the fog, but somehow he found his way to an abandoned barn.

Ray had found refuge inside the barn. It creaked in the wind, its beams and planks rotten from time and swollen from damp. Stacks of aged straw sagged in the corner, but it was enough to keep him warm. He closed his eyes to sleep.

That was when the girl had appeared.

"You're alone?" she asked Ray. Her voice was far off and had an ethereal quality. Her skin was translucent, a ghostly white.

Ray nodded, too frightened to answer.

"I'm alone, too. Maybe we could be friends?"

The girl extended a hand to Ray, and that was when he ran.

He dashed through the fields at breakneck speed, pausing only when a cow lunged at him in the darkness. He ran and ran, not caring where he was going, only knowing he needed to escape. That something was wrong with that girl, and if he stayed, he would join her.

The flashing blue lights of a police car woke him the next morning when the police found him curled in a ditch, shivering with cold. He had kept what he'd seen secret for so long. He hadn't even told his mother as she sobbed with relief and hugged the swaddled Ray in the back of the police car.

That feeling of strange cold overwhelmed him now. He wasn't aware of the sweat that peppered his brow or the crazed look in his eyes as he read. He knew that he had seen a ghost. They did exist. It was true. Here was all the evidence confirming what he'd seen.

The site gripped him. Zach drifted away, replaced by his new friend in the Shadows. She knew what he'd been through. She understood Ray needed closure and told him how to get it. A month later, Ray was frenzied with desire to repeat his experience.

He had to go back there and find the ghost.

He scoured the moor for days, hunting blindly for the barn with no reference point except the road he'd been found on. His mother watched him closely, worrying about how thin he was becoming and puzzled by his sudden desire to exit the house. The change in his character was not as alarming as his appearance. His face had grown gaunt, his eyes sinking into his head.

Ray had begun to believe that he'd never find the barn again, but his obsession kept him searching. He was losing hope when he came across it six miles from his house, in a wooded valley beyond the bramble perimeter of Farmer Mason's grazing land.

It was exactly as he remembered it, right down to the chill that penetrated his skin. He stood outside the barn for a few seconds, wondering if he was in a dream. He had hardly eaten over the last few days, and a small part of him had begun to wonder what was real and what wasn't. His house and parents, they weren't real. The words on the screen of his computer, that was real. Those people were the real deal. They were the real "woke" generation; his friends were aware of what existed beyond this life.

Ray entered the barn and was unsurprised to find it empty. Over where the straw pile had been was an empty corner. He turned to where he had seen the girl, but she wasn't there.

He waited for hours in that barn, shivering and desperate like the twelve-year-old him had done, eventually falling asleep against the wall.

Ray awoke at dawn when a cock crowed and slumped home, bitter sadness in his dark eyes. She had been real once. He was certain of it —*had* been certain of it. But now she wasn't there.

Had she ever been there?

Ray returned to the forums, where his friend was full of sympathy and advice about taking his search to the next level. He studied the rituals she sent him, and he found one that might work. A ritual that could not only prove that specters were real, but that would also restore his sanity.

Three weeks later, the first reports of Ray's arrest were logged. The news was splashed across the Dartmoor *Gazette's* front page:

Deranged local loner charged with murder.

A photo of Ray's beaming face took up the majority of the cover, along with a small caption beneath that read:

Raymond Uttleton, the self-proclaimed Dartmoor "Ghost Hunter," slays best friend in an effort to prove the existence of specters. Confiscated computer yields startling information.

CHAPTER FIFTY

<u>Alexandria, Virginia, USA</u>

Brendan Koa stared at his collection of screens, his eyes narrowed in concentration.

It had been three days since they had been forced to vacate yet another property in their efforts to hide from Jennie and the SIA. Made rich by his investments and a number of useful inheritances he had acquired from relatives, he had built himself quite an empire, ensuring that he held the licenses to a number of buildings across Washington and the neighboring states. Each building was equipped with a get-out-quick route, but he was getting tired of last-minute escapes.

He watched on the monitors two hours later as SIA agents finally found the hidden tunnels and followed them to Washington's Navy Yard.

Escapes by boat were some of the most difficult to track.

He watched them on the screen, flicking through the camera feeds like a retired cop flicks through the channels in his La-Z-Boy chair.

They had found a few of his cameras and disabled their feeds. That didn't matter much. Even if they tracked the wireless feed, they would only be led to an offshore server and looped into a network of endless proxies designed to confuse its hackers and alert Brendan to their progress. He had always been meticulous, having learned to cover his tracks early in life. His attention to detail was what had gotten him so far.

The remote had become an extension of his arm over the last few days. Julia arrived regularly, looking lost without Cole, to provide reports on developments with the acquisition of more mortal bodies to convert, but that didn't soothe him any.

Rogue was still out there.

"She'll have to surface sooner or later," he grumbled. He rubbed the silver-flecked stubble covering the lower half of his face. Bags hung beneath his eyes.

There had been no sign of Rogue since she had escaped. Part of him had assumed she had found her way back to the SIA, but he had been keeping careful watch over their HQ, and there had been no visuals of her.

He had even tracked her closest crew, those agents and specters who had come to rescue her from the Washington facility, but either she had found a way to become completely invisible, or she was hiding.

If she was hiding, he knew that would not be good news. He couldn't defend against an enemy he couldn't see.

"You should rest."

Brendan struggled to tear his eyes away from the screens, but he managed it. Standing in the doorway was an agent with dark eyes and a chiseled jaw. He wore blacks protected by Kevlar with the letters "SIS" on the chest.

Brendan's lip curled into a sneer at the sight of Spectral Intelligence Services Agent Oliver Clark.

The queen had sent them personally, gathering a force of a hundred of the best SIS agents and flying them across the Atlantic. Brendan hadn't asked for help, but the queen had demanded it, raising the heat in her latest phone call as her tune changed completely on Rogue.

Before she had requested he protect Rogue and bring her into the inner circle. Now it was, "Destroy the nuisance and remove her from the face of the Earth."

The only problem was that Brendan was in too deep. His eyes had been opened to the possibility of what having Jennie on his side could offer. She was a Pandora's box of mysteries, and he wanted to open it. Imagine what could be achieved if her secrets could be unlocked and her powers added to his already growing spectral arsenal.

Agent Clark was operating on the "Kill now, ask questions later" mentality, but Brendan wanted Rogue, and he wanted her alive.

Brendan turned back to the screen. "I'll turn it off during the commercials. It's just coming up to the good part."

Clark sighed and took a step into the room. "No sign of her yet?"

"None," Brendan replied. "If you Brits were as smart as you say, you would have tagged her long ago."

Clark's eyes were drawn to the screens. He held his rifle close to his chest, barrel aimed at the floor. "Have you ever tried tagging a rabid bear?"

"No."

The agent sighed. "It would be a damn sight easier."

Brendan chuckled softly. "She's up to something, Clark. I can feel it. Whatever it is, it's not going to be pretty."

"I understand your army is growing? You understand the limits to our arrangement?"

Brendan turned to Clark, eyebrow raised. "*Our* arrangement? I'm sorry, I didn't realize you'd grown breasts and become the queen of fucking England."

"I stand as the queen's proxy in her absence," Agent Clark reminded him icily. "Her arrangement is my arrangement."

Brendan stared at him and growled. He finally returned his gaze to the screens, raising the remote to continue flicking through the camera feeds. "Yes, I understand our arrangement. Your specters are your own, and mine are the ones I create. The Shadows have been instructed to only farm the mortals and specters we have been involved in birthing."

"And the results?"

There was a knock on the door. Julia hesitated under Clark's stare. "I can answer that."

Brendan remained silent. Clark gave a slight nod, indicating she should continue.

"We've birthed the first fifty Penumbra. All has gone according to plan, no hitches. The midwives are in the process of erasing the evidence via the cremation chambers."

"Penumbra? Midwives?" He turned to Brendan. "I thought you'd shown me the entire operation. You've been keeping secrets?"

If Brendan was alarmed or frightened, he didn't show it. He watched the screens with cool calm. "The midwives are what the Shadows have taken to calling the team in charge of the ritual. A more uplifting name than the 'Sacrificers' or the 'Homicide Squad,' don't you think?"

"And the Penumbra?"

"My army," Brendan told him with a smug smile. "The lightest part of the Shadows. Light is necessary to give power to the dark, don't you agree?"

Julia's brow furrowed, wondering if he was aware that Clark could see his every movement reflected on one of the screens.

"I want to see them," Agent Clark informed him curtly.

Julia looked at Brendan for help.

"As you wish," Brendan replied. "Julia, please take Agent Clark to the Maternity Ward and show him the babies."

Julia plastered a fake smile on her face. "Of course. Agent Clark, if you'd like to follow me."

She led him out of the room, leaving Brendan behind with his cameras.

Brendan's thoughts swirled with animosity toward the SIS agent, irritated by his presence in his operation. Did the queen not trust him?

Maybe one day I'll be lucky enough to have Agent Clark join my army. Would he be the specter or the mortal who died to produce it?

He supposed it didn't matter. Those under his control were dead either way.

And death was where the riches lay.

Washington DC, USA

"I can take on all three of you. Just stagger your entry."

Jennie couldn't remember how long it had been since she'd encountered specters who could put up a decent fight. Of course, these three were only this good because she'd been training them for the last few days, adding to their already excellent fighting skills.

She dodged a blow from Gavin, grabbed his wrist, and turned at the hip to throw him over her shoulder. She turned enough to feel his weight against her back, and Gavin hooked his arm beneath her armpit and held on tight.

"You're like herpes." Jennie grunted. "I can't shake your spectral arse off."

Gavin Connolly laughed. "Speaking from experience there?"

Jennie tried to put force into the throw, but he clutched her arm. She was wasting precious seconds. The others were about to come for her. The crowd was counting Olivia in, holding Jennie to her promise. They had enthusiastically accepted her challenge, but she was beginning to have regrets.

Jennie planted her feet. Gavin planted his. They tussled for a few moments, then Jennie dropped her center of gravity and swept her leg behind her.

Gavin went down when her foot crunched into the back of his knee.

Jennie twisted to land on top of him, knocking the wind out of him.

He wasn't done yet.

Before Jennie could pin him down, Gavin threw a punch to Jennie's jaw, catching her off-guard. Her head snapped to the side, and she saw stars.

Jennie recovered quickly and captured Gavin's wrists. "Don't you know it's wrong to hit a woman?"

Gavin growled. "Equal rights. What are you gonna do about it?" He raised his knee and planted a foot on the floor to gain traction while he bucked his hips in an attempt to throw Jennie off, but she held on like a cowgirl riding a bronco.

"Such a gentleman." Jennie laughed as she snaked her legs under his and pinned him to tire him out.

The specters forming the circle around them whooped and hollered. One shouted, "I wanted a fight, not porn!"

Jennie winked at the specter, then shifted her weight to put the hurt on Gavin. She twisted, contorting Gavin's legs into an uncomfortable knot.

Pain screwed his face shut as he pounded the ground with his fist. "Okay! I give! I give!"

Jennie raised her arms to celebrate, momentarily forgetting the other two specters.

Olivia Carter dived at Jennie and caught her from behind, throwing her forward onto her face.

The rough packed dirt left an irritated scrape on Jennie's cheek. She had let the specters pick their order of entry. She had hoped that Olivia would be the last.

Olivia gripped Jennie under the arms and dragged her to her feet. An ex-wrestler in her heyday, she certainly had the muscle to be a problem for Jennie.

Olivia gained enough momentum to hurl Jennie across the room, where the wall of spectral spectators shoved her back. She glanced at the three mortals who were watching her with patient, studious eyes and went for a strike on Olivia.

They sparred around the arena, Jennie using her speed to counter Olivia's bulk. Before she knew it, time was up, and Howie Viktor joined the fray.

"Two against one is hardly fair," Jennie told them, her chest rising and falling with each measured breath. "Call it quits?" She grinned, confirming to the others that quitting would never be an option.

Olivia laughed. "Surrendering already? The little girl's big mouth finally caught up with her?"

Howie winked at Olivia. "Ah, man, and I didn't get a chance to fight her yet."

"Cute, you think you have a chance," Jennie told them with a laugh.

The crowd went wild when the pair of specters rushed her.

Jennie ran straight at them, taking the opportunity to turn material so that they passed right through her.

They exchanged confused looks before finding her again.

"Cheap tricks," Olivia complained.

Jennie grinned, closing the gap between them. "It's not my fault if they work."

She threw a right hook at Olivia, catching her in the temple. Using her momentum, she whirled around and planted the heel of her boot into Howie's chest.

Howie staggered back, winded. Olivia attempted to grab Jennie while her back was turned, but Jennie was already in motion.

She ducked Olivia's arms and sidestepped, putting her balance onto her forward foot before spinning into a back roundhouse.

Olivia caught Jennie's ankle, stopping her in her tracks. Her strength was enough to unbalance Jennie and pull her toward her, causing Jennie to hop awkwardly to keep balance.

"Never turn your back on your opponent," Olivia preached. "It makes you vulnerable."

"Funny," Jennie replied. "Because Bruce Lee once told me the exact opposite. See, most fighters expect their opponents not to turn their back, but it's the element of surprise that turns the tide. Give them what they'll never expect."

Before Olivia could react, Jennie twisted and kicked Olivia with her free foot, catching the crease of her elbow and forcing her to release her. She transferred her momentum into a smooth roll.

Olivia roared her frustration as Jennie caught her fall with her hands and rolled to her feet.

Jennie swiveled one-eighty and ran at Olivia.

The pair of them looked set to collide, but Jennie darted left at the last second, catching Olivia's right hand. She swung the specter around, using Olivia's forward momentum against her so her arm was twisted behind her.

Jennie pushed her hand into the pressure point she'd just created. "Do you yield?"

Olivia winced as Jennie put a touch more pressure into the arm lock. The sudden injection of pain forced her to crash to her knees. She slapped the floor. "I'm tapping."

Jennie hopped off her back and brushed the dirt off her top. "Good job. Use your opponent's body against them." She gave Olivia space to move and cracked her knuckles as Howie squared up to face her. "I must say I'm enjoying this. It's like riding a vintage bike. Sometimes the emergency brakes just need a swift kick—"

Jennie hopped back, dodging Howie's fists. He glanced at her without emotion. He was the only one left to take on Jennie, and his demeanor was different from the others.

He took a breath and calmed himself.

Jennie took the opportunity to do the same. "You have some training, yes?"

Howie nodded. "Before my death, I dedicated my life to studying martial arts: Capoeira, karate, Brazilian jiu-jitsu, Muay-Thai. I've studied under the world's greatest masters and achieved tenth dan in them all. I've won tournaments, earned gold across the world, and used my skills in street combat. I look forward to showing you the skills of a master."

Jennie nodded, impressed even though he'd just handed her the key to beating him. "Not bad. Not bad at all, for a novice,"

"A *novice?*" Howie spat the word. The very sound of it was an insult.

"What?" Jennie shrugged. "Twenty-three years is a good start. I've studied combat for over a hundred. Do you know what I've found is the best way to take the teachings of these so-called 'masters' who believe their titles are the definition of success?"

Howie shook his head, uncertainty creeping in.

"A nice smile." Jennie flashed a winning grin, eliciting laughter from the spectral crowd.

This only angered Howie. "Very well. Let's do it your way."

Howie moved toward Jennie, hands readied in defense. She threw a left jab, and he blocked it. She threw a right jab, and he slapped it away.

Her hands moved fast, but he was just as fast. Every attempt to connect was batted away with a series of moves that could be likened to a style of dance Jennie couldn't remember the name of. The Robot? Body Pop? It had to be one of them. He was fast, able to land a jab to her collarbone and a hook to her ribcage.

It was when Howie's eyes narrowed and Jennie became aware that he'd taken her taunts to heart that she decided to end the fight.

Jennie stepped out of reach and beamed at him.

"What are you doing?" Howie demanded. "Fight me!"

"Smiling," Jennie replied, using distraction to do what she did best.

Jennie latched onto Howie and froze him in place.

He tried to move and growled when he realized what was happening.

Jennie advanced on him until her nose was an inch from his. "I expected you to hold your temper. This is a sparring lesson, not a bare-knuckle fight. Just remember, as good as your skills are, I possess skills that are not outmatched by any specter."

Howie couldn't speak, but the growl continued to rumble in his throat.

Jennie saw he was still angry. "Game, set..."

She kissed Howie's cheek. "Match."

With that, she hurled Howie backward, throwing him above the crowd until he hit the wall. He sank behind them, falling temporarily out of sight as the specters erupted in cheers and claps. "Do what you can to affect your enemy's emotions, but do not allow them to affect yours in return. Being reactive hands control to your opponent."

Jennie turned to Olivia and Gavin and offered them a hand to help them back to their feet. "You put up a good fight, guys. One of the best I've had in years. I think we all learned something today."

Olivia and Gavin gave appreciative nods, happy to have had the chance to jump into the arena with Jennie.

As they headed back into the crowd, loud claps came from behind. Jennie turned to find Ula, Triton, and Roman approaching her, distinguishable among the specters as the only other mortals in the group hidden beneath the city.

Jennie had discovered that the three of them were conduits the day she had been led into the chamber by Susannah.

Ula Huntington, Triton Ward, and Roman Long had impressed Jennie with their fighting skills, demonstrating them during a training session that had taken place that night. They were all ex-military, and all of them were beyond pissed at the state of affairs in Washington. Ula was an ex-Navy Seal, and Triton Ward was a retired US Marine. Roman Long refused to disclose his military history, but it was clear that he was a stone-cold badass from the aura of deadly capability he gave off.

But it wasn't in the tactical or the operational arenas that the three of them excelled. Jennie had watched in wonder as each of them stepped into the ring and demonstrated their combat skills. While Lupe was a conduit who could only see and hear specters to talk to them, these three were gifted with the ability to touch specters.

"Not bad. Not bad at all." Ula smirked. "Not the cleanest fight we've seen, but you came out smiling in the end."

"I had to pull a few dirty maneuvers to wriggle my way free. They were smart, putting the strongest in the middle. Gave me more to face earlier than I'd have liked."

Roman's face appeared to be made from concrete, the deep grooves in his brow wrinkled. Jennie had learned quite quickly that, though he appeared to be their leader, he was a man of few words and difficult to humor. "Be nice to see you win a fight without resorting to your powers."

"I play to win," Jennie replied. "Don't like dirty? Don't fight Jennie."

Jennie looked around at the specters in the room, all of them deep in conversation with one another. They really were a mixed bag of talents. Though there were plenty of fighters among them, there were many who were slow on the uptake and were still learning the basics of combat. Jennie wished she could provide them all with weapons, give them something to play with that would increase their chances of survival when they eventually did go up top. The only problem was that she couldn't just magic up spectral weapons.

"Who's next?" Triton asked, unconsciously flexing his bare biceps. He wore a dark tank top, with brown chinos and brown suspenders holding them up. To Jennie, he looked as though he should always have a cigar clamped between his teeth, the way that snarl seemed to be a permanent fixture.

"You, I guess." Ula laughed. "You seem eager."

Triton stepped into the circle and presented himself for the challenge. Soon enough, three specters were ready and waiting for him. He readied his stance, planting his feet and raising his fists to protect his face. The fight got underway.

"How much longer do you think we'll have?" Ula asked Jennie, eyes not leaving the fight.

"I don't know," Jennie replied. "We can't stay down here forever. The longer we're down here, the more time we're giving Brendan to plot and amass his army. But we need to train these guys and get them ready for the fight ahead. Only sixty percent of these specters are combat-ready, and that's being optimistic. Susannah is yet to have a breakthrough. It's all a goddamn waiting game."

Roman grunted. "Any sign of Brendan's latest location?"

Jennie sighed. "Not at last check, but that was twelve hours ago." Her hand moved to the cell phone in her pocket. The device was switched off since Jennie had quickly learned that she received no phone signal underground, and she also had nowhere to charge the damn thing. The last she had seen, she had been on fifteen percent battery. That wasn't going to last forever.

"Worth another check?" Ula suggested as Triton took a mean thwack to the stomach. He pushed off the floor to his feet and roared, charging at a lean woman with flowing hair and a smile on her pretty lips.

Jennie nodded. "You're coming with me."

Roman folded his arms and watched Triton in action as Jennie took the cell phone and left with Ula in tow. She was met by a sudden eerie silence when they left the main chamber. They made their way along tunnels she'd familiarized herself with during the days she'd spent below the surface of Washington until they came to a set of mud-hewn steps leading upward.

The stairs eventually reached a dead-end, and it was here that Jennie paused and turned the phone on. She was dismayed to see her battery had dropped to twelve percent. If it took three percent of the phone's capacity just to load the damn thing every time, she was going to be in trouble.

"Ready?" Jennie asked.

Ula nodded.

Jennie latched onto Ula and walked through the packed dirt until her head poked above the surface. Light streamed through the front arch of the Lincoln Memorial.

Jennie found the number and hit dial. The room was cold and echoey. While Jennie's head hovered out of the floor in the dark shadows, she could make out a cluster of tourists roaming around.

She waited with butterflies in her stomach while it rang. It looked as if it was about to go to voicemail when Baxter answered.

"Hey, Jennie. How are you?"

CHAPTER FIFTY-ONE

The Plaza, New York City, USA

"Hey, Jennie. How are you?"

Baxter waited apprehensively for a reply. Beside him, Lupe grunted and reached for the phone while Baxter held it far out of reach.

Jennie was quiet for a moment. "Remember, we have to make this quick."

"You're the one taking years to reply," Baxter joked. "Seriously, how are things down there? Any updates?"

"I was going to ask you the same thing."

Baxter smiled, although there was an emptiness behind it. "If this is how the conversation is going to go, we might as well hang up."

Jennie let out an audible sigh on the other end. "Things are okay here. The specters are getting restless, but it's not worth it to break free and storm the city yet. I've told them that until we know Brendan's location, we can't chance it. Not while they've got those machines. They're terrified of being exorcised on the spot."

"I can understand why," Baxter replied. "It's like when you've gotten to the end of a really difficult video game level and you're on your last life. You move slower and take care because you don't want all the effort you put into surviving to be a waste."

"What are you talking about?" Jennie asked him, thrown by the change of subject.

"You've never played video games?" Baxter asked.

Jennie was silent.

Baxter scoffed. "Oh, come on, Jennie. Even you must've played *something*."

"I played the one where you slot the bricks into each other and make a line," Jennie told him. "That was relaxing."

Baxter burst into laughter. "Tetris?"

"That's the one," she confirmed. "I gave it a go when all the kids were raving about it. It might've been the same year Virgin Airlines launched."

Baxter shook his head, thankful Jennie couldn't see his response. "Anyway, gaming aside, what else is new?"

"Nothing much," Jennie admitted. "We're training the specters in combat, trying to get the fighting virgins up to a good enough standard to last through a battle, if it comes to that. Susannah is still trying to understand the inner workings of the canisters, but who knows how long that'll take?"

"Between Hendrick's and Susannah's skills for the strange, I'm sure it won't be much longer," Baxter replied. Lupe had given up and was standing beside him on tiptoe to try to hear both sides of the conversation.

Jennie then asked what was happening on the SIA side.

Baxter told Jennie that they had yet to extract the information that they needed from Cole and his men. A few of the Shadows had killed themselves, apparently fitted with the cyanide tooth Jennie and Baxter had seen in Baltimore. "The agents restrained the rest and removed theirs before they could trigger them, and now there's a neat collection of poisonous teeth somewhere in the SIA HQ."

"What about Cole?" Jennie pressed.

"Cole wasn't fitted with one," Baxter told her. "Which seemed strange until they realized he was going to stay zip-lipped. Every time they've tried to interrogate him, he just stares at them with this weird smile on his face."

Jennie chuckled. "I bet that drives Daggro crazy."

"You know it," Baxter confirmed. "She can beat her fists on the table, scream in his face, or threaten the quality of life in the holding cell, but he doesn't crack."

Jennie sighed, seeing the downside to the agency having custody of Cole. "That's one negative about being on the side of good. There's too much law in place to protect the scumbags. That's not how interrogation works. Bad people acquire information because they have no limits. Peel toenails, hold scissors to eyeballs—those are real threats. Reading them their Miranda Rights and saying you'll be granted less time in prison doesn't break many people."

"You sound like you admire the dark side," Baxter told her.

Jennie considered that. "Not admire. I just know they get the job done. That's important. The law is meant to protect the innocent, not be used as a shield against justice."

Baxter went on to tell Jennie that the SIA had widened their search. They'd gained access to Brendan's live camera feeds in Washington, and they had brought in an analysis team from the FBI to work alongside them and find Brendan and the Shadows.

"That's something," Jennie enthused. "When will they get started?"

"They arrived this morning," Baxter told her. "They've just finished setting up, but soon we should have a clear direction on intelligence. Don't worry, Jennie. Brendan can't stay hidden forever."

"Wow." Jennie laughed softly. "You're beginning to sound like a real agent."

"As long as there's a light bright enough to flush out the shadows, we'll find them."

Lupe scoffed. "Okay, now you sound like a pretentious philosopher."

Baxter placed a hand on his head and shoved him away.

There was shuffling on Jennie's end of the phone. "I've got to go, Bax. This battery situation is shitty. Where can I find a charger at the Lincoln Memorial?"

"Try Lupe's handbag," Baxter suggested.

"Very funny. Call back in another twelve hours?"

"Sounds good," Baxter replied. "Talk then."

"Bye, Bax."

Baxter tossed the phone to Lupe so suddenly that he struggled to catch it. There was a troubled look on his face.

"What is it?" Lupe asked.

Baxter sighed. "We've got one more call, then we're out of contact with Jennie. We need to find a way to charge her phone."

"Or bring her a new phone?" Carolyn suggested, appearing at the doorway. She waved them both over. "Come on. Word is Hendrick has some news to share."

Baxter looked at the phone Lupe was still clutching tightly. "Why couldn't that have happened five minutes ago, *before* Jennie called us?"

Carolyn shrugged. "The dried-up old prune works in mysterious ways. He's also an impatient SOB. Come *on*."

For a man who looked like a human version of a naked mole rat, Hendrick had a surprising skip in his step. His glasses hung on precariously at the end of his nose as he examined the large glass case on the bench in front of him.

The case might have been mistaken for a fish tank if it hadn't been for the thick steel frame holding it all together, not to mention the misty silver liquid that swirled inside the tank. The liquid emitted a faint glow that, added to the lighted screen of Hendrick's tablet, gave him a ghastly appearance as Baxter, Carolyn, Lupe, and the lead SIA agents came in to see what all the fuss was about.

"Come in, come in," Proctor fussed.

Baxter wasn't surprised to see Proctor's excited expression. He had begun to anticipate the researcher's glee when he had made some discovery and was going to share it with his superiors. It was the same excitement he'd seen on children's faces when they handed parents a finger painting of a tree, or a crayon sketch of the family holding hands.

Proctor waved his hands in excitement. "What we've achieved… What has been… It's unbelievable."

"Why don't you try full sentences so we can all share in your happiness?" Hopkins suggested, his face the polar opposite of Proctor's.

Proctor gathered them around the tank. "Of course. It's just hard to begin."

"Jennie said the liquid is energy drained from specters?" Baxter asked, feeling the strange wash of mourning that came every time he was near a large amount of the stuff.

Proctor nodded somberly. "I don't know *how* they've done it, but we're working on that."

"*I'm* working on that," Hendrick interjected.

"Right. Hendrick is working on it. But what we have discovered is more interesting than you can imagine."

"How about we skip the intrigue and get right to the demonstration?" Daggro commanded.

"Right. Yes. Right." Proctor moved across to a workbench where a large sheet covered a number of objects. He rolled up one edge and revealed a Glock 19. "A mortal weapon, can we all agree?"

He passed it to the agents. They handed it around, weighing it in their hands before giving it back. "Real. Sturdy. Perfect for taking down criminals or putting a hole in your crazy ex-fiancé's door."

Carolyn raised an eyebrow, folding her arms. "I'm not sure it's your ex-fiancé who's crazy if you're shooting holes in their door."

A few of the others chuckled.

"Well, yes," Proctor replied, unperturbed. "But watch what happens when I do this."

He opened the small hatch at the top of the tank that was locked with a clasp and dropped the pistol into the silver liquid. The liquid clawed at the opening, moving as if it were trying to escape.

Proctor closed the hatch with a snap. "Now, watch."

The pistol fell to the bottom of the tank, sinking slowly through the viscous liquid. Its black sheen was only slightly obscured by the liquid, but then a strange thing happened.

The pistol began to float back up, stopping when it was suspended in the middle of the tank.

"Holy…" Rhone muttered.

The pistol began to glow, its black exterior pulsing with bright white light. It began in the center as though tremendous heat was pressurizing it into oblivion, but the gun kept its shape.

Baxter gasped. "It's like the gun is being exorcised."

The pistol vanished when the light peaked, replaced by a bright white afterimage. The swirling liquid swam and swarmed around it, creating a vortex inside the glass case. The tank wobbled slightly as the onlookers shielded their eyes.

"Are you sure this is safe?" Hopkins asked through gritted teeth, his face turned away from the light.

Hendrick, however, continued staring at his tablet, measuring readings with an almost passive expression. "All safe. All fine. Not long now."

The light reached a brilliant crescendo, flooding the room and leaving no shadows behind. It pulsed with a final intensity, then, as suddenly as it had all appeared, the light faded, and the room's gloom returned.

Baxter and the others uncovered their eyes and gasped at what they saw in the tank.

Baxter's mouth hung open. "The gun. It's spectral."

"If you'd like to do the honors," Proctor told Hendrick, standing back from the tank with a look of apprehension as Hendrick rolled up his lab coat sleeves, unclasped the hatch, and plunged his hand inside without a care for the way the liquid rushed toward him.

The liquid encapsulated Hendrick's hand and wrist, and for the moment it took him to snatch the weapon, they became immaterial. He retrieved the gun and placed it on the table beside the tank, moving faster than any of them had seen him move to shut the hatch.

Proctor danced on his toes excitedly.

Hopkins moved closer to the gun, only able to see the spectral shape through his SI goggles. "Can I touch it?"

"Please, by all means, try," Proctor offered with a motion of his hand.

Hopkins tried to pick up the Glock, but his hand passed straight through it. He swept his hand back and forth, but it was like trying to catch mist.

Proctor turned his attention to Baxter. "Your turn."

Baxter waited for Hopkins to give an approving nod before reaching for the gun. He picked it up with no issue, surprised at how light it felt and how comfortably it fitted his hand. "This is—"

"Impossible?" Proctor practically squealed. "Not anymore. Forget all the things you thought couldn't be done. This changes everything."

"What is this stuff?" Hopkins asked, moving closer to the tank. He placed a hand on its side and the silver liquid moved toward it, growing dense and following his movements. "You said it's spectral?"

Proctor opened his mouth to speak, but it was Hendrick who answered.

"We are yet to determine how it was harvested, from a scientific standpoint, but yes. Inside this tank is the essence of dozens of specters, filtered and extracted by the Shadows. It's pure spectral energy, the base components of what makes specters exist and gives them their powers."

Proctor wore a disappointed glare, unhappy not to have enlightened the others himself. "Thank you, Hendrick."

Rhone shook his head. "That seems—"

"Impossible," Carolyn finished, taking the gun Baxter offered her.

"This is revolutionary," Hopkins exclaimed, his eyes widening with excitement.

Lupe nodded eagerly. "This means we can arm the Spectral Plane specters and transform everyday objects into things that can be used in combat. Right now, unless you've been lucky enough to die with a weapon in your grasp, you have to steal a firearm or go without."

Carolyn tapped Lupe's shoulder. "What about the potential to give specters things they've had to go without since death? Oh! Oh! Can you put food into it? Does it work with food?"

Rhone chuckled. "You don't have a digestive system. You don't need food."

Carolyn fixed him with a stern glare. "That doesn't mean I don't miss it." She sighed. "Imagine never being able to taste chocolate again. No strawberries. No Prosecco."

Baxter whirled on them, suddenly intimidating. "Before you get carried away here, remember where this substance has come from. It's filtered from *us*. Specters. Our kind have been drained to make this for the benefit of the Shadows. They're upgrading their tech and using our essence to lace their weapons, and all you care about is putting a Hershey bar in your pie hole?"

Carolyn stared back with a "Can you blame me?" expression on her face.

"Think about it," Baxter told them. "Is this stuff incredible? Yes. But it's also the harvested souls of our brothers and sisters. Let's be a little more respectful in deciding what we're going to do with it."

Hopkins gave a stern nod. "Proctor, Hendrick, good work, but he's right. We should only use what we have so far. Those canisters are in limited supply, so let's find a way to put it to the best use."

"How many do we have?" Baxter asked.

Proctor walked over to a large cupboard and slid the doors open. Inside were four crates of canisters that had been seized from the Shadows' base.

Baxter felt nauseous. "Shit. There's enough there to—"

"Arm ourselves for the war ahead?" Hopkins replied. "That was my thinking, too."

CHAPTER FIFTY-TWO

Washington DC, USA

Hendrick hardly ever slept. He didn't need to. After years of experimenting with the vast array of earth elements available through his line of work, he had defeated sleep.

It had been thirty-four years since he had discovered the miracle elixir, a formula he was keeping to himself. Sure, he might share the secret before he kicked the bucket, but he knew he had a few good decades left. Many good years of contributing, helping those who needed help, and studying the secrets of the elements.

He knew it was late. He wore no watch and he could not see the moon or the sun, but he knew it, nonetheless. Uncountable years of existence and experience had made him accurate with the time to within a second.

Test him. Just try it.

Hendrick scuffled around the lab, his only light the silvery glow from the tank. He balanced his glasses at the end of his nose and squinted, but more light wouldn't have helped him to see any better. His eyesight was as good as it would ever be. Some things he'd just had to learn to deal with.

"Fascinating…" he mumbled, playing with the rods and connectors that fed off the tank. "Absolutely fascinating."

Hendrick paid no attention when a gentle knock came at the door. He waited until his visitor was almost directly behind him before he acknowledged his presence. "Baxter. To what do I owe this late-night pleasure?"

Baxter did a double-take. "For a man with such poor eyesight, you didn't have any trouble knowing it was me."

"You knocked," Hendrick replied.

"You didn't turn around," Baxter pointed out.

Hendrick chuckled. "I don't need eyes to see. I have plenty of other senses I am gifted with. Your smell, for example." Hendrick tapped a finger to his temple. "It's all logged up in here for me to recognize when you're nearby."

"My smell?" Baxter repeated blankly.

"Every specter has a unique energy signature. I happen to process them as smells or tastes." Hendrick pointed at Baxter. "Cinnamon with a hint of oregano."

Baxter's nose wrinkled. "Sounds nasty."

Hendrick shrugged. "Hey, it's your smell."

As Hendrick spoke, he continued what he was doing. He tapped away on his tablet as he fiddled with the coils and wires, inputting readings from the tank. The ability to multitask was something you were either born with or not, and he had been blessed.

He waited for Baxter to talk again but was left wanting. Finally, he broke the silence. "You wanted to see me?"

Baxter's eyes remained fixed on the tank.

Hendrick cast a glance over his shoulder, showcasing a gruesome smile. "You wanted to see *it?*"

"I don't understand," Baxter replied. "This all seems like some kind of weird magic. That mortals can harvest specters and use them for… what? Power? Energy? What is this?"

Hendrick flicked a small panel of glass and a needle shook behind it. "Believe it or not, none of this is new. The potential to harvest spectral energy has always been a possibility, in the same way that we could harvest mortals for power if we really wanted to."

Baxter's eyebrow raised. "Excuse me?"

Hendrick nodded. "I'm not saying that's something I've ever considered, but there's a lot of energy in the human body that can be harvested. Electrical signals, heat, iron, and other minerals in the blood. If someone wanted to do so, and they had the ability to gather enough mortals together, I'm sure something would happen."

Baxter's lip curled. "That's disgusting."

"Haven't you seen *The Matrix?*" Hendrick asked.

Baxter was taken aback by this question. He couldn't imagine the alchemist settling in for movie night with a bowl of popcorn. "No? Have you?"

"I have," Hendrick replied. "What do *you* do when you have a down night? I haven't always been this old, you know. And keep your voice down, or you'll wake that cretin Proctor."

Baxter looked over his shoulder as if expecting Proctor to appear. "What happens?"

Hendrick chuckled. "In *The Matrix*, or if Proctor wakes up?"

"The movie," Baxter clarified.

"Are you sure?" Hendrick asked. "Either one is a headache if you think too hard."

"I'm sure!"

Hendrick paused momentarily, looking at the dark shadows of the corner as if he was drawing the memory from there. "Humans are plugged into machines so the machines can harvest their energy, like batteries. Their thoughts, their dreams, their whole reality is a construct fed to them to keep them docile. They think they're alive when really their whole world is being fed to them by machines."

Baxter shrugged. "Sounds dense."

"It can sometimes take a few watches." Hendrick carried on with his work.

Baxter watched with great interest as he busied himself around the room. Hendrick paused to take notes on his tablet.

"You said that none of this is new," Baxter asked, finding his voice again. "Has any of this ever happened before?"

Hendrick looked at Baxter for the first time. "Of course."

"When? How?"

Hendrick sighed, resigning himself to an explanation. "For hundreds of years, there were few mortals in the know of the spectral world. The whole spectral world was considered the Holy Grail of existence, and most specters worked to keep it hidden."

"Most?" Baxter inquired.

"There's always a minority," Hendrick answered. "If history has taught us anything at all, it's that what is hidden can rarely stay lost. There have been recorded instances of mortals trying to manipulate the spectral world from as far back as history stretches. It was one of the reasons the paranormal court refused to work alongside any mortals except those within their royal bloodline who would one day inherit the crown."

"And then came Victoria," Baxter grumbled, knowing the answer already.

Hendrick gave a soft nod. "She inherited an empire and she wanted to keep it, although that was not how she presented it at the time. Victoria began to bring the mortals into the know, claiming she wanted the same progress she'd seen in her lifetime to follow her into her spectral life. She made affiliations with scientists, apothecaries, anyone who could help her get a leg up over the competition."

Hendrick's eyes grew glassy. He took his glasses off with stubby fingers and rubbed the lenses on his grubby lab coat. "My master was one of the first to make waves, obtaining a number of specters that were donated by the queen to further his work. I was only young when he mastered the funneling process. I was new to my craft, so I had no idea what he was doing, but I saw it nonetheless."

"You knew Jennie back then, didn't you?" Baxter asked. "When she was new to her work. You said so in New York. You made her perfume."

"*I* made perfume." He put the glasses back on and looked Baxter in the eye. "My master gave Jennie the ultimate gift. She has the only remaining proof that he had harnessed the power of spectral power and created something unimaginable."

Baxter's mouth hung open. "Your master *made* Jennie?"

Hendrick blew air between his lips in a wet raspberry. "No. Master Yungheim would never alter a human's genetics. Don't be so obtuse. I couldn't tell you what made Jennie the way she is."

"Then what are you talking about?"

Hendrick pinched the bridge of his nose. "You've seen the 'Big Bitch,' haven't you? Jennie never goes anywhere without it."

Baxter's eyes grew wide. "Yungheim gifted Jennie the Big Bitch?"

"*Master* Yungheim," Hendrick corrected.

"But I don't understand," Baxter told him, trying to piece it all together. "If your master discovered all of this, then why hasn't this been put to use already? Why was it all kept quiet?"

"Because Master Yungheim saw the danger," Hendrick replied. "He saw the queen donating criminals, thieves, murderers, and more so he could dissect them and drain them, and after a number of months, his conscience kicked in. He couldn't put specters through the process, knowing what it did to them. He gave Jennie her weapons, then he shut down his experiments and told the queen he wouldn't do it anymore. There are no apothecaries like Master Yungheim anymore. No one could carry the mantle."

Baxter sat on the workbench with his elbows on his thighs and put his head in his hands. "But you have no problem continuing his work?"

"Of course, I do!" Hendrick told him hotly. "I would never kill a specter or drain them for science. But when does a scientist ever have four crates of the stuff drop into his lap? These have already been processed; there's no saving the specters. All I can do is use the bad for good, find a way to help you and the SIA end this all. That's the kind of work I'm doing."

Baxter cocked his head admiringly. "You're a good man, you know?"

Hendrick raised an eyebrow. "Thank you. I needed your approval. My self-worth is tied up in your opinion of me."

Baxter laughed and hopped off the bench. He studied the tank for a few moments longer, hearing footsteps echo in the hall outside the room. "Did you really know Jennie as a little girl?"

Hendrick debated this, tapping the side of the tank and watching a coil of the silver liquid draw toward his finger like a hungry eel. "No. Not really. I don't think Jennie's ever really been a young girl."

<hr>

Rhone watched Daggro from the other side of the one-way glass. Cole was sitting with his arms folded, and a grim expression on his face, the same as he'd done since they'd apprehended him at the Shadows' base.

"Ready to talk yet?" Daggro adjusted a pile of notes on the table and paused for effect. Rhone and Daggro already knew that Cole was going to remain tight-lipped, but it was protocol to keep on trying.

Give the suspects a chance to speak. Give them everything they're "owed." Then, when that's all over, turn to the rough stuff.

Not that that had been Jennie's approach.

Daggro took an exaggerated breath and flipped the pages over. They had obtained a large amount of information on his extensive criminal activity after running his fingerprints through Quantico's database and unlocked a number of useful points about his past.

The most revealing information was from the file the FBI profilers had sent, outlining a troubled man who had never found a way to belong. A man who had never found stability in his life.

An ex-military man, Cole had served fifteen years in the US Army before leaving to marry his late wife, Kate Merriwether. The decade that followed Kate's death saw a man who had fallen into nearly every pit a man could fall into. The only thing that Cole had avoided had been drugs. On that front, he was cleaner than a college freshman who was yet to take a toke on something green and hazy. Alcohol and debt led to robbery, looting, car-jacking, and weapons charges.

But everything had changed for Cole when the Shadows had come along.

Rhone's best guess was that Cole had stumbled across Brendan in the same way all his other minions had. Only, with his institutional background and his longing for someone in his life who wouldn't leave him, Cole had fully immersed himself in the Shadows.

They didn't need Cole to admit his crimes. The only thing they needed was for him to open his mouth and tell them what they needed to know about Brendan Koa's operation.

"You're going to have to talk sometime," Daggro told him dryly. "We've played it nice so far, but it won't be long before we have to turn up the heat. Comply, or things will turn nasty."

Nasty? Rhone thought. *How nasty can you get when the law is on your side? A slap on the wrist? Withholding a phone call to a loved one? This should be counted as terrorism; then we could do what was necessary.*

Cole tilted his head to the side, a bored expression on his face.

Daggro gave a curt nod as if she had been expecting this. Rhone could sense her impatience, could imagine in his mind the moment when Daggro would yield to Rogue's techniques and hurl herself over the table at him.

But first, Plan B.

"Very well." Daggro collected the papers together and straightened them on the table with a couple of heavy taps. She filed them into a small manilla folder and rose to leave.

She stopped with her hand on the door handle. "Oh, there is one thing before I go." She turned and wagged a finger. "Just a small thing, but as a parent myself, I believe the least I can do is give you a heads-up before we upset the balance of things."

A flicker of something passed over Cole's face. The momentary movement betrayed his curiosity. Rhone put his hands in his pocket and watched closely, impressed by Daggro's acting skills.

Daggro rifled through the papers and pulled out a sheet with a large photo on one side and text on the other. She placed it on the table, photo-side-up in front of Cole, and then tilted her head to smile at him. "Lovely girl you have there, Cole. How old is Abby? I'd guess about eight? Nine?"

Cole's upper lip rose in a sneer, giving him the appearance of a cornered bulldog.

Daggro flipped the page over. "Abigail Kipman. Oh, I'm sorry. That's not right. She has her mother's surname, doesn't she?" Her eyes rose to Cole's awaiting a response. "Abigail Chatsley, a resident at 102 Southgate Corner, with her mother and stepfather, Erica and Philip Chatsley. Seems she's had a cozy life so far, hasn't she? All things considered..."

Cole's icy exterior broke. He rested on his elbows, leaning slowly toward Daggro. When he spoke, his words were a quiet growl. "My daughter has nothing to do with this."

"Oh, I know!" Daggro replied as though butter wouldn't melt on her tongue. "And it seems you've had nothing to do with her either. Well, apart from the money you send every month, huh? We tracked the transfers for child support on your account, and you never miss a payment. We know you care about the child. What happened? Did Abby's new daddy take over, and you thought you'd disappear into the shadows—excuse the pun—and let Abby have a father who wasn't a worthless pile of shit?"

Rhone moved closer to the glass, resting a hand on the panel. *Easy now, Daggro. Keep it calm.*

Although Daggro was treading the line, it was clearly having an impact on Cole. His eyes narrowed, and his face went sour. "She has *nothing* to do with this."

Daggro looked down at the paper, a pitying expression on her face. "It's a real shame, isn't it? That we'll have to tell Abby that her father has been sent to jail. That he refused to cooperate with the authorities, and now he's one of the bad guys. That'd break her heart—"

"*Keep my daughter out of this!*" Cole roared.

Rhone smiled. *That's it. She's broken him.*

Cole jumped to his feet, strained against the cuffs securing him to the table, and slammed his fists on the surface. His stare was molten, boring into Daggro, who gave him the faintest flicker of a smile as the two guards at the door aimed their weapons at him.

"Sit down and tell me what we want to know," Daggro ordered.

Cole's chest rose and fell. Confusion contorted his features.

"The power is in your hands," Daggro added softly.

Cole slowly lowered himself to his seat, eyes moving from Daggro to the guards. He folded his arms and closed his eyes, tortured by the options.

"I know you haven't seen her since she was a young girl." Daggro's words were soft but Cole heard her easily in the pin-drop quiet. "I know she doesn't know who you are and, you've done nothing but watch from the sidelines while another man raises her. One night stands do that. I know what it would do to you if we were to report to your ex-lover what your position is and the information found its way to your little girl, so let's just make this easy. Tell us where Brendan Koa is. Tell us everything you know about the Shadows, and we'll reconsider our position."

Cole took a deep breath and looked out from the shadow of his brow. He folded his arms tighter, then seemed to look directly at Rhone through the glass.

"Fine. Let's talk."

CHAPTER FIFTY-THREE

<u>Washington DC, USA</u>

Tanya's heart thumped in her chest as she crossed the road.

It wasn't so much that she wasn't used to danger. After the last few weeks, danger had followed her and the Spectral Plane everywhere they had gone. If anything, it had become something of a familiar companion.

If she was honest, her anxiety was because it had been a while since she had gone this long without being able to see Sandra, the little spectral girl who had come into their lives and granted Tanya the gift she had always been searching for. It was only with Sandra's powers that Tanya was able to turn spectral and unlock her mind to the spectral world around her.

And now she was mortal. Sandra had promised she'd remain nearby, just in case, but Tanya could neither see, hear, feel, touch, or smell her. She was alone, walking through Washington by herself.

It had been a while since she had done anything alone.

Tanya half-jogged up the street, ignoring the stares from the occasionally hungry male who was entranced by her blood-red lips and dark red hair. Her red cape flew behind her, her pretty face buried in the soft shadow of its hood. She was used to attracting male attention, had had to deal with it half of her life, she just could never understand what it was that made men feel entitled to cat-call, or to devour her with their stares. She wasn't a piece of meat. She was an intelligent woman who held a pivotal role in the Spectral Plane.

A car horn blared. Tanya would have jumped if she hadn't already met the balding man's eyes as he drove toward her. He stopped to allow her to cross the road, and she picked up her pace, keen to put as much distance between them as possible.

It was when Tanya found her way to the end of the estate and saw the wide-open common of the Lincoln Memorial that she paused and whispered, "Sandra. If you're here, give me some kind of sign."

She darted her head around, eliciting a few strange looks from a family of four who were excitedly navigating their way toward the large white building of the Memorial.

There was no reply. No sign. Worry ate at Tanya's stomach. She asked again and almost jumped when a sudden coldness washed through the center of her body.

"Good enough," she mumbled. "Unless that isn't you, Sandra. Then I'm officially freaked out."

Tanya looked around again, this time specifically looking for anyone who appeared out of the ordinary, or could possibly be watching her. They knew that the Shadows had eyes all around them, but they just didn't know where. As the only one of their order who had stayed relatively clear of the action, Tanya was the one asked to complete the mission.

"Hardly the noblest of missions," Tanya had argued when Rhone handed her the fully charged cell phone.

"Still, it needs to be done." Baxter had told her with a fatherly look on his face. "We need contact with Jennie, and she's not ready to leave her hideout until we track down Brendan and we're able to secure the specters' safety."

Tanya walked briskly across the lawn. Visiting the sites in Washington had always been on her bucket list, and she was almost disappointed that her first experiences of the Washington Monument and the Lincoln Reflection Pool were marred by a rapidly beating heart and the worry that the cult's spies were watching her.

Tanya approached a cluster of tourists being led along in a tight group by a loud-mouthed guide. She joined the back of the group as they ascended the stairs into the Lincoln Memorial, then diverted to her left when they were under the cover of its canopy.

Making sure to act like a tourist, she admired the nineteen-foot tall white statue of Abraham Lincoln. She laced her fingers behind her back and strolled slowly backward until she found the shaded corner of the building.

There she waited, her heart thumping with every single individual who came in, and hoping not to draw too much attention to herself. She checked her watch. There was still time for everything to go wrong.

Jennie appeared behind Tanya suddenly, putting an end to her worry. "Thank you *so* much," she told her with a smile. "I don't know what we would have done if you hadn't made it."

"Don't mention it." Tanya smiled warmly and handed over the phone. "It's the least I could do considering everything you've done for Sandra and me. Can you see her, Jennie? Is she still here?"

Jennie glanced down at the little girl who stood by Tanya's side, the hem of her dress swaying gently in the breeze. Jennie waved back when Sandra wiggled her fingers shyly. "Yeah, I can see her."

"Oh, thank goodness," Tanya sighed. "Honestly, I know I've been overprotective lately, but it's been so long since I've not been spectral, or at least able to see her. It's like a whole new world being fully mortal again."

"Don't worry, someday you'll be permanently spectral if you choose, and then you'll experience it all the time."

Tanya chuckled. "Sometimes I wish that day would come sooner rather than later."

Jennie shook her head. "Don't wish your life away. Would you really rather be at risk of being sucked up and exorcised by whatever tech that is that the Shadows have?"

Tanya shook her head. Then, when pressed for any updates from the SIA, Tanya told Jennie about what they'd discovered with the spectral energy capsules they'd confiscated from the Shadows. Baxter had informed all of the Spectral Plane the moment they had reconvened, and none of them could believe what they'd heard.

"So, the secret's finally coming out?" Jennie muttered to herself. "The tech they've been seeking all these years…"

"What do you mean? What secret?" Tanya asked.

Jennie shook her head. Aware of a middle-aged couple who kept turning their head their way. "You need to get going. Tell Baxter that it's all under control down here. I haven't told the SIA yet, but I've got help. Three more conduits who are skilled in combat."

"Why haven't you told the SIA?" Tanya asked with a note of concern in her voice.

"They haven't asked." Jennie grinned. She palmed the phone and held it up. "Thanks for this. I thought I'd be out of contact for a while."

Tanya knew a brush-off when she heard it. "What are you doing down there, Jennie? How long are we going to have to wait?"

"Three more days, tops," Jennie told her with surprising swiftness. "Tell the SIA to hurry up their hunt for the Shadows. They're not going to stay quiet for long. Not now that they know we're onto them. Pull in other divisions, bring in experts, do whatever it takes. Just find them so that we have the advantage."

Tanya nodded and embraced Jennie. She wrapped her in her arms so tight that Jennie struggled to breathe.

Jennie laughed. "This isn't goodbye."

"I know," Tanya agreed. "I just miss you."

She was talking to thin air.

Alexandria, Virginia, USA

Brendan strolled around his facility with his fingers laced behind his back and a permanent sour expression on his face.

He had liked his facility in Washington. The views were beautiful at sunset, the place had a certain charm, and he had begun to feel at home wandering its halls.

Painful remorse now worked at his stomach. This facility, a former factory used for the production of candy bars that had been discontinued after the great healthy eating revolution of 2004, left a lot to be desired. Brendan loathed that he had been forced out of his favorite facility and into one so sub-par. The place was gritty, the halls were cold, and it lacked the charm he had grown accustomed to.

Still, progress was progress, and progress was happening right before his eyes.

Julia walked five feet behind him, respectfully silent as Brendan opened the door onto the balconies way above the factory floor.

Hundreds of workers scurried around below, banging metal on metal, pouring the essence of harvested specters, and creating dozens of replicas of the machinery they'd need to remove the nuisances and complete their tasks.

There were stacks of exorcism traps in one corner—crude, square machines laced with holy water that were able to destroy specters within seconds. There was also a large crate full of assault rifles and handguns, every one of them filled with spectral bullets that could pierce mortal and specter alike.

Brendan nodded at the doorway in the far corner of the room that led to the place where the specters they'd captured were bound to their new mortal hosts. The midwife team was hard at work utilizing the possession spell to create Brendan's army.

"How many?" Brendan asked.

Julia checked her tablet. "Three hundred and sixty-one so far."

Brendan growled. "It's not enough. We want to take the city by storm. That's barely enough to fill a Starbucks parking lot. Why has progress slowed?"

"It's the body issue," Julia told him with regret. "We've made soldiers of nearly all our volunteers. We're running out of fresh meat."

"What about the callout?" Brendan countered. "I thought we were attracting all the fresh meat we could want?"

Julia's cheeks flushed. "Sir, there have been…incidents. People have, well, died from using the rituals we leaked online. People who weren't a part of our…your organization."

Julia rotated the tablet to show him the news article on the screen. A gaunt boy who looked more like a humanoid insect than a human, pictured beside his mother.

"Deranged local loner charged with murder?" Brendan read aloud, every syllable dripping with disgust. He perused the article, picking up scant details about the UK boy and his dabbling in the dark arts.

Brendan's dark eyes met Julia's, and she wilted under his stare. "How many more stories like this?"

Julia tapped a button and jumped back a screen, sliding her finger down to reveal two dozen similar articles. "It's made the news. According to the media, it's a crazy ploy from a psycho terrorist organization trying to bend the minds of the world's impressionable youth. The comments sections, people are in an uproar."

Brendan shook his head and pawed at his eyes. "Even when presented with bold evidence to prove that specters are real, the mortals will turn a blind eye. It's always been that way. Too many people are stuck in their cozy little lives, petrified of change, terrified of any alteration to their perfect little realities, unaware of the truth out there."

"Did you want the world to know?" Julia asked softly. "Surely mainstream belief would bring the mortal authorities into it worldwide."

Brendan debated this internally. "No, you're right. Not yet. It actually works in our favor that the blind believe we are a hoax. Those who are truly curious and hungry for the truth will find us."

Julia gave a subtle nod. "That's true. If only certain commenters on the forum wouldn't mar the truth." She showed Brendan the comments section under their post on the dark web conspiracy site. As many as there were who believed, there were twice as many that accused them of being scammers.

"We need to find a better way to get the word out," Brendan told Julia softly. "What we need is a horde of devoted followers looking for a way out of their miserable lives."

Brendan turned to stare out of the grease-stained window at the industrial estate beyond. A flicker of something orange caught his attention. He saw the bright color belonged to a homeless man sitting in the shelter of the adjacent wall. The man was wrapped in his filthy blanket with a pile of burning sticks before him.

A smile pricked at the corner of Brendan's lips. He rubbed his hands eagerly.

"I may just have the answer…"

CHAPTER FIFTY-FOUR

<u>Washington DC, USA</u>

Jennie knocked on the stretch of wall that led to Susannah's chambers. There was no door there, but Jennie felt it was common courtesy to at least warn Suzannah before startling the witch into a reactionary incantation.

"You took a bold risk back then." Susannah didn't turn, but her words were scornful. "The fate of us all rests in your hands."

"Not solely in mine," Jennie retorted. "Everyone has a part to play in what's to come. It's not entirely on me to fix everything."

Susannah chuckled. "If only you knew."

She was bent over a small bench made of packed earth. After the last few days, Jennie had gotten used to the very definition of "bare necessities." She'd eaten scarcely, not seen a real piece of furniture, and hadn't tasted a drop of alcohol while they bided their time underneath the ground.

"No one saw me." Jennie wasn't sure why she felt she needed to justify her actions to Susannah. Maybe it was the fact she had died at the stake as a witch. Maybe it was the fact that Susannah had easily healed Jennie with magic. Maybe it was nothing more than the fact that Susannah, in a strange kind of way, reminded her of her mother in her final years.

"Someone saw you," Suzannah stated. "The world isn't so blind as to not notice someone dressed like you appear from the floor of a renowned monument. You need to be careful."

"I needed a way to communicate with the others," Jennie reminded her. "I took minimal risks. Nobody saw me; I made sure."

"There are other ways than the modern electric curse."

Jennie walked closer into the room, taking a knee beside Susannah. The mud bench was littered with a variety of instruments that had been brought down from the surface before Jennie's lockdown. An array of weaponry, and steel objects with filed edges or bludgeoning capabilities.

Next to them were the canisters of liquid Jennie had stolen from the Shadows' base. One was already empty, while the other was down to the final third of its contents.

That familiar discomfort reappeared in Jennie's stomach when Susannah unscrewed the lid and tipped five drops onto a small dagger.

Jennie's hands moved to her center. As they did, the Big Bitch materialized by her side, appearing of its own volition.

Susannah's eyes darted toward the weapon. "This isn't your first encounter with this substance, is it?"

Jennie shook her head. "No, although I never witnessed it with my own eyes. I didn't know what it was either until I found those specters being drained. Someone close to me created my weapons from its power, and I took them. I never thought to ask where the magic had come from."

"There's no magic here," Susannah replied. She held the hilt of the dagger and brought it to her face. The dagger shone a gentle white, pulsing in and out of view as if it was simply fading from existence. "Extracting the essence from specters is an abomination, pure and simple. Getting the quantity right, that's science. Too much and the weapon is next to useless for humans, too little and it will hardly make a scratch on a specter."

"What about extraction?" Jennie replied. "Is there a way to remove the power once an object has been imbued?"

Susannah's eyes closed as if she was pained. "None that I've found so far. Its effects appear to be permanent." She shook her head again. "Who in their right mind dares to play with the dead? To harvest those already on their final lives?"

"We don't have enough, do we?" Jennie asked the question that had been plaguing her while she waited patiently for Susannah to work her magic. "There's not enough here to arm our specters and take the fight to them?"

Susannah sighed. "No, dear. We don't have nearly enough. I've converted at least a dozen rifles and pistols, but the rest was wasted in the experimentation, and there's little left to spare."

Jennie put a hand to her head. "Then what are we supposed to do? You know as well as I do that every day we sit down here, dilly-dallying and hoping that the SIA finds Koa's location, the Shadows are growing their army. If the queen is supporting him in this, who knows what else is going to come our way?" She stood and began pacing the room, ducking slightly so her head wouldn't scrape on the ceiling. "We need to speed this shit up. We can't stay down here forever."

Susannah smiled.

"What's so funny?" Jennie asked with a scowl.

Susannah rose to her feet, using the bench for support. "Come with me, child."

Jennie raised an eyebrow. "Where are you taking me?"

Susannah ducked through a tiny hole at the end of the chamber. "You asked only about the spectral liquid. You didn't ask about the other options on the table."

Jennie followed, crawling on the floor to keep up. The low passage was dark, with only the glow of Susannah to guide Jennie until they arrived in a dome-ceilinged chamber with an earthenware pot in the center.

Flames licked at its base, lighting the chamber. A gentle ribbon of steam curled into the air, filling the chamber was with the scent of sap and rock.

Jennie's mouth fell ajar. "What are these other options?"

Susannah chuckled. "I've been hard at work while you've been training your army."

"They're not my army—"

Susannah tsked. "Cut the modesty and claim what's yours. Soon the time will come when you will be challenged, and if you don't take what's rightfully yours, it will be stolen from you."

"Like your life was stolen from you?" Jennie asked. She wasn't sure why she felt like she was being led down a sloping tunnel with no control over what was happening.

"My dear, when I died, my life was *given* to me." She reached into a hessian sack that stood in the corner of the room and threw a handful of the black powder into the fire at the base of the cauldron. Sparks erupted and popped like fireworks and the liquid turned bright green, lighting up the chamber with an eerie glow. "All my mortal life, my magic was forbidden. It was a curse to my family, to my people, to my friends."

Susannah circled the cauldron, occasionally throwing handfuls of strange ingredients into its slowly bubbling center. "I practiced in secret, dabbling with the occult, playing with the dark arts, discovering the ways of Wicca, until I was able to do extraordinary things. When my accuser, John Allen approached me three nights previous to his accusation with rape on his mind, I escaped with magic and put a curse on his oxen, forcing them to drown themselves in the river."

She shrugged at Jennie's chuckle. "Of course, you can understand why that would upset such a man. He made my abilities public, and although I attempted to hide them, I was tried and found guilty."

Another handful of ingredients turned the solution orange. The scent of citrus filled the air, curdling rapidly into mold and dust.

"Over the past three hundred years, I have lived as a specter, mostly isolated and alone. I traveled to America in search of my past, hunted for my ancestors, and took revenge on those who persecuted my mortal Wiccan sisters and brothers. It was only in the last two decades that I let myself find peace and turned instead to mastering the wonder that is magic."

Susannah paused, eyes fixed on the center of the cauldron.

Jennie waved her hands in front of her. "Hold on, I *know* that magic isn't really real. As impossible as it seems, everything that we know and have accomplished has some foundation in science. The witches I know in London only make potions and brews. They don't lay curses or use incantations to create the impossible. They use real-world ingredients to make real-world products."

Susannah turned to Jennie. Her eyes were wide and excited. A strange smile was on her face. "You don't understand it, do you, Jennie?"

Jennie raised an eyebrow. "Understand what?"

"You're the very definition of magic. *You're* impossible."

Jennie's mind was thrown back to the pile of papers she had been presented with by Brendan. A promise to uncover her heritage and to learn what she truly was.

"That's some of the world's best magic if I've ever seen it." Susannah winked before returning her attention back to the cauldron.

Another few fistfuls of ingredients, including a rat's skeleton, and the mixture was ready. Susannah waved Jennie over to the bubbling mess.

Jennie studied the mixture for a few moments, seeing nothing more than the swirls of greasy colors. "What am I looking at here?"

"Stop looking, start breathing," Susannah instructed, closing her eyes and widening her nostrils to inhale the earthy scent.

Jennie followed suit. The heat stung her nose, but she persevered. After a few moments, a strange fog began to descend over her mind. She felt light-headed, and in her mind, she saw the ghostly projection of a city where the sky was a burning crimson, and the world cast in shadow.

Jennie was flying. She realized she was having an out-of-body experience when she was taken low to the ground, hovering over a long flat lawn that was punctuated by a large stone building with a tiered central structure pointing straight into the sky.

The fog returned. She was in the center of a street that she didn't recognize. Clean tarmac paved the roads, while the buildings around her were a quaint mismatch of oranges and whites, styled like a colonial town from the days before the revolution. She saw trees, a trading post, and a building that claimed to make art out of former torpedoes.

A little farther on from that was the water. The boardwalk led to a jutting pier and the docks surrounded by white sailboats. Not dissimilar to Baltimore's docks, but cleaner, and with far more in the way of a commercialized shopping district.

Another flash of fog and Jennie was in a corridor. The walls were stained, and she felt a sudden chill run down her spine when the temperature dropped.

She glided like a wraith through the building, stopping only when she saw two figures who wobbled with a distorted shimmer Jennie had only seen when heatwaves hit the UK and the tarmac sent reams of heat to distort the horizon.

Yet there was something familiar about those two figures.

Jennie crept closer until she was only a foot away from the pair. Although they were still not in crystal clarity, she knew the stance of Brendan Koa anywhere. And, across from him, a man she least expected to see in the same vicinity.

SIS Agent Oliver Clark.

Jennie moved her hand to cover her mouth when both men turned to look in her direction. Their eyes had no pupils, only bright shining white.

Jennie backed away, wanting nothing more than to escape. The two men who had been able to restrain her were standing together, and they had seen her. She was sure of it.

She turned to flee, and the corridor melted into shadows around her. She was suddenly outside of the building without moving her feet, the world warping around her. As the scene receded, Jennie caught sight of an old, faded sign.

Suddenly, she felt her feet hit solid ground, and she heard Susannah's heavy breathing.

Jennie pushed herself off the ground, momentarily disoriented and confused.

"Well…what did you see?" Susannah grinned, acting as though she hadn't seen the same herself.

But Jennie didn't answer straight away. She grabbed her phone and opened the memo app before she lost the clue she'd seen.

Susannah peered at the screen as Jennie typed.

Sylvester's Premium Candies. Est 1856.

CHAPTER FIFTY-FIVE

Washington DC, USA

There were over a hundred specters hiding in the caverns below the earth's surface, and not one of them was able to help her.

"I'm sorry, Jennie." Cadence, a woman who had left her mortal body during the middle of the twentieth century, replied with an apologetic look on her face. "But I've never seen anything like it. I was born and bred in Washington, too. If it was here, I'd know it."

"'Sylvester's?'" a specter with a long beard and sunken eyes inquired. "Weren't those the candies that always had a surprise in the middle? Toffee, and caramel, and—"

"Lime! With chocolate in the center." Olivia shuddered. "I always hated those. Who'd ever think of mixing citrus with chocolate? It's enough to make your eyes bleed."

"What about chocolate and orange?" Cadence offered. "That works."

Olivia stroked her chin. "Hmm, didn't think of that. Good point."

Jennie looked incredulously at the three conduits sitting beside her. After her induced trip, she had summoned the specters hoping that she'd be able to glean some knowledge from the pack.

The main problem was that most of the specters were locals. It was only in recent decades that humanity had started to travel the continent more. When cars were made accessible to all, people had more freedom to travel to the neighboring cities and states. If you went back a century or so, families lived near each other. Outside of the wealthy whose lifestyles involved it regularly, there was no reason to travel unless work demanded it.

Jennie shook her head and directed her question toward the only other three mortals below the ground. "You guys got any ideas?"

"We're not from around here," Ula replied. Roman and Triton nodded their agreement. "And, besides, if there was a candy factory around here, don't you think the locals would know about it? It's America. It'd be all the rage. You'd see posters on the freeway, great ribbons of rainbow smoke spiraling into the sky, the air would smell of sugar and…"

"I think you've sent Ula into a fantasy about Charlie and his friggin' Chocolate Factory." Roman laughed. "The world ain't kind enough to pump out sweets and fill the sky with rainbows."

Ula shot Roman a look.

"Then what was it I saw?" Jennie pondered, feeling the pressure to work it out before it was too late.

The man sitting next to Olivia curled his finger into his beard. "Have you thought that it might not even be in Washington?"

Jennie raised her eyebrows. "What makes you think it's out of state?"

He shrugged. "You said it yourself. We're mostly locals, and none of us have seen the factory nearby. Perhaps it's somewhere else?"

"Koa's really gone to a lot of effort if he's managing properties among three different states," Ula commented skeptically. "I've never known a psychopath go to such extreme lengths. Three buildings in the same city? Sure. Three in neighboring states? Possibly. But three different facilities across three different states entirely? Is it really worth it?"

Jennie's mouth straightened. She thought about the little that she knew of Brendan and asked herself the same question. Could the ex-military man who had turned against his partner for the sake of a power trip be meticulous enough to spread his facilities across such a distance?

Absolutely.

"It has to be true," Jennie stated, her conviction growing rapidly. "He's *exactly* the type of nutcase who would do whatever it took to cover his tracks and keep his operation going. He could have places in San Francisco, Austin, Oklahoma, Paris, for all we know."

"A property portfolio like that would leave a paper trail though, surely?" Roman interjected. "Someone would have records of all of his purchases."

"Unless he used a cutout," Olivia countered. "All he has to do is pay a third party to purchase what he wants."

Triton shook his head and grunted. When he spoke, his voice was deep, capturing the attention of the room. "There'd still be a trail. The only way someone would have managed an operation like this is with cold, hard cash. I've seen it too many times to count. Criminal scum know that cash is king. If Koa is smart, which I think we can agree he is, then he's two steps ahead at all times. That's how I'd play it. Plan for every eventuality, and leave a lot of options to run and carry my prize with me."

Jennie fell into thought.

An exclamation broke the silence in the crowded chamber.

"Wait! I might have something. Yes, I'm sure of it…"

Jennie looked into the spectral crowd at the person talking.

The man who had died in his middle years was looking through his pockets with an impatient expression.

He paid no attention to the eyes turned to him. He pulled fistfuls of ghostly receipts and papers from his pocket, letting them all float to the floor like fallen leaves. He patted his long coat with both hands, eventually plunging his hand deep into his inside breast pocket. Done emptying his pockets, he knelt and rummaged through them until finally, he pulled out a small golden wrapper.

He unscrewed the wrapper and straightened it out, moving it closer to his face to read. "A-ha, yes! Toffee Sucker. I knew it."

He looked at Jennie, realizing for the first time that he was being watched. An awkward laugh left his lips as he held the wrapper out to her. "They were my favorite, you know. Back before I… Well, before my heart gave out." He laughed again, looking at the wrapper with a sense of nostalgia. "After all these years, it's still in my pocket. Almost slipped my mind entirely. I think these had the manufacturer's information on the wrapper. Look at the edge."

Jennie took the wrapper and flipped it over in her hands. The writing on the back was small, but the words jumped out at her. "A product of Sylvester's Premium Candies, Est. 1856. Packaged and produced in Virginia."

"Virginia." Jennie blew air through her lips. "Well, at least we've got the state nailed down. Now to comb through every square inch of the damned place to find the factory."

Ula sighed. "Sounds like a riot."

Jennie was about to open her mouth to reply when a scream came from the tunnels. A blinding flash illuminated the cavern.

A moment later, a pair of specters sprinted toward them just as another flash filled the tunnels with light.

"They're here!" one of them shouted. "They've found us!"

The next thing Jennie saw was the specter's face drop as he was pulled suddenly backward, his entire spectral form vanishing down the dark nozzle of a Shadow's vacuum.

Agent Oliver Clark was dubious.

He didn't trust Brendan Koa, but it was his duty to obey the queen's wishes. It had been obvious ever since he had arrived that there would be a power struggle, and while Brendan obeyed everything that Clark had asked for on the surface, he was clearly up to something.

I've been in enough operations to know that no man who thinks he is at the top of his chain will abandon his throne willingly. The moment my back is turned, he's coming for me whether he knows what the queen will do to him or not.

So when Brendan had reported to Clark that Jennie had been spotted, it was with a dubious nod that he had agreed to send his team over to Washington to find her.

"Just know that if you're lying, we're going to have a problem," Clark warned.

Brendan sat back in his chair and clasped his hands behind his head. The screen behind him played the sketchy footage of two women in the darkened corner of the Lincoln Memorial. A tip sent from one of their undercover agents who had happened to be in the vicinity at the time.

Clark scowled and left.

The Lincoln Memorial was cloaked in darkness, the lawn lost to the night and the pool a mirror reflection of the stars. They swooped into the building, guided by a confused tour guide who showed them the only entrance into the underground tunnels that had been blocked off years ago.

The SIS stood at the rear, allowing the Shadows to enter first. Clark wasn't an idiot. If the whole thing was a trap, then the band of idiots in cloaks would be destroyed long before any of the SIS. While he was in charge, he needed to set his priorities.

His main priority was ensuring that the queen's people were kept alive.

The Shadows fired up their machines. They emitted a strange electrical hum. The contraptions looked like speakers with wide horns attached to them. The guide unlocked the door to the basement and stood back, allowing the Shadows to cautiously open the door and sneak in.

At the first flash of light, Clark felt the thrill of the chase, his heart beating with eager excitement.

Son of a bitch was telling the truth.

The tunnels became holes of instant chaos.

Specters scrambled left, right, and center. The tunnels were a flurry of movement, screams, shouts, and panic. Flashes lit the tunnels as the first of the Shadows came racing toward them with their devices turned to maximum, sucking up specters as though they were draining a pool.

"Shit," Jennie growled as specter after specter fell to an early exorcism. She turned to Ula, Roman, and Triton. "Arm yourselves. This is going to get messy."

She raced across the chamber to the tunnel's opening. Specters amassed, gathering behind Jennie as she made it to the tunnel's entrance and aimed the Big Bitch at her attackers.

"I'll give you one warning, and then I won't be held responsible for my actions," Jennie barked. Roman, Ula, and Triton stood beside her, their weapons aimed at the Shadows.

The Shadows momentarily froze, their faces masked by the dark of the tunnels. Jennie could just make out the beetle-shell glint of their eyes.

"Funny," one of the cultists called. "You're outnumbered, and yet you throw the first threat?"

"This isn't my first day on the job," Jennie replied, eyes narrowing. "One more step, and you're—"

A bullet whizzed past Jennie's head, whispering into her ear as it passed. Grunts of pain came from behind her as the bullet tore through three specters before coming to a stop.

Jennie reacted instantly, firing multiple times at her attacker. "I'll give you one more chance to save yourselves."

Mud rained from the ceiling, spraying dust into the tunnel. Muzzle flashes lit the tunnel like strobe lights. Chunks of dirt fell as the tunnel began to collapse.

Jennie whirled around to the specters. She was surprised to find Susannah stood in their midst, drawn by the sound of gunfire. "Run!" Her words were urgent, her command authoritative. "To the back of the tunnels. Head to the surface. It's the only way you'll be safe."

"We can't leave you," Olivia argued, face full of concern. "We're all in this together."

"Not if you all get sucked up into those vacuums," Jennie replied. "Go now. We'll meet you up there. I promise."

Ula gave Jennie a concerned look. "Don't make promises you can't keep."

Jennie smirked. "Believe me, I never have, and never will."

Voices echoed down the tunnel, magnified by the close proximity of the walls.

"*Now!*" Jennie shouted.

That kicked them into action. They all filed through the tunnel at the back of the chamber, clustering together in a spectral mass as they filtered through and toward the farthest reaches.

"What about us?" Roman asked, a cocky grin on his face.

Jennie shrugged. "We fight." She turned and ran toward where the specters had vanished.

"Where are you going?" Ula shouted.

"To take control of this shit show," Jennie replied. "If you're outnumbered, the only thing to do is funnel the enemy and even it up. Come on!"

The four of them made their way into the tunnel, stopping with enough distance that they could see the whole chamber from where they stood. Jennie aimed the Big Bitch at the roof of the tunnel opening and fired, dislodging enough dirt to provide cover for the four of them without blocking their line of fire.

Shouted commands preceded the arrival of a large group of Shadows, their faces lit only by their flashlights. Jennie had been sure to extinguish any lights that were remaining as she ran out of the chamber.

"Where'd they go!" One of the Shadows held up a hand and squinted at the darkness ahead. Jennie took this moment to aim her pistol and send a bullet into the middle of his forehead.

"Open fire," she told the others.

Roman, Triton, and Ula needed no further instruction. Roman aimed his twin Desert Eagles and shot into the chamber. Ula held a single Beretta before her with both hands, one eye closed as the other took aim, and sent a number of heads into explosion-mode.

Triton, on the other hand, drew an M16 from his waist and opened fire. The assault rifle sang as it sent a spray of bullets at the crowd, mowing down the front row with relative ease.

"I'm so sick of these sons of bitches," Jennie grunted, barely audible above the roar of the firearms.

The crowd of Shadows dispersed. They took cover wherever they could, losing themselves in the entrances to the chamber. While she had blocked the entrance to their tunnel, Jennie knew that they would regroup and come back for them. It wouldn't be long before the Shadows had them surrounded. They needed to work fast.

"Hold fire!" Jennie commanded.

The others obeyed Jennie instantly. She thought fast, and fired the Big Bitch at the roof again, collapsing the mouth of the tunnel completely. "That will give us some time."

A moment of quiet passed through the tunnels as the four conduits struggled to work out what was happening on the other side of the cave-in. The darkness pressed in on them.

"They've gone," Ula stated.

"No," Triton replied. "They're regrouping."

"We need to move," Jennie told them. She set off at a run, using the tunnel wall as her guide. "Press the offense. The tunnel is dark. That's our advantage."

"Until they get their gear in motion," Roman countered, matching her pace. "They've got SI goggles now, but a quick switch, and we're lit up like the Fourth of July."

"Isn't there a back entrance?" Ula asked, feeling her way as she moved hesitantly. "Another way out of this tunnel?"

"You know as well as we do that there isn't," Triton answered, hissing when he bumped into her. "One way in. One way out. Both the best and worst line of defense, depending on who your enemy is."

Jennie didn't slow. "Well, one way or another, we're getting out."

"How?" Ula asked. "None of us can see in the dark."

"What do you mean?" Jennie chuckled softly. "Didn't you eat all your carrots as a kid?"

Ula scoffed. "That's an old wives' tale."

A glow appeared directly ahead. "Is it?"

Susannah's voice made them jump.

Jennie looked at the old woman with a mixture of relief at seeing her, and annoyance that she hadn't followed the others out.

"What are you doing here?" Jennie scolded. "You need to get out with the others. This isn't safe for you."

"And four egocentric military types against dozens of enemies in a dark tunnel with one way in and out is safe? Shut up. You need me."

Jennie sighed. "Did you even go to the surface?"

Susannah nodded. "I did. Your entrance is surrounded. You're going to have a tough time wading through that quicksand, but it's your only option."

"Funny thing, that," Jennie replied, aware of footsteps growing closer. "I don't like having just the one option. It makes me feel claustrophobic. It makes me liable to do something risky."

"Oh, great," Roman groaned. "What exactly does that mean?"

"I've got a plan," Jennie told them. "But what I have in mind is not going to be subtle."

"Why am I not surprised?" Ula replied.

Jennie turned to the faint glow of Susannah. "Hey, Susie, can you provide us with some light?"

Susannah frowned. "I'll see what I can do. I do have one condition, though."

"What's that?" Jennie asked.

"Don't *ever* call me Susie again," Susannah told her.

Jennie smiled. "No promises."

CHAPTER FIFTY-SIX

<u>Washington DC, USA</u>

"I don't care about the specters. I want *Rogue!*" Clark shouted the instructions into his radio, alerting every one of his troops with an earpiece in.

He had foreseen the scramble, assuming that the specters would run at the sight of the Shadows' vacuums, and now he had the rabbits on the run. They were caught in the trap, ready to be caught and skinned alive.

The queen couldn't have been clearer in her instructions. Go to America and remove the nuisance. Squash the cockroach. Rogue had pushed her to her limits and made a mockery of her. It was time to say bye-bye to the bitch.

This was Clark's moment to shine.

He didn't want to kill her if he could help it. There was something impressive about Rogue that made it a shame to focus on killing her as the only option. But if he could catch her, maybe that would get him a bigger reward. To give the queen the opportunity to do whatever she wanted with her prize.

"Sir, there are more of them down here," an agent reported over the radio.

"More of them?" Clark repeated, confused. "More of what?"

"Mortals, sir," the agent clarified. "She's not alone. There are three others. They have weapons."

Clark rubbed his temple with one hand, throwing a cursory glance at Julia. He wasn't sure why Brendan had insisted that the woman accompany them. Maybe it was something to do with being able to control their first wave of zombies. Either way, she wasn't bad on the eyes. "You idiots," he told the agents. "*You* have weapons."

"Affirmative," the agent agreed. "But we don't have eyes on the targets. We're working on digging out the tunnel they went down. Everyone has their IR goggles engaged. We'll be through in a minute."

Clark waited eagerly, his radio near his head. Soon they would have her. There was no escape. She didn't have her specters to help her out of this one. By the sounds of it, it was just Rogue and the three nobodies.

Who are they, though?

It didn't matter. Not really. Clark looked down at Julia, then lifted the radio back to his mouth. "Prepare explosives. If it looks like she's about to escape, I'd rather the entire tunnel system collapse than let that bitch get free. Remember, that's our *last* resort."

A pause. "Affirmative."

* * *

Susannah could sense the mortals around all the exits as she walked into the main chamber. Since she'd spent a while in darkness, her eyes had adjusted enough to see their outlines and sense their movements.

The only saving grace she found was that they had swapped their headwear. They were currently looking for heat signatures instead of spectral frequencies.

Specters couldn't be detected that way since they didn't give off heat signatures.

Susanne found her way to the small pockets of free room among the mortals and prepared herself, rubbing her hands together to warm them up and get ready. She used this magic before to put such a fright into John Allen's great-great-granddaughter that her hair had turned white almost instantly.

Perhaps it would have that power once again. Hopefully, she'd be able to twist the spell to her purpose. Susannah saw that the cloaked cultists were backed up by a second set of attackers. These were equipped with Kevlar vests with the SIS logo on their chests. She found her starting pocket of space and moved into action.

The Latin rolled off her tongue like water. The ancient incantation powered the spell as her hands swirled around each other in patterns designed to call the magic to her. In the center of the pitch-black room, a light began to glow.

A moment later, that glow became an orb.

Susannah left it floating there, already moving toward her next location. The enemy was ignorant of its power, naive to the fact that Susannah had placed a spectral beacon that lit them all in a ghostly light only visible by specters and conduits.

The orbs lit the tunnels. After the glow of the first appeared, Jennie let her breath go. She hadn't been certain if Shadows had conduits among their number, or if they'd have soldiers ready for any sign of spectral activity.

In hindsight, she supposed if that were true, Susannah would have been discovered long before she lit the orb.

She could see the Shadows. They were illuminated like folk around a campfire, yet they were blind to the fact that they were lit with the spectral glow. The cloaked cultists squinted into the darkness, awaiting their next instruction.

There were a *lot* of them stationed at each entrance.

Susannah stalked her way back toward them, a satisfied grin on her face. "There are more down the tunnels. Trained men with guns, wearing armored vests with SIS on their chests."

"SIS?" Jennie couldn't process it despite her vision of Oliver Clark earlier. "You mean, SIA?" She knew what she was saying was stupid.

"SIA? They're the good guys, right?" Ula asked in a hushed whisper.

"No, it was SIS. Definitely SIS," Susannah confirmed. "Do you know them?"

Jennie's jaw clenched. She knew them, of course. Although, she could only take a guess at what they were doing there in Washington.

"Light them up," Jennie growled. "Let's get this started."

Susannah gave a curt nod and turned her attention toward her glowing orbs. She stretched her hands out in front of her, her fingers bending as though she were clutching a ball, and concentrated on saying the incantation.

Immediately the tunnel exploded into light as each orb transferred its power from the spectral world to the mortal world. The agents started at the sudden explosion, turning their guns toward the source of light, threatening those standing across from them with friendly fire.

"Now!" Jennie hissed. She waved the others into the open chamber, studying the bodies of the fallen. If they could find what they were looking for while the confusion ensued, then perhaps they could find a way to execute Jennie's plan.

Jennie hopped from body to body, searching them in the hope of finding what she was looking for.

A shout came from the tunnel. "There they are! Get them!" The shout was followed by gunfire and more shouts.

Jennie and the others dropped to the floor as bullets embedded themselves in the chamber wall where they'd been standing a second previously. However, just when the enemy thought they'd locked onto their targets, Susannah clicked her fingers and plummeted them back into darkness.

Those microseconds of confusion were enough for Jennie to continue her search. The others got to their feet and fired at the enemy, each clearing a separate tunnel entrance into the chamber.

Before the Shadows could react, Susannah snapped her fingers and the lights strobed brightly again, stunning the enemy. She started to snap her fingers randomly, flashing the lights until the enemy was forced to fire blindly.

Jennie took the opportunity to scan the rest of the bodies, but she couldn't find what she needed. She looked ahead past the Shadows and saw the SIS agents beyond.

The sight of them filled her stomach with a fire she hadn't felt in some time. Rapidly assessing the situation, she chose the tunnel closest to her and stormed into it with both guns held up in front of her.

Shadow after Shadow fell. The Big Bitch deafened the enemy while the lights blinded them. She sidestepped as a Shadow leapt at her, missing by inches and hitting the floor. A quick shot to her side and he was no more.

Jennie fired off another few rounds, clearing her path and sending the tunnel into a smog of dust and debris. Shouts added to the gunfire. In the adjacent tunnels, more shots were fired. She hoped that was Ula, Triton, and Roman overpowering their enemies.

Jennie reached a small recess in the wall where she ducked out of the way, taking a brief second to glance at the fallen SIS agent on the floor. Three hand grenades were strapped to the agent's utility built, ready and waiting to be used.

Aha!

Jennie peeked around the corner and quickly retracted her head when a bullet whizzed past her and hit the wall. She bent an arm around and fired a shot from the Big Bitch at the ceiling, adding to the rain of mud and dirt. Coughs followed from down the tunnel.

Jennie ducked, tore away the grenades, and shouted, "Now, Susie!"

There was a moment's pause where Jennie wondered if Susannah had heard before a shout came from the darkness. "It's *Susannah!*"

"Really?" Jennie yelled.

"Fine!"

The lights snapped off from mortal view, plunging the enemy into darkness, but the spectral glow of the orbs still remained for Jennie and the other conduits.

Jennie tore through the tunnels, joining up with her team as they emerged from the other tunnels and into the central chamber. They banded together, aiming for the tunnel that the specters had escaped through, managing to plummet into the darkness and out of danger before they heard the first, "They're gone!"

The telltale hiss of handheld flares was followed by a bright orange glow.

"This way!"

Jennie sped ahead, meeting Susannah and grabbing her hand to drag her with them. Susannah grunted but did not protest.

The tunnels seemed never-ending, but Jennie navigated them with determination, retracing her steps until she found her way to Susannah's cauldron room.

Ula stared in wonder at the cauldron, since the room had been off-limits to all but Susannah and Jennie until then. "How long has this been here?"

"History lessons later," Jennie told her, pulling the pins from all three grenades and tossing them in the pot. "Back out. Duck, cover your ears, and pray for the best."

Not needing to be told twice, Ula, Triton, and Roman ducked around the corner and crouched by the wall. Their eyes were screwed shut, their hands clamped their ears.

Jennie was almost out when she realized that Susannah was standing in front of the pot, staring at it with a distraught look on her face.

"Susie, come *on!*" Jennie grabbed Susannah around the waist and hauled her out of the chamber. Susannah went limp, allowing Jennie to do her thing, her eyes never leaving the cauldron. "Bad idea… That's a bad idea…"

"There are no bad ideas," Jennie grunted. "Just some that are ill-thought-out, and they lead to lessons."

She managed to get Susannah around the corner before the grenades went off. The explosion shook the earth around them.

The cauldron burst into a thousand pieces, its contents spraying the room as the heat and the debris was flung into the dome. The ground above gave way, dropping chunks of turf, rock, and root into the cavern and creating a crater at the far end of the memorial's lawn.

The tunnels began to collapse around them. Jennie yelled for the others to follow, but there was no way she could be heard. She had to depend on them to understand; they were trained for situations. She was relieved when they ran out from the raining dirt and joined her in climbing the slope formed where the lawn had fallen in on itself.

Jennie sucked in grateful lungfuls of chilly air when they emerged under a starlit sky. Not thirty feet away, the Reflection Pool still created small waves following the sudden deposit of debris into its usually calm waters.

Shouts and lights came from the entrance to the Memorial. A mass of armed agents in black was running toward the explosion site.

"Haul arse," Jennie instructed.

Roman grinned. "Crass, ain't ya?"

Jennie rolled her eyes. "Just get moving, okay?"

Susannah sent one last reluctant glance at the place that had been her home for weeks. "Bubble, bubble, toil, and trouble..."

Jennie took her hand and ran.

Alexandria, Virginia, USA

Brendan ran a hand down his face, torn between two emotions.

On the one hand, he was fucking furious. Jennie had escaped yet again. They'd had her trapped, they'd had the element of surprise, but she had still gotten away, accompanied by three more mortals who appeared to be hardened fighters. Their actions proved that they knew their way around firearms and were useful in a combat situation.

Yet, on the other, he felt a smug sense of satisfaction at the fact that Clark had failed. Even now, watching his face on the small camera planted at the Memorial's entrance, it was delightful to see the remorse in his features. The anger that poured off him as he shouted at his SIS agents and the Shadows they had sent into battle.

"You better get moving," Brendan murmured to the screen. "Best to get out of the way before the local authorities arrive. Leave that mess for the SIA to explain. That will make Rogers' day." He grinned again as he imagined the furious look on his former partner's face.

CHAPTER FIFTY-SEVEN

Washington DC, USA

Baxter rode shotgun while Hopkins, Rhone, Daggro, and Lupe sat in the back. The flashing blue and reds of the state police at the attack scene came into view long before the Memorial had.

"We're no longer playing in the Junior Division," Hopkins announced to the car after a brief news alert from the radio, detailing the destruction of a historic site. "These are the Big Leagues, boys. Strap in."

Daggro had enough experience not to question the use of "boys" at that moment. Some things just needed to be let go.

They parked a little away from the Memorial, where officers in tan uniforms were setting up a yellow and black tape perimeter. Behind them were at least a dozen cop cars, a pair of forensics vans. On the other side of the tape were a number of large white vans with news channel numbers painted on the side. Large satellite dishes were strapped to the roofs, while dolled-up men and women with micro-phones crowded as close to the scene as the officers allowed, each eager to be the first to report on the events that had taken place that night.

Hopkins cast an angry glance at the journalists, then walked briskly toward the cops with his hands in his pockets. The SIA agents all wore long, dark coats to cover their uniforms from the unblinking stare of the cameras.

Hopkins ducked under the tape and was immediately met by the open palm of a cop. "No unauthorized personnel. This is a crime scene."

Hopkins opened the inside of his jacket and showed the cop his badge. "Federal jurisdiction," he stated. "This is our scene now. Who's your superior?"

The man lowered his hand and leaned in closer to the badge. He checked the man's image against his face and, satisfied, led him toward a man with a short white beard, and a stern expression on his face.

The man turned with a flash of annoyance. "I thought I said no unauthorized personnel?"

"They're Federal, Captain," the cop replied. "They wanted to see you."

"Federal?" he asked with trepidation. "What are you, the bomb squad? You arrived faster than I thought. I was told you were out on the edge of State, dealing with a threat in the suburbs?" He shook Hopkins' hand. "Captain Michael Evans."

"Special Agent in Charge, Tom Hopkins. We're not here to deal with the bombs or the explosives," Hopkins replied dryly. "We're here to examine the scene and be on our way. Our interest isn't in the damage done to the memorial."

Captain Evans lifted an eyebrow. "Forgive me, Agent. But I was under the impression that a terrorist organization had just destroyed a major historical site. What is your interest in our scene if not to discover and aid in our investigation of what transpired here?"

"What evidence do you have of terrorism?" Hopkins asked.

Captain Evan's gave a derisive snort, then waved a hand around them. "You do see the hole, right? Witnesses reported a huge explosion and a group dressed in black with firearms leaving the scene. Do I need to say more?"

Hopkins fixed Evans with a studious stare. "Thank you for your information, Captain. We'll perform the checks we need to get done, then leave the site promptly. The FBI will likely send someone to assist you in your investigations, but this will be the last you see of us."

Captain Evans' eyes narrowed. "Just what department are you from, exactly?"

"SIA," Hopkins told him. "If you ask any more, you're at risk of being in breach of federal security. We'll leave it there."

Hopkins left the flummoxed Captain behind, and headed inside the Lincoln Memorial, aiming toward the corner where the entrance to the underground system lay.

Baxter only heard the beginning of Hopkins' conversation with Evans before he left the group behind and headed for the site of the lawn explosion.

He passed an anchor from CNN reporting live from the scene that they were currently awaiting updates from Washington State Police Department. Another from CWB detailing the moment the explosions came, and the history of the site itself. A third anchor from WBB was interviewing a woman who was physically shaking but appeared happy to have the chance to appear on TV.

Mortals, Baxter thought. *Even after an explosion, all they care about is their own ego. Being seen on TV is a higher priority than running for cover.*

He stopped to eavesdrop on a group of police officers examining the scene with flashlights, but none wanted to venture too far into the main crater for fear of further collapse.

"I can't believe someone would trash this place," a cop with a goatee muttered to his colleague. "Where do people get off destroying history?"

"Insane, right? Did you know there were tunnels down here?"

"Had no idea. What did you think they used them for?"

The other cop shrugged. "Smuggling shit?"

"Like what?"

"Drugs? People? Food? Times were different back then, weren't they."

"I suppose."

You have no idea. Baxter left the cops behind and jumped into the hole. He slipped and slid down the crumbling earth until he reached the bottom of the crater. He wasn't sure what he had been expecting to find. Maybe another few specters. Perhaps a note or some sign left behind to say which way Jennie and her specters had gone.

"If they've even survived, that is," he muttered.

Baxter knelt and examined the ground. There were traces of black powder, and after a bit of gentle digging, he found pieces of the grenade that had collapsed the tunnels. There was a strange smell in the air that he couldn't quite describe.

"Where are you, Jennie?" He wondered what had happened. Whether Jennie was free, or whether she was buried under all of this rubble. After everything she had been through, would fate bring her to her doom in the most unjust of ways?

Somehow Baxter doubted it.

Something glowed faintly in the moonlight above the rim of the crater. A small white dome, flourishing like a mushroom head. Baxter climbed out of the crater and stood on the lawn, seeing dozens of the things blossoming on the grass. White domed discs, some smooth and white, others with a strange fuzz on top.

It was only when the first mushroom continued to rise and grow that Baxter saw the face appear. The head rose out of the ground, eyes clamped shut until the air brushed its skin. The eyes snapped open, and Baxter looked into the angry face of the specter.

A sly grin appeared on the specter's face. "Our mortal bodies may have perished, but our spectral bodies will live on."

The man's hands rose and he pushed himself free of the earth. His SIS uniform still clothed him, and his weapons had the same spectral glow as his skin. All around him, other SIS specters were surfacing and clawing their way out of the ground. Among them were figures who looked like wraiths, but which Baxter guessed were the Shadows, or at least, the specters who had been channeled into the bodies of the mortals who had perished.

Baxter drew his gun and began firing, suddenly caught up in a perverse game of Whack-A-Mole. He backed away, feeling for the ridge of the crater as his bullets found the skulls of the dead, taking large chunks out of their heads and causing them to stumble.

They rose faster than he could attack. He hopped back, using the crater for cover, but they still rose, and the spectral army began to fire their weapons at him.

Baxter peeked over the top, sending bullets their way, hoping that someone might hear the gunfire and come to his aid.

Baxter wasn't aware of the figure approaching from behind until he felt a hand on his shoulder, and another clasp his mouth.

***

Lupe's ears pricked up. His head swiveled like a meerkat alert to danger when gunshots fired somewhere nearby.

"Er, sir?" He nudged closer to Hopkins, who was examining what was left of the tunnels. SI goggles were strapped to his face as he knelt next to the body of a fallen SIS agent.

"SIS?" he murmured to himself, remembering the dealings he'd had with the paranormal court and the SIS in the sharing of their intelligence. "How is this possible?"

"Sir?" Lupe repeated with urgency. More gunshots, unmistakable. He looked toward the surface with worry in his eyes.

Hopkins examined the man's pistol, goggles, and explosives. "All imbued with spectral energy. All the same tech they shared with us, only…what were the explosives *for*?"

"Maybe they're just a defensive tactic?" Rhone offered, examining another body nearby. "A way to incapacitate a mass group of specters without damaging mortals."

"They blew a crater in the lawn," Hopkins replied. "I don't think your theory lines up."

Lupe tapped Hopkins on the shoulder, eliciting a fiery glare from the agent. "Don't you know it's beyond disrespectful to interrupt a senior agent in the middle of an investigation?"

"With all due respect," Lupe replied. "You're not my superior. Also, there's gunfire on the lawn."

"Gunfire on the lawn? Don't be stupid. If there was gunfire, we'd have heard it." His face dropped when another burst went off. "Shit, positions! Get your asses outside. Ready your weapons and prepare for a fight."

They exited the tunnel at double pace, surprising Captain Evans and his crew, who had waited patiently at the entrance. They rushed past them, finding their positions around the columns at the Memorial entrance.

With their SI goggles on, they saw a couple of dozen spectral shapes out on the lawn.

"Clear the area," Hopkins ordered Captain Evans. "Remove the news crews. This is a high-security measure, and I'm instating total media blackout."

Evans peered around the corner at the empty lawn. "Are you mad? There's nothing here."

Hopkins glared the Captain into silence. "Captain, unless you want me to file an official report stating that you have obstructed a federal investigation, then I suggest you do as commanded."

Evans turned to his crew and gave the nod. "Do as he says."

The confused police crew dispersed, running toward the news crews to order them to leave while the SIA agents and Lupe got to work.

"Is there anything you need from me?" Evans asked, intrigue loading his tone.

Hopkins nodded. "Just forget what you're about to see. None of this will make sense to you, and that's okay."

With that, Hopkins gathered Rhone, Daggro, and Lupe, and sped toward the specters.

They had the element of surprise on their side since the specters' attention was all focused on something in the crater. Running at half-crouch in the darkness, they came up behind them with their weapons raised.

It was only then that Lupe noticed that Baxter wasn't among them, and his brain pieced it together.

What are you doing? Lupe wondered, keeping a step behind Hopkins.

Hopkins approached the first specter and shot him point-blank in the back of the head. He immediately turned his pistol to those flanking the specter, and let off two more shots, forcing the specters to collapse to the floor where they crawled around blindly.

The SIS and Shadows specters turned at the disturbance. They reacted as they would have in life by returning fire, only they had forgotten in the heat of the moment that they were no longer mortal —and neither were their weapons.

The realization hit them hard when their bullets passed straight through Hopkins, Lupe, and the others without so much as grazing them. Their eyes widened and they began to run, hunting for an escape route, some choosing to take their chances against Baxter rather than the four mortals mowing them down with spectrally imbued weapons.

"Take them down," Hopkins commanded, doing just that. Daggro and Rhone joined him, drawing the attention of a couple of persistent journalists who'd already had their cameras confiscated by the state police.

They advanced on the specters, bringing them down with steely calm. Although Lupe was almost certain that Hopkins hadn't seen action in some time, the agent hadn't lost anything of his edge. Every bullet found its mark, and the specters went down fast.

In fact, as they took down the last handful of specters, it occurred to Lupe that not one of them had put up a challenge. They were frozen like statues until the bullets found them and brought them down.

Hopkins gave a satisfied nod and walked through the crawling figures until he reached the edge of the crater. He peered inside and grinned at the surprise awaiting him at the bottom.

Jennie stood at her full height in the center of the crater, her hands outstretched toward the specters. "Fancy seeing you here."

Hopkins smirked. "Couldn't find your gun?"

Jennie lowered her hands, her chest rising and falling from exertion. "I didn't want to draw more attention. I assumed you strapping boys—and Daggro—would have it covered if I held them still. Was I wrong?"

Hopkins shrugged. "I like a challenge. Immobile targets don't give me that."

Jennie gave an understanding nod. "Sweetie, I'm all the challenge you need."

Jennie smiled up at Hopkins, her grin widening when she saw Rhone and Daggro and Lupe appear at his side. Rhone returned the smile, while Daggro simply rolled her eyes and scowled.

"Speak of the devil. This is not quite the reunion I had planned," Jennie told Hopkins. "Shall we take this to your office?"

"I think that would be wise." He looked around the lawn, eyes narrowing. "Where are your specter friends?"

"They're safe," Jennie assured him. "They'll need transport."

Daggro growled. "A hundred specters out in sight of Koa's cameras? Hardly subtle, is it?"

Jennie fixed Daggro with a hard stare. "Agent Daggro, I think the time for subtlety has passed. I'm going to take the fight to them."

CHAPTER FIFTY-EIGHT

<u>Washington DC, USA</u>

Although Jennie had only been in hiding for less than a week, it felt strange being back in the SIA HQ.

An artificial smell hung in the air. The cloying scent of mud and dirt was gone, and instead of the faint spectral glow of ghosts, she was bombarded by the bright strip lights in the clinical hallways.

Jennie's eyes hurt. There was a faint throb behind her temple. It was only now that she was surrounded by agents that she realized how messy she was and how dirty her clothes had become. She ran a hand through her hair, and her fingers met tangles.

Jennie sat through the debrief Hopkins called the moment they arrived back. She nodded but remained quiet, only just becoming aware of how tired she was. After five minutes of Hopkins explaining the situation and barking instructions at fellow agents, he dismissed Jennie, ordering that she clean herself up and get some rest before rejoining them all again. Usually, Jennie wouldn't appreciate being ordered about by someone who wasn't her superior, but in this case, she resigned herself.

The water was hot. It prickled her skin, but it wasn't unpleasant. The white basin filled with muddied water. Clumps of dirt clogged the drain, and she was forced to smoosh it with her toes to clear it. She rested her head against the cool tiles.

The reality of being out of the bubble of the underground tunnels set in. The battle had been initiated. It had begun. Although they didn't have all the pieces of the puzzle, they needed to march on the enemy.

Jennie already knew that her role was to lead everyone and guide both mortals and specters to peace. The weight of responsibility hung over her as she turned off the shower and patted herself dry. She dressed in some clean clothes and tightened her corset until there was almost no room to breathe. She gritted her teeth and bore the pain, knowing that it would only make her stronger. Pain was a cleanser.

When Baxter entered, Jennie was sitting on her couch with a neat shot of whiskey in a tumbler. She held the glass to her head, occasionally lowering it to take sips that induced a sharp inhalation of breath.

"Tough day?" Baxter asked, taking a seat beside her.

Jennie pressed the cool glass to her forehead. "Tough week. I don't know what I'd do without my friends." She scoffed. "That feels strange to say."

Baxter's eyes lowered to the floor. His cheeks flushed. "We've got your back, Jennie. You don't even have to ask."

Jennie glanced sideways at Baxter. "Oh. This is awkward. I meant alcohol. You know, gin, rum, whiskey, tequila. My friends."

Baxter looked at her with disbelief. Jennie winked and laughed. Baxter joined in.

"You look like you could use some sleep," he told her.

Jennie nodded. "I feel like it, too. There's no time to sleep. There's so much happening, and we need to move fast to press the advantage on Brendan and the Shadows."

Baxter sighed. "We've been trying. So far all we have is a team hunting for any financial records on him, and a captive who has revealed to us all of Brendan's sources of recruitment, but they're all hidden behind VPNs, so we're no closer to finding him than we were a week ago."

Jennie considered what other angles they could come at the situation from. "You've got agents set up, acting as possible recruits?"

Baxter rubbed his eyes. "Yep. We're doing our best to catfish them, but progress is slow. Seems the initiation process is pretty rigorous. They want a lot of answers and a lot of confirmation before they even get close to telling the guys where to go. So far, we've got two field agents out there, obeying instructions from the Shadows to meet in a specific location."

Jennie took a long sip of her whiskey. The burn followed down her throat and into her chest. "I may have something that can help us."

"You do?"

Jennie explained to Baxter the vision that had been induced by Susannah. She described the appearance of Clark and Koa, and the faded sign she'd seen on the wall.

Baxter's eyes were deep in thought. "That's got to be something we can track."

Jennie's smile was strained. "I hope so. We need to press the advantage and get this shit underway. Catch them before they can really do any damage. We've already seen what they're willing to do to catch specters."

"To catch you, you mean?"

Jennie looked at Baxter with surprise. "What do you mean?"

"Jennie, they weren't hunting specters. They were hunting you. Isn't it obvious? You're their prime obstacle. They're going to want you out of the way before they can do any real damage. Don't tell me you haven't thought of this?"

The truth was that Jennie hadn't considered this at all. From her perspective, Brendan and his men were seeking domination of the wider population, while Clark and the queen were pressing for control. It hadn't crossed her mind that they would line up their cross-hairs solely to eliminate Jennie. She had a history with the queen. They had made a truce.

A truce that has already backfired. Didn't she promise you she'd keep her nose out of your business? Leave America for you?

Yeah, right. Like she'd ever leave one of the largest land-masses to someone else.

That bitch was all about control.

Jennie held her head in her hands. "I suppose you're right."

Baxter placed a hand on her shoulder, his brow creased with concern. "Are you okay?"

"I will be," Jennie breathed. "But first I need to shake off this exhaustion. Is Hendrick still about?"

"Last I saw him was last night. He's working on understanding the spectral capsules. Once he's figured out its qualities, we're going to get to work on experimenting with various pieces of equipment that may help in the fight ahead."

Jennie let out a small chuckle.

"What?" Baxter asked.

"You're becoming one of them. *We're* doing our best. *We're* going to work on. When did you become a member of the SIA?"

She shook her head and left the room, Baxter laughing in tow.

Jennie wasn't surprised to find Hendrick still working away in his lab. Beside him, Proctor busied himself with a small Petri dish, examining a sample of the silver fluid under a microscope. It was funny, really. The more Jennie saw the two working together, the more obvious it was that Hendrick was slowly taking control of the lab and using Proctor as an assistant for his work.

Jennie asked for something to shake off her fatigue. Hendrick shuffled toward a far cupboard and drew four vials of a formula that would pep Jennie up and eradicate any tiredness she felt. She glugged one in front of them, then stored the others for later.

Less than a minute later, the exhaustion fell off of her like rain.

Satisfied and ready for action, Jennie headed to Hopkins' office and knocked on the door. She wasn't surprised to find Rhone and Daggro still sitting with him, deep in conversation with their heads gathered over the screen of a tablet. She was, however, surprised to find that Special Agent in Charge Kurt Rogers had joined them with his assistant, Ashleigh sitting beside them taking notes.

Jennie placed a hand on her chest. "Where was my invite to the party?"

Hopkins glanced at Rogers, then back at Jennie. "You've pepped up."

"There's nothing Hendrick can't put together to cure any ailment." She nodded at the tablet. "Looks like serious work."

Rogers leaned back in his chair. "We may have found a lead. We've stumbled across a series of rather heavy transactions that have been cross-referenced and matched against each other within a seven day period, just over a year ago. A number of abandoned factories that were paid for in hard cash, and that hint at a deliberate effort to keep the transaction of the buildings off the radar."

"Koa?" Jennie asked, feeling no need to expand further.

Hopkins frowned. "Possibly. The problem is, with no signed papers available and no digital records of the transactions, there's little we can find to lock them together."

Baxter chipped in. "Isn't it incredibly unlikely that a number of cash transactions of that amount would be made within a one-week window?"

No one answered.

Jennie realized the problem. "Oh." She repeated Baxter's question to the room on his behalf, cueing the others to place on their SI goggles.

Hopkins nodded. "Unlikely, but not unheard of. The world is full of reckless millionaires. That's no grounds to search the properties."

Jennie skirted the table and stopped behind Hopkins. "Where are they?" She leaned over his shoulder to look at the map. Four red pins showed locations across Washington, with an additional pin residing in Baltimore.

She wasn't surprised to find that two of the pins were in the same locations as the buildings she'd encountered the Shadows previously.

"Have we searched the other buildings?" Jennie asked.

"We've sent a crew for surveillance. We're yet to hear back."

Something in the corner of the screen caught Jennie's eye. She leaned over and zoomed out the image until the word "Virginia" was visible. "Is there a reason you've isolated your search to Maryland and Washington?"

"Baby steps," Rhone answered. "The team is still tracking the transactions, looking for appropriate patterns across the two states before we widen our search."

"You got a problem with that?" Daggro frowned.

Despite the burning stare of Daggro, Jennie swiped her finger over to Virginia and zoomed in until the State encompassed the whole screen. "Here's where we need to be looking."

"Virginia?" Rogers replied. He fixed Jennie with his piercing eyes that made her feel as though he could see through her. "Do you know something that we don't?"

Jennie reached into her pocket and drew the spectral sweet wrapper. She had forgotten to give it back to the specter after he had handed it over. She tossed it on the table in front of her.

Rogers reached for the wrapper, but his hand passed straight through it.

Rhone chuckled. "The world isn't polluted enough by mortals, so you're planning on polluting it spectrally, too?"

Jennie didn't answer. She unscrewed the wrapper and held it up for them all to see.

Hopkins read the wrapper. "Sylvester's Premium Candies? What's this got to do with anything?"

Jennie held her hands in front of her. "Okay, before I tell you what I know, just remember that the world is crazy, and nothing is impossible."

They raised their eyebrows as Jennie explained her encounter with Susannah and her cauldron. She told them of her vision and the sign she'd seen.

Daggro groaned. "Oh, you guys aren't going to buy this, are you? I've bought a lot of shit she's said and done, but this? You're telling us that you had a vision, and suddenly you know where our enemy is? Give me a break."

Rogers stared at Jennie, his eyes full of thought. "Has anything like this ever happened to you before?"

Jennie didn't lie. "Honestly? No. But I've lived through enough to know the feeling in your gut when you're fighting for the truth. This place exists, I just know it. And it'll be the last place he'll think we'll search, too." She pointed at the tablet. "Search for it on there. See if it's listed."

Rogers, unused to taking orders from anyone except his superiors, held Jennie's gaze a moment. He eventually nodded at Rhone to do as she asked.

Rhone took the tablet and tapped in the information. Google listings brought up the old candy brand, with a gallery of images of the old packaging, as well as photos of people from across the world enjoying their products.

He swiped across to a Wikipedia page detailing the company's rise and fall, tracking its trajectory from bestselling brand of sugary snacks, to the health food crisis of the late 1900s, eventually settling with a paragraph about the company's liquidation in 2004.

Jennie wasn't surprised to see that the logo on the right-hand side of the page matched the image she had seen in her vision. The information box also listed a Virginian city by the name of Alexandria.

"There," Jennie called out with a confidence that surprised even herself. "That's where they are."

Hopkins and Rogers exchanged a look. "You're sure?"

Jennie nodded. "Track the building's ownership history, view live satellite footage, knock on the damned door for all I care. I'm telling you, that's them, right there."

Rogers stared into her eyes for a few moments longer, clearly doubtful of her conviction.

Rhone leaned forward hesitantly and raising a finger. "If I may speak freely, sir, Jennie has been nothing but an asset to this division since her arrival. Sure, her methods may be unorthodox, but she knows things that we don't. Instead of being doubtful of her talents, I'd argue that we need to embrace them. She knows the spectral world a damn sight better than we do. She knows the power and—for want of a better word— the magic of it all. I think it's worth trusting her, even if we aren't able to see the scope of it ourselves."

Hopkins looked from Rogers to Rhone. His subordinate had never spoken out of turn or even passed an opinion over the top of him. He waited to gauge the Special Agent in Charge's response.

Rogers' face hardened. "Daggro, get intelligence to run the checks. See if there's *any* validity in Agent Rogue's suspicions before we blindly charge. Hopkins, while the checks are run, prepare your men and women for prompt deployment. If this is as Rogue believes it is to be, we need to be ready to go." His eyes found Jennie's. "That little bastard, Koa, is not going to get away this time."

CHAPTER FIFTY-NINE

Alexandria, Virginia, USA

Agent Clark's voice had an unsteady edge to it as he barked at the two cloaked sentinels stationed at Brendan's door. "Move out of my way. That is an order."

Brendan swiveled toward the door and slow-clapped. "That was quite a show, Agent. What happened? Outfoxed by a trapped rabbit?"

"Trapped rabbit, my ass." Clark tried to shove past the two guards, but they blocked his way. "I said, let me through."

A flicker of fear crossed over Clark's face as he looked into the stone-dead eyes of the guards. There was no life there at all. They might as well have been laid in an open casket at a wake.

Brendan snorted. "Do as he says."

At his instruction, the guards lowered their arms and took a small step away. Clark shoulder-barged past one of them and entered the room, unsurprised to find a number of the screens showcasing the news footage of the aftermath of the events at the Memorial. Beside them, a solitary camera situated at the Memorial's entrance showed older footage of the SIS and the Shadows arriving at the scene.

"You watched it all, like a telly show?"

Brendan reached for his glass of whiskey and took a sip. "It's all rather entertaining, don't you think? Better than Netflix."

Clark growled. "This situation is serious, if you think I'm here just to become some perverse star in your little games, you underestimate myself and the power of the paranormal court. I'm running this operation, and we're going to remove the obstacle. Queen's orders."

Brendan gave a smug grin and swirled his drink. The sour blend teased his nostrils. "If the queen cared so much about our affairs here, then where the hell is she?"

Clark growled. "I am her proxy. Be careful of what you're saying."

"It seems to me that the US is nothing more than an afterthought for Victoria." Brendan snapped his fingers and the two guards blocked the door behind Clark. "That it's more of a fancy, a petty jewel among the treasured hoard. If Victoria wanted to have the US on her squad so much, why would she send nothing more than a team of mortals to do her bidding?"

Clark's eyes narrowed. His hand moved to the holster at his waist. "You know nothing of what you speak."

"No?" Brendan let out a chilling laugh. "Is that so?"

He flicked a button on the remote control, then rose to his feet and laced his fingers behind his back. He began pacing the room. Behind him, the screens filled with a vintage feed of old documentary footage of a marching brigade of Britons from years gone by.

"The British Empire was once one of the greatest achievements of mankind. A dominion that spread across one of the largest landmasses in our history, crossing oceans and claiming islands. For almost a hundred and fifty years, the United Kingdom—one of the smallest islands of the modern Western World—spread its power beyond anything that could have been imagined possible and held onto a world far beyond its own borders."

Brendan waved a hand in the air. "Canada, Egypt, India, Australia, Africa, the stranglehold was a force to be reckoned with. It was an empire envied across the world. When Victoria came into the throne in, well, I shouldn't need to tell you, should I? You know your history."

Clark returned an intense stare, his lips pressed so tightly together they were nothing more than a slit on his face.

Brendan gave a dramatic gasp. "You don't know, do you? You serve under one of the world's greatest leaders of all time, and you don't even know her history!" He laughed, then drained his drink. He poured himself another measure from a crystal jug. "1837, in case you were interested. Victoria came into power in 1837 and already owned an impressive percentage of the world. Over her years of rule, her power only grew as she absorbed nations and introduced many to the new world. When she died in 1901, Victoria was the head of nearly a quarter of the world's population."

Brendan paused. His eyes grew vacant. "Just take a second to digest that. At the turn of the century, the world contained 1.5 billion people. Victoria ruled over 300 million of those. The very definition of a true queen. A true *Empress*."

Clark slid his hand past his holster and tucked it inside of his pocket. Brendan didn't notice the movement, his mind too focused on his thoughts.

"You speak about Victoria as though you admire her."

An enthusiastic beam spread across Brendan's face. "Oh, I do admire her. Queen Victoria was arguably the most important and powerful figure on the planet. I mean, no one else has even come close to that kind of respect and power."

"Yet, you talk ill of a woman to whom you will owe your very life, one day."

Brendan moved closer to Clark, pausing when he was only a foot away. The two men stared at each other, each trying to read the other's intentions. Brendan's voice grew dark. "You misunderstand me, agent. Victoria *was* one of the most powerful figures on the planet. Her rule ended in 1901, along with her life…"

"When her reign over the paranormal court began."

Brendan's eyes flashed. "And where has that gotten her? The most powerful queen to ever rule can't even maintain a hold on the United States of America? Where is her army? Where are her men and women? If she wanted America, why didn't she come and claim it?"

Brendan's nostrils flared, his face an inch away from Clark's. Spittle flew from his mouth and peppered the agent. "You know what I think? I think it's all bullshit. I think that Victoria has lost everything that made her great and that all this talk of her rule, her reign, her armies, her power in the afterlife is nothing more than empty threats designed to make people quake in fear. I've come across people like you before, messengers sent to coax people out of their security and inject a fear that leads to stupid decisions and makes people bow before any real threat has shown itself. I'm not falling for it, Clark. You came to *my* country. This is *my* empire I'm growing. You can either become a part of it or..." He closed the gap, their noses touching. "You can fuck off back to where you came from."

Clark pushed back against him. A smile curled his lips. "You really have no idea what you're up against, do you? I returned with the majority of my men intact. Your men were crushed in the tunnels."

Brendan held his position a moment longer before taking a step back and returning Clark's grin. "Let me show you what *you're* up against."

He crossed to the table and pointed the remote at the screen. The four central screens combined to one image, showing footage of the Memorial lawn after the explosion as the specters began to rise from the ground and attack Baxter.

"Although my mortals may perish, my specters live on." Brendan's eyes were wild with excitement. "An invincible army, executing my every command."

He studied Clark's face, the agent showing no sign of emotion or threat. He frowned, then clicked his fingers. The guards at the door took hold of Clark's arms and held him tight, drawing his hand from his pocket.

"You still don't see it, do you?" Brendan crooned. "We're almost ready to launch. Phase one of our plan is on the cusp of completion, and once my army is complete, we march on Washington. We storm the SIA HQ and remove the only government-led knowledge base of spectral activity on the East Coast. We wipe out the competition and offer our services to the US Government, only instead of us running by their rule, they will work for *us*."

Brendan laughed again, arms high as he took a deep breath. "All my life, I've seen the politics and the chaos of the American Presidential system. Finally, I'll have the trump card—excuse the pun—to right the wrongs and bring the nation under a united order. The darkness will spread. The world will be shadowed by the Umbra."

Clark struggled against the guards. "And what then? You'll never get that far."

"After that? Well, maybe I'll take a leaf out of your precious queen's book. Maybe after that, I'll extend my Empire, and show the world what a true mortal leader can do." Brendan addressed the guards. "Take him to cell B4. Strip him of his weapons. Make sure he's locked up tight. Initiate the order to subdue the remaining SIS agents." His eyes met Clark's once more. "It's time to prepare them for spectral conversion."

Agent Clark was dragged out kicking and fighting from Brendan's surveillance room. The guards showed no sign of emotion as they gripped him tightly and pulled him along with them.

Brendan returned to his seat and added another measure of whiskey to his glass. He kicked his feet up on the desk and smiled at the wall of screens, blissfully unaware that, at that very moment, Agent Oliver Clark's cell phone was dialed into Queen Victoria's cell, and the reigning queen of the paranormal court, had heard every last word Brendan had said.

CHAPTER SIXTY

Washington DC, USA

Caroline laughed and pointed at Lupe. "You'd think a short, stocky guy would be able to handle his liquor better than that."

Lupe was slumped in the plush armchair of Jennie's SIA quarters. His chin rested on his chest, and his eyes were glassy. On the table in front of him was an array of cocktail glasses of varying sizes and shapes, each drained of their contents.

Baxter joined in the laughter. "I thought Mexicans were great at holding booze. What about all those tequila rumors? Don't they pour that stuff on their cereal?"

Jennie's mouth fell open. "Really? You're going to jump straight in with the stereotypes? Does that mean *you* should be able to handle gallons of booze?"

Baxter raised an eyebrow. "Because I'm huge? I suppose that had something to do with it. I can certainly hold my own."

Lupe hiccupped, the movement preceding an impressive burp.

Tanya searched the crowd, looking for something. "Someone get him a bucket." She sat on the arm of the couch, a Pink Russian in her hand. The drink had left a white mustache around her lips that Sandra pointed at and giggled. "What?"

"Nothing… *Sir*," Sandra teased.

Jennie stood at the little cocktail bar and grinned. A warmth spread through her stomach. She had spread the word among her people that she was to have a gathering in her quarters to lighten the mood, build morale, and reconnect with those who had helped her come so far.

Crammed into her room was a mixture of Spectral Plane specters and mortals, off-duty SIA agents, as well as Ula, Triton, Roman, and a number of specters who had been rescued from the Memorial tunnels. Feng Mian was sitting with his mother and father, animatedly discussing something in Chinese. Jennie was surprised to see that even Ruby—the morally conscious teenage girl who had aided in the fight against the *sturmgeist* in Batsto—had received the message and was sitting in the corner, dressed in an agent-in-training uniform. The uniform made her look older than Jennie remembered.

The room was alive with conversation. Some talked about the coming fight, while others asked the questions they'd been dying to ask. Jennie wasn't surprised to see that most of the SIA agents wore their SI goggles and were deep in conversation with specters. Triton, Ula, and Roman were over by the far wall, looking uncomfortably out of place among so many others, their military backgrounds lending themselves better to a discussion with Jack and Clive.

For Jennie, the orders kept coming. She couldn't remember the last time she'd had a gathering like this, allowing her the opportunity to shake the dust off her old cocktail recipes and revive some formulas she hadn't worked with for decades.

Jennie called down to Hendrick, who had crouched and was rifling through the cabinet beneath the counter. "Pass me the activated charcoal."

Beside Hendrick was his own large leather bag of components and ingredients that would add unique flavors to the drinks.

Hendrick passed the black substance, and Jennie poured it all into a metallic shaker. She added the tequila, Koch Espadin Mezcal, lime, agave syrup, and Moles Bitters before capping it and shaking the container beside her head.

When she was finished, she popped the lid, turned her attention to the ice crusher, ground a handful of large cubes, and tossed them into a tumbler. She poured the dark black cocktail over the rocks and pushed it toward Susannah, who stood with her elbow leaned against the bar and a sour expression on her face.

"Oh, that's just cruel," the witch grumbled.

"It's not for you." Jennie winked. "Clark! Heart of Darkness! Get it while it's cool!"

Jack excused himself from the three conduits and took the drink from Jennie. "Where did you find those guys? They're incredible."

"Would you believe if it I told you a hole in the ground?" Jennie chuckled, already beginning her next concoction, adding sprigs of mint and crushing them into a glass.

Jack grinned. "If anyone else told me? No. Because it's you? Yes. Yes, I do."

"You found out about their background?" Jennie asked with surprise.

Jack shook his head. "No. No more than the fact they've seen action and served with different special forces. They wouldn't go into specifics. I think they've kept themselves guarded their entire lives, lived with secrecy as their creed, and now they won't open up." Jack sipped his cocktail and nodded approvingly. "Not bad."

"Thanks," Jennie replied. "I couldn't get much from them either. They're closed books."

"Can we trust them?" he asked.

Jennie looked past Jack to where the three conduits were in discussion with Clive. Triton remained fairly stoic, while Ula and Roman led the conversation.

Jennie half-shrugged. "I've met a lot of people over the years. I liked to think that it made me a fairly good judge of character. But then again, I thought the queen was doing good, so what do I know?"

Hendrick placed a couple of vials on the counter, reading Jennie's next moves as if they were communicating telepathically.

"So, yes?" Jack smirked.

Jennie looked up once more. Although Triton remained relatively silent, his eyes were kind. His mouth showed the faintest glimmer of a smile. "I'd say so. If they were working for the enemy, they'd have tried to kill me the moment I arrived with the others. They didn't. That speaks volumes."

An explosion of laughter mixed with disgust erupted from the center of the room. Jennie glanced over to see Lupe's head stuck in a bucket while Tanya and Baxter rubbed his back.

"I suppose we should remedy his ailment," Jennie suggested to Hendrick.

Without a word, Hendrick reached into his bag. He pulled Lupe's head out of the bucket, shoved a vial into his mouth, and forced him to swallow.

Lupe's consciousness returned immediately. His eyes widened, and his cheeks flushed with embarrassment. He joined the others in their laughter.

The party lasted until well into the night. Agents and specters came and went, while Jennie remained at the bar and provided the social lubricant. Music played from a cheap set of tinny speakers smuggled in by Ruby, and at one point in the night, Tanya was merry enough to jump on the table and start dancing.

It was around four AM when the gathering disbanded and Jennie's room emptied of people. Hendrick had looked ahead and created enough elixir to cure everyone of their drunkenness and alleviate any future hangovers. He handed them out to everybody as they left.

Finally, Ruby, Jack, Clive, and the conduits closed the door behind them, leaving only Tanya, Lupe, Baxter, Sandra, Carolyn, and Feng Mian behind. Feng Mian's parents waved goodbye and headed to the quarters the specters had been provided by the SIA.

Jennie slumped on the couch and brushed a lock of hair from her face. "Well, I think that was successful."

"Sure," Carolyn replied sarcastically. "Get the soldiers wankered before they have to set off into battle. Great idea."

"Wankered?" Sandra asked, innocence in her voice.

Tanya shrugged.

Jenny grinned. "She's trying to be funny. Wankered means drunk in English. Nice to see you're practicing the lingo, Yankee Girl."

Carolyn gave a curt bow of her head. "I try."

Baxter turned in his seat. "Doesn't 'wanker' also mean something else in English?"

Carolyn interjected, "Can you believe how many people came?" She caught Jennie's eye and they exchanged looks. "Who'd have thought earlier this year, that we'd be partying in a top-secret federal department, getting ready to take on bad guys with God complexes and black magic? I know I didn't."

Lupe shook his head. "Me neither."

Feng Mian grunted.

Nor me." Tanya smiled as she turned to look at Jennie. "Do you really think we've got what it takes to take them all on? They've got technology that we don't. They've got black magic that we don't have access to. They're sneaky as hell and seem to always be one step ahead."

Jennie chewed her lip, knowing that it wasn't the time to shake the team's confidence. She needed everyone believing in their mission and rallying behind them. A true leader united her squad and filled them with hope.

Hope. The enemy's greatest enemy.

She smiled at the group. "We've got insider knowledge on our side. I know the game, and I've played it before. Believe it or not, this isn't the first egomaniacal dictatorship I've had to battle it out against."

"You've fought mortal dictators before?" Baxter asked in earnest.

"Not exactly," Jennie admitted. "My work in this arena tended to exist around specters."

Tanya sat up straight in her chair. "Then how are we going to make this work?".

"Because we've got the element of surprise," Jennie told her. "We've got each other. We've got the US Government on our side. There's nothing we can't do, as long as we stick together, rally the troops, and prepare ourselves as best we can."

Baxter shuffled his feet awkwardly. "They'll see us coming from miles away" He apologetically bowed his head as he cast doubt on Jennie's words. "A convoy this size can't cross the state border unnoticed."

Jennie nodded her agreement. "No, you're right there. But we have two advantages on our side."

A sly grin crept onto Lupe's face. "And they are?"

Jennie counted on her fingers. "Number one, we have reinforcements on their way from New York. George is leading a convoy straight toward Washington, and they should be arriving as we speak."

"You're welcome." Lupe held up his phone and shook it at everyone in the room.

"Number two?" Tanya nudged.

Baxter and Carolyn snorted with laughter.

Jennie smiled. "Oh, real mature, guys. Number two is that we have a secret ingredient that is currently being trialed by Hendrick and Proctor that should lead to a nice little surprise for the Shadows and the SIS."

Lupe reached for his water on the table and shook his head. "All these abbreviations are ridiculous. SIS. SIA. It's hard to keep track of who's who."

Baxter drew his attention. "Here's your clue. You're on the good guy's team. Focus on that and get everyone else."

The room fell quiet shortly after that. One by one they fell into slumber as the night passed to morning.

All except Jennie.

Jennie tiptoed across the quiet room, treading carefully past the snoozing specters and mortals. She found the door in the darkness and let herself out.

Tonight had been invigorating for her, a reminder of where it had all started. Cocktails, fun, specters, and friends—that was the world she wanted to strive for. A place where specters and mortals could live in harmony and enjoy whatever years they had left. If there was one gift she could bring to the world before she died, it would be that.

Baxter caught Jennie by surprise, causing Jennie to turn in the quiet corridor. "Where are you going?"

Jennie smiled. "Honestly? I don't know. I couldn't sleep."

"It's even harder if you're walking," Baxter smiled. When he saw the look in Jennie's eyes, he added. "What's on your mind?"

Jennie took a deep breath, unsure whether to tell Baxter the truth. It was a question that had plagued her mind constantly over the last century, and one that had been inflamed by the recent attack on the Memorial. A question about her very existence that had been exacerbated under the knowledge that she was being targeted by two organizations across two contrasting realms.

But to admit that it was a concern, would that show weakness? Would that make them think any less of her? It was the same curiosity that, she was ashamed to admit, had made Brendan's offer to investigate her origins a severe temptation. She had almost signed the paper, had placed the tip of the pen on it and intended to sign her name. It had only been the vision of her parents in her mind that had prevented her.

"Jennie?"

Jennie met Baxter's eyes and found her resolve. Of everyone she had met in her life, she had never met anyone as loyal, kind, and honest as Baxter. Through it all, he had stuck by her side without question, surpassing any relationship she'd had with any of the queen's stooges.

Baxter was good people.

She sighed. "We're heading into the danger zone, Bax. There's no knowing what they've got up their sleeves, or what they'll do to me if I get captured. I'm the missing piece of a puzzle no one knows how to solve."

Baxter moved closer. "What are you talking about? You're Genevieve King. You're *Rogue*. There's nothing that can stop you."

Jennie's eyes sparkled. "What about death?"

Baxter opened his mouth to answer, then closed it. He hadn't expected that question. After a moment, he answered, "If you die, you become a specter, and you kick ass in the afterlife."

Jennie's eyes grew glassy. "How do we know? I'm not like you were. I'm not like any human I've met. I've been cursed with longevity, and I have no idea why. What if this *is* my afterlife, and all it'll take is a bullet through the heart to end it all?"

Baxter took Jennie's shoulders in his massive hands. "That's never going to happen, Jennie. You know as well as I do that you're untouchable. Your powers, your life, it's a blessing, not a curse. Whatever your genetic makeup is, I'm sure you'll always have an extra round in the chamber. Those shitbags out there? They've got nothing on you. You'd be stupid to think otherwise."

Jennie gave a small chuckle and wiped a tear from the corner of her eye. "You know, it wasn't all that long ago that if someone called me stupid, I'd find a way to punish them."

Baxter chuckled. "The only punishment you could give would be to leave us all and disappear into the wild."

Jennie grinned. "Who says I won't?"

Baxter held her gaze. "I do."

Without another word, Baxter pulled her into an embrace. His arms were thick and wrapped her almost wholly in his biceps. Jennie tensed, then relaxed and allowed the hug to warm her, despite the chill of his spectral presence.

When they broke apart what felt like a long time later, Rhone rounded the corner behind them and let out a small exclamation. "Oh, Jennie. I thought you'd be asleep."

"I'll sleep when injustice does," Jennie stated. "What is it?"

Rhone's face turned serious. "We've found it. We've matched the records and found him. We've got Brendan in our scope."

CHAPTER SIXTY-ONE

Buckingham Palace, London, England

The palace lay in silence. Moonlight filtered through the floor-to-ceiling windows, sending motes of dust swirling lazily in its beams.

Victoria exited her chambers, her face contorted into a grim mask. The power she exuded washed over the lines of specters, who stood to attention, creating an alley that guided her all the way to the palace's exit. Beefeaters, lords, ladies, aristocrats; the hundreds of specters who had remained loyal to the court and who were witnessing the undertaking of an event that hadn't occurred in centuries waited patiently.

The two burly guards flanking the doorway awaited. They spoke little, which was perfect for Victoria, who could talk *at* them for hours and know that they wouldn't tell a soul her secrets. She took each of the arms they proffered in her dainty hands and glided along the hallways.

Every specter she passed took a knee, folding in a strange wave that followed them through the palace. Victoria held her chin high, a small part of her wondering if she'd ever come back here. After a century of residing within its walls, or at least in its general vicinity, she wondered if her trip would end with her finding her way back, or if the final death was going to meet her abroad.

Power oozed off her in pulses. The specters glowed brighter in her presence. The title of Paranormal Majesty offered more than simple specterdom, and it was something that she didn't take for granted.

She strode out the front door and down into the quad where Elizabeth II and all of Victoria's descendants and predecessors had wished hellos and bid farewells to the powerful and mighty for hundreds of years. The air was still as if it were also holding its breath as she stepped onto the pebble-dashed pathway and took a moment to admire the crowd gathered around her.

Every square inch apart from her aisle was filled with specters, those who had pledged their loyalty and wished nothing more than success for their queen. There were small outbursts of tears from the specters who admired the queen so much that the thought of her not being in her residence was more distressing than the pain of their own deaths.

Victoria gave a satisfied nod and continued down the aisle. Her guards guided her along the curving track until they reached the front gates of the palace, to where a large black horse and carriage were waiting for her.

Victoria scoffed at an elderly Beefeater with wrinkled skin and a large pair of spectacles. "Is this the best you could do?"

The Beefeater bowed low. "I'm afraid Elizabeth has taken the Bentley to Sandringham, Your Majesty." He offered her a hand.

Victoria took his hand and climbed into the carriage.

The entrance to the palace was choked with specters in the wake of her departure. All eyes were fixed on her. Gathered in a long line behind the carriage were specters obediently standing in lines, armed with weaponry.

The door shut behind Victoria, and she was on her way.

Washington DC, USA

Jennie had not noticed the extra staircase leading to the final basement level of the SIA HQ before. She wondered where Hopkins was leading her as he found the final locked door and pressed his thumb against the pad.

"I thought you gave me access to all of the SIA?" she asked.

Hopkins opened the door. "C'mon, Rogue. You of all people should know that every organization has its secrets. We didn't know you from Adam. We're hardly going to give a stranger access to every corner of our HQ."

Jennie grinned. "That's why I like you guys. You're smart."

Hopkins led the way down a set of stairs that turned back on itself enough times to make Jennie question how far below the surface they were.

"Ugh, I've had enough of living like a mole."

Baxter laughed.

They passed through another door and walked along a short corridor, then Hopkins opened one final door. Light flooded toward them, and Jennie's breath was caught as they emerged into the underground chamber that looked as though it took up the entire surface area of the main building. Long rows of halogen lights illuminated a gathering such as Jennie hadn't seen in some time.

The front row was taken up by SIA agents, the highest-ranking first, followed by those decreasing in hierarchy behind them. In a small section on the far side of the front were a group of serious-looking older men and women who Jennie had never seen before, as well as Cole, flanked by two agents handcuffed by one wrist each to the prisoner.

Following behind them were rows upon rows of SIA agents. The chairs seating the SIA agents gave way to the hundreds of specters who had banded together to assist. Jennie recognized the faces of the Spectral Plane troops, as well as the Spectral Plane mortals who had accompanied Tanya during her early days of trying to prove the existence of the paranormal.

There were also the specters from the Lincoln Memorial, with Susannah and Hendrick standing side-by-side, and Jennie even picked out George from among the lineup.

At the back were a number of specters Jennie had never seen before, who she could only assume were the specters who had worked alongside the SIA before the arrival of Jennie and her team, those who knew little of what was being asked of them but wanted nothing more than to help bridge the gap in relations between the two worlds.

Jennie nodded in approval. "This is quite an impressive gathering."

Hopkins grinned and led Jennie over to the center of a raised platform. Daggro, Rhone, Rogers, Ashleigh, Lupe, and Tanya sat on chairs behind a glass podium. Upon Jennie's arrival, Rogers stood and motioned for Jennie to take a seat, then took to the podium to address the crowd.

His voice was calm yet authoritative. All eyes were fixed to the front. "Welcome all, and thank you for joining us here today. A threat has fallen over our city, and our security is being tested. I would like to stand here and tell you that the city is not in crisis. I would like to tell you that we have everything under control and that you will be deployed imminently to neutralize the threat and bring this state to order."

Rogers' eyes narrowed as he rested his hands on the podium. "That's what I would *like* to say. However, the reality is much more severe. It is not just the state that is under threat. It's our country, our nation, our world, and our very *existence.*"

Every ear was bent toward his words. There were no coughs, no sniffles, just a room full of enraptured specters and mortals, whose hearts were beating at an increased pace.

Rogers continued in the same serious tone. "Over the last year or so, I have made it my mission to control spectral and mortal relations, in order to make sure that our country is safe. The SIA's purpose is to develop intelligence and technology to work alongside the spectral realm and ensure that peace resides." He took a deep breath. "But that was never the intention of my close associate and former partner.

"Brendan Koa, codename Umbra, has raised the stakes and is experimenting with dangerous magic, unseen and unused before by anyone on Earth. Koa has built a resistance to our justice system—the Shadows—and is plotting to utilize specters and mortals to overthrow what the White House has specifically ordered us to do. They are committing homicide and repurposing the dead, encroaching vastly on the spectral relations we once held dear to our organization."

Rogers paused, noting the blank looks in the crowd. He looked over his shoulder at Jennie, then returned to his speech. "The paranormal court is the largest spectral organization on this planet. Run entirely by the former British monarch, Queen Victoria, the paranormal court, and their mortal allies, it was feeding us information and assisting us in our developments within the spectral arena. Not too long ago, the paranormal court went silent on us. We have since learned that it is working with Koa's cult and that the SIS and the Shadows have partnered and are on track to build a fighting force so large that we pale in comparison. We cannot allow this."

He banged a hand on the glass in front of him. "It is our duty to neutralize the threat. We are deploying all forces to Alexandra, Virginia since we have strong intelligence to suggest that the rebel scum are holed up there. They do not expect our arrival. This operation will take every ounce of stealth, cunning, and firepower we have. I have explicit orders from the President that they are to be taken down with extreme prejudice. No mercy. These rebels form a direct threat to our national peace, and *that* is something that we cannot stand for."

Rogers' eyes scanned the crowd, taking in the new recruits at the back. "For some of you, this will be your first field operation. For others, it may be your last. Although there are still a lot of unknowns surrounding the Shadows' operations, I can assure you that we have the best field agent on our side. Someone who has spent more years than I care to say battling for justice and equanimity between the spectral and the mortal worlds."

Jennie's stomach fizzed. She was pleased Rogers kept her true age under wraps, knowing that people would not believe how many years she'd been gifted with.

Yes, Bax. Gifted.

Rogers motioned toward Jennie. "Agent Rogue is a stellar addition to our team and one of the finest field operatives in the arena of spectral combat. Her talents know no bounds, and she has been an invaluable asset to our team in discovering the true nature of Koa's operations."

"All right, don't hype me up too much, I won't be able to deliver on people's expectations," Jennie quipped, eliciting a murmur of laughs from the crowd.

Rogers' thin line of a mouth broke into a grin. "Over to you, Agent."

Jennie walked to the podium and shook Rogers' hand. She held onto both sides of the podium, able to feel the eyes of everyone in the room. Some of the agents farther back craned their heads around those in front to see her better.

Jennie took a steadying breath. "Thank you for the kind words, Special Agent in Charge, Rogers." A mischievous smile appeared on her face before she shouted. "And *thank you, Glastonbury!*"

A mixture of confusion and laughter washed over the crowd as Jennie held her hands up, her pinky and forefinger raised in the sign of the heavy metal rocker. Never before had the SIA agents experienced such a strange turn of serious to playful during such a dire situation.

"Sorry, I've always wanted to do that," Jennie commented, settling back to the podium. "In all seriousness, I want to thank Agent Rogers for the kind words. What we're facing today—what we're *all* facing is unlike anything I've seen before. I hail from across the seas and have worked alongside the paranormal court for the best part of my life. I've encountered psychopaths, lunatics, ghouls, wraiths, and poltergeists, but these don't stand up to the mortal operation happening because of Koa.

She shook her head. "You might think you've seen action. Hell, you might have fought a couple of specters yourself, but I promise you that nothing will compare to the fight ahead. We must go in hard, and we must win. If we don't, well. It won't be long before Koa's army grows large enough to be able to go back to the state of what once was. A world of dictatorship and war. We need you. We need *all* of you, and we need your best. When this assembly closes up, we'll be out and on our way. Follow orders. Stay strong, and we will see each other on the other side."

Jennie sat back down as she allowed her words to sink across the room. The specters and the Spectral Plane mortals clapped, then quickly stopped when the SIA agents dutifully remained silent.

Rogers returned to the podium. "You heard the agent. Pony up. Bring your A-game. Let's roll."

CHAPTER SIXTY-TWO

<u>Alexandria, Virginia, USA</u>

Jennie stuck by Rogers' side as the deployment of troops was staggered across the next three hours.

First came the helicopters. The birds, as Rogers referred to them, scattered in all directions, some heading east toward Delaware, a handful heading north toward Maryland, and others heading west toward the upper borders of Virginia.

"That'll do something to shake them off our scent," Rogers approved, with a small nod of his head.

They didn't know how far Koa's cameras could see. They knew, for sure, that Washington was under watch, and there was evidence of their presence in Baltimore. For all they knew, there could be cameras littering Alexandria and its neighboring towns, so as long as they funneled into Virginia at the planned intervals, they'd be able to get close without alerting them.

Next came a series of speedboats and cruisers, half taking the southern route, while the other half would race north where they would station themselves until the signal was called.

"Surround them and trap them in a pincer," Jennie mumbled. "No escape."

"That's the hope," Rogers replied.

They deployed a series of trucks and vans, each crammed to bursting with mortals in some, and specters in the others. When they reached their various exits, they headed in all directions once more, doing whatever it took to shake off any worry from Koa.

"You know that the HQ is being monitored?" Jennie asked, remembering the footage on Koa's screens.

"We've eliminated a number of cameras," Rogers informed her.

Jennie's brow furrowed. "You think that's enough?"

"No," he admitted. "It never is. But it's all we can do for now."

Once the main horde of vehicles was on the road, Jennie and the key players within the operation were given radio sets that remained permanently nestled in their ears. She called the checks to ensure that everyone could hear her and heard the calls back from Ula, Roman, Triton, Rhone, Daggro, Hopkins, Sade, and a handful of additional SIA agents who had been given the chance to step up and lead a unit in the field.

"Best get down to your vehicle," Rogers instructed. "Time to step into the batting cage."

Jennie saluted but wasn't sure why.

Rogers returned the salute with a smile. "Don't let me down."

Jennie grinned. "Tell your men not to let *me* down, and we'll be just fine."

Jennie curled her lip, a small groan of discomfort leaving her mouth.

Baxter sniggered. "Oh, come on."

She rubbed her hands along the curve of the smooth leather steering wheel and shifted in her seat. "Nothing feels right. Nothing feels comfortable in here."

Jack snickered. "Well, I'm sorry that the SIA won't allow you to ride your Mustang into Virginia, but I'm pretty sure that a sleek Mustang like yours might raise suspicion, given the fact it was the same vehicle you drove to the Shadows' facility just over a week ago."

Jennie didn't approve of Jack's sarcasm, but she let it slide, given how distracted the car made her. She adjusted the rearview mirror and played with the toggles for the wing mirrors. No matter how long she spent trying to adjust the various toggles and dials of the Chevrolet Suburban SUV, nothing fit her the same way that her Mustang did.

Jennie pointed across the parking lot. "But it's over there. We could just take it and go. They'd be none-the-wiser."

Baxter turned to the merry gathering crammed into the car. Lupe and Tanya were sitting side-by-side, with Jack in the third row beside Ruby. Sandra, Carolyn, Feng Mian, and his parents were floating in spaces between the seats, all looking as uncomfortable as each other.

Baxter laughed. "I don't think we all fit."

Jennie's mouth fell open. "Most of you are specters! Melt into the exhaust and hold on, or something."

"The pipes get hot," Carolyn complained.

"I repeat—you're a specter!" Jennie shook her head. "You could put up with a little discomfort once in a while."

"Like you and your seat?" Carolyn quipped.

Feng Li whispered something into Feng Mian's ears in Chinese.

Carolyn narrowed her eyes. "What was that?"

Feng remained silent.

Carolyn shot him a dangerous look. "Feng Mian, I'm warning you…"

"He asks why the big man is in the front seat by himself," Feng Mian's mother replied with a wag of her finger. "We're all cramped here, and he gets the luxury."

A smug grin appeared on Baxter's face. "Special orders from the SIA. Rogers named me as one of the leading specters of the operation. Great deeds deserve great privileges. I don't make the rules."

"Bullshit!" Carolyn's voice was loud inside the car.

Tanya clasped her hands over Sandra's ears. "Watch your language."

Jennie rolled her eyes. She started the car and winced at the chugging of the loud engine. She pressed the gas and rolled them out the lot. As they cruised along, a radio segment on the news spoke of the homeless population suddenly shrinking in Virginia. Jennie made a note of it, then switched off the news and plugged in her phone, ready to play mobile DJ.

They took Route 695 out of Washington and passed the Navy Yard toward the Potomac River. The midday sun was hidden behind a rift of cotton clouds, and the roadway ahead was a mass of grey concrete. They left the city behind, turned onto Route 295, and covered ground through the edge of Maryland until they finally turned west and headed across the river once more toward Alexandria.

The journey took a little over an hour, yet Jennie was glad when she could finally switch off the engine and exit the vehicle. No amount of the Spice Girls blaring through her speakers could put an end to that discomfort.

Sandra looked at Jennie with bright eyes. "What does 'Zigga-zig-ah' mean?"

Carolyn answered. "It means the dance grown-ups do."

"What dance?" Sandra inquired.

Tanya stared at Carolyn with eyes of fire. "Nothing! It means nothing."

Carolyn looked at the others for help, but no help came. "Sorry. I keep forgetting you're a kid."

Jennie shook her head and led the way.

The office block was situated in the heart of Alexandria and offered one of the best views of the city that they could find at short notice. Stretching twenty floors into the sky, Jennie and the others made their way to the rooftop to search for the old factory and see what else they could find. There were still a few hours left until night-fall. The operation would begin under the cover of darkness.

Baxter leaned his chin on the lip of the building as he lay on his stomach beside Jennie. "Would they really be stupid enough to hang around the building in the daytime?"

Jennie kept a pair of red-lensed binoculars to her face. Beside her, Lupe and Tanya scoured the city.

"Not if I know them how I think I do, but we still need to remain vigilant. If they get so much as a sniff of what we're up to, they'll dash faster than that vindaloo left Lupe's bowels in NYC."

"Hey," Lupe whined. "That was one time, okay? I had a bug."

"Whatever helps you sleep at night," Jennie replied without missing a beat. "We all ate the same thing, and none of us struggled with the brown water."

Baxter shuddered.

She scoured the city, familiarizing herself with its layout. Over near the docks, she spotted the disused industrial district and found the Sylvester's Premium Candies logo half-eroded on the side of the building. If the Shadows were there, they had certainly done a good job of hiding their tracks. There wasn't so much as a puff of smoke coming from their chimneys or any sign of activity inside.

To the north, she could make out the quaint city, a mixture of modern architecture combined with colonial buildings that gave the city a feel of the Old World, as seen in dozens of films over the years. Replica flame-lit lampposts lit the city, and cars drove along neat streets with red-brick sidewalks.

Greenery filled the area, with small flower beds and trees dotted along the sidewalks. There were shops with striped awnings pulled down to protect their customers from the elements as they entered and exited the buildings.

Jennie breathed in the fresh air. "Takes you back, doesn't it?"

Baxter and Carolyn caught each other's eyes. At their silence, Jennie removed the goggles and turned to Baxter. "No?"

"New York was very different from this while I was growing up," Baxter informed her. "I've never known anything like this. The city has always been a city for me. High-rises and stonework everywhere, a perfect concrete jungle."

Carolyn nodded. "Yeah, and I died, like, this year, remember? You were at the morgue. The only way I'd know about anything like this is from old-timey movies."

A lazy smile crept onto Jennie's face. "Right. I forget how young you are sometimes."

"I remember."

They all looked at Sandra with curious eyes. She was standing beside them, staring out at the cityscape. The wind billowed her hair.

"This is the closest thing I've seen to what I'd consider my home," Sandra went on. Her voice was delicate and soft, almost quiet enough to be stolen by the wind. "If you erased these large buildings and kept the ones with the wooden beams between the brickwork, and got rid of the cars, it would be almost like my hometown."

Tanya knelt beside Sandra, her head at the same height as the girl's. "Where were you from?"

Sandra's head shook slowly. "I don't remember. It was too long ago. I think it'll all be gone now."

Jennie understood this completely. The world had changed a lot over the last hundred years alone, let alone the additional centuries from when Sandra was first imprisoned in rock. And when you added the developments of the last fifty years in modern civilization, as well as industrialization and the advances in technology, the modern world resembled the old world in the same way that a raisin resembled a grape.

"The old world is still around," Jennie soothed, her voice reassuring. "It takes more than a sewer system and transport links to erase the old. Without the old world, we'd never have gotten this far. Sure, it might be tough to take in at first, but there are reminders everywhere of what came before. Gravestones, dig sites, protected historical buildings. Everything else lives in the books Tanya is teaching you to read."

Sandra tucked a lock of hair behind her ear. "I just wish I had more time."

"We all do," Baxter replied. "Unfortunately, time is not something we can control. All we can control is what we do with the years we've got left, and you've got plenty, Sandra. That's the blessing of being a specter."

Sandra nodded, her face resolute. Tanya brought Sandra into her arms and squeezed her tight, whispering soothing words into her ear. Jennie took the opportunity to turn back to the skyline and peer through her binoculars.

Another hour passed. Jennie's skin prickled from the chill air. Although there had been no sign of the Shadows or the SIS, she had begun to notice signs of the coming SIA operation.

They came in one group at a time, creeping along the streets and finding places nearby to park. Every ten minutes, Jennie would receive a word in her ear of another unit checking in. Boats reached the docks and undercover agents disembarked, finding a nearby cafe or bar to wait in.

Carolyn laughed when Jennie pointed out a helicopter on the horizon. "It's like the world's most aggressive flash mob."

Feng Chen's ears pricked up. "What's a flash mob?"

She huddled beside Feng Mian and Feng Li, which made Jennie laugh internally. Feng Mian had been fiercely independent and quiet before reuniting with his family, but they had since formed a tight unit, with Feng Li apologizing unendingly to his wife about the position they had been put in with the Dragon. Each second was an opportunity for them to catch up and exchange words, although mostly it was Feng Chen and Feng Li talking over the top of Feng Mian.

Carolyn gasped. "You've never heard of a flash mob?" She turned to Jennie for reassurance, but Jennie shrugged. "Jennie, I'm disappointed in you."

Jack mockingly placed his hand in the air. "I have."

Ruby told them that she had too.

Jennie lowered her binoculars. "I'm sorry, flash mobs haven't entered my wheelhouse of knowledge, either. I'm usually preoccupied with, you know, saving people and nullifying specters or criminals." She raised the binoculars back to her eyes for half a moment before resigning to her curiosity and asking, "What are they?"

Carolyn waved her hands. "Flash mobs are, like, when you're in town doing some shopping and people come out of nowhere and start dancing or performing. At first, it's only one person, then another joins them, and people keep adding to the theater until the whole street is alive. They do it in Times Square all the time."

Feng Chen scrutinized Carolyn with narrowed eyes. "Why?"

"For fun!" Carolyn laughed. "Or have you all forgotten how to have fun since you've discovered the spectral world?"

Jennie exchanged glances with Feng Chen. "I'm going to go out on a limb and say flash mobs might not have made their way into Chinese culture. We're not all American millennials from New York."

"Hey!" Ruby complained.

Carolyn feigned offense with a scoff and a hand on her chest. "Jennie! You wound us with your words."

Jennie smirked. "Be thankful it ain't my guns." She returned her attention to her binoculars and tracked movements on the streets around them. The sun had begun to dip in the sky, and the world was going dark. A little bit longer, and they'd be ready to strike.

"Time to get changed, folks," Jennie ordered the others. "T-minus one hour until the world's first SIA flash mob reaches full throttle."

Brendan and Clark, you sons of bitches. You're not going to know what hit you.

CHAPTER SIXTY-THREE

Alexandria, Virginia, USA

The robe fit her better than she'd have liked to admit, drowning all parts of her except the glint of her eyes and the lowest parts of her face.

The SIA had repurposed the long dark cloaks they'd confiscated from the Shadows they had arrested in Batsto. Clothed in black, the disguise allowed the SIA agents to wander through the city toward their location with relative confidence that they would meet with less suspicion from the Shadows if their cameras were to pick them up.

Not that they diverted any looks they received from passersby. Everyone they passed darted across the street out of the reach of the mortals dressed like Grim Reapers. They couldn't see Tanya, made spectral by Sandra, Baxter, Carolyn, and Feng Mian's family following them.

"Mordor's that way!" one emboldened youth called across the street through cupped hands.

Jennie turned his way and the youth increased his pace, his smile quickly vanishing.

They wound along the red-bricked sidewalk until the houses began to vanish around them and the riverside industrial estate loomed ahead. Here, the streetlights' glow stopped and left nothing but darkness before them.

Jennie approached the first building and skirted the corrugated iron walls. She sidled to the corner of the building and peered ahead.

The way before them was empty, as Jennie had predicted it would be. She touched a hand to her headpiece. "No sign of the enemy. The coast is clear thus far. Confirm you receive, over."

A series of "Confirmed, over" returned to Jennie's ear.

"Wow, you sound like a professional," Baxter teased. "I thought you only dealt in solo operations?"

Jennie looked over her shoulder at the others. "I've had to play with others sometimes. Never on this scale, but you don't lose the skills."

Her eyes were caught by the smallest of the cloaked figures around her. Ruby looked at the stars, her eyes twinkling with their reflection.

Jennie saw her nerves. "You okay, Ruby? I know this is a lot, but if you're with us, I need you strong, okay?"

Ruby met Jennie's eyes. "I'll be fine. It's just a lot, is all."

Jennie gave her a sympathetic look. "Are you worried about going back into the heart of it all? Going back to face the Shadows?"

Ruby gave a small nod. "I never imagined this could have gotten so big. Wearing this cloak again, it's like it's all come rushing back to me. We were supposed to be doing it all for good. I had no idea that everything we were doing was just practice and research for Koa and his people."

"Well, you have a chance to undo what has been done." Jennie gave a reassuring smile. "A lot of people don't get that opportunity, much less get the chance to join the SIA as a starter agent with zero experience."

Jack placed a hand on her shoulder. "You've got this, kid."

Ruby smiled and, even though she was lost beneath his shadow, Jennie sensed her face hardening. "Let's do this."

They broke free of the building and ran along to the next, pausing with every opportunity of cover and listening for any sign of the enemy. They would only have one chance to get this right, and Jennie wasn't about to screw that up. The Big Bitch was already in her hands, its reassuring steel providing comfort to her palms as they neared the factory they had viewed from afar.

All too soon, the factory fell into sight.

It was larger than the others. Its roof peaked into a hazardous spike, the metal rusted and corroded around its frame. Where the front steepled, the large Sylvester's logo was displayed in all its dying glory—a relic of the old world before society grew culturally conscious of its health agenda.

Baxter let out a scoff. "It's funny, really."

Tanya turned. "I don't see the funny side of this situation."

Baxter's gaze was fixed on the logo. "I mean, that this place would shut down, while other sweet manufacturers lived on. If the world was that conscious of health, wouldn't it have stopped producing chocolate, hard candies, and other forms of sweets?"

"Sylvester's had a unique formula that relied on impure sugars that rotted children's teeth at double the pace of its competitors," Jennie informed them. "When you think of that, coupled with the number of lawsuits and human rights violations they were up against, their stock lost value pretty quickly, and their investors had no choice but to shut the operation down."

Carolyn chuckled softly. "Well, someone has managed to find their way around Google."

Jennie winked. "You can't do an op without doing your research." She peered around the corner once more. "Okay, here's the final hurdle. It's about fifty feet from here to the walls of the facility. Time to secure the area and prepare for the invasion."

"Aye-aye captain," Baxter jested, surprised when the rest of the party followed suit. Even Feng Mian and his parents lifted a hand to their heads and saluted their leader.

Jennie chuckled. "You guys are the worst. Sandra, are you ready?"

"As I'll ever be," Sandra replied. She stood up straight and placed a hand to either side of her head. Her eyes screwed shut as she focused her powers on more than just cloaking Tanya. Small threads of power emerged from her body and found Jack, Ruby, and Lupe, snaking around them and fading them all from the mortal realm.

"Damn, this is so freaky." Ruby's chest rose and fell as she examined her new form. She could see right through her arms, her outline throbbing with a faint spectral glow.

Jack laughed and wiggled his fingers. "You're telling me. Is this what you feel, Jennie? A kind of...cool surge, as though you've been plunged into water?"

Jennie, who had latched onto Baxter to save Sandra from expending more energy she didn't need to, shrugged. "I don't notice it anymore. After a hundred years of this, you grow numb to it."

"Lucky son of a bitch," Jack muttered.

Jennie gave him a gentle slap on the head. "It's *daughter* of a bitch. And, well, if you call my mother a bitch one more time, you'll find out what it's like to get shot as a specter."

Jack held up his hands. "Understood."

Jennie broke free of cover. The others followed closely behind. They reached the edge of the building, and it was there that Jennie paused and listened closely through the walls.

The silence didn't surprise her, the stillness of the night did. Dark clouds began to roll overhead, covering the stars and blocking the moon, the sky holding its breath before the downpour of what was to come.

Somewhere far off, the sound of an ambulance faded into the distance, a strange reminder of the normality that resumed in the city behind them.

Jennie raised a fist. "Wait here." She took half a step through the wall.

"Hold on." Carolyn's eyes narrowed. "You're not running off without us again. We're all in this together, remember?"

"I'll be back. I'm just doing the preliminaries," Jennie smiled. "It's nice to know you already have separation anxiety."

"Separation—" Carolyn began to protest, but Jennie was already gone.

Jennie emerged behind a series of crates that blocked her view of the factory proper. In the ceiling, large panels of grime-covered glass gave her a grim glimpse at the world beyond and provided little light to see everything through.

Jennie slipped around the crate, her ears cocked for any indication of the enemy. She wasn't surprised to discover that a pair of guards were roaming along the factory floor.

Their faces were buried in their cloaks, but she could see the glow of their SI goggles. Their footsteps were soft, but their voices were not. The factory carried every word, as though it wanted Jennie to hear.

"They deployed earlier today, heading off somewhere into the neighboring states," one of the Shadow guards laughed. "Honestly, it's like they sent out some sort of search party. They have no clue where we are."

The second guard was dubious of this information. "How do you know all of this? You talk as though you watched it all yourself."

"I overheard the Umbra telling William. Sounded pretty pleased at his efforts."

"I would be, too. The last thing any of us need is the SIA on our backs. Imagine how much faster all of this would happen if we didn't have to keep upping and moving all the damn time."

Jennie kept her gaze on them as they passed a series of broken-down vending machines. The glass fronts were smashed, but behind them were old packets of Sylvester's candies that had been forgotten by time.

Could make for some interesting cocktail ingredients.

"At least you haven't been put forward for conversion," one of the guards mused. "How long do you think it'll be before it's mandatory?"

The other guard paused his pacing. "It would be an honor to be asked to represent the Shadows as a spectral vessel."

"I didn't mean anything by it, I just...I like being alive."

"Mortal or specter, I don't mind which." Even from afar, Jennie could see his eyes flash. "Don't tell me you're growing yellow. The Umbra wouldn't like that very much, now, would he?"

The first guard held his hands up defensively. Jennie was dismayed to see an assault rifle gripped in one hand. "I meant nothing by it. Just that, I don't think *all* of us need conversion. Some are loyal to stand by his side and take orders when he gives them. I believe in what he's doing here; it's groundbreaking. We're changing the course of the world, and I'd *prefer* if I could have my memories and consciousness intact when it all happens."

The second guard fixed him with a look.

"But, if it came to it," the first guard resigned, "I'd accept whatever the Umbra wants from me. I am but a humble servant."

Satisfied, the second guard began walking once more, the first guard catching up and falling in step.

What is with all of these freaks? Jennie wondered. *Why would anyone just give up their lives for something like this?*

When the guards drew nearer, Jennie waited in silence until they'd passed and begun their next lap. Satisfied she was clear, she melted back through the wall and told her party everything she had seen.

"Thinking what I'm thinking?" Baxter asked.

Carolyn's smile broadened. "Secure the area and lock the two guards down?"

"I was thinking more of inviting them for a game of soccer, but I suppose your idea will do," Baxter chuckled.

CHAPTER SIXTY-FOUR

Jennie waited until everyone was in position. She could just make out the faint glow of Baxter across the way as the two guards continued to chat amongst themselves.

She pressed a finger to her ear. "Autobots, roll out. Over."

Carolyn's tinny voice came back to her. "I thought you said the codeword was 'Go?'"

"This is more fun. And you didn't say 'over.' Over."

Carolyn returned, "Yeah, that's what we need in this situation. Fun."

"Are we going, or what?" Lupe's demanded.

"On my count," Jennie instructed. "And you need to say 'over.' One…"

Lupe added, "Over."

Jennie took a hiss of breath. "Not now. Over."

"Okay," Lupe replied.

Jennie waited.

"Over," he added.

"Okay. One…Two…*Three.*"

Jennie leapt out of her hiding place and aimed her two guns at the guards. For a moment, they continued to walk, blissfully unaware of their presence until Jennie cleared her throat and drew their attention.

Their eyes fixed on Jennie, confusion on their faces as they studied her cloak and saw the two guns aimed at their chests. Then, when they noticed the others, they turned on the spot, hands moving to their own weapons in a flash.

"I suggest you leave your hands where we can see them," Jennie stressed. "Unless you want us to turn them into bloody stumps."

The first guard leered. "Why? Is your aim that bad that you can't aim for the heart?"

"What is this?" The second guard raised his hands and glanced uneasily at the others. "Are we being summoned? Is it our time?" A glimmer of hope crossed his face.

"Oh, it's your time for something," Jennie replied. An idea struck her then—a way to ensure a quiet takedown. She could go in all-guns-blazing, but that would raise the alarm, and that was something she wasn't prepared to do just yet. She lowered her weapons and tucked them into the folds of her cloak. "Follow me, please, gents."

The others looked at her with discontent, wondering what Jennie's plan was. She waved them closer, and they surrounded the pair, turning the group into a mass of black.

"Follow me, please."

Jennie led, and the others obediently followed. She wondered how dumb the pair could be to follow a complete stranger, but she had seen enough examples of pack mentality to know that those within cults or dictatorships would follow any instruction if she gave it with enough confidence.

She led them to a restroom at the side of the facility. The smell of stale urine filled their nostrils. What was once white ceramic was stained yellow and brown, and the mirrors had been smashed some time ago.

"Your initiation is about to begin," Jennie asserted, ushering them into the center of the room and encouraging the others to gather around. She reached forward and lowered the two guard's hoods.

They were normal men, as far as 'normal' goes. Both were in their late thirties, with shades of stubble on their faces.

The second guard stared eagerly at Jennie as if awaiting his prize. The first guard was more uncertain. There was an innocence to both of their faces, a fairy-like quality of wonder and hope.

I can't kill them, Jennie thought. *They don't deserve to die.*

"Strip them of their weapons," Jennie ordered.

Jack and Ruby went straight to it, patting the pair down and removing the assault rifle from guard number two, and a pistol and knife from number one.

"On your knees," Jennie commanded.

They hesitated. When Jennie moved her hand to her gun again, the second guard obeyed, while the first one began to shake.

"No, please! I-I have a family. I didn't want to. I'm sorry, okay? I can do more as myself than I ever will as a penumbra. Please."

Knowing she needed to keep up her facade, for the time being, Jennie lashed a leg out, swept it behind the guard's, and brought him to his knees.

"No. No!" The first guard's voice raised, echoing around the bathroom.

Jennie's eyes widened, suddenly fearful that she was losing control of the situation and that the guard would alert others to the situation.

Jennie dropped to her knees and took the guard's face in her hands. His cheeks were warm, flushed. "Calm yourself, soldier," she reassured through gritted teeth. "If you can't keep your shit together, how can we ever trust you when it comes to the important matters?"

The second guard stared daggers at the first guard and shook his head.

The first guard eventually gave an approving nod. His lip quivered as he took a steadying breath.

"That's better." Jennie gave a satisfied nod. "We're not going to hurt you, kill you, or turn you into penumbra. What I *am* going to do is show you the light. Would you like that?"

The first guard shook his head eagerly. The second one began to grow suspicious. "You're not going to turn us into penumbra?" He narrowed his eyes. "Who are you?"

Jennie removed her hood and palmed one of the vials from her waist pocket. She looked at them through her tinted shades and raised an eyebrow. "Just a friend, ready to smash her foot through your glass ceiling and send the pieces shattering to the floor."

Before the guards could cry out, Jennie poured a measure of silver powder from the vial and blew it from her palm into the faces.

They gasped involuntarily, taking in the powder. It clumped in their throat, drying it out, forcing them to swallow. Within seconds of the powder entering their bloodstream, they were asleep on the floor, snoring lazily as their eyes fluttered.

"What is that stuff?" Carolyn asked.

Jennie pocketed the empty vial. "A Hendrick special. I try not to question the guy."

"I could find a lot of uses for that stuff," Ruby told her admiringly. "My brother used to terrorize me as a kid. Imagine popping him to sleep instantly."

Baxter scoffed. "Don't be naïve. You're still a kid."

Ruby glared at Baxter.

"Two down," Jennie chipped in, breaking the flow of conversation. "Think it's time we began our search, don't you think? Find the hidden entrance and alert our troops to start the invasion."

"*Our* troops?" Jack asked. "Since when were you official SIA?"

"Sweetie," Jennie cooed. "It doesn't matter what hierarchy you set. Women rule the world, remember?"

She left Jack confounded behind her and made a move for the exit. She pushed the door open when an alert came over the radio.

"Alpha-Niner, this is an urgent alert. A convoy is heading your way, over."

"Stand down," Jennie instructed. "We have yet to find the entry-way. Stand down. Over."

"Negative," came the reply. "The convoy is not ours. Three vehicles on the move toward your location. Unable to identify their origins. Estimated time to arrival, T-minus thirty seconds. Over."

"Thirty seconds!" Carolyn gasped. "Who is it?"

"How is Jennie supposed to know?" Tanya snapped. Sandra was huddled against her legs.

Jennie waved a hand. "Shh." She moved her finger back to her ear. "Give me a description upon their exit from the vehicles. This could be trouble."

Silence on the line.

Carolyn leaned closer with a visible amount of joy on her face. "You forgot to say 'over.'"

Jennie ignored her, awaiting the information she requested.

"Headcount: four mortals and twelve specters. The mortals are in dark uniform, while the specters are a mix of origins. All remained silent and focused on their entry into the building. Over."

Jennie's heart sank. "Do any of them have lettering on their chests or backs? Over."

"Affirmative. Mortals have 'SIS' listed. The specters are wearing a large golden badge on their chest."

"Shit," Jennie exclaimed.

"What is it, Jennie?" Ruby asked. "Who are they?"

"They're the queen's guards," Jennie replied softly. "They're scouting ahead."

Ruby moved her hand to her chest. "Why?"

Only one answer came to Jennie's lips. She knew how the queen worked, her strategies, and precessions. Her throat went dry. "They're clearing the path for the queen to arrive."

Baxter's brow creased. "How long do we have?"

"Depends on her transportation." Jennie pinched the bridge of her nose. "Shit, shit, *shit!*"

"What do we do?" Carolyn asked.

Jennie raised her head. She had suspected the queen might get involved, but she had never anticipated Victoria joining them directly in the country. Things must be serious, to have drawn her over the ocean and to the US.

"We lie low. See what they want, then we continue." Jennie's back straightened. "We've got a job to do."

They entered the building from the front door, having no need to hide their arrival as they made their way inside.

The SIS agents were hardened soldiers, the best of the best, trained personally by Clark, himself. The queen's specters, on the other hand, were unused to such derelict quarters, and their noses wrinkled as they followed the agents who searched for the entry into the underground facility.

The agents held their rifles close to their chests, hands positioned in a way to deal damage the instant a threat might appear. Their footsteps were heavy, and their eyes were dark behind their SI goggles.

A practiced, aristocratic British accent spilled from a specter with a pointed chin, and a mole painted on his right cheek. "Where are the doormen? I understood that we were to be greeted and shown into the quarters. This will not do, indeed. Will *not* do for Her Majesty."

"Perhaps we have the wrong building?" A woman in a flawless white ball gown suggested, her 'r' sounds rolling off her tongue like a drum roll. "Are you sure that we are in the correct place, chaps?"

One of the SIS agents turned back to her. "Yeah, we're in the right place, all right. Can't you smell it?"

"Smell what?" the lady replied.

"The stench of specters." He burst into choking laughter at the sight of the lady's crestfallen face.

"You'd do better to respect your superiors," she scolded. "Lady Catia does not stand for such brutality and offense, particularly from you mortals." She tossed her nose in the air and huffed.

"Ladies, ladies," the first specter calmed. His articulation was immaculate, having spoken the Queen's English all of his life—and death. "Let's remember why we've come, shall we? We must ensure that the pathway is clear ahead of Her Majesty's arrival. She wouldn't do with us bickering while she is sitting on the road awaiting our seal of approval, would she?"

The agents and the specters nodded in approval

"Besides," he went on, "Mr. Clark provided us with additional instructions before he went radio silent. The entry should be over in that direction, should it not?"

"Fantastic," Lady Catia moaned. "That's exactly what we need—a plan filled with oughts, coulds, and shoulds."

CHAPTER SIXTY-FIVE

Jennie waited until the group was gone before crossing to the far corner of the room. They found the hole closed. The aristocrat had performed the ritual and poured his own energy into the seal, then sealed it behind himself.

"It's the same pattern as the other two," Carolyn exclaimed.

Baxter nodded. "Did you expect anything different? This is clearly some kind of sigil for them. A way for them to stamp their seal across their properties."

"I wonder how many other places they have," Carolyn added.

"It doesn't matter," Jennie told them flatly. "This is their last stop."

She drew a vial from her waist and held it up to the light. The others were surprised to see the spectral fluid inside, a sample taken from Hendrick to aid on their quest.

Ruby spoke without thought. "It's so beautiful."

"That's the essence of a specter," Baxter retorted. "There's nothing beautiful about it."

Jennie let the liquid fall toward the seal where it took ahold instantly, navigating its force around the deep channels in the seal and illuminating the pattern in bright blue light. A click indicated that they had gained access. Jennie hauled the lid open on its hinge and stared into the blackness below.

She raised her head and blew a puff of air. "Seriously. Always underground."

"You'll be fine," Baxter reassured her. "This is the last time, for a while, at least. Don't forget, I'll be going down, too."

Baxter's eyes widened as he realized what he had said.

"I mean, with you. *With* you."

The others hid their laughter behind their hands, trying not to draw too much attention to themselves.

Jennie placed a hand on Baxter's shoulder. "It's all right, Bax. Sometimes a girl has needs, you know." She bounced her eyebrows and grinned. Baxter waved his hands in protest.

"No, I definitely didn't mean that! I… Oh, forget it."

Keeping her eyes on Baxter, Jennie engaged her radio and called to the others. "We're in. Showtime, people. Over."

"Roger that. Over."

Jennie took a step back from the hole and asked Jack to ensure it remained open. She stood, her eyes drawn to a nearby pillar. She moved over to it, knowing the SIA would need a minute or two to crash in on the scene, and ran her hand over a series of long cables that ran along the pillar's length.

Most of the tangle of cables were covered in a layer of dust, their color faded from years of neglect. One wire, however, looked as though it had been disturbed more recently than the others.

Or someone had installed it not too long ago.

"Feng Mian, over here."

He rose without complaint and stood by Jennie. "Think you can overload these cables?"

Feng Mian's eyes slid to the cable. It snaked into a hole in the floor and split in a dozen directions at the top of the pillar.

Feng Mian placed a hand on the wire and closed his eyes. His hands began to throb a brilliant blue, and seconds later, bolts of electricity appeared on the wires and danced like white-blue pixies along the cable's length.

The wires hummed at the top, where the electricity split across the network. Small pops indicated to them that cameras had shorted from the sudden burst of power.

Another few pops exploded around the room before the electric hum stopped altogether. Jennie wondered if the circuit was a series or a parallel. One would short just a small section of the facility, while the other would break the entire network.

"Nice work," she told Feng Mian.

"Thanks," he replied.

"Risky move," Jack muttered. "But at least backup has arrived."

The first of the engines could be heard outside, alongside the calls and orders of the lead agents and their crew. They poured into the facility through every door with their weapons at the ready. Some found their way into the overhead balconies, while others cleared the room to ensure that no enemies had been missed.

"You could just trust me," Jennie chided, approaching Hopkins, who she was surprised to see out in the field. "We'd already checked."

"No offense meant. It's our duty to double-check. Protocol. You understand."

Jennie couldn't work out if that last part was an apology or a question.

"You ready to storm a base?" Hopkins asked.

Jennie smirked. "It wouldn't be my first, would it?"

Hopkins grinned.

"What about air cover?" Jennie continued. "Do we have the place surrounded?"

"All units are in position," Hopkins confirmed. "If the rats run from their hole, then we'll get them before they get too far. Rogers has tracked the blueprints to any underground networks nearby, so there's no escaping this time. Once you're in the hole, there's no going back."

Jennie bit her tongue. "Not the first time I've heard that in my lifetime."

Jennie moved over to the entrance and lowered her legs into the hole. She took the smoke grenade offered to her by Hopkins and threw it into the darkness.

Nothing happened for a few seconds, then a small flash of light indicated its successful detonation. Smoke filtered around them, and Jennie lowered herself inside, moving quickly to ensure that she could counter any ambush that was waiting for them.

Clever move, Koa. A single hole to filter the enemy through. You're using Spartan tactics against us...clever.

Jennie reached the bottom. Her party followed closely behind, then came the agents and the remaining specters.

They funneled in like hot water into an ant's nest, moving as quickly as they could down a number of long corridors. Compared to the last facility, this one left a lot to be desired. Mold and cobwebs covered the ceilings, the windows in the smaller rooms were missing or smashed, and the smell of earth infested their passage.

A few minutes into their run through the corridors, they encountered their first enemy. A group of three Shadows dressed in their long dark cloaks, appeared around the corner, marching in step as if the whole thing had been practiced.

Jennie called a warning to her team, then opened fire on the Shadows. She blasted them in the chest with the Big Bitch before they could so much as pull their itchy trigger fingers.

The three were sent backward into the wall, the force of it creating a small fracture on its surface.

They turned right, following the long, snaking corridor until a red door appeared before them. A yellow triangular warning sticker was in the center. Jennie could make out figures moving beyond the frosted glass.

She held out her arm and activated her radio. "Bogeys ahead. Looks like it might be the main chamber of the facility. They're preparing. Over."

"Neutralize the target," Hopkins ordered. "Take no prisoners. Over."

Jennie steeled herself, turning to perform a quick check of those behind her. She nodded to Rhone, who had worked his way through the horde toward the front, and he prepared with two flash-bangs in either hand.

Jennie raised her boot and kicked in the door. It swung open, and Rhone threw in his flash-bangs.

Jennie found it strange that shouts didn't greet the surprise of the door opening, then remembered the dead stare she had seen in the Shadows' eyes below the Lincoln Memorial, the possession ritual stripping their enemy of any emotion.

Undead soldiers. Nice touch.

A blinding light lit the way ahead as the flash-bangs exploded. They pressed the advantage with Jennie leading the pack as she took down anyone who came her way.

They made it onto a gantry high above the facility floor. Shadows were all around, lining the walkways and the stairs, disturbed at the intrusion of the explosives.

As Jennie's finger worked the trigger, she was aware of at least a dozen more smoke grenades being thrown from behind her, filling the area with a thick haze of smoke.

Bullets fired around them. They pinged off the metal walkway. Some made their way through the mesh and came precariously close to hitting Jennie. A few found their marks in the Shadows. The sound of surprised shouts and screams filled the room.

Jennie used the fallen bodies of the dead Shadows to create a bridge beneath her and protect herself from the bullets fired from below. Shadows appeared through the smoke as she worked her way along the gantry, and Jennie wasted no time in snuffing the light from their cold, dead eyes. It was impossible to know where she was going, but she followed the direction that the Shadows were coming from.

Another three explosions rang out as the SIA ensured their cover, allowing time for the rest of the squad to file inside. The noise reached dangerous levels, with gunfire adding to shouts and explosions. Jennie wondered how far there was to go, only having glimpsed the room briefly upon entry.

She found the top of the stairs and began to descend. As she curved back on herself, flashes of white caught her attention from the ground below. The flashes looked like balls of lightning in the midst of a storm. When shouts of protest followed, Jennie knew she was needed. Battle was all about priorities, and this was hers.

A wall of Shadows blocked her path, Jennie took hold of the handrail and swung herself over the edge of the gantry. She lowered herself down to the lowest rail, then let herself drop, hoping that her sense of direction was intact and that it wouldn't be too big a drop.

She landed sooner than she'd expected and ran until she could find a place that was quiet and where she could think, which was easier said than done when all of her senses were being attacked.

Jennie closed her eyes and placed her fingers against her temples. She focused on her breathing as she felt around for spectral frequencies.

This is why I prefer my own method of creating smoke. At least then I can see fine and be able to identify specters. With smoke grenades, all parties were blocked from view, and it was down to her raw talents to figure out where everyone was.

She identified them one-by-one. Her power extended beyond her, acting like a kind of sonar until she had nearby specters in sight. She could see them behind the closed lids of her eyes as white silhouettes against a dark background. She was dismayed to find a number of them lost their firmness and simply disappeared, disappearing from existence as the light flashed in the real world.

Those fucking vacuums. The specters stand no chance against them.

Seeing red, Jennie kept her touch on the specters so that she could navigate through the smoke, and worked her way toward the area where she had last seen specters disappearing.

Emotionless Shadows appeared along the way. These she took down with a quick punch to the nose, chin, temple, or mouth, depending on whatever took her fancy.

The first spectral vacuum operator she encountered was a beast of a man. Standing at nearly seven feet tall, he loomed out of the smoke. His face was hauntingly neutral as he scanned the area nearby and activated the vacuum whenever a specter came in sight, popping it off like a juggernaut with a rocket launcher, only this weapon sucked the victims inside instead of blasting them sky-high.

"Hey! Big guy!" Jennie wasted no time in distracting him from the specter he had in his sights.

The Shadow turned toward Jennie, and she wondered if he was really some kind of Grim Reaper, and this was the universe's way of telling her that her time was up. For a fleeting second, she was taken back to the tombs of London, standing beneath the hovering form of Canute the Great. Then, with a shake of her head, she was back, and it was time to take him down.

The Shadow chuckled as he switched on his machine. Jennie was alarmed to discover that she could feel its pull. Whatever spectral power resided within her was affected by the vacuum. She pulled against it, raising her pistol. She clenched her teeth as she felt *something*—she wasn't sure what—being pulled out of her. The radar location she had on the specters vanished instantly, and she was alone in the smoke.

She shot at his foot, or where she imagined his foot to be. The bullet ricocheted off the ground, getting lost in the folds of his dark cloak.

He shifted, moving closer toward her. Even though she couldn't see his face, she could feel his grin. A strange power came off of him. She took another shot, but he was too close, and one swing from his cubic vacuum was enough to knock the pistol from her hand.

Jennie fell to her knees, unsure of what was happening. She had never considered any part of her biology as spectral, had in fact always been convinced of her mortality. But at that moment, she wasn't so sure. Something was being drained from her.

She fought against the pull, feeling as though she were engaged in a tug of war that she was losing. A deep, demonic chuckle came from the asshat with the vacuum as he closed the gap and—

Baxter's wrench smacked against his head.

Beneath the cloak, the Shadow's skull shattered, giving under the thick metal of Baxter's melee weapon. A strange gasp escaped his mouth and then he collapsed, almost disappearing beneath the bundle of cloth.

The vacuum twisted as it dropped to the floor. Jennie shouted at Baxter to move, and he dodged out of its mouth just in time. Jennie dived over to the machine and flicked the off switch, relieving them both from its yawning mouth of death.

"Good timing," Jennie breathed.

Baxter panted. "I would've got here sooner. There are so many of them."

As if to illustrate his point, a number of Shadows were thrown toward them. On the edges of their vision, they could make out SIA agents wrestling with Shadows, and doing everything they could to take them down.

Jennie's eyes darted around the smoke. "We're never going to find Koa in all of this chaos. We need to move faster. Get ahead somehow. For all we know, he's in a capsule somewhere, jetting off through underground tubes to his next location."

"The place is surrounded." Baxter ducked at the sound of a nearby explosion. "They've got nowhere to go."

"This is far from over, Bax," Jennie told him. "This is merely their warm-up. You think they wouldn't have measures in place to deal with an attack like this?"

"I thought we had the element of surprise?" Baxter countered.

"We did. But Koa has the element of wisdom. He's not stupid enough to not prepare for this. Trust me."

Baxter nodded. "I always do."

They dived back into the fray, Jennie making a beeline for the vacuum-wielding Shadows. One by one, she jumped on their backs and choked them out. Whatever had happened with the first vacuum, she did not want to repeat. She worked alongside Baxter to stop the eradication of specters by the strange devices.

The sounds of fighting began to wane as the smoke cleared from the room. By the time it was thin enough to see again, the room had fallen eerily silent. SIA agents and specters scanned the room, still poised and ready for any threat that may come. Instead, they found nothing more than scores of fallen bodies—from both home and away teams.

"This can't be all there is." Rhone wiped a sheen of sweat from his head. His eyebrows knit together, his arm hung limply by his side, gun pointing to the floor. A large gash ran from his brow to his ear, and his uniform was torn in places. "Where are they all?"

Jennie pointed to a door at the far end of the room. "They're regrouping. The body count here isn't half of what I saw when we first entered. My guess is that they're retreating, warning the others, sending the alarm floating to the surface."

Jack approached. His normally neatly groomed hair was a mess, and he limped as he walked. "A floating alarm? What are you talking about?"

Jennie sighed. "It's an expression. Sailors would attach warning lights to buoys when they found treasure beneath the waves. The lights would draw the main crew to its location so they could investigate further."

Jack nodded. "Oh."

Jennie raised her voice, addressing the room. "We cannot linger. We must press on. Those who are wounded, report back to the top. Hopkins has medics waiting. Those who are well enough to continue, come with me."

To her joy, a good number of the agents were still able to follow. That didn't discount the pain Jennie felt at seeing the number of bodies that lay on the floor, the SIA agents recognizable among the masses of cloaks thanks to the bright white lettering on their chests.

Specters gathered around the room. They hadn't been as helpful as they'd have liked, with many of them unable to get involved in mortal affairs like Baxter.

"Feng family, up front with me." Jennie ushered them forward and prepared to exit the room.

The family obeyed, appearing at Jennie's side in a matter of moments.

"What is it?" Feng Li asked. "You spotted someone ahead?"

"No," Jennie told him. "Not yet, anyway. That's why I need you.

Feng Mian, it's been my experience that some families carry traits in their bloodline that pass down to relatives and deceased family members."

"I have seen similar, in some circles," Feng Mian agreed.

Jennie nodded. "Good. Do you know what your parents' powers are yet? Their spectral gifts?"

Feng Mian gave a minute shrug. "Mother shows signs of my own powers, but she needs training. My father, I still do not know."

Feng Chen appeared at their side, her face a thundercloud. "Feng Mian. It's rude to discuss us as though we're not here. We raised you better than that."

"*Duìbùqǐ*," Feng Mian replied, hands together as he bowed.

Jennie looked between them, then continued as if there had been no interruption. "I've got an idea, but it might take the three of you. Particularly if I'm looking to get as many people as I can across the finish line."

Feng Li spoke with a fierce determination. "Try us."

Jennie nodded. "Feng Mian, work with them. Get your shields ready to cast. I'll be back in one second."

"One." Baxter smirked, counting on a single finger.

"Ha-ha," Jennie snarked. "When did you become a comedian?"

"When your influence started rubbing off on me, I guess."

Jennie left the group at the door and caught up with Rhone. She found him among a cluster of agents who were reporting various losses and taking stock of those who had fallen.

"What's the count?" she asked.

"At least thirty dead so far," he replied sadly. "Another fifty or so injured. I've sent word to Hopkins for medical assistance."

Jennie pointed at her ear. "I know. I heard you."

Rhone wasn't in the mood for humor. "We can keep a troop behind to watch over the injured in case any come out of the woodwork while we press on. I've already assigned Sade and her team to watch over them."

Sade saluted. "I've got it covered."

"Good work," Jennie praised. "The aim of the game is to lose as few as possible. Ideally, the total tally would be zero, but let's be real here."

She trailed away as a strange thing happened. Rhone stared at Jennie and raised his weapon, pointing the barrel at her. Jennie cocked an eyebrow. "What do you think you're…"

"Move," Rhone barked. He brought the gun up and swept Jennie aside.

She turned and made sense of what was going on.

Specters were rising in their dozens from both sides, a mass of spectral bodies rising from the dead. Even in death, there was a stark difference in the demeanor of the two factions. While the SIA agents awoke with confused expressions, investigating their bodies and breathing relief that they were somehow alive, the Shadows' specters were rapidly scrambling to their feet and readying their weapons. They had been forewarned of this event, Jennie was sure, and they were prepared to fight again.

Jennie's head fell back, and she muttered to the ceiling, "Two lives. Everyone lives two lives."

"What do you want us to do, Rogue?" Rhone asked.

Jennie was surprised by the question, knowing Rhone's reputation among the SIA. It seemed that Rogers' speech had permeated the hierarchy at last. She really was in charge here.

"Specters, engage," Jennie called loudly. "Mortals, press on. This isn't a fight for you."

CHAPTER SIXTY-SIX

The horses came to a stop as they entered Old Town, a small quarter in the city of Alexandria not too far from the docks.

It wasn't a gradual stop, either. It was almost as though they'd hit an invisible wall. Victoria let out a shocked gasp and gripped the window to steady herself, tsking beneath her breath as all fell quiet around her.

"What is the meaning of this?" she demanded.

Her two guards shrugged their shoulders and exited the carriage to examine what was going on. Despite the unplanned stop, Victoria couldn't help but be taken by the quaint city. As someone who had lived most of her life during the 1800s, she had something of a fondness for cities that could blend the old with the new. Cities that respected the ways of the past, while allowing technological and architectural advancements to weave between the fibers of its history, rather than destroying them completely.

This city was exactly that.

The guard returned. "Your Majesty, there's a problem."

Victoria was unsurprised by this. Nothing was ever straightforward these days. There was always a problem somewhere down the line.

"Is it something that you can handle?" Victoria asked lazily.

"The Spectral Intelligence Agency is aware of our presence. They've barricaded the roads and streets into the base. They've got the Shadows surrounded."

Victoria's smooth line of lip twisted into a curve of displeasure. It only lasted a moment, though. A second later and she was smiling, speaking as though nothing negative had crossed her mind at all.

"Not a problem," Victoria replied. "It's a little earlier than anticipated, but I suppose now's the time to make a statement."

A little man with a mean stare appeared at her window. "What do you have in mind?" His arms were thick—thicker than they should be for someone of his size, reminding Victoria more of a gorilla than a man. Moonlight bounced off his shaven head.

"Agent Tiptry, I didn't know the SIS were in the habit of eavesdropping on the private matters of royalty."

While others may have turned a shade of scarlet, Tiptry held Victoria's gaze. "Your Majesty, with the greatest of respect, Agent Clark is radio-silent, and the Shadows have turned on our order. I believe it is hardly the time for subtlety. You need a strong leader for the SIS in place of Clark, and that's what I'm offering."

"Just because you're the standing agent in charge, that doesn't give you the right to invade my privacy."

To Victoria's amusement, Tiptry ignored her comment. "You need to execute. I'm here to carry out your orders. If there's something needs doing, I'm far more capable of spreading the messages than those two spectral trolls."

The queen's guards growled.

"No disrespect, boys," Tiptry added with a grin.

"I'd be careful of them, Agent Tiptry," Victoria warned. "They bite when aggravated."

"Well, I guess that makes three of us." Tiptry held up a gloved hand with two veins of green lights running down the sides and nine more running up each finger. At the tip of each was a small circular pad throbbing with the same green light.

Victoria laughed. "Agent Tiptry, execute the order. Operation blackout."

Tiptry stared at the spectral guards for a moment before nodding and saying, "Absolutely, Your Majesty."

He hopped down from the carriage and disappeared from sight.

"He's right, you know," Victoria teased playfully. "You two *are* somewhat trollish."

Hopkins watched the events unfold from inside the factory with practiced patience. A dozen or so medics were making their way into the hole, ready to accompany and heal those who had been injured in the initial fray.

He summoned Daggro, her face as surly as it ever was. She held an AK47, its ammunition imbued with spectral energy.

"The scum are here?" she growled.

Hopkins nodded grimly. "Birds report a three-block tailback of specters. Our teams have blocked the road, and their advance has stopped. A horse and carriage are leading their procession."

"A horse and carriage?" Daggro repeated. "What is this, the 1920s?"

"For all we know, it could be." Hopkins scratched his chin. "Assist the agents at the barricade and prepare for a battle in the streets. Set up a perimeter to block any potential broadcasting or media capture of the event. It won't be long before the press wants to be involved."

"Of course," she told him. "Anything else?"

Hopkins thought for a moment. "Stay alive."

He watched as Daggro rallied the agents around her and headed out of the facility. The last thing he wanted was to stretch their numbers and not hold steady together, but they had little choice. If the others were to complete their operation below, they needed backup on the surface.

Hopkins pressed a finger to his ear and had got as far as saying, "Rogue, update…" when all sources of power around the facility were cut. There was a small pop. It was faint but physical. Hopkins could hear nothing through his radio, and everything around him was plunged into total darkness.

He tried the radio again. No luck. His eyes adjusted to the darkness since the only light available was from the thin sickle moon through the grim windows above. Some agents were beating their flashlights in their palms to get them back on, and others were trying their radios, but there was no response.

"Sir." Clive appeared beside Hopkins with alarm on his face. "They've done something. Every piece of our electrical equipment has gone down. We've got no tracking, no lights, and no communications."

A sudden haunting realization hit Hopkins. The world was silent, deadly silent, whereas only moments before there had been…

His eyes widened, and he shouted the command to all agents. "Find cover! Clear the facility."

He indelicately shoved Clive forward and led the way by sprinting toward the exit doors of the building. Less than a second later, a high-pitched whistling preceded the crash as the roof crumpled beneath the weight of the falling helicopter.

It came down like some great bird from the sky, the metal folding in on itself as it slammed into the ground, nose-first. The agents inside were immediately crushed as the fuel tank caught fire, and seconds later, the force of the explosion hit any agents remaining in the building.

Hopkins watched it all from the safety of the doors, ducking out of the way as a blast of heat pushed toward him. The inside of the facility lit up under the glow of the fire, and all that could be heard where the moans of the injured and the crackle of the flames.

———

Jennie felt a slight tremor in the ground but had no time to contemplate what that could mean. Hopkins' voice had come and gone so suddenly that she had no doubt that something was wrong, but she was in no position to fix that right now.

She could still hear the sounds of combat as the Spectral Plane and any specter who had accompanied their mission fought the new rising tide of specters. Jennie was confident that since their number was greater, they would no doubt overpower the opposition, but she also knew that in battle, no victory could be assumed.

They pressed on through the corridors, making impulse decisions on direction and following their gut. Feng Mian led the way with his mother and father beside them, deflecting any oncoming bullets from the enemy as they charged the corners.

To give him his credit, he was a good teacher. Feng Chen's shield proved to be a useful addition on a number of occasions as she flanked Jennie's side. On the other hand, Feng Li was still in the process of understanding his powers. His shield appeared in bursts, flickering like an old VHS feed, and causing him to grunt with frustration. He was ignoring Feng Mian's advice that calm was the way to power.

They rounded another corner, and the walls opened to reveal a wide reception area. Once it might have been welcoming to arrive at this room, but now tables were overturned and chairs were rotting. An old desk in the corner indicated where the receptionist had once sat.

Jennie wondered if this had been a meeting hall for a secret society. The world was littered with them, people who found the spare recesses that were out of sight and gathered to talk about their business. They weren't always sinister affairs, either. Sometimes people liked the isolation of remaining out of sight.

Though, for the most part, it is *the bad guys hiding out of view of the law. And here comes exhibit A.*

At the far end of the hall were three doors. Each of these was occupied with the strangest grouping of people Jennie had ever seen—and she had seen some sights.

They were a grizzly bunch, none of them were dressed in the cloaks of the Shadows. They wore ill-fitting clothes, covered in stains and tears. The men sported messy beards, and both sexes had hair so greasy and thin that they looked unnatural on their heads.

The worst, though, was their eyes. They were blank white marbles, staring at them with no conscious thought whatsoever. What human intelligence they'd had was missing, and all that was left was a husk.

Jennie's throat went dry. "Jesus Christ."

The sentiment was reflected by the gasps of the other agents. A moment later, the smell hit them in full force—the smell of city streets and abandonment.

Jennie looked forlornly at the line of former vagrants. "Ready your weapons." She didn't want to hurt them, but if she was going to look at the larger picture, and end Koa's reign, then that might be the only option they presented.

A single vagrant took a step forward. His shoes made a strange squelching sound.

Guns cocked around her. Jennie put an arm up and held them back. "Hold…"

She took a few tentative steps forward, her hands poised and ready on her weapons. The gap between the two seemed to stretch like taffy as she walked, each step an effort, each move a concentration.

The horde waited patiently, none of them making an effort to move toward her. Her breath caught in her throat. The smell became overwhelming, but she trudged on as she holstered her pistol and held a hand before her as if approaching a dangerous animal.

Baxter took a step out of line, and Jennie halted him with a wave of her hand.

"You're too close," Baxter hissed. "It's a trap."

Jennie's eyes were fixed on the vagrant. "No. I don't think it is…"

She stopped when she was within ten feet of him, her hand still in front of her, her back bent slightly, prepared to make a dash and move if needed.

"You're stuck, aren't you?" She spoke softly, trying not to spook him. "You don't want to be in there. You've been dealt a shit hand, and this needs fixing. I can help you."

"What is she doing?" a voice hissed from behind.

Jennie ignored it, instead choosing to focus on the spectral aura gravitating toward her from the possessed. Although the specters were inside the bodies of the homeless, she could still sense them, could feel their discomfort, their anger.

"Hold still…" Jennie felt for their energy, connecting with them each in turn. Their signatures were strange, different than what she would normally feel, as though they'd been tainted in some way. It was as though someone had dropped a dot of black ink into crystal clear water. She drew their energy toward her and tried to latch on.

The vagrant took another step.

Jennie closed one eye as she focused, keeping the other on the vagrant. In her head, she could almost hear the words of the specter, as though they were speaking through the glass of an aquarium—a far-off, indistinct voice that shouted and protested in anger.

I can't hear you, Jennie called in her head. *Speak louder.*

The vagrant took another step, and Jennie narrowed her focus.

Again, the words were muffled. She could make out individual syllables, but could not blend them all together.

She detached from the others and focused solely on the vagrant before her, staring into his lifeless eyes as he took another labored step.

Finally, the words became clear: *You're dead, bitch.*

The vagrant closed the gap with a powerful leap, arms outstretched and gunning for her throat.

Great, Jennie thought. *The wittle homeless man wants a hug.*

CHAPTER SIXTY-SEVEN

Jennie swept her forearm in front of her, blocking the vagrant's arms and sending him sprawling to the side. He grunted as he hit the floor, then sprang back to his feet, his limbs moving as if he were being controlled by a puppeteer.

He went for Jennie's legs, trying to pin them together and cause her to lose her center of balance. His mouth hinged open, revealing a set of yellow and black teeth, gaps dotted along the gum. He pulled himself toward her and went for the bite.

Around her, shots rang out as homeless began to charge but fell under the impact of the SIA's bullets.

Jennie ripped her leg from the vagrant's grasp and kicked him in the chest, causing him to fold into a V. She took a step back, moving from his clutches and shouted, "Incapacitate them, don't kill them!"

Rhone closed the gap and drew closer to Jennie. "What are you talking about? They're the enemy."

"They're enemies without guns," Jennie replied. "Knock them unconscious, bind them up, do whatever you can to save them. It's not their fault they were brought into this shit. Save them, if we can."

Rhone furrowed his brow but echoed the order. The gunshots

silenced, and in their place were grunts and cries of effort as agents and the homeless possessed engaged in fisticuffs.

Something tugged at Jennie's leg. She sent another kick into the vagrant's face, then was shoved to the floor as two bowled into her and knocked her down.

If she thought the smell was bad before, it was worse now. They drooled and growled in her face, the stink of their breath a mixture of halitosis and rot. Jennie headbutted one and threw them off, then wrestled with the other, doing whatever her mind told her to do to neutralize the threat with minimal damage.

"Girl, you need a Tic-Tac," Jennie managed before the vagrant was lifted from her. From where Jennie was lying, all she could see was the scuffling feet of others as Triton tossed the woman clean across the room and offered Jennie a hand to help her to her feet.

"I thought you were a strong fighter?"

Jennie wiped a glob of drool from her cheek. "My forte is specters. Can't say I've wrestled a tramp before."

Triton threw an elbow behind and knocked a man unconscious in one blow. "The principles are the same. You just can't use your spectral powers."

"The hell I can't," Jennie replied, an idea springing to her mind.

The helicopter was an unanticipated touch, but it was something that made Victoria smile.

The aftermath of the pulse was immediate, a piece of technology that shorted all the circuits within a one-mile radius—give or take a few inches. It served as a blockade, a way to dim the light in the surrounding city, and throw the SIA into alarm. Sure, they may be trained to work in such conditions, but that didn't mean it wasn't a hindrance to them.

She strode through the streets with a steady gait, her fingers laced in front of her. Around her, SIS agents sprinted ahead, led by Tiptry, who shouted orders and pulled them into action. They moved like shadows, while the wall of specters wandered behind her, following at her pace, savoring each step as they approached.

How long had it been since Victoria had *seen* action? She sniffed the air and savored the scent of burning, relishing the eruption of gunfire. Flashes of muzzles flickered ahead as the fire worked its magic and caught the facility with its tongue.

Flames snaked up the beams. Smoke billowed into the sky. If the SIA were smart, they'd halt the fire services and contact the local authorities to stay back. This was no place for the local man, now: a war was starting.

She advanced on the building without pause. The SIS had her covered and were locked into their battle with the mortals. It was interesting to see the similarities. She had spoken to the SIA indirectly, but would never have imagined how similar the two factions might be.

Perhaps there's an opportunity here for a merger? A way to unite the two and bring the SIA under my wing? Act as my serving force, alongside *the Shadows.*

No, it was too late for that. Somewhere beneath them, she was certain that Brendan Koa was fighting his own battle, but it wasn't him she cared about. As long as she could control the situation and guide the chaos to the best outcome to suit her, that would be just fine. Erase the traitors, and earn the respect and loyalty of those who were willing to bow before her.

And save Agent Clark. After everything that's happened these past few months, I've grown something of a soft spot for him.

<hr>

The situation looked dire.

Hopkins hadn't accounted for this. He had learned from Jennie that the SIS were somehow involved, but he had made the mistake of assuming their numbers were already tied up in the current operation with Koa. Who could have guessed that more were to come, that Queen Victoria would show her face and engage in the battle?

He could see her from afar as a portly white shape rolling toward them like a thunderous cloud. It had been years since Hopkins had experienced anything akin to fear, having trained his mind to serve in some of the most nerve-wracking situations across the world in his years of service, but he felt it then. A discomfort in his stomach that confused and startled him.

She was a vision exactly as he had imagined, the woman he had seen in numerous magazines and online articles. Hopkins had done his fair share of studying history, but nothing had prepared him for meeting the real deal in person.

If he even managed to get close enough to meet her.

Bullets sprayed around them. Voices were raised and angry. He gave his commands and pulled his agents back toward him, wondering what the best line of command would be. For each SIS agent they took down, one of his own was killed.

"Retreat!" he called, sending off his own bullets and taking down two agents with rapid speed. "To the hole! Retreat!"

The SIA agents worked their way back, their focus entirely on the enemy. They used the flaming corpse of the helicopter for cover and made their way into the hole, sprinting through the flames and ducking into the cool safety of the darkness beneath.

Hopkins waited at the entrance. As the captain of the ship, it was his duty to ensure his men were safe. He waved and encouraged SIA agents back, heart pumping as he shouted encouragement and covered their backs, his aim with his rifle impressive and true.

When the last agent dropped into the tunnel, he gave one last look around the burning building, feeling the effects of the heat on his skin. His hands and face felt raw, dry, and somehow cloying and damp at the same time.

A bullet whizzed past him. A second caught him in the shoulder.

Hopkins grunted and dropped down into the coveted safety of the world below, one hand gripping the ladder, while the other hung limply from his side.

Victoria strode through the flames, her spectral entourage following in step. The SIS agents awaited her arrival, their guns trained inside the flaming building on the off-chance a survivor might be waiting for them.

The flames were roaring now. Great billows of smoke concealed the moon and stars.

Victoria paused alongside Agent Tiptry, whose eyes were fixed inside the broken shell of the factory. The walls had begun to collapse, creating large holes around the outside of the building, making it look more like a whale skeleton than the facility it had once been.

"All clear," Tiptry told her.

Victoria stared ahead, finding the flames beautiful to watch. They had always fascinated her, the sporadic curls and licks of a power that could eat through nearly anything on the planet. The oranges and reds acted as some amorphous thing feeding itself on all it consumed.

Victoria walked ahead.

Tiptry's back straightened. "Your Majesty?"

She ignored him, walking straight into the flames. They didn't affect her in any way, shape, or form. She passed from sight, and for a long moment, the only sound was the crackling of the fire.

A shot rang out. The SIS agents readied their weapons. The specters shifted uncomfortably.

Two bodies emerged from the flames. Victoria carried the spectral SIA agent by the scruff of the neck, holding him up to the others as though she were presenting some kind of gift. There was a bullet hole in her chest that was already rapidly healing, and before she had emerged in her entirety, it was gone.

"Agent Tiptry, you've forgotten the first rule of spectral warfare." She closed her eyes and placed her free hand on the wriggling agent's heart. "The double-tap."

Her hand suddenly glowed with a brilliant light that spread over the shape of the SIA agent. His eyes widened, and before he could so much as shout or scream, he was gone. Any trace of him had evaporated.

Awe passed over Victoria's followers. She walked back to Tiptry and loomed over him. "Clean up the rest of the mess, will you?"

"Of course," he replied before calling forward a team of agents who all held their own versions of the spectral vacuums. These were neater and more compact than the crude mechanisms of the Shadows' but proved to be just as effective as they worked their way through the building, taking care to avoid the fire as flash after flash exploded with each exorcism.

While all of this was going on, Victoria strode back into the building, searching for the tunnel's entrance. She stood above the hole and stared into its dark eye.

Her lips peeled back into a grin. "You can hide, but you can't run."

Chaos reigned around the chamber. Agent versus vagrant, vagrant versus agent. Fists flew, and kicks were delivered; the combat skills of the agents were put to the test.

Nearby, Jennie, Triton, Ula, and Roman came into their own, neutralizing threats with a series of grabs, tosses, and throws. They moved like whirlwinds, their opponents finding it near impossible to track their movements before they ended up on their backs on the floor.

Not that that stopped them. Whatever driving spectral force that had been stuffed inside the vagrants like Babushka dolls was relentless. Although the mortal body was damaged and beaten, the spectral power drove them on.

Spectral power, Jennie mused. *At least some part of them is spectral. That has to mean something.*

Jennie fought off her own enemies, shaking off the rust of the skills she'd honed over the years. As she used elbows, knees, palms, and feet, she kept her feelers on the alert to detect any kind of spectral signal she could control. She had almost done something with the single vagrant earlier. That had to mean there was a gateway in.

Her overpowering theory was that there had to be at least one person controlling the vagrants. An antenna that broadcasted its directions to the hundreds of spectral vessels. But as she swam ever onwards through the aggressive horde, she began to think that perhaps there had to be another way.

A blast of spectral energy sent a handful of vagrants flying. Jennie drove her palm into the stomach of her most recent attacker and gave herself a few microseconds of breathing room. Her eyes found Feng Mian and his parents, who were sending shockwaves from their shields to propel the enemies backward.

Jennie aimed for them.

She ducked out of the way of an oncoming blow, and returned the favor with a swift kick to the vagrant's kneecap, reversing its bend and causing the snapped bone to break the skin. A fist came from nowhere, catching Jennie between her shoulder blades. She turned and punched another vagrant in the face, her knuckles catching the vagrant's jaw and sending her spinning to the floor.

"Nice one!" Ula laughed, before taking a punch to her chest.

Jennie called, "Thanks! *Focus.*"

Ula waved a hand.

Soon enough, she'd made it to Feng Mian. She gathered in the hollow between the Mian family. "Good to see you guys."

"Likewise," Feng Mian returned.

"Have you got a plan here?" Feng Chen asked. "I don't see Koa among these assholes."

Jennie, disorientated from the wave of bodies, hunted for the door where the vagrants were still emerging from. "We have a one in three chance of finding the right door."

Feng Chen's face filled with motherly concern. "That's lovely, dear, but we can't get anywhere without finding a way to stop these people."

"That's why I'm here," Jennie replied. "Keep me covered, will you?"

Feng Li smiled. "We've got you."

Jennie held her fingers to her head again and extended her power into the crowd. The readings were overwhelming, with the specters not only clouded behind the mortal bodies but also all shouting in their own voices, too. Jennie tried to filter through the noise and static, hunting for something that could benefit them.

There it was. It was slight, but it was there.

Jennie sifted through the noise, moving slowly toward the signal. In her mind's eye, she could make out the faint shapes of specters. It was as though she were a bird flying through the crowd and hunting for the morsel of food that would satisfy her. She was aware of the flashing power of the shields around her but fought against the distraction.

A single signal called to her, more powerful than the others. She flew above the specters until they divided into three lines.

The three doors...

She followed the one with the most power—door number three. A line of specters filed back until they faded into nothingness. At the end of the line was a powerful thread of spectral energy, attaching to nothing whatsoever.

Jennie couldn't understand it. What non-spectral force could be exuding spectral energy?

The only thought that came to her, then, was, *Me?*

Jennie snapped out of her reverie with such suddenness that, for a moment, she forgot where she was. The chaos coalesced around her as another flash of energy came from Feng Mian's shield. "Not to rush you, Jennie, but our power doesn't hold forever."

"I've got it," she told him. "Door number three. The answer is back there. Take them down, and the rest might fall."

"Might?" Feng Li questioned. "There's a lot at stake that rests on 'might.'"

Jennie's face was pained. "I can feel it. And my gut is usually right."

"But not always?" he inquired.

Jennie arched her eyebrow. "Now's not the best time to question my abilities."

A flash of Feng Li's shield pulled his attention. While Feng Mian's shield covered almost his entire height, Feng Li's was just large enough to prevent direct hits, as long as he moved it into the trajectory of the vagrants before him.

Jennie looked over the crowd to the door, wondering how she was going to navigate her way past, and what would await her on the other side.

Triton's words came back to her. "You can't use your spectral powers."

No. But I can use other specter's powers.

"Feng Mian, I'm going to latch onto you and your family. Are you ready for power like you've never felt before?"

Feng Mian gave a resolute nod. His shield flashed.

Jennie nodded. "Sweet. Let's do it."

CHAPTER SIXTY-EIGHT

There was something satisfying about hacking into a specter's powers. As the energy flowed through Jennie, she felt alive. A buzz of adrenaline coursed through her body as she felt the defensive powers activate within her.

She took a stance beside Feng Mian and held her hands out to the crowd, palms first. Energy sparked from her fingertips, erupting into a shield that encased her body entirely. She looked around her bubble with approval and winked at Feng Mian.

"Always have to go one better, don't you?" he joked.

Jennie laughed. "I don't know why I haven't done this before."

The shield was tested almost immediately when the vagrants in front of them attacked her. Each time a fist connected, the area where they had hit flashed with an angry white light and repelled them a few inches backward.

Let's see what this bad boy can do. Jennie took a step forward, and the shield came with her. A thin tendril of power remained connected to Feng Mian, Feng Li, and Feng Chen, and it was this she knew she needed to keep control of.

She took another step. The vagrant army was subsiding in front of her. Each step pushed them away from her and around the bubble.

Apart from the physical force, the shield did little to block the intensity of the fight. Sounds came through with crystal clarity, to either side she spotted agents and mortals involved in the fight.

She passed Rhone, and Ula, Triton, and Roman, Jack and Clive, and Ruby. She was impressed by Ruby's combat skills, moves she'd picked up quickly in the short time she'd been with the SIA. Jennie was also surprised to see the efforts of Lupe and Tanya, who remained close to one another and used Sandra to power them in and out of the spectral realm at the right time to avoid blows before dishing them out.

But soon the agents were left behind, and Jennie was left in a sea of vagrants. The further into the crowd she got, the angrier they became, attacking Jennie with such ferocity that she wondered if there was any human left in them at all. Their teeth were bared, snarls and growls directed her way. The shield was flashing so regularly that Jennie wouldn't have been surprised if she'd somehow found the attachment for a strobe light inside.

There's an app for that.

She shoved her way forward, finding that the farther away from the Fengs she got, the more she needed to concentrate to keep her shields up. Feng Mian did his best to follow behind, but couldn't match her pace. She gritted her teeth and pushed ahead, her eyes closed against the near-constant flashes of light.

By the time she made it to the door, all she could see was white. The vagrants funneled into tighter hordes, and as she pressed her way through the entrance the shield squashed vagrants against the wall. She was a freight liner carving her way through the thick ice of the arctic, and all would give way.

They leapt at her. The vagrants took every possible opportunity to try to slow Jennie down, but to no avail. By the time she neared the source of the power, she knew there was only one thing left to do.

She stopped. She needed to see what was ahead. Even though the shield would protect her, it would do nothing to help her eradicate the nuisance that was binding this all together.

"Okay, Jennie. Count to three, then it's berserker time." She patted a vial attached to her waist.

Jennie relaxed her shoulders and opened her eyes wide. The shield flashed again and again. She reached her final countdown and bared her teeth at the enemy.

The shield disappeared, and Jennie immediately stepped out of the way of those who were forcing themselves forward and found that their obstacle was no longer in their way. Torches lined the wall, flickering and casting them all into a dizzying mass before her.

Standing on the fallen, Jennie laid out a series of punches and kicks, taking one pop at each of those surrounding her. She grabbed the vial and quickly drained its contents, feeling the warm solution surging through her. Her focus narrowed, and her blood pumped around her body. Her movements increased in speed, and all of her training came back to her in a sudden flurry of memories.

She grabbed a wrist in front of her and twisted it. Simultaneously, she kicked the vagrant behind her. With a tug on the wrist she held, she drew the enemy toward her, elbowed the back of his head, and then spun away from another blow. She caught a second fist in her hand on the upswing, then shoved backward before throwing a left jab, two rights, followed by a left hook.

The bodies piling up on the floor beneath her gave her a height advantage over the others. As she rose higher, she saw what she was looking for. A dark figure in a cloak stood at the end of the corridor, a set of stairs led upward behind them.

Jennie leapt.

Dozens of eyes traced her trajectory, watching Jennie arc over three, then four vagrants, before her feet landed on the shoulders of the fifth. She used his sturdy frame to push onward, jumping across them like stepping stones. Although each jump was different, and some sank while others remained as sturdy as stone, Jennie closed the gap and cleared the final vagrant with one final push.

She bent her knees upon landing on the stone. When she rose, she was surprised to find the Shadow halfway up the stairs.

"Oh, no, you don't."

Jennie drew the Saber of Holy Divinity from its sheath and hurled it toward the figure. It spun in the air before piercing the Shadow's cloak and pinning them to the wall where the stairs began to double back on themselves.

The Shadow wrestled with the sword, its metallic length vibrating from the impact of Jennie's throw.

Jennie ran fast, aware of the vagrants behind her, and jumped the stairs two at a time.

"Show yourself, Koa," Jennie growled, taking a fistful of cloth and pulling the hood back.

Her breath caught. She had been expecting to see Brendan's face beneath the hood, though she wasn't sure why. Instead, she looked into a set of eyes she recognized instantly. Ruby-red lips and the high cheekbones gave Julia something of an elfin appearance.

Jennie pressed the Big Bitch into her stomach. "Call them off."

"Please," Julia whined. "I don't want to die. I'm only following orders."

The vagrants closed in, and they reached the bottom of the stairs.

"*Call. Them. Off.*" Jennie's words slipped between gritted teeth.

"You don't understand."

Jennie drew her pistol with her free hand and pointed them at the vagrants. "One last chance."

"You… You won't kill me," Julia stuttered.

Jennie's lip curled. "I'll do what I have to do."

They were halfway up the stairs.

Jennie screamed in Julia's face. "*Call them off!*"

Julia gasped but was frozen in terror.

In a sudden bout of rage, Jennie whipped the Big Bitch away from the woman and fired half a dozen shots at the ceiling above the vagrants.

Julia screamed. The ceiling groaned and crumbled from the impact of the bullets. The vagrants disappeared behind a wall of rock and earth as Jennie tugged the saber from the wall, sheathed it, then dragged the terrified woman out of the way of the collapse.

At the top of the stairs, Jennie waited until the dust had settled.

They could faintly hear the ongoing sound of the fight, but there was little chance of any mortals passing through the tunnel now.

"You best hope that there's an alternate route out of here," Jennie scolded. "Because, one way or another, I'm finding your boss and handing him over to the authorities."

Julia muttered a series of incomprehensible sounds, her eyes glassy and dazed.

"I'll give you one thing. You're loyal. That's to your own detriment." Jennie shoved Julia ahead. "Show me where he is. You make one move to escape, I'll turn your brain into fucking pâté."

Julia nodded eagerly, then took a few steps in front of Jennie.

"Oh, one more thing."

Julia turned.

"Deactivate your minions," Jennie ordered. "I've got friends down there who I've grown rather fond of. I'd hate for them to have to blow your army sky high."

"I don't know if I can through the blockade," Julia replied softly. "I don't know if it'll work."

Jennie didn't buy that for a second. "You can try, can't you? I'll give you a gold sticker."

Julia closed her eyes and stretched a hand toward the staircase. She muttered, "Stand down," then met Jennie's eyes.

"That it?" Jennie asked.

"That's it."

"Great. Now, show me the way to Amarillo."

Julia looked confused. "I thought you wanted to find—"

Jennie gave Julia a shove to get her moving. "Oh, will you just fucking go already."

***

Baxter watched the whole thing from afar. First, Jennie catching up with Feng Mian and his family, then the appearance of the shield, then her march into the unknown.

He had been caught in the melee. Usually, he would have just walked through the mortals and found his way to Jennie, but these weren't just mortals. There were specters inside them, and those specters were a pain in his ass.

His wrench had never seen so much action. He swept it around him in wide circles, holding his arm steady against the vibrations as he hit specter after specter.

The worst part about it all was that the mortals were affected by the hits, too. They held their hands to their heads and fell to the floor, blinking stupidly at the ceiling. Jennie had told them not to kill the homeless, and that's what he intended. But he hated the idea he might accidentally be damaging their brains in the process.

Then shots were fired. The tunnel shook, and Baxter threw vagrants aside—or rather, their spectral counterparts—and charged toward the entrance.

But even he was not as strong as all that. The vagrants slowed him down to the point where he felt as though he were swimming through a pool of tar. He lashed his wrench around, but they just kept on coming. Jennie was in trouble, and he couldn't reach her.

"Sons of bitches!" he shouted.

His rage grew, and vagrants were thrown in every direction. Yet, he only got so far as the doorway, when a strange thing happened.

They stopped. As suddenly as they had all launched into battle, the vagrants stood stupidly on their feet, swaying slightly. Their eyes were still vacant, but their limbs hung by their side. At the back of the chamber, the rest of the agents and specters were coming to the same realization. They weren't fighting back. They'd just…*stopped.*

Baxter prodded a finger at the middle of the vagrant's forehead in front of him. The vagrant rocked back on his heels, then wobbled toward him as though he were nothing more than a toy finding its balance on a rounded platform. "What the…"

Lupe pulled by his side. "She must have found the trigger."

Carolyn carved her way through the vagrant sentinels. "The trigger?"

Lupe examined a nearby vagrant and waved a hand in front of her eyes. "The thing that holds them all together. In every ritual, there's a power trigger. Someone who can call the commands and set the specters in motion."

"But where is she?" Baxter asked.

They reached the tunnel entrance, collecting Feng Mian, Feng Chen, and Feng Li as they passed, and stared inside. Only a few of the torches remained after the dust had drifted from the tunnel's collapse. They squinted ahead, but could only see where the tunnel ended.

"Shit," Baxter uttered.

Feng Mian peered into the mess. "She's somewhere ahead.."

"How do you know?" Baxter asked.

"We saw it," Feng Chen replied. "From the mouth of the corridor. Jennie found a woman with long hair and red lips. She told her to call off the…whatever they are, but she refused. She blocked the tunnel to prevent them from getting her."

Lupe sighed.

Carolyn gave the others an incredulous stare. "So? What's the problem?"

Lupe tore his eyes away from the vacant vagrant. "Easy for you to say. Mortals can't pass through walls that easy."

Tanya and Sandra poked their heads around the door.

"Aren't you forgetting something?" Tanya asked.

Lupe looked down at Sandra. "Bingo." He tiptoed over to her and scanned the ensemble of agents working their way forward and weaving through the crowd. "With Jennie gone, the SIA is going to want to take control of the situation. Come on, if we're going to get ahead, let's do it now before they see us."

From afar, they could hear Rhone delivering orders, asking his agents to search ahead for Jennie.

"Fine, quick," Tanya conceded. "Sandra, are you okay to guide people through?"

"Of course," Sandra beamed. "Anything to help."

CHAPTER SIXTY-NINE

The corridors were silent apart from their footsteps, the way illuminated by the emergency spotlights that lined the ceiling.

Every turn was an imminent threat in Jennie's mind. She was prepared for any eventuality, holding Julia at gunpoint as she led the way ahead.

Could she trust Julia? History had taught her not, but she was certain that even Julia wouldn't be so stupid as to try anything that might put her life in danger. Julia was loyal, but you couldn't be loyal when you were exorcised and dead.

The double-tap. Hadn't that been one of Victoria's tips?

"How much further?" Jennie nudged Julia as they passed a series of open doors leading to small offices. Inside, desks stood askew, chairs had been kicked back, and laptops were either closed or half-open with their backlight gently lighting their keys.

Do they have wi-fi down here? She shook her head. *Concentrate, Jennie.*

"Just a little way ahead," Julia replied. Her voice had grown some of its confidence back, but there was still a hesitation there. "Though, I don't know if I have the code for the door."

Jennie shook her head. "Oh, I think you're lying about that, aren't you, Julia?"

Julia didn't reply.

They took another set of ascending stairs that doubled back on themselves. On the walls were faded signs for emergency exits, and posters showing the proper ways to work with dangerous chemicals.

Once again, Jennie wondered what the original purpose of this building once was. An underground bunker for a secret political society? An illegal operation playing with dangerous chemicals? Was this how the Sylvester corporation had discovered the original formula to create candies, by using dangerous toxins and illegal compounds? Jennie had heard that Coca-Cola had once actually contained cocaine in its formula, but had thought that was just hearsay.

The 1800s were a different time, baby. Almost anything was legal if it was kept on the DL.

They passed another series of doors before Julia started to move ahead. Jennie paused, her attention caught by something flickering in a room to her right.

"Julia, let's not get ahead of ourselves."

Julia looked over her shoulder, noticing that Jennie was a good distance back. Her eyes darted ahead.

"Don't even think about it, sweetheart," Jennie warned. "I think you know that I'm a quicker human than you."

"Are you human?" Julia asked, emboldened by distance.

Jennie shrugged. "Who's to say? Get your arse over here now."

Julia considered both options, then with hesitation, she followed Jennie. Jennie took a step back, forcing her inside the room before she stepped inside—to an exact replica of a room Jennie had been in before.

"Man, this is trippy," she breathed as her eyes explored the wall of monitors. Dozens of small screens showcasing various camera feeds from around the world outside.

While a number of the screens showed nothing but static, a fair few showed locations she recognized instantly. Three showed different angles of the external of the SIA HQ. One showed a street in

Alexandria, which Jennie recognized due to the style of the buildings displayed. Another dozen or so showed the interior of the facility, including a current projection of the main building above ground and the various chambers below.

"Oh, no," Jennie gasped, taking in the mass of flames covering what looked to be the surface-level area of the facility. A strange metallic frame could be made out through the flames, but whatever it had been, Jennie had no clue. White silhouettes of specters were filing into the tunnels, some of whom she recognized from her many years prowling the halls of Buckingham Palace.

She studied the screens beside them and found the footage of specters in the initial chamber, the Spectral Plane having overpowered those who had risen from the bodies of the SIS and the Shadows. The footage showed their progression through the next set of doors toward the final chamber where the vagrants had been—and where Hopkins and a number of SIA agents were deep in the middle of a heated conversation with the other agents. Already they were assembling into a formation that would allow for them to form the best defense against the coming storm.

A pang of guilt formed in Jennie's stomach. She was alone, ahead, and had trapped the SIA and her specters in a chamber from which they could not escape without facing the queen's army. Her final horror was realized when a large white shape appeared in the first chamber, and Jennie looked into the cold eyes of Queen Victoria.

Rage unlike anything Jennie had felt before boiled inside of her. The audacity of the queen, to travel across the ocean and interfere in her affairs after giving her blessing for Jennie to take care of things in the US. The hand holding the pistol at Julia's back shook, and a small grin appeared on Julia's face.

"She's coming for you, Rogue," she taunted. "She's coming for you and your friends. Go back and save them before it's too late. You know that only you can."

Jennie was faced with a dilemma. To head back and take the helm of the fight against the queen and her army, or to go ahead and chase

Koa. Either way would lead to the capture of enemies to the state, yet, each option left the possibility that another might escape.

"You've still got time," Julia teased. "Let me go, then run and help your friends. Without you, what hope do they have? You know the queen better than anyone, right? I read your file, and I know your history. Only you can stop her."

To Julia's surprise, Jennie fired the pistol at the screens, popping them all off, one-by-one. A startled scream came from Julia's mouth as she crouched and clapped her hands to her ears.

Jennie returned her gun to point at Julia. "You wouldn't be trying so hard to change my mind if I wasn't close to Koa. Show me where he is. *Now.*"

"It's too late," Julia protested. "He's gone. Go back to your—"

"Bullshit!" Jennie cut her off. "Take me to him *now.*"

Julia looked into Jennie's fiery eyes and swallowed hard. She rose and led Jennie quickly down the corridors toward a wall where a large ornate painting was fixed. It was out of place among the other décor—or lack thereof.

Julia pressed on the face of a painted young woman, setting a chain of events into motion.

The painting moved sideways, revealing a keypad that lay naked and flat against the wall. There were no signs of a door anywhere, but when Julia tapped in the code—encouraged by the cold steel of Jennie's pistol against her spine—a series of clicks were heard.

"Rogue, you don't have time—"

Jennie cut her off again. "Every interruption from you grants me less and less. Get your arse in gear."

Julia stepped back and kicked the wall. A rectangular section pushed back on a hinge that hadn't been there before and revealed a large circular tunnel.

"It's always tunnels with you guys, isn't it?" Jennie grumbled, the smell of domestic waste hitting her nostrils. "The sewers, really? That's your out?"

Julia looked at Jennie. "I don't make the rules," she managed before being shoved roughly ahead.

Jennie glanced at the floor, hoping to see Julia's shoes, but they were covered by her cloak. "I hope you're wearing running shoes because that's what we're going to do."

Julia groaned and increased her speed.

Hopkins' shoulder throbbed. They had ushered the remainders of the spectral allies through to the chamber, and they were in position. He ignored the pain and held his rifle steady, using the space between his pectoral and shoulder to hold the gun in place. All firearms were trained at the door.

The specters took the front rows, while the mortals took the back half. He had no idea what to expect. Despite all of the warfare situations he had found himself in over the years, he had never encountered a spectral battle on this scale. He knew the queen's army had SIS agents, although he didn't know how many were left after their skirmish above ground. He had no idea how many specters were involved, and that was what worried him most. He had never gone into battle blind like this before.

Intelligence is the winning force of any fight.

Not only that, they were blocked in. The only way out was back the way they had come.

At least he had Daggro and Rhone by his side. His trusted leads flanked him and zeroed in on the doorway. They could hear them advancing, but they were yet to appear. The whole room held its breath.

"I hope Rogers has something up his sleeve," Rhone muttered, only loud enough for Hopkins and Daggro to hear.

Me too, Hopkins thought. *Me too.*

A sudden aura of light glowed from the entryway. It started as a small flicker and grew to a blinding light.

A shape appeared before them, portly and beaming. "Hello, my friends."

It was strange to hear the British accent and round tones coming from a long-dead queen. Her voice was friendly, yet there was an edge to it that spoke of mistrust, as though she was choosing her words in the same way a chess master chooses his next move, always one step ahead.

She held her arms wide, the glow slowly fading until she was looked like a regular specter. "You need not fear the coming tide. Change is a strange and delicate thing to negotiate, and I understand you have been fed a series of misinformation and lies to make you see us as the enemy. I am not your enemy; I am nothing more than a potential friend and a powerful ally who could grant you an alternative path to the one you believe lies ahead."

Hopkins narrowed his eyes and moved forward, weaving through the specters even though he didn't need to. It was force of habit. He scoffed. "A friend who just mowed down half my agents and set the place on fire? Come on, Vicky. You expect us to believe that?"

Something flashed behind Victoria's eyes at the shortening of her name. Despite this, she smiled and addressed Hopkins. "And who might you be?"

"Senior Special Agent Tom Hopkins," he informed her.

Victoria smiled. "Senior? So, you're not the agent in charge?"

Hopkins' lip curled. "I'm the agent in charge of this operation. You want them, you go through me."

Victoria gave a curt nod, exchanging a glance with an SIS agent who moved ahead and stood by her side. "Agent Hopkins, this is my man in charge of mortals, Agent Tiptry. He's not the head of our agency. Agent Oliver Clark has been declared missing. I'm certain that if we work together, we can come to some kind of arrangement where I can find and rescue my SIS leader, while you still get what you want."

"What is it you think we want?" Hopkins asked.

Victoria chuckled. "Order."

Hopkins growled. "You're in the wrong place."

"I don't think you understand the position you're in," Victoria responded. "I am the head of the paranormal court, and with that comes special privileges that make me very dangerous when provoked. Consider me a hornet's nest. You can either kick the nest or scurry back into your holes with your tails between your legs and surrender. I'd like to say the choice is in your hands, but there's only one option here that won't end in your deaths." Her face darkened. "And in death, I'll be sure to have you."

Hopkins nodded and lowered his rifle. "I guess we only have one option then, folks." His eyes narrowed, and he fixed them on Victoria. "Break down your force until you have no option but to surrender."

The specters leading the formation all ducked at once, allowing room for the agents behind to fire their weapons. Hopkins joined them on the floor, groaning as he was forced to use his injured arm to balance himself. A spray of bullets peppered the entryway, taking down Agent Tiptry instantly and filling Victoria with bullet wounds.

She was forced backward, her limbs windmilling. The bullets passed through her and the specters behind her, tearing through the mortal agents woven in-between and down the tunnel. Groans and cries and grunts were lost below the sound of gunfire.

Victoria's back hit the wall. Her eyes closed, and her body went limp.

The SIA continued to pound her with spectrally imbued bullets until they were satisfied that she was down.

Hopkins held up a fist. He pushed himself uneasily to his feet. A commotion farther down the tunnel indicated the rest of the force making their way forward. He ordered the first line of agents to advance on the door and continue firing to send shots blindly into the tunnel to hit whoever was there.

Hopkins, on the other hand, moved toward Victoria. Silver blood leaked from her wounds, and her dress was torn in a number of places. Parts of her body were missing, and a hole in her cheek showed the inside of her mouth.

Hopkins trained his gun on her. He knew specters required exorcisms for them to be fully erased from the world, but he had seen them suffer enough injuries to incapacitate them for some time.

Rhone offered a supportive shoulder for Hopkins to lean on. "Is she down?"

"Yeah. For now," Hopkins replied. "Funny, out of all the things I envisioned doing with my life, I never thought I'd take down a monarch."

Victoria's eyes flashed open. "You still haven't."

She stood up suddenly, moving as though the pain didn't exist and she hadn't been hit.

Before Hopkins could issue a command, Victoria swept her arms wide and sent out a pulse of power.

CHAPTER SEVENTY

Jennie soon lost her bearings on which direction they were running. Julia expertly navigated the sewers, only occasionally slowing down to sidle past a thick puddle of waste, or to study a series of scratches on the wall. Above them, a gentle glow of light filtered through the gaps in the drainage that led to the open air.

Story of my life, Jennie grumbled inwardly. *Wading through shit and trying to find some clarity and direction.*

When Jennie felt as though they'd been running for miles, Julia pulled to a stop. They were at a dead end with a circular valve handle against the wall.

Julia huffed, fighting off a stomach cramp. "They're just inside."

"No funny business?"

"No funny business."

Jennie could read no malice on Julia's face. "Open it."

"Can't you just pass through?"

Not without a specter nearby, but Jennie wasn't about to tell Julia that. "I can. But you're my shield. I wasn't born yesterday."

Julia sighed and gripped the wheel. At first, she could not get it to budge, but then a grinding squeal announced movement, and it span open freely.

"After you," Jennie offered.

Julia pulled the door open and stepped inside.

The room was pitch-black. A layman might assume the way ahead was clear, but Jennie knew better. "Koa. It's over. Show yourself."

At first, there was no response. Then, a match flickered to life, limning Brendan with a ghostly glow. It reminded Jennie of the campfire games she'd played as a kid, holding the flame low to extend the shadows across her face.

"I continue to underestimate you," Brendan admitted sourly. There was anger in his voice, frustration at being foiled again and again.

"It's okay," Jennie told him without inflection. "Most people do."

Brendan scowled. "I gave you every opportunity, Genevieve. I offered you the opportunity to find out the truth to the question you most wanted answers to. We could've built something. We could *still* build something together. It could be beautiful."

Jennie's stare hardened. "I don't negotiate with arseholes. The world deserves better than to have a tyrannical scrotum forcing his agenda on the world. If you want to work together, you're going to want to come over to my side. It's rare I change my position."

"But not unheard of?" Brendan sneered.

Jennie remained silent.

Brendan continued, sounding more like a disappointed father than the egomaniac she knew he was. "It's a shame, really. I've tried over and over to give you what you want, but my patience is running thin. The queen was right, you know. You're impossible."

"I think you mean improbable," Jennie corrected. "If I was impossible, I would not exist."

"You're tiresome."

"Sticks and stones, my friend."

Brendan sneered. "So, we're friends now?"

"Why take everything so literally?"

"Because it's fun."

Jennie took a deep lungful of air. Her pistol rested against Julia's head. The Big Bitch was aimed at Brendan. "Last chance to surrender, Brendan. I don't like killing as a rule, but I'll do it if I'm pushed to act. Give yourself up, and you can live. You don't want death, trust me."

Brendan slowly shook his head, his eyes on the floor. "But don't you see, Genevieve? It's in death that the possibilities open, and the impossible becomes, as you say, the improbable. You'll learn that soon *enough*!"

At his final word, Brendan shouted and extinguished the match, plunging himself into darkness.

Jennie acted fast, pulling the trigger and sending a number of bullets ricocheting around. The bright flashes of her weapon were enough to illuminate the wider spaces of the tunnel, and suddenly Jennie grew afraid.

"Missed me!" Brendan called back, an impish cackle following him as he wandered around the darkness. "But you didn't miss my contraptions, did you?"

Jennie didn't. In the brief flashes of light, she had seen six large metal containers gathered in a semicircle around the dark room. Great, gaping nozzles the size of cars were pointed in her direction, each one reminiscent of the vacuums she had been under the influence of in the first chamber of the underground facility.

Brendan cackled. "Impressive, aren't they?"

A match lit to her right, and Jennie shot immediately. The light was snuffed out, and Jennie realized at that moment she hadn't shot Brendan but had taken the life of a Shadow.

A decoy.

Another match to her left and she took aim, dismayed to discover that it was another Shadow. One by one, they lit torches until a dozen Shadows were viewable in the flickering light.

There was no sign of Brendan.

"Koa!" Jennie called. "Show yourself. Don't hide behind your cheap tricks and your soldiers. Fight me like a man."

"That would be unfair, wouldn't it?" Koa called back. "For you are not a man, are you, Genevieve? You're not even human, are you? Of course, we could discover the truth if you called it a truce, but I think we both know what your final decision is going to be."

"Your death," Jennie growled.

Koa laughed. "Shame. That's the one thing I can't promise you. I'm already halfway to freedom, lost in the umbra of our coming eclipse. Enjoy spending time with my penumbra, Genevieve."

Jennie detected the tinny edge to the speaker that played Brendan's voice. Somehow he had activated a radio in the darkness, and he was no doubt fleeing down the tunnels to freedom.

Jennie shoved Julia forward.

Julia landed on her hands and knees and cried out to the tunnels that stretched endlessly ahead, past the strange machines. "Umbra! Come back! What about me?"

"He's abandoned you," Jennie told her, eyes darting to each machine as loud whirring indicated the initiation of a series of high-powered fans. "He's abandoned all of you to death."

Julia turned back to Jennie. "Those machines aren't designed to kill me. They're designed to kill you."

"That may be, but I'm designed to kill, and I think I've had just about enough of you."

"No!" Julia's scream was almost as loud as Jennie's gunshot.

Jennie stepped over Julia, taking advantage of the fear she could invoke by simply shooting near her.

Jennie's focus turned to the silent guardians of the machines, the Shadows standing as still as statues and waiting for the machines to reach their full power.

"Why didn't you shoot me?" Julia muttered behind her.

"I don't kill in cold blood," Jennie replied, already feeling a strange tingle as the fans began to roar.

In a frenzied burst, Jennie shot each of the Shadows in the kneecap, and they folded to the floor, twelve perfect shots in quick succession.

"If you want to run, now's your chance," Jennie told Julia without looking. "But I promise you, if your choice is to catch up with Brendan and forget my generosity, I'll shoot you both."

Julia went wide-eyed and ran, shoving herself crudely to her feet and darting toward the machines. She curved around the back of the central machine and disappeared from sight.

"Well, I guess you've made your choice," Jennie murmured. She looked at the machines, the devices lighting up as they drew power and began to fully engage. The roar was growing deafening, and Jennie could feel the pull increase. She took a step back, then another, wondering how she was going to switch them off without getting dragged into their sucking current.

"Think, Jennie, think."

She took another step back, her foot catching on the rise of the doorway into the chamber. She almost fell over, but instead was caught by a sturdy set of hands. "Bax?"

The large specter smiled down at her. "Don't worry, Jennie. We've always got your back."

Jennie arched an eyebrow. "We?"

Carolyn, Lupe, Tanya, Sandra, Feng Mian, Feng Chen, and Feng Li were behind her with determined expressions on their faces.

Jennie laughed. "Hey, guys, fancy seeing you here..." Her words trailed into a grunt as the machines reached their full power. She tried to step toward her friends, but her feet slid across the floor.

"Jennie!" Baxter grabbed her hand, little realizing the threat before him. While he tried to hold her, he too was drawn in by suction's power. Carolyn, Feng Mian, Feng Li, Feng Chen, and even Sandra were affected, bracing themselves against the door to avoid the suction.

"Get back!" Jennie cried. "Jump back! You can't come any closer. Get yourselves to safety."

Lupe and Tanya stared at them, helpless and unsure. The suction was growing more powerful by the second, threatening to pull the door closed and lock everyone inside.

Jennie slid a few more inches.

Carolyn scanned the room for any kind of solution. "Latch onto us, Jennie. Use us all as leverage."

"That'll put you in danger," Jennie told her. "We might all perish."

"Just do it!" Carolyn screamed, afraid they were going to lose Jennie.

It was strange having someone bark commands at her. Normally, Jennie was the one in control, the one who knew what to do. She shook off her moment of incomprehension and did as she was told, extending her power to every other specter as she latched onto them for control.

It was just in time, too. Jennie's feet slid from beneath her, and she hovered, her arms stretched toward the specters, her legs pulled toward the fans. Jennie wondered what would happen if she lost her grip and flew into the darkness. Would she be exorcised first, or would the internal fans shred her mortal body?

"Pull!" the specters shouted. Tanya shouted something in Sandra's ear, and the next thing they knew, Tanya and Lupe had turned spectral, too. They all banded together to tug at Jennie and try to draw her back.

Baxter's arms were tense, his muscles as tight as knotted rope, yet he still began to slip forward again. He shuffled his feet backward, but lost all momentum and flew off past Jennie and toward the fans.

"No!" Jennie held her connection with Baxter and kept him in position, just ten feet away from the hungry machines. Baxter's eyes met hers as the other specters failed to hold on.

"Let me go!" Baxter shouted.

"Never!" Jennie's words were choked. "I can't!"

"You need to let me go," Baxter urged. "If you don't, we're all gone. The world needs a Jennie King. It doesn't need a Baxter Scampton."

Jennie's tears flew away as they fell and were sucked in to be devoured by the machines. "*I* need a Baxter Scampton," she countered. "I need you."

Baxter gave a small smile. "Let me go. If you don't, the machines will take me with you anyway. Save yourself."

Jennie lurched. The specters at the door had been pulled another few inches. She turned back and saw that Carolyn had added to Baxter's security. Her own tendril of power latched onto the beast of a man, the same power she used to draw the pistol to her in the depths of Buckingham Palace. She pulled both of them toward her.

Jennie's grin was strained. "I told you, Bax. We're all in this together."

Baxter's face softened just as the most powerful lurch came. The specters on the ground were dragged again as the machines built momentum. The group struggled to hold on.

Lupe and Tanya tried to hold onto the door, but it swung closed behind them. They let go in time to not trap their fingers and flew toward the machines. There was nothing left to hold onto. A few more seconds and they would all be eradicated.

A voice cried out, then a loud popping noise came from somewhere they could not see, and as suddenly as it had all began, the machines began to power down. All at once, the fans slowed to a stop, and the specters who were being dragged toward them fell to the floor, landing on top of each other in an awkward heap.

Jennie pushed herself off the ground and scanned the room, her guns held in front of her as she rotated to cover the room.

"Don't shoot! You promised!"

Jennie searched for the voice and saw a head poking around the back of one of the machines.

Julia waved a hand, an awkward smile on her face.

Jennie kept the gun aimed at her, then lowered it and began laughing. A moment later, Julia was laughing too.

"You really chose your moment, didn't you?" Jennie told her.

"Call it a moral crisis," Julia replied. "Is this enough to count as my redemption?"

"It's a start," Jennie replied. "If you want to be fully absolved, I'd suggest helping us close in on that fucking Umbra."

Julia nodded. Her face turned resolute as she came out from her hiding place—the large switch behind the machines, the single power source that controlled them all.

Jennie recalled the loss of power back at the facility. She was certain they were far enough away from the EMP pulse that the power here hadn't been affected. It just wasn't possible.

Satisfied that they were safe for now, Jennie ran over to the rising Baxter and threw her arms around him. "I'm glad you're safe."

"You too, kid," he agreed. "You, too."

Jennie slapped his chest. "I'm older than you, dickhead."

Baxter chuckled. "You're a sucker for a tease."

Jennie ran a hand down her face. "Can we not talk about sucking, please? I've had enough suction for one day."

Jennie ignored the sniggers from the others.

CHAPTER SEVENTY-ONE

The battle raged on inside the chemical plant.

Victoria took center point in the room, keeping her enemies at bay. Her wounds healed quickly, but that didn't mean that the opposing forces weren't still trying to break her. It was infuriating that she could use her powers on specters but not on mortals.

She hated having to rely on mortals.

Gunfire sounded all around. The mortal agents aimed at each other while her specters poured into the room. They navigated around the vagrant army, though there were undoubtedly some casualties from the whole affair.

Pretty soon, Victoria grew tired of waiting and left the battle to her followers, sweeping across the room and pushing all those who opposed her out of the way.

The specters were repelled from her, as though she were the negatively charged magnet to their negative force. The few mortals she passed through were left momentarily dazed, confused, and chilled to the bone.

Shouts came from behind, calling for her to stop, but there were few who would be able to make her. She hadn't come this far in her reign to just bow down to a few upset federal-types and specters.

When she reached the doorway to the blocked corridor, she found a surprise waiting for her.

A woman and two men, dressed in a strange combination of army fatigues, blocked her way. While the other fighters had worn SI goggles, these wore none.

Victoria smiled. "It's rare to see a conduit among your order, much less three at once."

They remained tight-lipped and readied themselves in combat stances. The last of the bullet wounds on Victoria's chest healed before their eyes.

"If you're planning on preventing me from reaching my goal, I'm afraid to tell you that this won't end well for you."

Again they stayed silent.

Victoria sighed. "Very well, then."

She glided rapidly toward them, expecting in her mind to bowl them over and pass straight on through. To her surprise, she was shoved backward so roughly that her foot caught on her dress, and she had to pinwheel her arms to stop herself from falling over.

"Interesting," she muttered.

She glided toward them again, this time with her face contorted harshly. When she reached them, they prepared to shove her once more.

This time, Victoria twisted out of their way so quickly that it seemed impossible for a woman of her size. Ula, Roman, and Triton tracked Victoria and grabbed her limbs, working together to drag her backward as she let out a banshee cry and a shadow gathered over her features.

She was back where she started, and she was pissed. "So, you can touch specters. I wonder, can we touch you?"

Victoria snapped her fingers, and a gaggle of specters rushed toward them. She shouted an order, and suddenly Ula, Roman, and Triton were engaged in combat with a dozen specters each.

Not the best fighters, but they'll serve their purpose, Victoria thought as she chose to pass through the tunnel wall beside her instead of attempting to pass the conduits. She reappeared at the wall by the blockade and looked over her shoulder.

Ula, Roman, and Triton tried to fight through the specters to reach her, but she was gone before they could gain any ground.

Victoria melted through the rubble and continued her journey.

Julia huffed as they ran along the tunnel after Brendan. "There's only one way we can fix all this and free the specters who have been trapped inside the humans."

"Mortals," Jennie corrected.

"What do you mean?" Julia asked.

"Most specters are human, but not all humans are specters. We differentiate by mortal and spectral."

"Is now the time to argue semantics?" Carolyn cut in. She was doing a good job keeping pace. It was only Lupe with his shorter legs and Tanya carrying Sandra who slowed them down. "She's handing you the information to end all of this right now."

Jennie rolled her eyes. "Sorry, go ahead."

Julia took them left at an intersection. A thin layer of waste splashed beneath their feet.

"The Umbra has an override," she told them. "A way he can communicate with everyone in his army at once. He planted a network of remote speakers across all of his properties and has access to it via his phone. There are antennas on the surface to capture the signal and feed it down to anything it can reach."

Baxter screwed his face up in thought. His footsteps were the loudest of the lot, not that they fell on mortal ears. "But aren't the specters only going to be responsive to your commands? Aren't you the one who created them all?"

Tanya scoffed. "Every sentence that comes out of your mouth makes it seem like it should be impossible." She turned to Lupe. "Remember when specterdom was just a pipe dream? In the quiet days where we doubted life beyond death?"

Lupe gasped, his hand massaging the stitch in his side. "I always knew it was true."

"Every new recruit was programmed to respond to three separate leaders," Julia continued. "Me, the Umbra, and whichever Shadow leader was in charge of their unit. He has ultimate control over the pack. His word trumps mine."

"So, how do we get to his phone?" Carolyn asked.

Julia gave her a strange look. "We take it from his pocket."

"Oh, really? That simple?"

Jennie grinned. "Not everything in life has to be overly complicated. Some things are as straightforward as that."

Carolyn furrowed her brow. "Oh, it's just that... I thought..." She turned to Feng Mian, who was keeping pace neatly beside her. "This is the same guy who created massive machines to exorcise Jennie, right?"

The sounds of the outside world rumbled through grates above their heads, and soon they could hear frantic footsteps. They increased their pace, determined to catch up with Koa and put a final stop to all of his madness.

The sound of metal clanging on metal came from up ahead, magnified by the tunnels. Something ground against concrete.

"Brendan's making a run for it above ground," Jennie growled. "That was a manhole cover, right?"

A final turn and the open hole above them confirmed their theory. They scaled the ladder one by one and found themselves on a quiet road.

The fresh air soothed their skin and took away the stench of the sewer. The streetlights were all out. Jennie could still see the billowing smoke from the factory fire in the distance. A fence clanged, and Jennie saw Brendan Koa, the Umbra, in all his glory, with his foot caught in the chain mesh of a waist-high fence he had attempted to vault over.

An arm's length in front of him was someone else. It took Jennie a moment to recognize who.

"Stay back!" Brendan shouted, wriggling his foot free of the fence's grasp. He reached the other side, where a manicured baseball field lay desolate in the night. He pulled himself free and crawled a few feet along the ground before pushing himself up and sending a warning shot toward Jennie.

It missed by at least six inches. Jennie fired back, catching Brendan's fingers and blowing the gun from his hand. Agent Clark stood behind him, stripped down to his pants and wearing a pair of metal handcuffs. He flinched at the sudden gunshot.

Brendan grunted as blood poured from the place where two of his fingers had been. He stood up, squaring his shoulders as Jennie and her crew approached.

"Your reign is over, Brendan. Your time is up. Now *you* have a choice. Come quietly with us, and we'll hand you to the authorities." Jennie closed one eye and trained her pistol at Brendan's forehead. "Or die."

"That's murder," Brendan growled. "You murder me, and you'll do time."

"They'll have to catch me, first," Jennie replied without concern, her pistol still poised and ready. "I hope you don't think you'd be the first shitsack I've sent into the abyss?"

Koa's eyes dropped to the ground. "I thought you'd understand my vision, Genevieve. I thought we could make something beautiful together. A world at peace. A world where all of this pettiness, all of the conflict and war is erased. Isn't that what you've always wanted? Total, supreme justice for the world? A place where Genevieve King isn't needed to solve all the problems because there are none left to solve"

Carolyn whispered, "He's kidding, right?"

Jennie lowered her gun. "That's a pipe dream. I fight for justice because I fight for freedom, and I fight for humanity. What you're talking about is a dictatorship. At its heart, it's unjust for one man or group to hold the ultimate power. The beauty of life for mortals and specters is the unpredictability of it all. That we can make mistakes and atone for them. Lord knows I've made enough of my own over the years to fill the pages of a book, but you? You don't see humans or specters as complete and whole, do you? You see them as something that needs to be fixed. That's the problem here."

Brendan held Jennie's gaze for a few moments. It looked as though he was coming around to her way of thinking when he suddenly dropped to the ground and reached for his gun.

Jennie shot three times in quick succession. Another of Koa's fingers was lost, and the other two shots pushed the gun farther back.

Jennie tsked. "I guess that's your choice made."

"I'm not coming with you." Brendan bared his teeth, then sighed when he felt the barrel of his own gun pressed against the back of his head.

"Either way, you're coming with one of us." Agent Clark held the gun awkwardly between his cuffed hands. "Down on your knees, fuckstain. We're done here."

Brendan reluctantly obeyed, placing his hands in the air and crouching until he was on his knees.

Jennie kept her gun on Brendan as she advanced toward them.

"Be careful," Baxter warned.

As Clark held his gun on Brendan, Jennie fished through the Umbra's pockets and found his phone, a key, and a handful of pieces of folded yellow paper. Jennie unlocked Clark's handcuffs, and they used them to bind Brendan's hands behind his back.

Clark mumbled as he rubbed his sore wrists. "You do understand that this doesn't make us friends."

"I get that," Jennie replied. She eyed the red marks on his arms. "How the hell did you climb a ladder with handcuffs on?"

"With great difficulty," he admitted.

Jennie bit back a laugh, then looked down at the pitiful excuse for the leader of the Shadows. "Brendan Koa, you have the right to remain silent. Anything you say can and will be used against you in a court of law. You have the right to an attorney. If you cannot afford an attorney, one will be provided for you. Do you understand the rights I have just given to you? With these rights in mind, do you wish to speak to me?"

"Really?" Clark scoffed. "You're offering him an attorney?"

"Nah." Jennie chuckled. "I just always wanted to read someone their Miranda Rights. This son of a bitch has no rights. He's been caught red-handed, and it's for the SIA to deal with him now."

Clark moved with impressive speed, raising his gun arm to Jennie so that she was looking into the cold dark eye of his pistol.

Jennie gritted her teeth. "This terrorist is on US soil. He is under my jurisdiction, as laid out in mine and Victoria's truce. Lower your weapon, Agent, or I'll have to find another way to nullify you."

Queen Victoria's voice came from behind them. "I say, just shoot her." She rose ungracefully from the manhole and laced her hands in front of her. She took a few long steps toward them, causing Jennie's party to fall back in shock.

"Hello, Genevieve."

Jennie sighed. "Of course. Right on cue."

CHAPTER SEVENTY-TWO

Victoria clicked her tongue. "Dear me, Genevieve. Always with the theatrics. Drama is embedded in your blood, isn't it?"

Jennie narrowed her eyes at Victoria. "Speak for yourself. Every time I see your face or hear your name lately, there's some shit popping off. You make a great liar, too. A performance like that is easily worth a BAFTA."

"What's a BAFTA?" Carolyn whispered.

"Kind of like an Oscar, but British," Tanya replied.

"So what is this all about, Vicky?" Jennie continued, doing her best not to smile at Tanya and Carolyn's exchange. "Couldn't handle not being the supreme leader of the world, so you decided to employ a psychopathic madman to run your mortals and give me a run for my money? Well, that ended well for you."

She nodded toward Clark's bare body. The chill wind did nothing for his downstairs area. Clark twisted his hips away from Jenny's view as he pressed the gun into her temple.

"All right, all right," Jennie grumbled. "You've made your point. I'm at gunpoint now. No need to be a stroppy bollocks."

Victoria chuckled. Her head cocked to the side in the irritating manner Jennie's father used to employ. The one that made it feel as though she was being studied from head to foot. "I've always liked you, Genevieve. You know that."

Jennie sighed. "Okay, before you continue, can I remind everyone that it's 2019? If you're going to use my Christian name, I'd prefer it if you went with Jennie, since it's far more contemporary. No one is called Genevieve anymore." She kicked Brendan in the back. "That includes you, too. You're not a Victorian aristocrat. You're a lowlife piece of shit born in the sixties."

Victoria placated Jennie. "Fine. You've always been my number one, Jennie. The one I could rely on to ensure that what needed to be done got done. No task has been set that you cannot complete, and that's something that is incredibly useful to my court."

"Your court across the ocean." Jennie stared intently at Victoria.

The queen continued, undeterred. "My only concern has been that you don't play well with others. Every specter I've set to your service has torn themselves from duty and returned scarred and bruised. Dolly Farrington, Evan Tweedy, Louis Tharrell, even Worthington Conrad; they were either damaged or destroyed by you."

At the mention of Worthington's name, Sandra's eyes lowered as she began to make the connection of who the queen was talking about.

Victoria continued. "Over the years, I worried that we'd never find someone to make the partnership work, but it turns out I was going about this all wrong, wasn't I? I couldn't *give* you a specter. You had to take one for yourself."

Victoria turned to Baxter and the others and was greeted with hostile stares.

"I never took them," Jennie replied. "Each and every specter and mortal here has *chosen* to follow me. They're more than some stowaway loan from Her Majesty. They're my friends. They're family."

Victoria's eyes flicked nervously.

Jennie wondered what the notion of family meant to a woman who had abandoned her predecessors and destroyed her successors in her desire to maintain the throne.

Victoria uttered a short laugh. "Family? Don't make me laugh.

They fear you, Jennie. The world has feared you for as long as you've had the ability to control the things you don't understand. *I'm* your family. I raised you, brought you into the spectral kingdom, gave you a place to belong, a place to call home. For years I gave you everything you could ever want, money, weapons, a *purpose*, and this is how you repay me?"

Jennie blinked, and when she opened her eyes again, Victoria stood right in front of her. The movement seemed impossible, yet here she was.

Victoria's voice lowered, a conspiratorial secret for her ears only. "Think about it. The advancements that have been made in mortal-spectral relations since the SIA and SIS have been in action has been incredible. The technological advances are ensuring that the two worlds will one day interact. Specters are sacrificing themselves for a higher purpose, and finally, I can begin to rebuild my empire and reclaim what those who followed me were too weak to hold onto."

Victoria's hand brushed Jennie's cheek. She shuddered at her touch. "Look at you, Jennie. As pure and beautiful as the day we first met. You haven't aged a day, have you?"

Jennie batted her hand away and gripped Victoria's throat.

Clark's finger twitched on the trigger, but Victoria stopped him with a sharp look and a shake of her head.

"It wasn't all that long ago that you were hiding in your cozy little palace and painting while others did your dirty work," Jennie growled. "What happened to you? Upon returning to power, did your hunger and your idiocy grow? Did the sudden influx of oxygen fuck with your head, or are you just susceptible to influence? Has the idea of owning what you once had muddled your mind?"

Victoria held her gaze and, even though her words were choked by Jennie's grip, she didn't struggle. "You don't know what you're talking about."

"*We had a deal!*" Jennie roared, her voice cutting through the night. "You looked me in the eye, and you promised me this territory. You promised you'd stick to your borders, and you'd leave me alone. You promised, Victoria. You fucking *promised.*"

Victoria's mouth twisted into a smile. "Show me the treaty I signed."

Jennie's nostrils flared. A warm flush of irritation coursed through her.

On the ground, Brendan turned his head to look at the two women locked together.

Jennie spoke in a voice so low that only Victoria could hear it. "Where I came from, a woman's word was law. In our era, a promise was sacred. Vows were holy. Do you think you can get out of this on a *technicality*? You're wrong. One move and I could have you and your two little goblins dead and buried."

"You may have found a way to exorcise Worthington and the Messino brothers, but you've got a lot to learn about exorcizing royalty," Victoria told her. "Don't turn this into a fight you can't win."

Jennie lowered her eyes and exhaled. She dropped her hands from Victoria's throat. "Very well."

A swift elbow into Clark's ribs knocked his aim off-center with the pistol. The shot passed inches from Jennie's ear and smashed the glass window of a little hut at the side of the baseball field.

Clark groaned and tried to pull back, but before he could, Jennie grabbed his wrist in one hand and slammed her forearm onto his elbow, forcing the limb to bend at an unnatural angle.

The gun fell to the ground. Before Jennie could reach it, Victoria grabbed her arm and spun, pulling Jennie around with surprising strength.

Jennie was tossed, her flight only stopping when her back smashed into the trunk of a nearby oak. She slid to the ground and groaned.

Baxter raced toward Victoria. Through blurry vision, Jennie watched as he fired shots with his pistol that did nothing to stop her. He neared Victoria with his wrench and was ready to strike, but a swift move of her hands sent out a shockwave that repelled him backward.

Jennie pushed herself to her feet. Her specters charged Victoria, fired up and ready to engage. Jennie carved a path to the side, staying out of Victoria's line of sight as she moved to where Brendan was crawling after the fallen pistol.

Clark spotted the movement. He dropped to his knees and pursued the gun. Each movement sent pain up his arm, but he used his good arm to scrap for it.

Jennie drew the Big Bitch and aimed it in their direction. "Leave it!" she shouted.

This caught Victoria's attention. With Feng Mian, Feng Li, and Feng Chen as her next obstacles, Victoria drew up her shield and kept them at bay with one arm, while with the other, she allowed Carolyn through and grabbed her by the neck.

She lifted the girl as though she were a pebble. "You know I could extinguish you in a heartbeat."

Carolyn choked. "Then you better fucking do it."

Victoria grinned and hurled Carolyn toward Jennie.

Jennie dropped the Big Bitch and held her arms out to catch Carolyn. She put her down and checked that she was okay.

Carolyn nodded. "What a day."

"You're telling me," Jennie replied before shoving Carolyn to the ground again and twisting her shoulder to escape Clark's shot.

Annoyance washed over Clark's face and he lined up again, but before he could pull the trigger, Brendan was on him.

The two fought, then fell to the ground. Brendan placed a foot on Clark's broken bone, and the agent screamed in pain. Although he was in agony, he wouldn't relent, knowing that the minute Brendan got the gun, he'd be a goner.

Victoria shoved the Fengs backward and left them sprawled on the ground. Jennie was surprised to see that the only people still standing were her, Victoria, Sandra, and Tanya, who were currently hiding behind a nearby tree. Tanya had her hands wrapped tightly around Sandra, and her eyes were closed.

Jennie weighed her options. Normally her instincts would kick in about now and she'd go for the strike, but something was holding her back—the very thing she had always feared when connecting with other people.

She knew that a wrong choice could put others in danger, and Jennie was a protector. Which decision would result in the least amount of casualties? With so many friends on her side, it was impossible to tell.

Luckily, Victoria made Jennie's decision for her.

She dashed toward Rogue, appearing in front of her in a heartbeat. Jennie was lifted high above Victoria's head. She looked down into the anger-fueled eyes, and for a moment, it was just the two of them on the field. No one else mattered.

"I didn't want this, Jennie," Victoria told her. "You were like a daughter to me, but you fueled this fire, and now you're going to burn."

Fire?

A sudden flurry of memories came to Jennie. She was back in New York, in the Statue of Liberty with Worthington and the rival specters. She dove from the statue and swam the Hudson. A battle raged, with only one way to call off the troops. Somewhere, a hundred stories above the city, a little girl exorcized Worthington.

Exorcism, the only way to kill a specter.

Jennie was hurled to the ground by Victoria, this time so hard that the wind was knocked from her lungs. In her narrowing peripheral vision, Clark and Brendan still struggled, but they wouldn't be affected by what was to come.

Jennie raised herself onto her hands and knees, surprised to see drops of blood spilling from the corner of her mouth. That was going to hurt later.

"Speaking of fire," she gasped, recovering her breath. "Your little stooge Worthington had a friend who was experienced with spectral flames. Did you know he set the Statue of Liberty on fire?"

Victoria gave Jennie a pitiful look. "You never were much of a storyteller, were you? Always more of a hired goon with a walnut knocking around in your skull."

Jennie chuckled. "Oh, the stories I *could* tell."

Victoria kicked Jennie, and she rolled twice before coming to a stop. "Don't waste my time on your legends and myths." Victoria scowled, her anger coming in waves. "Why do I care what putrid vomit spews from your calloused little mouth? You had your chance with me. You had every chance, and you've chosen your fate. Now just lie there and accept it as I purge you from this world and erase the nuisance that is Genevieve—"

"Jennie." Jennie coughed.

"King."

Victoria went to stomp on Jennie, but she rapidly rolled out of the way.

Jennie shoved herself to her feet and swayed unsteadily. "Let me ask you a question, Victoria. How do you kill a specter?"

The amusement came back to Victoria's face. She liked the games. She loved the chase. "I think you know the answer to that."

"There are a number of ways. The first is holy water." Jennie drew a vial of clear liquid from its pouch and shook it in front of the queen.

The queen's confident facade was shaken for a second. She recovered quickly. "It's nothing without the divine words of the true—"

Jennie interjected, her eyes narrowing. *"Deus est; Et inimicos eorum dispersus est..."*

Victoria made a perfect O with her mouth. She raised her foot to kick Jennie in the chest, but not before Jennie threw the vial of water on the monarch.

Victoria shrieked, the sound like a banshee in agony. The water passed straight through Victoria and sprinkled the turf beneath her feet. She patted her body down, turning frantically for any sign of damage. She found none and turned back to Jennie.

Jennie held one hand to her stomach and shook the empty vial. "Evian, bitch."

Victoria rushed toward Jennie and was met with resistance as Jennie's specters and mortals gathered behind her. Baxter fired three times into Victoria's back, making her shrug and lose her momentum. The Fengs created a shield and blocked her intrusion, and Carolyn took a fighter's stance, ready for combat if it came.

Sandra and Tanya were nowhere to be seen.

Victoria shouted a jumble of vitriol and curses, but she could not penetrate their blockade easily. She pushed against them and made slow progress, which gave Jennie enough time to continue.

"Another way to exorcise a specter is to use another specter." She said the words as though teaching a lecture on Spectral Exorcism 101. "Some specters have *extraordinary* power. Of course, you know that, since your goons were exploring New York and trying to take what we already had."

"Preach all you like, King," Victoria spat, her face animalistic and furious. "Death won't avoid you forever."

Jennie smiled sweetly. "One thing you should know. Worthington didn't die at my hands. It's amazing the power that can be found in small packages."

Fear flickered over Victoria's face and she froze, her advancing steps stopping in an instant. Jennie told the Fengs to lower their shields. Somewhere nearby, a gunshot rang out as Clark's and Brendan's fight neared its conclusion.

Victoria was almost still. She moved as if in slow motion.

Jennie peered around Victoria's girth to see Sandra standing a short distance behind her, both hands aimed at the queen, her fingers bent and twisted as she focused on holding her still.

"Hey, Sandra."

Victoria tried to look behind her but couldn't. Jennie added to the queen's immobilization by latching her own power onto her and keeping her as still as a statue. She could feel power rolling off the queen such as she'd never felt before. It felt like a strange intrusion to dominate the woman who had acted like a parent in her mother's absence, but what other choice did she have?

While other specters' essences often felt like trying to hold onto a steady stream of spring water, the queen's was like a torrent of boiling lava. Assisted by Sandra, she managed it, but with every second that passed, the queen was slowly fighting them off, pushing her own power against that which held her.

Tanya remained near the tree but had stepped into sight with a worried look on her face.

"Tell me, Sandra, how did exorcizing Worthington feel?"

"Like the removal of something bad," Sandra replied, her voice maintaining its edge of innocence. "Like scrubbing out a stain."

"*She* did that?" Victoria mumbled through frozen lips. "Bullshit."

Jennie inclined her head. "Sandra, show Queeny what you mean."

Sandra looked from Jennie to Tanya, then began mouthing the words. Her hands glowed vibrantly white, and Victoria's eyes locked fearfully on Jennie's.

The center of Victoria's stomach lit up with a glowing orb. It began as a soccer ball, then stretched and grew inside of her as though she were pregnant and the baby of light was growing beyond all reason.

Tanya broke her silence and stepped forward. "No! Jennie, stop this!"

Sandra's head snapped to Tanya, her eyes glassy and wet. Her power ebbed.

Tanya ran toward Sandra and placed her arms around her, shielding her as a mother would. "Jennie! We can't put this burden upon a little girl. She'll have to live with the fact that she destroyed the reigning queen of the paranormal court for the rest of her life. The queen's followers will come for her, the spectral kingdom will brand her a traitor forever, and her name will go down in history as a murderer."

In the heat of the moment, Jennie hadn't considered that, but Tanya was right. The weight of what she wanted to do shouldn't rest on the shoulders of a young girl, even if she *was* centuries old.

"Fine," Jennie conceded, eyes returning to Victoria's. "There was always a third option anyway. Sandra, release her."

Sandra turned to Tanya for confirmation, then released the queen from her power. She slumped, drained from the exertion.

Tanya caught her in her arms and mouthed a thank you to Jennie.

Jennie held onto Victoria, but without Sandra, her power wasn't enough. The queen began to move again, slowly at first, but faster with every second. She advanced on Jennie with a murderous look in her eye.

"That's why you'll never rule," Victoria growled. "You don't have the strength to do what it takes, no matter who stands in your way. As strong as you think you are, there's a weakness inside you that holds you back. You'll never make it here."

When she was only inches from Jennie, Jennie whipped her hands to her side and drew the Saber of Holy Divinity in one clean move. She held the blade a hair's breadth from Victoria's chin.

"A toy you picked up on your journey?" Victoria crooned.

"Something like that," Jennie told her. "A little relic that exorcises specters on contact."

Victoria grinned. "I don't believe you."

Jennie shrugged. "Try me."

Victoria's humor faded when she saw the truth in Jennie's eyes. Her smile morphed into a frown, eyes occasionally flicking to the keen edge of the shiny blade.

"You wouldn't exorcise me, Jennie. You don't have it in you." Although her words were clear, there was uncertainty beneath them.

"That's where you're wrong, Vicky," Jennie replied, exhaustion beginning to settle over her. "I'll do anything to protect the people I love. I'm happy here. I've found a place I belong. This is your last chance to give me what you promised me and fuck off. There's still a deal to be had here. You take your territory, I'll take mine. We can find a way to work together."

Baxter stepped forward, eyes darting between the pair. "How can you still trust her after everything she's put us through?"

"Because Tanya's right," Jennie replied. "The paranormal court needs stability. Killing Victoria would end in anarchy across the Empire. We'll be fighting off specters by the thousands, unable to ever make this place a safe haven for my and your kind."

"Or I could just kill *you*." Victoria grabbed for the sword, managing to take the handle from Jennie in her distraction. She swung it, and Jennie ducked out of the way. On the return swing, the sword vibrated in Victoria's hand and did something that no one was expecting.

It shot out of her hand and sped toward Baxter and the other specters, finding its place in Carolyn's outstretched hand. Her face was a mask of concentration and surprise.

Victoria unleashed another wailing cry and charged at Jennie.

Carolyn held the sword toward Jennie. "Jennie! Go!"

Jennie grabbed the sword and swung it at Victoria's neck. Victoria's mouth was cavernous as a scream leaked out, her eyes were two full moons. Jennie arced the sword downwards, the blade whistling toward her neck…

Then stopped.

Victoria, who had closed her eyes in the final moments before impact, opened them. "What are you doing?"

"I'm considering," Jennie muttered.

Victoria tried to move but realized that she couldn't. Sandra had once again taken hold of the monarch at Tanya's command and frozen her.

"Final last chance," Jennie offered.

Brendan screamed in delight as he finally wrested control of the pistol, sending three bullets into the Agent Clark's skull. He turned frantically and held the gun up at Jennie, but in his exhausted state, he was too slow. Jennie raised the Big Bitch and fired without looking, Brendan's head exploded into a thousand droplets of brain matter.

"What do you say?" Jennie pressed. "It's my way or nothing."

Victoria's chest rose and fell for a few moments. She exhaled and dropped her shoulders. "I never thought I'd see the day a seven-year-old could exorcise a monarch."

"And she's not going anywhere," Jennie stated. "So, tell me. Truce, or no truce?"

Victoria fought herself, debating internally. Eventually, she sighed. "Truce."

Jennie nodded. "Good. Now, let's find somewhere where you can fill in some fucking paperwork. I'm not falling for that trick twice. Sandra, don't let go until we get what we want."

CHAPTER SEVENTY-THREE

They led Queen Victoria back through the sewers and toward the underground facility. When they arrived at the chamber of the vagrants, the battle was still raging. Each side fought relentlessly. The noise was unbearable, and everywhere they looked, there was carnage.

It was almost impossible to tell who was on which side. The fight had descended into a free-for-all, but the guns had been abandoned through fear of taking down an ally. They fought with their fists and feet, and those who fell returned as specters to join the other side.

Upon entering, Victoria sent out a shockwave to draw the attention of everyone in the room.

Jennie waited with bated breath, understanding that this could be the moment Victoria betrayed her and everything exploded once more.

Luckily for her—Victoria, that is—that didn't happen.

Victoria ordered the SIS to stand down. Jennie commanded the specters of the paranormal court and the specters of the Spectral Plane to stop. The SIA took the instruction of Rhone and Daggro, with Agent Hopkins mysteriously absent, and they listened with open ears as Victoria declared their official truce and spoke of unity between the two nations.

While Victoria spoke—with Sandra not far behind her—Jennie took in the devastation created in so small a place. She realized then that they would have to pass through tunnels filled with casualties before they made their way to the surface. And even when they got there, they would have to tackle the media and the local firefighters to ensure that the truth of what had occurred never came out. The journey was unending.

The specters marched from the room and into the tunnels. The SIS followed. Victoria stayed with Jennie as they trailed behind, stepping over the bodies of the dead as they made their way once more to the surface.

Something caught Jennie's attention. "Wait a second."

Jennie pulled away from Victoria and ran across the room. A pile of bodies was stacked by the far wall, the empty shells of what had been mortals. In amidst the corpses was an SIA logo sticking out like a sore thumb.

That wasn't what caught Jennie's attention, however. It was the hardened military face of Agent Hopkins. His eyes were black marbles, his mouth agape. Bullet wounds peppered his body.

"No," she muttered. A heavy hand appeared on her shoulder. She didn't need to look to know it was Baxter.

"He was a good man," Baxter told her. "One of the best mortals I've met. Sturdy, loyal, and strong."

"And soon to be the best specter you've ever met."

Jennie turned and smiled with relief as Hopkins appeared behind them. He looked strange in his spectral form, as though she were looking at a low-res, washed-out version of him. He held his assault rifle in his hands, and his uniform was permanently attached to his spectral form.

Jennie laughed. "I wondered if you'd choose to become a specter over the abyss."

"A difficult choice," Hopkins replied. "But there's much more work to be done, and I'm far from finished."

To his surprise, Jennie moved forward and hugged him. "I'm glad you're still around."

"You too, kid. You, too."

Baxter laughed. "She's older than—"

Jennie cut Baxter off with a wave. "Not now, Bax."

The next few hours passed by in a blur. The helicopter fire was almost out when they resurfaced, and Rhone and Daggro came up with a false explanation of what had happened to the facility. Media crews gathered around the fenced-off perimeter, but Hopkins managed to help the mortals stay out of sight by taking a series of hidden routes and passages he'd come across with his blueprints of the city.

The specters from both factions passed through the barricades unnoticed. Those from the Spectral Plane went back to their vehicles to head toward Washington and the SIA HQ. The remaining SIS and paranormal court specters gathered around the queen's carriage and followed in a long procession as it made its way along the roads and away from the action.

Victoria was held by Jennie's and Sandra's power until they made it the SIA HQ. A strange kind of surrealism hit Jennie as she marched the monarch through the corridors and into the meeting room where she had had her first encounter with Special Agent in Charge Kurt Rogers.

Rogers stood up as they entered. He had been alerted of their arrival by Ashleigh, but with the radios down, there had been no other warning.

They sat for some time in that room, discussing the terms of the truce and negotiating their boundaries. Jennie was careful to ensure that the truce still worked for Victoria and her Empire, but that each clause was crafted to protect Jennie and those within her jurisdiction in America. She wanted free reign of the US—not from a dictatorial standpoint, but from a protector's view. Any spectral activity that happened on the continent of America, both North and South, would be under Jennie's purview. She would stand as a guardian of specters and mortals alike and would work alongside the government to ensure that relations remained strong, controlled, and, most of all, just.

The meeting lasted longer than Jennie cared to remember. Hendrick provided enough doses of his formula to bypass sleep in the process, but eventually they had the document on the table, printed and ready to be signed by all three parties.

Jennie took the pen and signed it first, feeling a sense of accomplishment as she did so. Queen Victoria signed next, binding herself to the agreement with a pulse of spectral power. As well as Jennie knew the queen could be tricksy, she also knew that she had never gone against a written oath. Some things still held power in this world.

When it came to the final signature, Rogers took the document and sealed it in a manilla envelope. He wrote the address and added, "FAO The President of the United States of America."

Jennie chuckled. "Isn't it funny?"

"What's that?" Rogers asked.

"I just find it ironic that the truce between paranormal forces is signed in the same city where the Founding Fathers settled the hub of democracy after finally earning their independence from the UK."

Victoria chewed her lip. It was less than an hour later that the document was returned with the final signature.

"Now that this is in order, may I request my freedom?" Victoria asked in a voice that sounded as tired as she looked.

Jennie nodded to Sandra, and they released Victoria from their holds. Victoria thanked them both, then stood up and crossed the room. She paused by the door.

"Problem?" Jennie smiled. "I'd have thought you'd dash your ass out of here and reunite with your squad?"

Victoria's face was thoughtful. "Brendan might have been the wrong choice entirely in choosing a US ally, but he was right about one thing."

"What's that?" Jennie asked.

"You're a mystery, Jennie King. A mystery that can be solved. You were offered the chance to side with us and discover your heritage. After everything that happened to your mother and father, after all the long years you've lived, I can't understand why you wouldn't take such an opportunity. The world could benefit from you."

Jennie considered her answer for a moment, then replied with nothing more than, "I guess the past just belongs in the past."

The Sylvester's Premium Candies fire was the headline event on the news for a week afterward. Chyrons showed an ongoing array of theories and so-called "evidence" of what had transpired at the facility, but nothing ever came close to the truth.

TV screens played the news around the room, the volume low enough that no one could hear what was being said. As specters and mortals gathered together in the giant hall beneath the SIA HQ, footage of fires, witnesses, and local authorities flickered in a montage that no one present paid attention to.

"To Jennie!" Baxter cried, raising an empty cup into the air.

All around Jennie, people raised their glasses. She choked on a glug of her Bloody Mary and laughed, raising her own glass and responding with, "To *freedom*!"

"To freedom!" the attendees chorused.

Things had been quiet for Jennie in the week that followed the events with the queen and the demise of the Shadows. While the SIA had worked to cover up all that had happened, using their connections with key societal figures, and supporting the survivor vagrants from the fight, Jennie and the others had rested up, finally getting some downtime to recover from all that had transpired.

In all truth, Jennie had grown bored. She was used to vacations, but there had always been something to keep her busy. With the queen's connections across the country, there was almost always some bad guy or gal to take down, but now that the SIA was recovering its links and once more getting its communications up and running, there was a lull in potential missions.

Jennie drank with Baxter and the others, then wandered the

facility until her feet were tired. She spoke long into the night with Hendrick and assisted with his study of the spectral liquid. Sometimes, late at night, she simply wandered the city, hoping to encounter something that would demand her attention and get her back in the game.

The surprise party was something she had never expected, but just at the point when Jennie thought she could take no more sitting around, she had been summoned to the underground hall.

Every surviving agent and specter from the SIA had gathered to celebrate their victory and to toast to the future. They danced, they drank, they laughed, and soon enough, the crowd began to disperse, all gunning for Hendrick's stash of what was referred to as his "Hang-over-B-Gone" formula.

It was as Jennie was preparing to leave, wanting nothing more than to lay her head on her pillow and grab some shuteye, that Hopkins called her over.

He was sitting on the edge of the platform she had addressed the agency from. She was still getting used to his ghostly form, resisting the temptation to latch onto him and read his gifts. She had too much respect for him for that.

"Quite a journey we've been on." He nodded. "A hell of a journey."

"You talk as though it's come to an end," Jennie replied. "In my experience, it never ends. This is just the calm before the storm."

"It's funny you should say that." Hopkins half-turned and drew a folder from beneath his buttocks. "We've got something for you—your first assignment under the new agreement. I hope it's enough to keep you busy. People can go stir crazy with nothing to do."

"You're telling me," Jennie agreed.

Baxter approached and took a seat on the other side of Jennie. "What are you two lovebirds talking about?"

Hopkins arched an eyebrow.

Jennie elbowed Baxter playfully. "Let's see, shall we?"

She opened the folder and pulled out the piece of paper. Her eyes scanned the document, and a coy smile grew on her lips.

Hopkins drained his drink and winked. "What did I tell you? The fun never stops."

"No," Jennie replied. "No, it certainly does not."

The End

AUTHOR NOTES MICHAEL ANDERLE

FEBRUARY 3, 2020

Rogue called any other name (and she has been called a few) is still Rogue ;-)

Thank you for reading this story. We have enjoyed writing it for you!

So, the cover artist for the Rogue series (a woman by the name of Mihaela Voicu out of Romania - https://www.mihaelavoicu.com) came to me a few days ago and said that the big gun we used as the 3d Model on the first Rogue cover didn't have a commercial license to go with it...

OH SH#%!

Which would mean we have to find a new gun, if it is too different in the books we might have to deal with edit changes and other situations. It wasn't something I had dealt with in over 600 previous covers.

A 3D model that didn't have commercial license? (Ok, not including ones that obviously are models of famous ships like Tie Fighters or the Millennium Falcon etc.)

Mihaela started down the path of finding something sort of close, and then found some filigree work that she could use to enhance existing rifles to provide that old world look and then...

She found the SAME model on another sight WITH a commercial license. Mihaela reached out to the artist and received permission … CRISIS AVERTED.

I think 2020 is going to be a good year ;-)

Diary: Sunday Jan 26th – Saturday Feb 1st

First, the fun part. WOOT, *Goth Drow*! It's a new series I'm happy about, and it will be coming to you in early March as one of our LMBPN Large Releases of about 180k words.

Like *Witch of the Federation* or *The Steel Dragon* size.

This week, I spoke with ALLI (Alliance of Independent Authors) on a recorded video call for their symposium on selling foreign rights (with others, including Judith Anderle, our CMO for the company, who honestly spoke the most for LMBPN since it's her area of expertise.)

I finished a book titled **In Cold Type** by Leonard Shatzkin, written in 1983. The book helped open my eyes to the issues in the book-selling business. I hope to figure out a way and implement a solution for selling paperbacks (which is about .02% of our income, if that much.)

I greenlit (well, maybe only in my mind) *Cryptid Assassin 05…* but don't have a clue on where I want the story to go yet.

(I might want to get on that.)

Before I do that, I have two story beats to review and approve and *Opus 5* editing to finish.

I've been ill for the last forty-eight hours and had to learn to respect my body once again. It has probably been twelve months or longer that I have gone without any serious sick downtime. There is nothing like experience to foster sympathy through empathy, at least for me.

There is going to be a big author signing/fan get together or something going on the Friday after the 20Booksto50k Event here in Las Vegas in November (the show runs Tuesday to Thursday 10th-12th). Yes, yes, I know that is Friday the 13th ;-). I didn't set the date—ask Martelle about that one! The event will be held at Sam's Town Casino and Hotel (about twenty minutes east of the Strip driving straight over.)

For those who know, I'm doing a weight loss "thing" with my older brother. My goal was to be under 220 by Feb 1st. I weighed in at 218.8.

Go, Team! (I imagine being sick and unable to eat much helped, but what the hell. I'm keeping that W on my side.) I need to finish on June 30th at UNDER 202.0 lbs. If it looks like I might miss it, you may see Anderle doing all sorts of crazy stuff to drop weight.

I'm going to wrap up this diary post since I'm about two days past due on a lot of work. Take care of yourselves, and I'll chat with you in the next… OH OH!

New Universe coming 2020! (Well, uh, that's not even a big deal anymore—it's LMBPN. *OF COURSE, THERE IS A NEW UNIVERSE COMING!)*

Enjoy.

Michael Anderle

CONNECT WITH THE AUTHOR

Connect with Michael Anderle and sign up for his email list here:

Website: http://lmbpn.com

Email List: http://lmbpn.com/email/

Facebook:
www.facebook.com/TheKurtherianGambitBooks